MW00587459

THE PERFECT FIT

SADIE KINCAID

RED HOUSE PRESS LTD.

Copyright © 2023 by Sadie Kincaid

All rights reserved.

No part of this book may be reproduced in any form or by any electronic or mechanical means, including information storage and retrieval systems, without written permission from the author, except for the use of brief quotations in a book review.

The moral right of the author has been asserted

Cover Design: Red House Press Ltd

Editing: Baker Street Revisions

Formatting: Red House Press Ltd

All characters and events in this publication, other than those clearly in the public domain are fictitious and any resemblance to any real person, living or dead is purely coincidental and not intended by the author.

For anyone who has ever been told that they couldn't have it all - you absolutely can!

And if that includes wanting to be railed by three insanely hot men who know how to use all of their appendages, then you're definitely in the right place.

Love Sadie x

PROLOGUE

WEST

It's the crying I hear first, and I can't help but sigh. Always the crying. This time it's closely followed by the sound of footsteps thundering down the hallway. My concentration broken, I discard the magazine I was reading and glance across the room to Xander. Rolling his eyes, he pushes himself up from the sofa and goes to head her off so he can prevent another tantrum.

Xander's always been her favorite—the one who could talk her down. I suspect she's only stuck around for as long as she has because of him. However, I doubt even he can convince her to stay now. I must admit that with her experience and previous references, I thought she'd last longer than this, even if her presence has made the atmosphere in our penthouse increasingly tense.

Ebony—currently headed along the hall and into Xander's waiting arms—is our latest test subject. Our guinea pig, as Zeke likes to call them. She's lasted three months, which is longer than most. But that's because Zeke has been on his best behavior for her. Until today. We warned her how he could be, and she swore she could handle it. Seems like she can't.

She's pulling one of Xander's old hooded sweatshirts over her head when she comes into view, but I catch a glimpse of the bite marks and purple welts on her torso. "He's a fucking animal," she cries, wiping tears from her cheeks.

I grind my jaw, forcing myself to keep my mouth shut and let Xander handle this. He found her—it's up to him to let her go. But Zeke is no animal. He has issues, sure, but don't we all? Ebony included. Fuck me, does she have issues.

Xander whispers words of comfort in her ear, and she clings to him, her hands fisting in the fabric of his T-shirt even as he gives her his well-practiced speech about how it's time for her to leave. He had such hope this one would work out. Not because he's particularly attached to her, but because we swore she'd be the last one we attempted this with.

On paper, she seemed like the perfect fit. But no woman will ever come between Xander, Zeke, and me, although that hasn't stopped every single one of them from trying.

CHAPTER
ONE

LILY

"Hey! Watch it, jackass," I shout at the disappearing taillights of the taxi that splashed freezing rainwater all over me. It's the first week of April and the weather should start warming up any day now, but I'm still waiting. Betty—my bike—creaks as I cycle faster in an attempt to keep my rapidly numbing legs warm. I swear she's going to completely give out on me one day soon.

"Just a few more weeks, baby," I say quietly, giving the frame a gentle tap. "As soon as I get my big break, I'll retire you."

Turning right, I head toward Central Park. Where do tired old bicycles retire to anyway? The scrap heap? Not my Betty. I give her another reassuring pat on her handlebars. "Maybe you can be one of those bougie garden ornaments at some fancy house in the country," I whisper as the imposing XWZ building comes into view.

In the lobby, I'm hit by a rush of warm air. Oh, that's nice.

Pulling off my helmet, I shake out my curls and sigh. I hate wearing this thing, but I love my undamaged brain more, so ...

After parking Betty at a bike rack near the stairway, I open the zipper on my coat and study the fancy interior on my way to the reception desk. I've cycled past this building thousands of times and have always wondered what it looked like inside. It's exactly how I imagined it would be. All glass and steel and marble. Cold and detached. Much like the three men who own it, I suspect.

A stern-looking man wearing a dark gray suit and a powder blue tie sits behind the desk, eyeing me as I approach. "Can I help you?"

I reach for the thick padded envelope in my backpack. "I have a delivery for Mr. Archer. It requires his signature."

"I can take it to him," someone says, walking up behind me.

I roll my eyes. If I had a dollar for every time I've heard that. Exactly what part of *his signature* do people not understand? I spin around. "It needs his ..." *Holy mother of fucknuggets. Did this guy just walk off a photoshoot for some fancy designer cologne?* My jaw hangs open, the rest of the sentence caught in my mouth as I try not to drool.

He cocks an eyebrow at me, no doubt used to eliciting this kind of reaction from women. "It needs?"

"H-his ..." I swallow the dreamy sigh that wants to roll from my lips. Straightening my shoulders, I tilt my chin and look him in the eyes, which has to be safer than staring at that chiseled jaw. "Signature."

One corner of his mouth curls up, and damn if it doesn't make him look even more handsome. "I can sign it on his behalf." He holds out his hand, and I tighten my grip on the white envelope. I tilt my head, studying his features more thoroughly now that I've grown somewhat accustomed to his presence—as accustomed as any straight, red-blooded woman could be, anyway. "Are you Mr. Archer?"

That half smile turns into a full-on smirk, and my knees almost buckle. How does this man get through everyday life looking like he does? Do women just drop their panties when he walks past them in the street? "No. But trust me when I tell you that he won't mind me signing for his papers." He edges closer until he's invading my personal space, not so much that it would appear obvious, but just enough that I feel it. In every single part of my body. He smells good too. What is that? Cologne? Or maybe he just naturally smells as good as he looks because the stars were in perfect alignment the day he was born.

"So?" he asks, reminding me that he's waiting for my answer.

I want to clear my throat so I can be sure my voice won't come out in a squeak, but that would clue him in on the effect he has on me. I'll be damned if I let this arrogant, good-looking stranger think he has me rattled. "It requires Mr. Archer's signature," I reply, my voice surprisingly calm and steady despite my trembling knees.

He laughs softly.

"Can you tell me where I'll find him?"

He runs one hand over his jaw, his narrowed eyes searching my face like he's assessing whether I'm worthy enough to meet the great West Archer. Like I'd even want to meet that heartless douchebag by choice. I'd rather deliver his package inside a flaming bag of dog turds than hand it to him myself, but this is my job and it's the only one I have—for now. So, what is this guy's deal?

After the longest few seconds of my life, Hot Guy finally speaks. "Sure, I'm headed to his office myself. I'll show you the way." He inclines his head toward the elevators, then turns and walks away. With a quick glance at the guy behind the desk, who nods his approval, I fall into step beside Hot Guy.

We step inside the elevator a few moments later, and he leans against the back wall, hands splayed out on either side of him, gripping the polished chrome handrail. The elevator is bigger than the kitchen I ate my breakfast in this morning, but he still manages to dominate the entire space. I stand in the corner, as far from him as possible, and try to ignore the way he's watching me, his blue eyes twinkling with amusement.

A flush creeps over my cheeks as I become painfully aware of my appearance. The left leg of my jeans and the bottom of my thick coat is soaking wet. I've cycled twenty-eight miles today and this is my last stop, so no doubt my hair is at peak crazy. In sharp contrast, he's groomed to perfection. Clean shaven. Sandy blond hair, styled within an inch of its life. His white shirt is crisp and crease-free. He wears an impeccably tailored suit and the finest leather shoes. I might be penniless right now, but I have plenty of experience with the finer things in life and enough knowledge of men like this one here to know that he has the kind of wealth that makes him untouchable. It also makes women like me easily dispensable.

My skin grows hot under his gaze. "For a place this fancy, you'd think they'd have better security." I say, the need to take back control of the situation too strong for me to ignore.

His brow furrows in a slight frown. "Huh?"

I offer a casual shrug. "I mean I could be anyone. I could have all kinds of nasty stuff in this envelope here." I hold it up to emphasize my point.

He pushes himself off the wall, and in one step he's standing right in front of me. "Are you *anyone*, Lily?" My name rolls off his tongue like a raindrop from a leaf.

"H-how do you know my n-name?"

He glances down at my chest, which heaves with the effort of breathing. "It's on your ID badge."

My gaze follows his and intense relief washes over me. Of course it is.

"And *do you* have any nasty stuff in that envelope of yours?" His voice takes on a completely different tone, one that makes me regret saying that. His whole demeanor has shifted.

Dear god, I can't breathe. If smiley Hot Guy was hot, then growly Hot Guy with a hint of danger is pure fire. I shake my head, making my curls bounce around my shoulders. "Just papers."

He gives me a satisfied smile and steps back, his eyes locked on mine as he returns to his position against the rail.

CHAPTER
TWO

WEST

Xander stares at her ass as she sashays from the room, her dark curls bouncing with every step she takes. As soon as the door is closed, he flashes me a grin. "She was cute, right?"

I glance at the envelope on my desk. The papers she just delivered need my attention. Any further delay in this merger is going to make me gray before I'm forty, which is only two years away as Xander likes to remind me.

He flops into the chair opposite my desk. "West?"

I glance up, running my tongue over my bottom lip. "What?"

"I said she was cute."

"Kind of." I shrug and use my letter opener to slice open the envelope.

He scoffs. "Kind of? I saw the way you looked at her."

My head snaps up. Yes, I was acutely aware of the flush on her cheeks and the way her bright green eyes sparkled with defiance. I also noticed the bead of sweat running down her slender neck and wondered for a brief second what it would be like to lick it from her olive skin. "I didn't look at her like anything," I bark. Within these walls, I pride myself on being a professional. Unlike my partner here, I don't openly salivate over women every chance I get.

He laughs, throwing his head back far enough that I see the tattoo peeking out from beneath the open collar of his dress shirt. "Relax, buddy. She wouldn't have noticed. But I know you too well."

I snort but otherwise don't respond.

"Yeah." His voice drops an octave, and he leans forward, placing his hands on my desk. "You had that look in your eye. The one you get when your cock is twitching in your boxers."

"Fuck you." I concentrate on the papers and try to ignore him.

He sighs dramatically. "What's crawled up your ass today? Are you pissed at me for something?"

I'm pissed about a lot of things. Mostly this goddamn merger that he's preventing me from dealing with. I glare at him. "You're clean shaven."

He runs a hand over his jaw. "Yeah, Zeke was bitching about my stubble."

Tension works its way into my neck and shoulders. "You shaved for him?"

He rolls his eyes. "It'll grow back by tomorrow. I shave all the fucking time, West."

I clench my jaw, grinding my teeth together.

He cups my chin in his hand, his strong fingers flexing against my cheek as he forces me to look into his bright blue eyes. "And if you're pissed about me shaving, I think it's time we try to find a new addition to our little unit, don't you?"

I try to shake my head, but he holds me still. "We said we wouldn't do it again."

"I know what we said, but come on …" He tightens his grip on my jaw. "We're really giving up?"

"How many women have there been, Xander? Twenty? Thirty? I've lost fucking count."

His fingers slip from my face, and he runs a hand through his hair and sighs. "Twenty-two."

I stretch my neck in an attempt to alleviate the tension there, but it doesn't work. "Let's not add another to that particular body count."

"Maybe number twenty-three will be the one?" His hopeful smile and puppy dog expression make me wish I shared his enthusiasm and his sunny outlook on life. Too bad I'm a realist.

I shake my head. "I can't do it again. It's too much trouble and it never fucking works out."

"It doesn't have to be so much work, West. The NDAs. The contracts." He throws his hands in the air. "We could simplify things a little, you know?"

A frown furrows my brow, and my temples start to throb. "The fuck?"

His eyes soften and he leans across my desk, tracing a finger over my jawline. "It doesn't have to be another fucking merger is all I'm saying, West." He nods at the mountain of paperwork in front of me.

I swallow down the ball of emotion lodged in my throat. Anger and frustration eat away at my insides, and this man right in front of me deserves none of it. But the goddamn pressure of this Grayson News Corp merger is making me crazy. Sensing he's not about to let this go, I change tactics. "It's not good for Zeke … he blames himself every time. I can't stand to see him tear himself apart when it ends."

Disappointment flashes across Xander's face, and I feel like a jackass for putting it there. But he knows I'm right. He stands straight, stuffing his hands into his suit pants so that the already tight material stretches across his groin. The outline of his huge cock stares me directly in the face, and I run my tongue over my lip. That simple action makes him smile. "Then stop acting like a jealous asshole because I shaved."

I clear my throat. "I'm not jealous. I'm fucking stressed."

"All the more reason you need some pussy," he says with a wicked grin. "How about we go to the club tonight? The three of us? You need to relax, buddy. And Zeke ... well he's wound tighter than a coiled spring."

I sink back in my chair.

"It's Friday night. Wall-to-wall pussy," he adds with a chuckle.

I sigh. "Fine. Make the arrangements."

He winks at me. Cocky fucker. "Consider it done."

Xander heads out, and I return my focus to the papers on my desk but call out as he reaches the door. "Hey, Fitch."

He turns, his smile bright, probably because I used his nickname. "Yeah?"

"You look way better with some scruff on your face."

He barks a laugh and disappears from view.

CHAPTER

THREE

LILY

I t's still raining. Dammit. I stifle a groan as I strap my helmet back on, then take Betty from the bike rack in the lobby. My legs continue to shake after my encounter with West Archer. I almost passed out when I saw those steely gray eyes and square jaw. It's been fourteen years, but he's barely changed at all. Well, discounting the fact that he's now a super successful billionaire. At least he didn't recognize me, but I was just a little kid the last time he saw me. I had no idea the man responsible for the takeover of the magazine I work for was the same guy who ... Long-buried memories invade my consciousness, ascending from the deep recesses of my brain and causing my eyes to swim with unshed tears.

No. I shake my head. I won't think about it. I won't think about *him*.

Betty squeaks in protest as I wheel her through the WXZ tower's lobby and drags me back to the present. I wipe my eyes and focus on being here right now, in the greatest city in the entire world. "I know, girl. I don't like the idea of cycling home in this rain either, but we gotta do what we gotta do, yeah?"

She squeaks again, loudly, forcing me to look down at her and check if the chain gave out on me again. "Please don't give up on me now." Cycling to Brooklyn in this downpour is still a whole lot better than walking in it.

I'm so focused on Betty that I don't see the giant mountain of man muscle rounding the corner, and I wheel right into him, then bounce off like he's made of stone. Betty clatters to the floor, and I fall unceremoniously onto my ass. Ouch!

"Do you always talk to your bike instead of looking where you're going?" a gruff voice growls at me from above.

"Sorry, I was just—" I finish rubbing my bruised ass cheek and look up at the face of the man I just collided with. Holy mother of all that is divine and holy. Does every man who works in this building look like they fell from heaven, or have I just had the pleasure of meeting the three finest looking men on the face of this earth in the past ten minutes? Is the universe really so cruel that she would do this to me on today of all days, when I resemble a drowned rat and I'm acting like a lunatic who talks to bicycles?

His expression is fierce as he holds my gaze. I can't look away. I've never seen such dark eyes before. They're not even brown; they're black. And they smolder like charcoal. Or the darkest pits of hell. A shudder skitters along my spine. Irrational terror grips me, and I'm tempted to call for help, but I can't tear my gaze from his.

He holds out a hand. I can see it in my peripheral vision, but I don't take it. My cheeks flame with heat and I'm not sure if it's entirely because I just fell flat on my ass.

Maybe he sees my fear because his eyes soften just a little. "Are you okay?" His voice is deep and dangerous, but it serves to break the spell he seems to have me under. I blink rapidly and drop my gaze to his outstretched hand, which is almost the size of my head. Black ink snakes from beneath the sleeve of his crisp white shirt and wraps around his knuckles. My heart rate spikes. I catch a glimpse of his Rolex, and the cruel memory of another man who had a fondness for expensive jewelry is more than enough to snap me from my daze.

"Let me help you." He reaches for my elbow when I don't take his hand and hauls me up as though I weigh nothing. Heat from his fingertips penetrates through my coat and my sweater. His grip is tight, too tight, but I find myself wishing he'd squeeze harder. I want him to bruise me so I can look at it later and remember those dark eyes and tattooed hands while I …

I shake my head. *Bad Lily!* "Th-thanks." I brush the back of my jeans and coat before I risk looking at his face again. He's still glaring at me. So fucking intense. What the hell, dude? I mean I know I bumped into him, but I figure he barely even felt it. He must be at least six-four, and his shoulders are wider than a linebacker's. "I'm sorry I crashed into you."

"You should be more careful." He lets go of my arm, and I swear I nearly whimper at the loss of his bruising grip. He lifts Betty from the floor and straightens her up, and she doesn't squeak when he moves her. Traitor!

"I will," I whisper, my cheeks burning hotter with each passing second.

He moves Betty closer, holding her handlebars and indicating I should take them from him. His tattooed fingers brush mine, and my legs almost buckle as hot sparks of electricity shoot up my hands and skitter through my entire body. I hold onto my bike for dear life, knuckles turning white as I struggle to remain upright. Our eyes meet again, and the intensity of his stare makes it even harder to stay on my feet. "And you really shouldn't go around talking to your bike." One corner of his deliciously full lips lifts, hinting at a smirk.

Wow. I wonder what it would take to get a full-on smile from him. Not that I plan to find out. It would probably render me immobile.

He leans closer, and I forget how to breathe. "People will think you're crazy." His breath dusts across my forehead and goosebumps break out all over my body. Then he walks away, leaving me wanting. I spin around and watch him head for the stairwell. Even the way he walks is hot. Shoulders rolled back and huge arms swinging at his sides. So sure of where he's headed. Like our little interaction didn't affect him at all. Not one iota.

I wheel Betty toward the exit. The sooner I get out of this building, the better.

WRAPPING my wet hair in a towel, I wander into the kitchen and rifle through the stack of takeout menus clipped to the fridge. Dim sum sounds amazing. It will eat into my budget for the weekend, but … my imagination conjures the taste of steamed pork dumplings, pan fried noodles, and deep-fried eggplant, and my stomach rumbles loudly, voicing its opinion. Dim sum it is then.

The front door slams closed. "Lily!" Jen calls.

"Right here," I say.

She rushes toward me, breathless like she sprinted up the stairs, her cornflower-blue eyes wide with excitement. "You are going to freaking love me," she squeals.

"I already do," I remind her.

She tilts her head and runs her tongue over her perfect

white teeth. "True. But you're going to love me even more when I tell you what I managed to score for tonight."

"No." I hold out my hands and shake my head. "No more edibles. Last time I thought I was the king of the fairy underworld. Kevin from down the hall still looks at me funny whenever he sees me."

My beautiful best friend howls with laughter at the memory and wraps me in a hug. It takes her at least two minutes to regain the ability to speak. "No more edibles. This is even better." Reaching into her back pocket, she brandishes what looks like two tickets and squeals. "I got us passes for Marché de Viande!"

My shoulders slump, and I let out a loud groan.

"Lily!" she admonishes. "It's literally *the* hottest club in New York."

"It's also the most expensive," I remind her with a dead-eyed stare.

"These tickets are *free*." She waves them in my face for emphasis.

"The drinks inside aren't though." Despite my argument, I know I'm going to give in, and I mentally kiss my dream of eating dim sum in my pajamas goodbye. Whatever Jen wants, she gets. She's the only person I know who can talk just about anyone into anything, even me. Plus, I do kind of owe her. I'd be homeless if it wasn't for her willingness to share her one-bedroom apartment. Unfortunately for me, delivering documents and packages doesn't pay enough to afford a place to live in New York City.

She gives me her best puppy dog eyes. "We'll just have a few sodas."

I let out an exasperated sigh. "You do know the name literally means meat market in French, right?"

Her whole face lights up, and I have to bite my lip to hold back a laugh. "Really? That's so hot."

I shake my head. I should have known that wouldn't deter her. "It's really not."

She fixes me with a stare like she's trying to peer into my soul. She can't. Nobody can. "Hell yeah it is! When's the last time you got any action that wasn't of the battery-operated variety?"

"I'll have you know that my womanizer is rechargeable. Plug it in for thirty minutes, and I'm good to go for hours. No batteries required." Grinning triumphantly, I wink.

She snorts a laugh but quickly turns serious. "Lily. You need to get out there and have yourself some fun. You're twenty-four and you currently live the life of a nun."

"I do not! I'm just ..." I sigh. "The last guy I hooked up with at a club turned out to be in breach of his parole, remember? I mean he was cute, but ..."

"Yeah, didn't the cops bust into his place while you were doing the deed?" She snort-laughs again, and I shake my head. I have the absolute worst judgment when it comes to men. "This time just try and steer toward the guys who don't have tattoos on their hands, okay?"

My bottom lip pops out a tiny bit. I love tattooed hands. "That is an outdated and offensive stereotype, Jen."

She plucks the takeout menu from my hands and grabs my wrists. "Please come, Lils. You can wear that red dress you have stuffed in the back of my closet."

Now I'm really pouting. "I've had a stupid busy day," I whine. "My legs are aching. And I got soaked by a taxi."

"Awww." She pulls me in for another hug and pats my back. "I'm sorry, girl." Gripping my shoulders, she tilts her head and gives me a bright smile. "A night out might be just what you need. We can be home by two. Promise."

I can either spend my night arguing with her or just give in and go. At least if I give in, one of us will be happy. "Fine," I grumble, defeated.

She nearly deafens me with her excited shriek before kissing me on the forehead and dashing out of the room.

ZEKE

Xander squeezes my thigh. "Relax, big guy. Tonight will be fun."

Grunting, I continue to stare out the car window as we pull up outside our club. The queue is already around the block, a fact that will please West. Marché de Viande was his idea, and it's one of our most profitable ventures.

"Will you two lighten the fuck up?" Xander demands. "Or I'm going home with some stray tonight and leaving you two the fuck to it."

Quick as lightning, I take hold of his jaw and turn his head, forcing him to fix all his attention on me. He is such a fucking brat. But I'm grateful that his petulance pulls me out of my bad mood a little. "You find a stray, you bring them to our place. You don't go anywhere with her. You got me?"

He grins wickedly and runs his sinful tongue over his bottom lip. "I know the rules."

I squeeze his jaw tighter and slide my other hand up his

thigh until my fingertips brush his semihard cock. "Don't fuck with me, Fitch."

"Oh, I am gonna fuck with you two all night long." Laughing, he sinks back against the seat and wrenches out of my grip.

West catches my eyes and rolls his. He needs to cut loose for a few hours even more than I do. He always gets this way when we're close to closing a huge deal, and it puts me on edge whenever he acts like a grumpy asshole. I have no idea how Xander puts up with the two of us. He's a sucker for torture. I guess all three of us are gluttons for punishment in our own way.

Xander whistles and cranes his neck to look out the window next to me. "Would you look at all that pussy. Please tell me you're both planning on getting laid tonight."

West rocks his head from side to side. "Fuck yeah."

"Zeke?"

Probably not. But I don't reply because I don't need to. They both know me well enough to know my answer. And my reason why.

Xander squeezes my shoulder. "Will you at least get drunk and chill out a little then?"

"I'll get drunk if West does."

West's eyes narrow. "Now, why do you want me drunk, Zeke?" His deep voice is an octave lower than usual.

My cock twitches at the memory of the last time we both got drunk together. We were in his office with a bottle of fifty-year-old Macallan, celebrating a deal. And fuck, did we celebrate. "So I have someone to talk to while Fitch is knee-deep in pussy."

Smirking, Xander jerks his chin at me. "Balls-deep."

The car rolls to a stop and Xander jumps out, smoothing his hands down his dress shirt and over those hard-as-fuck abs of his. The women standing in line actually fucking scream when they see him, like he's some kind of celebrity. Which I guess he is around here. He's the face of our business for a reason. Charming as hell with a sunny disposition that could make Darth Vader crack a smile. It doesn't hurt that he looks like the love child of Chris Hemsworth and Scarlett Johansson either.

I step out behind him and fasten my jacket, followed closely by West.

"Sirs." One of the bouncers nods a greeting before moving the thick velvet rope and gesturing for us to enter the club. "Your usual table is ready."

HUNDREDS OF WOMEN, most of them hot and barely clothed, are packed in the club. Ours for the taking. None of us have ever had a problem getting laid, it's finding a woman who will stick around that we have an issue with. Not a single one of them grabs my attention tonight. I'm not like Xander and West, who could probably fuck any woman anywhere if the circumstances were right. I need some kind of connection first, and that's why I rarely screw around with anyone.

"You see anyone interesting?" Xander asks as he takes a seat beside me, discreetly nudging my thigh under the table. I resist the base urge to force him to his knees and make him suck my cock at this booth.

I shake my head. "You?"

"At least a dozen," he says, and I can't help but laugh. "Looks like West has his eye on someone." He nods to the dance floor, and I scan the sea of faces until I see him talking to a guy. Rage bubbles in my chest, and I'm surprised I don't shatter the glass I'm holding with my bare hand.

Xander laughs and strokes my thigh beneath the table. "Not him, big guy. You know he'd never fuck around with other guys. He was just talking to the girl behind him a second ago."

I grunt before downing my Scotch in one gulp.

He cocks his head, watching me with curiosity. "It's so fucking funny how you two get this jealous about other guys."

"It's funny how you don't," I snap.

"Nothing to be jealous about. Girls or guys, all the same to me. Just because you fuck other people doesn't diminish what we have."

I slam my glass onto the table. "So you wouldn't care if I fucked some random guy tonight?"

He presses his lips together, and after a few seconds he finally shakes his head.

"Well, that's easy to say when you know I'd never do that." I'm not into *men*. I'm into West and Xander.

He leans closer until his lips are pressed against my ear and his hot breath dusts over my neck. "And you know I'd never do that either, don't you?"

I groan. I'm a man on the fucking edge, and right now he's the only one who can offer me any kind of relief.

"Not tonight, big guy," he says with a soft laugh that rolls through me. "I need to fuck someone, and as you would *never* let that happen, I guess I should go find me some sweet, sweet pussy instead."

I sigh. "Then go."

Wrinkling his nose, he sits back and takes a sip of his Scotch. "I'm still deciding. You could at least help me, even if you're not indulging yourself."

I shake my head and refill my glass before scanning the crowd again. West is talking to one of our bouncers now, and they appear deep in conversation. He needs to switch the fuck off from work and get himself some sweet pussy too. Maybe that's what we all need. My eyes drift to the bar and linger on a perfect ass showcased by a skin-tight red dress. Her long dark hair falls in soft curls all the way down her back, stopping directly above the aforementioned fine ass. Red Dress turns her head toward the woman standing next to her and laughs. A wide smile spreads across my face. Well, she certainly looks different without her bike helmet and her giant padded coat, although I can't say which look I preferred. Cute as fuck, either way.

Xander nudges me. "You see someone you like?"

"Maybe."

With another laugh, he crosses his legs and rests his ankle on his thigh. "Well, point her out then."

"What if it's a guy?" I can't help teasing him, but he just stares at me, refusing to take the bait.

I look back at where she's still laughing with her friend. "At the bar. Red dress. Ass you could sink your teeth into."

"Holy fuck. Lily."

What the fuck? I glance at him. He's staring at her with his mouth hanging open. "You know her?"

"Yeah." He shakes his head. "I mean no. I met her today. She delivered a package to West. We thought she was cute."

"We?" My eyebrows go up. "He met her too?"

His eyes still on the vixen in the red dress—Lily—Xander grins. "Yeah. She was a firecracker. Such a smart fucking mouth." The sound that comes out of him sounds like he's imagining that smart mouth on him right now.

I frown. She didn't come across like that to me at all. "She was talking to her bike when I met her."

"You met her too?" he asks, his excitement palpable.

"Yeah. She ran right into me. Literally."

"Fuck," he mutters, then turns his attention back to the bar, a dopey ass grin on his face. I watch her too. Tossing her hair over her shoulder as she chats animatedly to the woman next to her. A friend? Or maybe her girlfriend.

Not that it matters. If West and Fitch think she's hot too, it's probably best if all three of us stay the fuck away.

I sip my Scotch, about to suggest that Xander look elsewhere for his hookup, but I'm distracted by the guy walking up behind Lily. He puts his hand on her beautiful ass and squeezes, and I wonder if she's with him.

Until she turns around and punches him square in the jaw.

CHAPTER
FIVE

LILY

J en half laughs, half shrieks as we both stare at the guy
sprawled on the floor at our feet, out cold. "Holy fuck,
Lils." The people who were crowded around the bar have
stepped back and everyone is now ogling and pointing
at us.

Dammit. I just reacted. I didn't mean to knock his ass out,
but he shouldn't have grabbed mine. But we're going to get
kicked out of this fancy club, and Jen will be so disappointed.
Bouncers are making their way toward us, their heads bobbing
above the crowd.

"I'm really sorry," I blurt as soon as they're close enough to
hear me. "But he—"

"Miss, we're going to have to ask you to leave." One of the
bouncers grabs my arm.

"Take your fucking hands off her. Now." The deep voice cuts
through the noise and the hand on my arm disappears.

"Apologies, Mr. Cavanagh," the bouncer mumbles.

I look up to see the same dark eyes from earlier today in the lobby. Oh my god, what's he doing here? I swallow the knot of anxiety clogging my throat, but I'm unable to keep my body from trembling.

He glances at the guy on the floor. "Get that piece of shit out of here and don't let him back in ever again. You hear me?"

"Yes, Mr. Cavanagh," another bouncer replies.

Jen stares at me with her mouth hanging open, and all I can do is shrug at her. I have no idea what the hell's going on either. The stranger steps closer to me, his dark eyes burning into mine.

"I-I, h-he grabbed me."

He frowns. "I saw. Are you okay?"

I nod, my tongue darting out to moisten my dry lips. "I'm fine."

"You have a habit of getting into trouble wherever you go, Lily?" he asks.

"H-how do you know my name?"

"You met a couple friends of mine today," he says, amusement dancing in his eyes.

Oh, wow. He's Ezekiel freaking Cavanagh, business partner of West Archer and Xander King.

"Before you recklessly tried to mow me down in the lobby of my building," he adds.

"What? I did not."

A smirk tugs at his lips, and damn, it makes him even more intimidating than he was a few seconds earlier. He's teasing me. Jackass. "At least let me buy you and your friend here a drink for the inconvenience of having to do our bouncer's jobs for them."

"You don't have to. We're good," I say, taking Jen's arm and signaling we should head to another part of the club.

Jen stays rooted to the spot, her gaze trained on Ezekiel. "I'd love a drink." She flutters her eyelashes, and that smirk of his grows wider. Oh, I see what this is now. He's into Jen. Most guys are. She's stunning.

"Come join us at our table." He nods toward the private booths on the balcony—the ones that cost upward of ten thousand dollars a night to sit at.

"Ooh, yes please." Jen glances at me and silently claps her hands together, and I barely resist the urge to roll my eyes. I guess we're going to his fancy-ass booth then.

~

JEN'S KNEELING on the plush velvet bench and peering down at the crowd. "Wow! It is freaking incredible up here. You can see everything."

"You sure can," the guy from the elevator today, who I now realize is Xander King, says with a grin.

She turns to face him and flashes him her killer smile. From the moment she saw Xander sitting in this booth, Ezekiel—or Zeke, as he introduced himself—has been well and truly sidelined. I can't say I blame her. Xander is ridiculously hot. Like you'd walk down the street behind him drooling at his ass hot. Not that Zeke isn't every bit as alluring, but in a different way. Dark and dangerous and brooding. The ultimate bad guy. But where's West Archer, the devil himself? Also known as the third member of their Unholy Trinity, which is what my colleagues call the three men who are about to take over Grayson News Corp, the company I work for. At least that's what the rumor mill's been saying.

Zeke pours a glass of champagne and hands it to me. "I don't think I've ever seen you in here before."

Those dark eyes narrow, and I scoot back a little as I murmur my thanks and take a sip. I feel like he's trying to see into my soul, and all he'll see in there are the things I keep hidden. "Do you know every single person who comes to this club?"

He shakes his head and laughs. The sound is dark and unnerving, and it sends a shiver of excitement down my spine. "But I would definitely remember you."

I suck in a stuttered breath. Is he flirting with me? No. He's an absurdly sexy billionaire. I'm dreaming. I must be.

"Lily?" A voice cuts through the steady thrum of the club. My pulse races as I drink in the delectable sight of West Archer. The devil himself, looking sexier than hell in a perfectly tailored suit and a crisp white shirt. I knock back the entire glass of champagne and hope for the second time today that he doesn't recognize me as the ten-year-old girl he met all those years ago.

CHAPTER
SIX

XANDER

The look on West's face when he sees Lily sitting at our booth is priceless. I wish I could take a picture. It's not often we see the ice man lost for words, at least not in public anyway. He stares at her, and then his gaze flickers between me and Zeke and finally to Lily's friend. A hint of a scowl creases his forehead, but he recovers quickly, and I doubt anyone but Zeke or I noticed.

"Hi," Lily says softly, giving him a little wave. Meanwhile, Jen spins around, plonking her ass on the seat for the first time since she climbed into the booth. Her eyes almost bug out when she sees West. I stifle a laugh. Handsome fucker tends to have that effect on people.

He clears his throat, all his attention on Lily now. "Hi. It's ... *interesting* to see you again."

I suppress a grin. He thinks I invited her up here. I know it.

Lily sinks her teeth into her pillowy bottom lip, and it makes me want to do the same—right before I sink them into her juicy, round ass. "It's interesting to see you too."

West opens his suit jacket. His nostrils flare and the thick vein on the underside of his jaw pulses. He's so fucking into her. He comes over and puts his lips by my ear so nobody will hear what he says. "Lose the fucking friend."

I bite back my grin. Oh he is *so* fucking into her. West takes a seat, sandwiching Lily between him and Zeke.

"Well, this is fun." Jen giggles and tops up her glass from the bottle of Dom on the table. "How do you all know my best friend here?"

"She tried to viciously and brutally run me down with her bicycle today," Zeke replies, deadpan.

Lily gapes at him. "I did not. I bumped into you by accident."

He cocks his head and lifts his glass to his lips. "Semantics." He takes a sip of his Scotch, and she smirks at him.

I stretch my arms over the back of the bench seat and stare at her until she makes eye contact. When she does, I wink at her. "We shared an elevator. Most interesting two minutes of my entire day."

Her cheeks flush pink, and it's goddamn fucking adorable. Is she too innocent for us? Would she run as fast and far as she could if she had any idea of the filthy thoughts that are running through all three of our minds right now? Although if she is as innocent as her sweet blush makes her seem, then that might be even hotter, because what I wouldn't give to corrupt her.

"She delivered me a steaming pile of elephant shit," West says with a shrug.

She glares at him now. "I did not."

"Figuratively speaking." His lip twitches, his tell that he's fighting the urge to laugh.

Lily rolls her eyes and turns to her friend. "I delivered a package to their building today."

"And now you're at our club. And in our booth," West says,

his narrowed eyes raking down her body. *Poor girl doesn't stand a fucking chance and she has no idea.*

Lily's blush creeps down her neck. "Well, your friend Zeke here invited me."

West glances at me, and I nod to confirm it's true, not missing the puzzled frown that flickers across his face. *Yeah, surprised the hell outta me too, buddy.*

"She punched out some asshole who grabbed her ass, and one of your bouncers got all handsy with her," Jen explains.

"Which guy and which bouncer?" West demands.

"I'll handle the bouncer," Zeke assures him. "And the guy is gone. She knocked him out cold."

West returns his attention to Lily, his gray eyes full of admiration, despite Jen's best efforts to direct them at her. But her crossing her legs and flashing him her panties ain't gonna work because he has a hard-on for the bike messenger. And the fact that this pint-sized, curly haired firecracker just dropped a man two times her size only makes her more intriguing.

I down my Scotch, make a lame excuse to leave the table, and head off to find one of our most loyal employees. Trey's standing near the bar, and I wave him over.

"You okay, Boss?"

I rub a hand over my jaw and glance at the booth. "I have a job for you."

He grins. "Okay."

"You see that redhead up there sitting with us?"

He scans the room until he finds her. "Yup."

"I need you to take her home."

His grin widens.

"Be a fucking gentleman, Trey. Unless she doesn't want you to, of course. But be respectful. Show her a good time and get her home safely. You understand me?"

31

He drags a hand over the stubble on his chin. "Same deal as last time?"

"Yeah. All expenses paid, buddy. Who do you fancy being tonight? Movie star? Billionaire tech genius?"

"Hmm." His eyes narrow. "I think I'll go with movie star."

"Perfect."

SEVEN

WEST

Trey Ferguson could be an actor given the Oscar-worthy performance he gave convincing Lily's friend that he's a movie star who's been watching her all night. Of course, Xander helped him out, playing his own part exceptionally well. It took a little persuading to make her consider leaving Lily behind, but Trey is a smooth, good-looking fucker, and Jen was putty in his hands by the time he gave her his well-practiced spiel.

As soon as Jen leaves, Lily starts chewing on the inside of her cheek.

"Like we told your friend, shorty, we'll make sure you get home safely," Xander assures her. Once Trey gave Jen a glimpse of his six pack and the keys to his Lamborghini—technically, Xander's Lamborghini, but Trey's for tonight—Lily knew she was on her own.

She downs her glass of champagne and jumps to her feet. "Yeah, but I should probably just go home now. I can take the subway."

"Why?" I ask her.

"Because ..." She chews on her cheek again, her green eyes dark as they search my face. "So you guys can get on with your night. I don't want to cramp your style. And now that Jen's gone ..." She looks out at the crowd.

Xander takes her hand, and she flinches at his touch. Unfazed by her reaction, he gives her a reassuring smile, and she doesn't pull away when he curls his fingers around hers. "How are you cramping our style?"

"Well ... you might want to ... uh, you know ..."

Her legs are trembling. She is so fucking cute. But as fun as it is to see her so nervous, I need her to be comfortable with us.

"We want to talk to you, Lily." Taking her other hand, I pull her back down onto the bench to sit between Zeke and me.

She eyes me suspiciously. "Why?"

Unable to stop my eyes from raking over her delectable body, I lean back. What I'd give to strip her out of that dress and explore every goddamn inch of her. She'd look so good on her knees for me. Stuffed full with all three of our cocks. I take a sip of my Scotch and clear my throat. "Many reasons."

"Have another drink. I promise we don't bite. Unless you ask nicely," Xander says, already refilling her champagne flute.

Her tongue darts out, moistening her lips. I bet she's a good girl, raised to believe that it's wrong for a woman to want three guys at the same time. And that only makes me want to show her what she's been missing.

Two hours and three more glasses of champagne later, Lily is drunk and way more relaxed than she was earlier. It's a joy to see her so open and chatty. Still, I'm disappointed that she's such a lightweight when it comes to alcohol, but only because we can't take her home and fuck her six ways to Sunday. Maybe that's for the best though, because I want more than one night with her.

"I should go," she says, checking her watch. Even after spending all this time with us, she seems completely unaware that we all want her.

Xander leans forward, and I can see the telltale bulge in his suit pants even if Lily can't. "Come for dinner tomorrow?"

She arches an eyebrow. "With you?"

I lean close and the scent of her fills my mouth and nose. I lick my lips, desperate for a taste, but I hold back. "With all of us."

Her eyelashes flutter against her pink cheeks. "Like ... a date?"

"Like dinner," I say.

"With all three of you though?"

Zeke drapes his arm over the back of the bench. "That is what all of us means."

She narrows her eyes, her gaze flitting between us. "But why?"

"It's just dinner, Lily," Xander replies, not taking his eyes off her for a second. They rake over her curves, lingering on all the parts I know he's dying to touch. He wants her as badly as I do. And Zeke? Well, the fact that he was the one to invite her to our booth tells me how much he likes her. He's never done that before.

"I know that. But ..." She chews on the inside of her cheek. I've come to realize it's one of her nervous tells. "Why me? What do the three of you, who could get literally any girl in this club, want with a bike messenger from Brooklyn?"

I shuffle closer, and my breath ruffles her hair, making her shiver. Oh, I fucking love the way her body responds to mine. It's primal and pure, and fuck me, she has me hard as stone. "Well, you are kind of funny, even when you don't mean to be."

Her cheeks redden.

I brush her hair back from her neck, trailing my fingertips over her bare skin. She squeezes her thighs together, and I suck in a stuttered breath. She's going to look so incredible with my hand around her throat while I fuck her. "You're sweet," I whisper, edging even closer until my lips brush her ear.

"Am not."

Her feeble protest makes me chuckle. "And you're hot as fuck, Lily." Her soft moan has my cock throbbing against my zipper. Fucking hell.

Her body leans into mine, like she's allowing her instincts to take over. Or maybe it's the champagne. "This club is bursting with hot women. You could take any of these girls home right now," she says, her voice husky.

"True." I force myself to back away before I lose control and end up fucking her right here at our table. She exhales and her shoulders slump. "But we're talking about dinner, and we only want that with you."

Once again, she studies the three of us and frowns. "So this isn't about one of you wanting to take me home for a quick hookup?"

Fuck yes, I want to take you home and feel those pretty lips around my cock. But that isn't all we want.

Zeke answers before I get the chance. "No."

A fleeting look of disappointment flashes across her face, but she masks it well. She glances around the club. Her throat thickens as she swallows. She wants to come home with us, likely only one of us though, and that's just not going to work. Not with her. But there's no use getting ahead of myself. Xander will make sure she gets home safely tonight, and he'll do whatever's necessary to convince her to have dinner with us tomorrow.

CHAPTER
EIGHT

LILY

I fumble my key after fishing it from my purse, and it clatters to the ground. Xander stoops to pick it up for me, which I'm eternally grateful for because my head is spinning and I'm not sure I could have bent down without falling over. I rarely drink at all, and I must have consumed almost an entire bottle of Dom by myself. I chalk it up to nerves. I mean, who wouldn't be nervous sitting with three of the richest, most powerful men in the country? And they were definitely flirting with me. Even if it was only to have a little fun at my expense, the memory of their teasing has me squeezing my thighs together to quell the throbbing ache.

Xander's fingers brush mine when he hands me my key, and a jolt of electricity shoots up my arm. I stare up at him. "So damn handsome it should be illegal."

He chuckles, and I realize I said my thoughts aloud. Staring up into his deep blue eyes, I exhale a dreamy sigh. He's been the perfect gentleman all night, even while he sat next to me on the ride here. It doesn't make sense for him to be interested in a girl like me, but ... the way he looks at me. As though he might be interested in something more, if only for tonight. And I so need to blow off steam.

Leaning against the doorframe for support and trying to look as sexy as possible, I clear my throat before any more of my thoughts spill from my lips. "You want to come in for a beer?"

He bites on his beautiful lip and shakes his head.

Dammit. Of course he doesn't. I look at the floor to hide the embarrassment burning my cheeks, but he cups my chin, tilting my head until I'm staring into his hypnotic eyes once more. "Don't think for a second it's because I don't want to, shorty."

I blink at him. Champagne is clouding my senses. "So what is it?"

He takes a half step forward, closing the distance between us until our bodies are mere inches apart. My pulse throbs against my skin. My legs tremble. My breath hitches. I feel like I'm standing too close to the sun and I'm about to get burned. He dusts the pad of his thumb over my lips. "Because you're drunk and it's taking all of my goddamn restraint not to slip my hand inside your panties and find out how wet you are, Lily."

My heart races into overdrive. Holy fucknuggets, I'm definitely going to pass out.

His lips are so close to my ear that his breath ruffles my hair. "I'm hanging on by a fucking thread here, shorty. So don't ask me again, because if you do, you're likely going to be bent over something real fast and I'll be balls-deep in your sweet pussy before you have a chance to change your mind."

Molten heat sears between my thighs and coils deep in my core, making me gasp. Without any further thought, I wrap my arms around his neck and pull him to me, sealing my lips over his. He groans, his hands sliding to my ass and yanking me forward, our bodies so close that his hard cock pushes into my stomach. God, he's huge. I curl my fingers in his thick hair, and he slides his tongue against mine, possessive and dominating as he takes control. My head spins. My pussy throbs. I shut my eyes and lose myself in the delicious pleasure of his kiss. It's incredible. He tastes of Scotch and fire and fresh air, and I want more. But all too soon, he pulls back, leaving me breathless and needy.

He takes my key from my hand and unlocks the door, then pushes it wide open. Taking a step away, he passes me my key back. "Go inside, Lily," he says in a low, commanding growl.

I sway on my feet. I should do what he says. If I beg him to come in with me, I'll only regret it in the morning. Better to remember that perfect kiss for the rest of my life. I step inside Jen's apartment, my eyes not leaving his. I don't want whatever this is to end.

"I'll see you at dinner tomorrow night," he reminds me.

I'd forgotten about that. I thought they were kidding around. "But where?"

He winks at me. "We'll be in touch, shorty. Now go get some sleep."

NINE

WEST

Xander leans against the kitchen island with his signature cocksure grin on his face.

"Did you do anything?" Zeke asks.

Xander shakes his head. "Well, nothing more than a kiss. I was a good boy. As much as I wanted to take her up on her invite to come in for a beer."

Leaning forward, I rest my hands on the countertop. "She invited you in?"

Of course she fucking did. He looks like Ryan Gosling's better-looking younger brother.

"I told her I'd see her at dinner tomorrow." He checks his watch. "Or more like tonight now, I guess."

Zeke pours himself another Scotch and sits on a stool. "So we're doing this again?"

Xander hops up and sits on the counter while I stare at Zeke, his face etched with worry and a deep-seated sadness that makes my heart feel heavy. "Do you want to try this again?" I ask.

"It's not my decision to make," he replies with a shrug, staring into his glass.

"No. It's all of ours, Zeke."

He lifts his head, his dark eyes piercing into mine. "But you and Fitch want to, yeah?"

I glance at Xander who nods. "I do. I mean I love you both, you know that. But ..."

"We're a lot to handle on your own," I finish for him.

He closes his eyes like it pains him to admit that, but I get it. Zeke and I are pretty full-on.

"*I'm* a lot to handle," Zeke adds before downing his drink.

Xander runs his hand through his hair. "I never fucking said that, Z."

"It would be a whole lot easier if I could just fuck random strangers like you both can though, wouldn't it? Or if I wasn't so messed up that I made all the others go running for the fucking hills as soon as they find out the shit I'm into."

"You are not messed up," I tell him. "They didn't all leave because of you. They left because the three of us together were too much, Zeke."

Xander runs a hand through Zeke's thick hair and gently tugs his head back. Zeke doesn't pull away from his grasp, which is unusual for him. "It's all three of us or none of us, Z. Like it's always been."

Zeke's eyes land on mine again. "You want to do this, West?"

I didn't think I'd want this again. When we agreed that Ebony would be the last one, we meant it. But that was before Lily. With her sweet laugh and sparkling green eyes. And legs I can't stop imagining wrapped around my neck. I knew in my office today that Xander and I liked her, but now that Zeke does too ... "I think it's worth one more shot."

He shakes his head. He's fighting this, even though I know

he wants Lily just as much as we do. But something changed on the ride home. Like once he knew she was a possibility, he closed himself off again. "What makes this one any different than the others?"

"We all met her separately and liked her, despite not knowing how the other two felt," I say. "That's never happened before."

Zeke shakes his head. "That's a nonissue. What matters more is how she'll respond to us. The women we've done this with before have been ..." He rubs a hand over his thick beard.

"Been what?" I ask.

He sucks on his top lip, as though he's searching for the right word. "Experienced. They weren't some kid fresh out of college who works as a fucking bike messenger."

Xander snorts and drops his hand from Zeke's hair. "Judgy much?"

"You know what I mean," he says with a heavy sigh. "We've always found women through recommendations. Women who we knew would be into group stuff. She's so fucking young and naive."

"Young, yes," I admit. "I don't get a naive vibe from her at all. And if you're going to hold her job title against her, may I remind you of Helena?"

Xander snorts a laugh, but Zeke frowns. "Helena?"

"Guinea pig number three," Xander answers. "She did those singing telegrams."

Realization dawns on Zeke's face, and he rolls his eyes. If I recall, she barely lasted a month, so she probably wasn't the best example. "Maybe something different is what we need," I add, before he gets lost in the memories of all the women who haven't worked out for us. My gut tells me that Lily's worth taking a risk on.

"Maybe we do everything different?" Xander suggests.

I scowl. "What do you mean?"

"I mean …" He slips off the countertop and runs a hand thought his blond hair. "We've always approached this like a fucking business arrangement rather than a relationship. Maybe that's why it always kinda felt like a contract instead of something that might last."

Zeke's eyes narrow as he stares at our best friend. "Are you suggesting we don't have an NDA?"

Xander shoves his hands into his pockets. "Fuck yes, I'm suggesting that."

I breathe out a sigh. "But what if—"

"Fuck your what-ifs, West. How about we just fucking tell her what we want and don't make her sign anything. How about we just do this like it's something we all want and not like some business deal."

I run my tongue over my bottom lip. We've never done this without some kind of contract in place. The NDAs were my idea to begin with, but Xander and Zeke were on board. Having things in writing offers us protection when these things inevitably go south.

Xander's blue eyes lock on mine. "How do we start something that might last forever when we go into it preparing for it to end?"

I swallow hard. I guess he has a point. But still …

Zeke looks between Xander and me. "So what? We just tell her we want a relationship with her? All three of us? No contract, no boundaries?"

Xander throws his hands in the air. "There's boundaries in every relationship, Z. Most people don't feel the need to write them into a fucking twenty-page contract."

That's an obvious dig at me, but I let it go. I'm tightly wound enough at the moment without dwelling on my neurotic tendencies.

"So we just invite her to dinner tonight and tell her we all want to ..." I stop short of saying *fuck her*, but that's all I've been able to think about since I saw her in that sinful red dress that hugged her curves like it was painted on. Fuck, it's practically all I've thought about since she came stomping into my office with those papers.

"Yep," Xander replies with a firm nod. "I don't know about you two, but I've been thinking about sinking my cock between those full pink lips from the first moment she opened them," he adds with a chuckle, defusing the tension in the way he does so well.

"What do you think, West?" Zeke asks.

I stare up at the ceiling, running through the pros and cons.

"Stop overthinking and just fucking answer, West," Xander admonishes me.

I suck in a breath. Maybe he's right. Maybe we do need to try something different. I look at Xander, who's now standing behind Zeke with his arms wrapped around his shoulders. "Fine. Let's do this your way and see how it works out."

"Great." A slow, sexy smile spreads across his face and he kisses Zeke's neck. "You okay with this too, big guy?"

Zeke merely grunts and wraps a thick arm around Xander's neck, pulling him closer. Rolling my eyes, I go to leave.

"Hey," Xander calls, stopping me in my tracks.

"Yeah?"

He cocks his head, motioning for me to come closer. With a sigh, I step toward him. He places a hand on my cheek and says in a soft voice, "Thanks."

"I hope we don't regret it, Fitch." With that, I leave them to it and go to bed alone with a raging hard on and thoughts of Lily swimming in my head.

STARING OUT THE KITCHEN WINDOW, I look down at Central Park and watch the morning joggers and the dog walkers with a pang of something that I can't quite identify. The soft pad of footsteps comes from behind me, and a few seconds later, the heat from his hard chest warms the bare skin of my back. He plants his hands beside mine on the counter.

"You okay?" he asks in his gruff voice, still heavy with sleep.

"I'm good."

"I'm sorry if I've been monopolizing Fitch's time."

"It's fine," I say with a sigh.

"Is it?"

"I just fucking said it was, Zeke." I instantly regret snapping at him.

His warm breath dusts over my neck, and I close my eyes. A second later he puts his hot mouth on the side of my throat, trailing his teeth across my skin. When his hand slides across my abs, I stifle a groan. He pulls me back as he rocks his hips and presses the hard length of his cock against my ass.

I hiss out his name, my aching cock leaking precum. It's been too fucking long since I had any sort of release.

"You always pull back from us when you're stressed. It's not good for you."

I pinch the bridge of my nose. "This merger is fucking exhausting, Z."

"I know," he says softly, teeth and lips teasing my skin and pushing me closer to the edge. "But this is *our* merger. You don't have to carry the weight of everything alone."

"I know that." The truth is I do have to carry it all though. I'm the one who's responsible for every t being crossed and every i being dotted. If I fuck up one single thing, the whole deal could fall to pieces. Of course, the other truth is that I thrive on the pressure. I always have, and I don't see that ever changing.

His hand skates lower, dipping into the waistband of my sweatpants. "Is there anything I can do?"

I groan. "You can stop doing that for a start." I don't have time for whatever he has in mind, no matter how tempting he may be.

His teeth clamp down my neck for a second before letting go. "Masochist," he grumbles. But he does as I asked, and soon the warmth of him is gone and I'm standing alone in the kitchen.

CHAPTER

TEN

LILY

My head throbbing, I blink my eyes open. Sunlight streams through the gap in the curtains in Jen's bedroom and blinds me. She sent me a text at 3:00 a.m. to tell me she was spending the night at Trey's hotel suite, so I slept in her bed instead of the sofa. My back already thanks me for it as I stretch out beneath the duvet.

My phone pings, signaling a text. I roll onto my side and grab it from my nightstand.

Hey shorty. Be ready at seven. No need to dress fancy, we're eating in. Bring an overnight bag too. But don't worry, we have a guest room. Your virtue will be safe with us. Xander x

I try to swallow, but my mouth is too dry. Xander? How did he even get my number? Did I give it to him? A vague memory of drawing it on his arm with my black eyeliner in the car returns. God, I made such a fool of myself. I invited him in. I kissed him.

But oh, what a kiss. Butterflies swirl in my stomach as I remember his lips. His tongue licking mine. His hands on my ass. Dear lord, how will I have dinner with all three of them?

Throwing the covers over my head, I kick myself for getting so drunk last night. Why on earth do they want me to come for dinner? What the hell is that even about? And taking an overnight bag? Like that's ever going to happen.

~

I SHAKE MY CURLS, watching as they fall over my shoulder. "Do I look okay?"

Jen comes up behind me and wrinkles her nose at my reflection in the full-length mirror in her bedroom.

Lips pressed together, she assesses my outfit. "You look cute."

I glance down at my knee-high boots, skinny jeans, and tight turtleneck.

"You couldn't be just a little more covered up though?" she says sarcastically.

"It's cold out and it's only dinner."

She pulls a face in the mirror. "Yeah, right."

"It is just dinner," I insist, even as nervous excitement and trepidation curl in my gut. I glance at my overnight bag. The one I swore to myself that I wouldn't take. But it's just a precaution, right? It never hurts to be prepared. I can still leave after dinner if things get weird. "Do you think I'm crazy going to this thing? I mean, I don't even know them."

She arches an eyebrow. "Everybody knows them. They're the three most powerful men in New York."

"Exactly. They could sell me to a drug cartel or something and nobody would be able to prove anything because they'd buy everyone off."

The spot between her brows pinches in a cute frown. "Why on earth would they sell you to a drug cartel?"

"Dunno." I shrug. "Maybe that's how they got so rich. Selling the unsuspecting women they invited for dinner."

She looks at me like I've grown a second head. "Pretty sure they got rich taking over failing companies."

A pang of guilt gnaws at me. One of those companies is the one that's about to give me my big break.

"Also pretty sure one of them just wants to fuck you," Jen adds with a giggle.

I shake my head and look over my outfit one more time. Maybe I should change.

"You think the other two like to watch?" she asks, her wide eyes locked on mine in the mirror.

"Jen!"

She wraps her arm around my shoulder. "I'm playing with you, girl. And if they do harvest your organs or sell you off to some cartel, trust me when I say that no amount of money will buy me off. Pinkie swear." She holds out her little finger, and I laugh. But I still can't help wondering what the hell the Unholy Trinity wants with me.

ELEVEN

LILY

S tanding in the private elevator on my way to the penthouse apartment of the most expensive building in Manhattan, I can't stop my legs from shaking. The interior is gold and glass and bigger than Jen's living room. My knuckles turn white around the handle of my overnight bag.

What the hell am I going to talk about with the three richest men in the city? Which of the five boroughs has the best slices of pizza in the city? What series I'm binging on Netflix this week? There's no way we have anything in common. Well, I guess there's one thing—I'm currently working in the mail room of the Grayson News building, and they're about to buy the company.

The elevator doors open to Xander leaning against the wall, arms folded across his broad chest. How the hell does this man make low-slung faded jeans and a plain white T-shirt look hotter than a bespoke suit?

"Hey there, shorty." He steps forward, his hand held out for my bag. I reluctantly release it and take in my surroundings.

The floors of the hallway are white marble, and the walls are a muted olive green. Simple but tasteful.

He nudges my arm. "Cat got your tongue, shorty?"

"I'm not short," I retort. "I'm five-five. That's like average height."

Granted, he does tower over me, all six foot whatever of him, and I have to crane my neck to look into his eyes. He winks, and my ovaries explode with the memory of his kiss last night. I'm pretty sure he had his hands on my ass at some point. My face heats.

"Let me take your coat too. You look a little warm." Grinning wickedly, he holds out his hand. I shrug out of my coat and pass it to him.

"I'll show you to the kitchen and then put your things in the guest room." He walks down the hallway and indicates I should too. I follow him and the mouthwatering scent of roasting meat into the kitchen.

Zeke is seated at the island looking at his cell phone while West stands over the stove.

"Our guest is here," Xander announces, and they both look up.

"Lily," West says with a hint of a smile. "Take a seat. Dinner won't be long. Zeke will get you a drink. Use the end guest room, Fitch." Then he turns back to the stove.

"Fitch?"

Xander rolls his eyes. "My nickname. Zeke came up with it. He used to call me Abercrombie, but it was a bit of a mouthful, hey big guy?"

Zeke scowls at him.

"Like Abercrombie and Fitch?" I ask.

Wearing a sheepish smile, Xander shrugs and nods.

A laugh bubbles out of me. That is the best nickname he could possibly have. "Because you look like a catalog model?"

"Apparently so," he answers, then walks out of the kitchen carrying my bag.

Zeke slips off his stool. "Wine?"

"Um." I tug at the sleeves of my sweater. "Can I have a soda?"

He frowns at me. "Soda?"

Do they even have soda in this place? Or do they only drink wine, champagne, and the elixir of the gods? I clear my throat. "Please."

Zeke rolls his eyes. "Hey West, what soda goes best with roast lamb?"

West laughs softly. "Don't be a dick and get the girl a coke, Z."

I flash him my sweetest smile. *Yeah, Z. Don't be a dick.*

By the time Xander gets back, Zeke has barely spoken two words to me, but his gaze scalds me while I look around. The kitchen is huge. Full of expensive gadgets and marble counter-tops, but's it's somehow warm and homey. Not at all what I was expecting. West has been chatting with both Zeke and me while working on dinner. To my surprise, he looks completely in his element. I never would have pictured West Archer whipping up a home-cooked meal. Probably because I figured that they'd have a team of servants to cook and clean for them.

Xander maneuvers around West, grabbing silverware and napkins and setting places around the island. Zeke hands West a pair of oven mitts without being asked, and I rest my chin on my hand, watching the three of them and admiring the way they seem to communicate without words.

"We have a dining room, but we prefer to eat here," Xander says after he grabs a stack of plates from a cabinet. "That okay with you?"

"Sure." I'd much prefer to eat here than at a fancy dining table anyway.

"Perfect." West pulls a tray of golden roasted potatoes from the oven and nudges Zeke's arm, tilting his chin toward the lamb joint resting on the counter. "Can you carve?"

Zeke grumbles but goes to grab a large knife from the block. Something about the way he holds it in his hand sends a shiver down my spine.

~

DESPITE MY NERVES and the worry that we'd have absolutely nothing in common, two hours have flashed by, during which time I ate some of the best roasted lamb and potatoes I've ever tasted in my life and laughed until I cried at Xander's funny stories. Even Zeke's grumpiness has faded a bit, giving me a small glimpse of the man I met at the club last night.

Inevitably, it's not long before our conversation turns to Grayson News.

"So, you work in the mail room?" West asks.

"Technically, yes. But I'm rarely in there. I'm one of the bike messengers, so I'm out riding around the city most of the day."

"And you like it?" Xander asks, leaning forward as though he's genuinely interested.

I shrug. "Yeah, but it's not my dream."

"What is your dream then, Lily?" My name rolls off Zeke's tongue like it belongs there.

"To be a writer for the magazine." A skitter of excitement runs through me as I think about how close I am to finally achieving that dream. "I've had a couple of small articles published so far, but I'm working on a bigger one right now. I'm hoping Julian—he's the editor—will use it as a feature."

West nods and takes a sip of his wine while Zeke stares at me with curiosity. It suddenly occurs to me that they might think I had an ulterior motive for coming here tonight. "That's not why I came to dinner, by the way. I-I would never want to have an article in the magazine unless it got there on its own merit."

Xander laughs softly.

Zeke scratches his neck. "Why would we think that was why you came to dinner?"

My eyes dart between the three of them. "Well, I know you're in the middle of a takeover of Grayson News Corp. Everyone who works there does."

"A merger," West says coolly.

"A what?" I blink at him.

"You said it's a takeover. It's a merger. Two different things."

I pull at the collar of my turtleneck. Is it hot in here? "Oh. Okay. I just know people are worried about their jobs."

"No one is going to lose their jobs, and Jensen Michaels should be reassuring every single employee of that fact," West says, his jaw clenched in annoyance.

Jensen Michaels is the current CEO of Grayson News Corp. I've never met the guy, but he's considered a god in some circles. The devil in others. "Yeah, well, he doesn't really speak to us in the mail room." I shrug. "But it's good to know there won't be any layoffs."

West takes a sip of his wine. He could be blowing smoke up my ass about the whole job thing, but I don't get that vibe from him. In fact, I don't get a bad vibe from any of them, not even Zeke's grouchy ass. I've spent a large portion of my life surrounded by cruel men who do terrible things, and I'm good at reading people. The Unholy Trinity have been impeccable hosts. Or dates. Whatever this is. They've welcomed me into their beautiful home, cooked me a lovely meal, and been the perfect gentlemen. I mean, that latter part is kind of a shame because the three of them are insanely hot, but the night's still young.

I sip my soda, and the three of them share a look that makes goosebumps pop out all over my body. A shudder runs down my spine. Did I think that too soon?

"Seeing as Lily was so open about why she *hasn't* come here tonight, should we tell her why we invited her?" Xander asks. His voice drops about two octaves, and it makes heat sear between my thighs.

My eyes bounce between the three of them, and my throat suddenly feels drier than the Mojave Desert. They stare at me, and West licks his lips like a lion about to feast on its prey. "Why did you ask me here?" I ask, my voice little more than a whisper.

Zeke sucks on his top lip and looks at the ceiling. Xander smiles at me. It's not his warm, friendly smile though. It's different. Dangerous. Sexy as hell.

West takes a deep breath. "We have a proposition for you, Lily. It may seem like an odd request, but it's not the first time we've done this. We want you to hear us out and then take a few days to think it over."

I take a gulp of my soda, and my hands tremble as I place my glass down on the counter. My heart rate has doubled in the span of ten seconds. I feel faint and hot and dizzy. Because despite no one saying anything remotely to do with sex, the sexual tension in the room has ratcheted up about two hundred levels. I clear my throat. "What's your proposition?"

"We want to date you, Lily. All three of us."

Holy fucknuggets. He's gotta be screwing with me. "At the same time?" I croak.

"Yes, at the same time. Although to the outside world, it will appear like you're only dating one of us."

Xander shoots a glare at West before directing his attention to me. "Well, it's more than dating."

I frown. "More than dating?"

West nods. "We'd like you to move in here with us for three months."

Now I know he's messing with me. A laugh bubbles from my lips, but none of them are laughing or even smiling, so I humor them. "Three months? And then what happens after? I just go on my merry way and we pretend we're friends? Or we never speak again? How does that part work?"

Xander sighs. "Three months is just the starting point. To see if this thing between us works. If it does, then ..."

I tilt my head. "Then?"

Xander shrugs. "Then you stay here."

I open my mouth to speak but no words come out, so I merely sit and gape at the three of them.

"I told you we should have taken this slower and drawn up a contract," West grumbles.

I almost fall off my stool. "A contract?"

West nods. "We told you we've done this before, Lily. Many times. But we usually don't spring this on someone the second time we meet. And we usually draw up a contract explaining all the rules."

This is sounding freakier by the second. "The rules?"

"He's making it sound weirder than it is," Xander says, shooting West another warning glare.

My mind races with questions, all of them begging to be asked first. "So, what happened to all of these other women you tried this with?"

West glares at me, his jaw ticking. "They didn't work out, obviously."

I wrinkle my nose and shake my head. "Three super-hot billionaire dudes ask a woman to live with them and 'date'"—I actually use air quotes for that word and hate myself for it—"them, and it never works out. What the hell is wrong with you all?"

Zeke snorts into his wine, and that makes me smile.

Xander arches one eyebrow. "You think we're super hot?"

I roll my eyes and fix Xander with the hardest glare I can muster. "Oh, come on. You own mirrors. Like you don't already know that."

West lets out a deep sigh and draws our attention back to him. "Maybe it wasn't us. Perhaps there was something wrong with them."

Of course. Always the women's fault, right. Misogynistic assholes. "Ah, I see now." With a nod, I slide off my stool.

"You see what?" Xander asks.

"You just use them up for three months and then toss them out, is that it? I mean are these poor women supposed to satisfy all of your needs every single day and night? It must be exhausting." Despite my argument, what they're asking has my panties wet and I haven't even been touched. But that's just the fantasy of it all, right? "I bet the reality of dating you three means constant blowjobs with minimal return."

"Actually, Xander and West give incredible blow jobs, so that wouldn't fall entirely on you," Zeke replies coolly, and I realize I said that last part out loud.

But wait. What? Now this just got a whole lot more interesting. Studying the three of them, I wait for someone to say that I'm being punked, but they're all wearing dead-serious expressions. I must admit, they are the finest looking men I've ever seen, and the thought of them together as well as with me—I have to clench my fists to keep from fanning my face. The visual alone is enough to make a girl come in her panties. But what on earth do they see in me?

Xander licks his lips. "And it's less like minimal return"—he glances between his two friends—"and more like three times your investment back."

"I'd say more," West adds, and his eyes twinkle with deviousness. "The number of times we make *a return* has never been an issue."

I swallow the breath that sticks in my throat. Triple the orgasms. My pussy clenches, letting me know she approves, and I squeeze my thighs together to silence her. "So, you're all together." I wave my hand in the air. "Like with each other too?"

Xander grins. "Yeah."

"So, who's a top and who's a bottom? Or do you all switch?"

West cracks a smile, but it's Xander who replies. "Zeke and West are tops. I'm a bottom."

I nod, fascinated by their dynamic. I had no freaking clue they were together like that, but I guess what they do in private is their business. *And maybe mine now too?* "I'm a bottom by the way. Just FYI."

For some reason that makes Xander and West laugh, and even Zeke shows a trace of amusement.

"What? Some women top."

At this point, West slides off his stool and walks around the island. He stands so close to me that I can smell his fresh masculine scent, and it makes the space between my legs ache with need.

"If you agree to this, Lily, there's not a single scenario where it won't be you getting fucked by one of us. We know you're a bottom, princess."

I swallow hard. Holy cow, I so want to be fucked by all three of them. I mean not all at the same time—*or maybe at the same time?* Shaking my head to clear it, I wonder what the hell is wrong with me. I breathe in West's scent, and it must scramble my senses because I'm actually considering this. "H-how long do I have to make a decision?"

He leans closer, his lips dusting over my hair. I think he's going to kiss me, but he reaches behind me and grabs my glass from the counter. "Take a few days."

Licking my lips, I nod.

His cloudy gray eyes narrow on my face. "We're discreet about our lifestyle, Lily. Whether you agree to this or not, we ask that you keep this to yourself."

"Of course," I assure him. What I don't tell him is that keeping secrets is my thing. That I have so many secrets of my own, I sometimes forget what the truth is supposed to be.

CHAPTER
TWELVE

WEST

Zeke disappeared straight after dinner, claiming he had work to do, but Xander and I know him well enough to know that he's freaking out. Lily is better than we could have hoped or imagined. This thing with her might actually have a shot, and that scares the shit out of him. Because he really fucking likes this one.

I walk Lily down the hallway toward the guest room. Xander got to take her home last night, and the charming little fucker kissed her, so it's my turn to escort her to bed. I stuff my hands into my pockets to stop myself from touching her. She's covered from her neck to her fucking toes, but in some ways that's worse because I can't stop thinking about peeling those clothes off her body and running my hands over every goddamn inch of her skin.

My cock aches for a little relief, and it would be so fucking easy to slide myself inside her and stay there until sunrise. She glances sideways at me, a shy smile on her lips. Her dark eyelashes flutter against her pink cheeks.

"You have any more questions?" We spent the last hour discussing our likes and dislikes—most of them anyway; we left out Zeke's particular kinks for now—and what the expectations would be if she took us up on our offer.

She sinks her teeth into her soft bottom lip. "No. I think you explained everything."

"Okay. Good." I come to a stop outside the guest room, and she peers inside.

"Wow. That's a big bed," she says with a soft laugh, and my cock jumps in my pants. *She's not inviting us into it, asshole.*

"Actually, I do have one question." Her voice sounds like a purr and only makes me want her more.

"Yeah?"

"What you're asking is a huge commitment, and we don't even know if we're ..." Her cheeks turn a deeper shade of pink.

I take a step closer, and I don't miss the way her breath hitches. "Don't know if we're what?"

"Compatible," she whispers.

"Wasn't that what tonight was for? I think we all got along pretty well."

She presses her lips together, and I enjoy watching her squirm. "I didn't mean that kind of compatible."

She shivers when I grip her chin and tilt her head. "We're all adults here, Lily. If you can't even say the words, how are you going to survive the three of us?"

Her eyes burn into mine, and she hardens her gaze. "Sexually, I mean."

I dip my head and dust my lips over hers. She lets out the sweetest, sexiest moan I think I've ever heard in my entire goddamn life. The skin on her neck now matches her face. Her pupils are blown wide. I have no idea how far I should take this, but she's driving me fucking crazy, and I don't know if I'll be able to stop once I start. "How wet are you right now?"

She blinks, and that cute blush deepens further. "What?"

"You heard me, Lily. You're concerned about us being sexually compatible." I edge closer until my body is pressed against hers, and there's no way she can't feel my hard cock rubbing on her stomach. "You can see and feel how hot I am for you, so I think it's only fair that you give me some indication of how turned on you are."

"Yes, but ..." The words come out as a pant, her breaths coming faster.

"I know you're attracted to me. I can tell by your breathing and how your pupils are so big that I can barely see the green in your eyes anymore, but tell me ..." I run a fingertip across her jawline and down her collarbone. "How wet are you?"

She flutters her long eyelashes but keeps her gaze trained on my face. "Why don't you find out for yourself?"

Fuck. Me. This woman is a fucking spitfire. My cock will most likely explode if I don't get some relief soon, but I shouldn't do this. She hasn't agreed yet. What if I scare her off?

Or what if she comes so fucking hard that she can't help but run back for more? That's the only option that will work for me because I haven't been able to stop thinking about her for longer than a second. Haven't been able to stop imagining how perfectly she will fit into our penthouse. Into our lives. I have no idea why I'm so certain of that. I barely know her.

But I want to know—I want to know and feel and taste and claim every single part of her. I give her one last chance to back out. "You sure?"

"Yes," she says on a moan.

"Jesus Christ, Lily." With no further consideration for how I might fuck this up for everyone, I tug open the button on her jeans, pull down her zipper, and slide my hand inside her lace panties. I quickly find her clit, swollen and slick with her arousal, and rub the pad of my finger over it. She whimpers, rocking her hips and grinding against me. I sink my hand deeper into her underwear, gliding two fingers through her wet folds.

She throws her arms around my neck and bites down on her lip to stifle the groans that come from deep inside her. When I reach her entrance, I swirl my finger around her tight hole, and her juices coat my fingertips. I'm not going to be able to hold off from driving into her much longer, and definitely not while she's staring into my eyes, silently pleading with me to continue. I slip one finger inside her silky wet heat and her back bows.

"Fuck, West," she gasps as she bears down on me.

I press my mouth against her neck and inhale the scent of her skin mixed with the smell of her arousal slicking my finger. "Jesus, you're not just wet, princess, you're fucking soaked."

"Oh, fuck," she whimpers, riding my hand as I drive deeper inside her.

"You're so fucking tight too. I can't wait to fuck you, Lily. Can't wait to feel you squeezing my cock."

"Yeah?" she says with a breathy moan.

"Fuck yeah, princess. You're going to feel so damn good when I sink balls-deep into you."

"Y-you have a dirty mouth."

"Oh, you have no fucking idea."

Her fingertips drift down my chest and into my waistband, but I catch her wrist with my free hand and place her hand back on my shoulder.

"But what about you?"

Jesus, fuck. What about me? We purposely didn't stock up on condoms before tonight because we knew we were asking a lot. We wanted her to take adequate time to make a decision, and having protection would practically guarantee we pressured her into deciding in our favor immediately. The three of us have been tempted to take her since the moment we laid eyes on her. "Tonight is all about you, princess. And if you get him out, I'll have to fuck you, and I don't have any condoms here. So just let me take care of you, okay?"

She smiles at me. The kind of smile that could bring a man to his knees. And I put that look on her fucking face. Me. I slip a second finger inside her, and she cries out my name.

I nip at her neck. "We're gonna have an audience pretty soon if you keep doing that."

She rakes her nails down my back and smirks. "Don't they like to watch?"

"Yeah, but they prefer to participate. The last thing you want to do, sweetheart, is have the three of us all riled up and desperate to fuck you when we don't have any protection."

She presses her lips together, and her pussy walls clamp around me, milking my fingers with hungry squeezes. I bite back a laugh, thrilled that the thought of all three of us at the same time elicits that kind of reaction.

"You gonna be a good girl and come for me?"

Her arousal runs down my palm. "Oh, fuck. Yes!"

I work my fingers harder, rubbing the knuckle of my thumb over her clit as I drive faster and deeper. Her body tenses. Her eyelids flutter and her eyes roll back. "That's my girl. Give me everything you got."

Her hands fist in my shirt as she lets go for me, her back arching off the wall. She rides the waves of her orgasm, whimpering my name while she comes. When I've rubbed the last tremors from her body, I slip my fingers out of her and place them in my mouth, keeping my eyes locked on hers while I suck them clean. Her delicious cum floods my senses. Her scent. Her taste. Her silky sweetness coats my tongue. "You taste fucking incredible, princess."

"Thank you," she whispers, averting her gaze.

I grab her jaw and tilt her head so she's forced to look at me. She doesn't get to act shy now, not after she's the one who prompted all this. My heart thumps like a bass drum. My cock is harder than a steel girder and is currently leaking in my boxers. I'm desperate to get away from her so I can jack off with her scent still in my nose and her taste in my mouth. "So, compatible then?"

Her lips spread in a slow, sexy smile. "Very."

I lean in and give her a gentle kiss on the lips. I need to tear myself away from her while I still can. "Goodnight, Lily."

"Night, West."

When I get to my room, Xander is sitting on my bed in just his boxers. Just like it does every time I see it, the tattoo on his chest—Poseidon and his trident—reminds me how lucky I am to have him and Zeke in my life. He grins at me, a mischievous look in his eyes. "You made her come, didn't you?"

I shrug. "Maybe."

"I heard her moaning your fucking name."

"Then fuck yeah, I made her come."

He palms his cock through his boxers and grunts his approval. "How did she feel?"

"Like fucking heaven, Fitch. Hot and wet and so goddamn tight. She's so fucking sweet. But I dunno." I shake my head and suck in a breath. "She's a little dangerous too. Inexperienced for sure but not shy. She loves the thrill. And despite what Zeke says, she's not naive."

He scoots back and lies on the pillows with his arms behind his head. "You think she'll agree to our proposal?"

"I don't know. I sure fucking hope so, because she tastes even sweeter than she looks."

He glares at me. "You tasted her?"

"I sucked her cum off my fingers."

"Fuck, West," he groans.

I sit beside him on the bed and run the two fingers I just had inside her over his lips. He opens his mouth and I slip them inside, allowing him a taste of her too. His blue eyes darken as he sucks greedily, swirling his expert tongue over my knuckles and making my already aching cock throb painfully.

"You're so fucking good at that," I growl, pulling my fingers out of his mouth and replacing them with my tongue. His hands slide through my hair, and he tugs me to lie on top of him. I grind my hard cock against his, and he moans into my mouth, letting me swallow the sounds he makes.

"Fuck me, West," he pleads. "It's been too long."

I press my forehead against his. "I'm sorry. I know I get crazy when we're close to closing a deal."

He grazes his knuckles over my cheek. "You get distant, not crazy."

"You staying in here with me tonight?"

His tongue darts out, licking his bottom lip. "Yeah."

"Is Zeke okay?"

He nods. "Yeah, he's just processing."

Pushing up onto my forearms, I rake my eyes over his face and down his toned, muscular body. He's right. It's been way too long. I arch an eyebrow at him. "Suck my cock like a good boy and I'll fuck you."

He flips me onto my back and rolls on top of me. "You're such an alpha-hole sometimes, you know that, right?"

"You fucking love it."

He works his mouth down my body, all teeth and tongue lashing over my skin. I push his head lower, trying to move him closer to my aching dick, but he chuckles, enjoying my torment. He's such a fucking brat.

"The more you tease me, the more I'll make it hurt," I snap.

"Why do you think I'm teasing you?"

I growl. "Suck my fucking cock, Fitch!"

He licks a trail across my abs before swirling his tongue over the crown, humming appreciatively as he cleans off the precum already collecting there. Then he swallows me whole, wrapping his sinful lips around my shaft and taking me balls-deep into his throat.

I fist my hands in his hair, holding his head still while I thrust my hips and fuck his mouth. "You're so fucking good at that too."

He looks up at me, his bright blue eyes watering as he chokes on my length. I swipe the pad of my thumb over his cheek. "You take my cock like such a good boy."

He winks at me, his cheeks hollowing as he sucks harder, and a few moments later, I come down his perfect throat.

I LEAN against the door frame, arms folded across my chest as I watch her and Xander chat over breakfast. I can't hear their conversation, but she keeps giggling—he does too. The sound of their combined laughter reverberates around the expansive kitchen and makes me smile. They look so good together, and the thought of fucking the two of them, or of fucking him while he's inside her, has my balls tightening and heat tingling at the base of my spine. Zeke comes up beside me, and we both stare at the two of them. I'm sure he's thinking the exact same thing I am.

After a few seconds, he clears his throat, reminding me I have somewhere else to be. The car is waiting for me, and I need to leave. I straighten my tie and roll my shoulders back. *Fuck giving her time. She's ours, and she needs to accept that sooner rather than later.*

I press my lips against Zeke's ear. "I want her, Zeke. Make it happen."

CHAPTER
THIRTEEN

LILY

"I'm sorry I didn't come home last night." Jen's voice is quiet on the phone. Her boss is a tyrant, and she isn't supposed to make personal calls during work hours. "I really wanted to hear about your date Saturday, but Trey took me to this party, and then after—" She sighs dreamily instead of finishing her sentence.

"Don't worry. I love sleeping in your bed," I remind her. "And I watched that movie with that actor you hate."

She laughs. "I have so much to tell you, Lils. Trey is perfect."

I roll my eyes. Trey the movie star, who turned out to not be a movie star at all. Apparently he's a bouncer and he only used the whole movie star bit to get Jen to hook up with him. Lucky for him, my friend isn't the shallow type and he told her soon enough that she didn't feel betrayed by his lie. She's into him, and she's happy. Hell, I'm seriously considering the Unholy Trinity's offer, so I don't think I have the right to judge any woman for her choice of bed partners at this point. "We can catch up tonight. I'll cook dinner."

"Perfect." She gasps. "Shit, I have to go. I have a meeting that started five minutes ago. Talk later, girl."

"Bye," I say, but she's already hung up.

⁓

JEN IS STANDING in the hallway when I get home from work, surrounded by bags and suitcases and holding a pillow under her arm. Two guys stand beside her, one of whom I recognize as Trey from the club, and the other wears navy coveralls and looks like he works in maintenance. My mouth goes dry. What the hell happened?

Jen shakes her head, and Trey puts a comforting arm around her shoulder as I jog down the hallway. "Hey, what's happened? Is everything okay?"

Jen turns to me, her eyes wide. "Roaches, Lil." She wrinkles her nose.

I peer inside the apartment, and a shudder runs the length of my spine. "In your apartment?"

She shivers and leans against Trey for support. "So this guy says." She nods at the stranger.

"And you are?"

"Carl." He points to the name badge sewn into his uniform.

"And you think we have roaches?"

"Yep. Got a complaint from a neighbor. The super let me in so I could take a look around, and this is where the nest is."

Bile surges up my throat. "*Nest?*"

Jen places her hand over her mouth. "I know. It's gross. How will we ever go back in there?"

"Give me a few weeks and it'll all be cleared. Like they've never been here," Carl says with a smile.

I gape at him. "A few weeks?"

"To make sure they're all gone. Yeah." He nods, rubbing his meaty hand through his hair.

"But …" I look between him and the apartment, then down the hallway. "Where are we supposed to go in the meantime?"

Carl shrugs. "You got any friends? Family you can stay with?"

I glance at Jen. She's my only friend. My only person. She bites her lip and glances at Trey, who now has his arm slung around her neck. "Trey has a sofa."

"Yeah. You can both stay with me. My place is small, but it's clean. No roaches," he adds with a wink. "The sofa's a two-seater, and the living room is also kind of the kitchen, but I'm sure you can squeeze on. Sometimes my buddy, Razor, crashes on it. He's like five foot ten, so you should fit. He'll just sleep on the floor if you're on the couch."

I close my eyes and take a moment to think. Just two more paychecks and I might have enough to put down a deposit for my own place. But until then, do I really want to sleep on a tiny sofa in Trey's apartment, listening to him and Jen bang all the time while a guy called Razor keeps me company?

I look down at my meager belongings which Jen kindly packed up for me. I'm beyond grateful that they're not sitting in the roach-infested apartment.

She places a hand on my forearm. "I think I got all your essentials, girl."

I nod. I'll take her word for it because now that I know what's beyond that door, I can't imagine stepping foot inside her apartment ever again. Not that Trey's sofa sounds all that much more appealing.

"So, my place?" Trey asks.

I fish my phone out of my pocket. Am I really going to do this? Because accepting their offer doesn't only mean accepting a room, albeit a room in the lap of luxury that's bigger than

Jen's whole apartment. It means I'm dating them. All three of them. But damn if a thrill of excitement doesn't shoot through me at the prospect. It's been two days since they made their indecent proposal, and I've thought of little else in that time. I want to be all in, but something has been holding me back. Maybe this is exactly the push I need.

"It's okay. I think I have somewhere I can crash."

Jen's face breaks into a huge smile. "You do? Where?"

"With that guy I told you about." I give her a look that I hope conveys what I'm thinking—*please don't ask me about all the juicy details right now in front of Trey. And Carl, the roach guy.*

"The guy from your date on Saturday?" She reads me so well. "Th—I mean, he said you could stay there?"

My face heats, but I nod.

"Lils ... are you sure?"

"Yep. I got it covered. It's all good."

"Cool." Jen beams at me as Trey presses a kiss on her head. I'm pretty sure he's as relieved as I am that I'm not about to be living in his kitchen/dining/living room with his friend, Razor. "You need a ride?"

I think back to the message Xander sent me earlier today.

Let me know as soon as you've made a decision and we'll send a car.

The decision I was always going to make has now been made for me. "Nope, I've got one. Thanks."

TRUE TO HIS WORD, Xander sent a car as soon as I messaged him to confirm I was taking them up on their offer. And now I'm in their private elevator once more, my knees trembling and heart racing while sweat trickles down my back. This is not at all how I expected my day to end up. Dating three guys is not what normal women do. Dating three insanely hot billionaires is not even in the same realm as normal. But then, what about my life so far has been?

The doors open and my fingers instinctively tighten around the handles of my bags. *This is it, Lily. No going back now.* The first face I see is Xander's. He's smiling widely, and for some reason I start to laugh. This is insane, right? My gaze doesn't linger on his face for long because he's shirtless and wearing a pair of gray sweatpants. And holy mother of all that is sacred, his abs look like they've been chiseled by the gods themselves. And that V. My eyes drop lower, to the outline of his incredibly impressive ... Holy fucknuggets.

"Let me get those for you." West says, snapping me out of my daze. Pretty sure I just dropped at least eighty IQ points. His warm fingers brush mine when he takes my bags from me.

"Thanks," I whisper. Looking into his deep gray eyes, I feel something stir in my core.

"Yeah, let's get you settled," Xander adds as he relieves me of my heavy backpack.

"Before we do, I have a confession," I blurt.

The two men stare at me, frowns on their handsome faces.

"My friend's apartment, where I've been staying, well it has a ..." Shuddering, I take a deep breath. "A *roach* infestation."

Xander holds my backpack away from his body and scrunches his face.

"Oh, god, you think they're in there?" My hand flies to my mouth. "The guy said he sprayed our stuff, but—"

West nudges Xander, who winks at me. "Just teasing, shorty. I'm sure you don't have any hitchhikers in here." They both start to walk down the hallway in the direction of the guest bedroom.

"Wait. That's not my confession." I wring my hands, and they both turn and stare at me again.

"So, what is?" West asks, his deep voice smoother than melted chocolate.

I swallow and take a breath. "That's why I decided to come here. Because I needed a place to stay." West and Xander share a look, but they don't seem mad. "I mean, I hadn't made a decision about the other thing yet. I was still thinking it over."

Xander shrugs. "So think it over here."

As if there's anything to think about. I was torn before, but it only took one look at Xander's chest and West's thick forearms for the decision to be made for me. Not to mention the man mountain that is Zeke, wherever he is. How the hell will I survive them? But if I don't, what a way to go. "I don't need to." I chew on the inside of my cheek. *Just say it, Lily.* "I want the other thing too. All of it."

Xander sinks his perfect white teeth into his bottom lip and tilts his head to the ceiling, letting out a loud groan that makes me giggle. West stares at me, his eyes dark and full of longing. His tongue darts out to lick his lips. Oh god, what I wouldn't give to have that tongue on any part of my body.

"Is that still what you want?" My voice is barely a whisper. "All three of you?" I glance around, hoping to see Zeke, and he obliges me, stepping out of the shadows and approaching us.

"Fuck yes." West's voice is a rumbling growl.

"Yeah," Zeke says quietly.

I have no idea how this is going to work. No idea at all what the hell I'm doing, but something about it feels very right. Xander looks at me too, and the heat from their gazes alone makes me wet and needy. "Hell yeah, shorty."

FOURTEEN

XANDER

We ate Chinese takeout for dinner because that's what Lily asked for and I figured it would make her feel more comfortable. Especially since her decision to move in was kind of forced on her. What West Archer wants, West Archer gets.

Zeke says he simply expedited the process, but whatever he did to make the whole roach nest situation happen, I fucking love him for it. Now we have this sexy, funny, sweet-as-cherry-fucking-pie woman sitting in our kitchen, snort-laughing because her fortune cookie says *your cup will overflow with happenis*. That typo would be hysterical regardless, but given the fact that she just agreed to be the beneficiary of three dicks for the foreseeable future, I totally get why she can barely breathe.

Tears roll down her cheeks, and even Zeke is watching her with amusement shining in his dark eyes. West looks at me and shakes his head, as if to ask me what the fuck we've gotten ourselves into with this one, but he has a huge-ass smile on his face. It's true that Lily is different from the other women we've tried this with, but maybe that's why it will work this time.

She wheezes loudly, doubled over on the stool as she tries to catch her breath. "Jesus, Lily, you don't have asthma, do you?" West asks, genuinely concerned.

She shakes her head, making her thick dark curls bounce wildly, and it only makes me laugh harder. When she finally calms down and sits up straight again, her cheeks are red and streaked with tears. She wipes them with the sleeve of her sweater. "I'm so sorry," she pants. "That was just so freaking hilarious."

I wink at her and start to clear away the empty takeout cartons. "Never known a fortune cookie to be so scarily accurate before."

That sets her off again, and West rolls his eyes, but his shoulders shake from suppressing his own laughter.

"As fun and indigestion-inducing as this dinner has been, I have a shit-ton of work to do." Zeke pushes his stool back and stands up. "I'll see you all in the morning. Goodnight."

That at least stops Lily's giggle fit, and she mouths *goodnight*.

"Night, buddy," West says, but he watches Zeke leave with narrowed eyes.

I place my hand on the back of West's neck and squeeze. "He'll be fine. You know how he gets."

He gives me a faint nod. He knows better than anyone the demons that Zeke battles.

"You sure it's okay, me being here?" Lily asks in a quiet voice.

West turns his attention back to her. "Princess, it is more than fucking okay." His low growl makes her breath visibly catch in her throat, and the atmosphere in the room turns on a dime.

After dropping the empty cartons into the trash, I head back over to her, leaning against the counter and sandwiching her between West and me. "We've been waiting for you to call and tell us you wanted to take us up on our offer since you left Sunday morning."

I glance over the top of her head and lock eyes with West. Would it be too much to have both of us together on her first night? He bites his lip, and I know that he's thinking the same thing.

"You have?" Wide-eyed, she studies the two of us.

West tucks a curl behind her ear, and I don't miss the way her neck turns pink at his touch. She sucks in a deep breath. "S-so, how does this work exactly?"

West spins her stool until she's facing him, and I press my chest up against her back. "How do you want it to work, princess?" he asks, his tone dark and dangerous. She opens her mouth, but no words come out. Poor girl has no fucking clue what she's letting herself in for.

He goes on staring at her, waiting for her to reply. "I don't know," she finally says. "How does this usually work when you do this kind of thing?"

His hand rasps over his five o'clock shadow. "This isn't how we ordinarily do things at all. We've never had someone move in after only knowing them for a couple of days."

Her pink cheeks turn a shade darker. "Oh."

I bend my head and rest my lips against her ear. "So this is kinda new to us too. We can take it slow if that's what you want."

She shivers.

"Or fast." West shrugs, and fuck me if a shudder doesn't run the length of our girl's spine. Her breath hitches. The blush on her face races south, disappearing beneath the neckline of her sweater. I want to follow it with my hands. With my mouth. My dick twitches in my sweatpants. I want to taste her. Not from West's fingers like before, but straight from the source.

She sinks her teeth into her full bottom lip, and I have to force myself back a step so I don't do the same. "And fast would be?" Her voice is a breathy whisper.

"Whatever you want it to be, princess."

I take her trembling hand and lace my fingers with hers, loving how West is willing to give her a little control tonight. At least a semblance of it anyway. It doesn't come easily to him. And if the fiery look in his eyes isn't enough to let me know how hot he is for this girl right here, then the outline of his hard cock in his suit pants surely is.

"How about we accompany you to your room and see where the night takes us," I suggest, trailing my teeth over her jaw.

She slips off the stool, her hand still clasped in mine, and while she doesn't say the word, West and I both take that as a yes.

Less than two minutes later, we're standing in Lily's room, watching her peel off her sweatshirt. I groan when she reveals the green tank top underneath. I was hoping to see more of her, but I guess from the mischievous look on her face, and the fact that me and my buddy are practically drooling here, that she's about to be naked *very* soon.

"So?" She flutters her eyelashes, and I can practically hear West's restraint snapping like a tightly wound rubber band. He crosses the room before she can blink, and he has one hand fisted in her hair and the other on her perfectly round ass, crushing her against him as he slams his mouth down on hers and devours her. He swallows her desperate moans, and without wasting another second, I step up behind her. Pulling her hair aside, I glide my tongue along the column of her neck.

She presses that fine ass against me, trapping West's hand between us. He rubs a knuckle over my semihard cock, and I bite back a groan as I inhale Lily's sweet scent and relish the soft sounds rolling in her throat.

West tugs on Lily's tank top. "I want all of these clothes off, princess. Now."

She nibbles her delicious bottom lip as we work together to get her naked. Crouching on the floor, I peel her skin-tight jeans and superhero-themed cotton panties down her perfect peach of an ass, trailing my fingertips along her silky tanned legs and imagining it's my tongue instead. When I stand again, West finishes stripping her top half, and I grin at him over her shoulder.

This is going to be so fucking good.

CHAPTER
FIFTEEN

LILY

West lets out a guttural groan. "Jesus, you're so fucking beautiful, Lily."

"She sure fucking is," Xander murmurs.

My cheeks flush at their praise and at the sensation of their hungry eyes on my naked form. Despite being sandwiched between their hard, molten-hot bodies, I feel a shiver run the length of my entire body and goosebumps pop out all over my forearms. The contrast of Xander's skin at my back and the soft cotton of West's shirt at my front is tantalizingly sensual. But I want to feel West's skin. I want to see that toned torso that I've only felt through his clothes in all its glory. I need to run my fingertips over the hard pecs that I had pressed against me a few nights ago, the ones currently rubbing against my achingly hard nipples.

I reach for the buttons on his shirt, but he catches my wrists and arches one eyebrow. "You want this off, do you, princess?"

Biting down on my lip, I nod. I'm so turned on I feel like I might implode. They've barely touched me but already my knees are trembling and slickness coats my inner thighs.

Xander brushes my hair to one side and trails sweet kisses along the back of my neck. Shivering, I watch West's deft fingers make short work of his buttons. He opens the white cotton shirt, exposing his flawless olive skin beneath. And as he moves lower, his fingers skate over his toned abs, and I can't help but join him, brushing my fingertips along each solid ridge of muscle. He tugs the fabric, freeing it from his waistband, and my eyes drop to the impressive outline of his rock-hard cock straining against the material of his suit pants.

My skin blooms with heat and my breath sticks in my throat. "I think our girl likes what she sees, West." Xander's breath dances delicately with the hairs at my nape as he chuckles.

West hums and pulls his shirt down his arms, revealing toned biceps and wide forearms, lined with thick veins. Xander rocks his hips against me, letting me feel how hard he is. The size of the bulge digging into the small of my back is no less impressive than West's.

West cups my jaw, angling my head so that I'm looking up into his handsome face. "Do you like what you see, princess?"

"Yes." The word comes out in a hoarse whisper.

With a wicked smile, he dips his head and seals his lips over my own, sweeping his tongue along the seam until I part them and allow him entry. He flicks his tongue against mine, exploring the recesses of my mouth. My body sags, melting between him and Xander so that they're the only thing holding me upright. Xander goes on kissing my neck, his mouth growing increasingly more fervent and persistent, matching the pace of his tongue to West's. My pussy flares with liquid heat, and my moan is muffled by West's mouth as my head spins with euphoria.

Xander's hand skates over my hip and down my stomach. He taps the inside of my ankle with his foot, and I obey his wordless command, spreading my legs wider and allowing him to slip his hand between my thighs. He drags two fingers along my folds, swirling the pads over my clit before sliding to my entrance and teasing me there. "Oh, our girl's so fucking wet, West," he says with a growl that vibrates through every nerve ending in my body.

West murmurs his agreement without breaking our kiss. His hands coast down my back to my ass and palm my cheeks, squeezing hard. My skin heats with equal parts shame and desire. This should feel wrong, but it might just be the hottest, most fiercely intense pleasure I've ever felt. My skin sizzles with electricity.

And when Xander slides a thick finger inside me, fireworks erupt in my core. Spurred on by my body's reaction, he fucks me harder while West trails his lips lower, covering my neck and chest with tiny bites until he reaches my nipples. He sucks a turgid peak into his warm mouth and nips gently, and a rush of arousal slicks Xander's finger.

Whimpering shamelessly, I rock my hips, all heat and desire and pleasure as I lose myself to the feelings evoked by their hands and mouths. I close my eyes, tilting my head back and resting it on Xander's shoulder as I let them work their magic, coaxing the longest and most intense orgasm of my entire life from my trembling body.

And when my knees are shaking so violently that I can no longer stand, Xander slides his finger out of my pussy and West lifts me, wrapping my legs around his waist and carrying me to the bed.

When I finally catch my breath and get my bearings, I see Xander has removed his sweatpants and is lying on the bed beside me, stroking his huge cock. A bead of precum collects on the tip, and I unconsciously lick my lips, making him chuckle.

"Oh, yeah," he grunts. "I've been thinking about those juicy lips around my cock from the moment I saw you in our lobby, Lily."

I suck in a breath and study his incredible body, desperate to taste him. West is discarding the rest of his clothes, and when he stands straight, my heart skips a beat or three at the sight of his naked form. His cock is thick and veined like his forearms. Shit. How the hell am I going to satisfy them both? Maybe I haven't thought this through enough.

West wraps his hand around his shaft and tugs hard, making his crown weep with precum too. A deep growl rumbles in his chest, and his stormy eyes burn into mine. "I'm so desperate to fuck you, Lily."

I pant, struggling to breathe and think straight at the same time.

Crawling onto the bed, West pushes my thighs apart and stares at my pussy like a lion eyeing its kill. Without any further warning, he sinks two fingers inside me, and my back arches off the bed.

"Holy fuck," I cry.

"I know, princess," he growls. "I fucking know." He curls his fingers deep inside me, sweeping the pads over a sensitive spot that no one except my vibrator has ever touched before, and my body practically arches in half. "Jesus, fuck, I need to take you bare, Lily," he pleads, his eyes searching mine for permission.

"N-no, you can't." I shake my head.

"We need to get you on some birth control." He slowly withdraws his fingers, then plows them back inside.

"I'm on birth control. An imp-plant," I stammer as his fingers drive in again.

He bites his lip and shoots Xander a look that I don't understand, but whatever it is has Xander jumping from the bed and grabbing something from the pocket of his sweatpants. "Are you clean?" West asks.

I blink at him, but the pleasure coursing through my body makes it hard for me to focus on anything else. "Y-yeah, but I'm not concerned about me."

"Fitch?" he says, and Xander passes him his phone. West holds it up to my face, his fingers pausing their relentless rhythm but remaining inside me. "You see that, Lily?"

I scan the email attachment on the screen. It shows that Xander has a clean bill of health and is dated last week. I nod, and West flicks to the next screen, which shows the same results, only with West's name, then he shows me the same for Zeke. The reports look legit, and they're from a private clinic that I know rich people use. I glance down at West's thick cock again and shake with the desperate need to have it inside me.

"Can we trust you, Lily?" he asks, his voice deep and gravelly.

Holy fucknuggets. I need him now. "Yes, I swear I'm clean."

A growl rumbles in his throat. "Good girl."

Xander lies back down beside me and fists his shaft. "I need you too, shorty."

West arches one eyebrow. "You gonna suck his cock while I fuck you?"

You bet your ass I am. I nod, unable to form words at the moment.

Xander hums, licking his lips. "You are a good fucking girl."

West slips his fingers from my pussy and sucks them clean. The look on his face when he tastes my cum has me panting. I roll onto my front and wrap my hand around the base of Xander's shaft. He threads his fingers through my hair, guiding my lips to where he wants them. My tongue darts out, sweeping over his crown and collecting the precum beading on the slit. He hisses out a breath, and his fingertips dig into my scalp. Swirling my tongue over the length of his shaft, I taunt him a little before taking him into my mouth.

Grunting, he tightens his grip. "Oh, a tease, huh?"

"Shall we tease her too, Fitch?" West chuckles as he moves to kneel behind me. His warm, wet tongue licks a path from my clit to my pussy entrance, and my mouth drops open on a cry, allowing Xander to push all the way inside until he hits the back of my throat.

My gag reflex kicks in, but I push past it, breathing through my nose the way I was taught a long time ago. "Oh, you're good at that, shorty. Your mouth is as hot as I knew it would be."

"You think it's as hot as her pussy?" West asks, his words vibrating through my sensitive flesh and making me whimper.

"Only one way to find out," Xander groans, rocking his hips and brushing my hair back from my face. He swipes away a tear that's been squeezed from the corner of my eye, and the overwhelming sensation of being cared for warms me from the inside. Real tears prick at my eyes, and I sniff.

Xander frowns. "You okay?"

I murmur that I am and give a faint nod.

West grabs my hips, fingertips digging into my skin as he positions the tip of his cock at my dripping entrance. He inches inside, and my moan is muffled around Xander's cock. He fills me, his girth stretching me and making my pussy burn. "Fuck, Lily, I'm barely inside you and my cock's already ready to explode."

West pushes deeper, and my mouth goes slack as I lose the ability to form a single rational thought.

"So fucking tight, princess." Each word West speaks is punctuated with a grunt.

"You need a little help, shorty?" Xander asks.

I merely moan my agreement, and Xander grips the back of

my head with both hands and rocks upward, fucking my throat while West sinks all the way inside me. His cock fills every inch of my pussy. He bottoms out, his hips slamming against my ass. Stars pepper my vision. My inner walls flutter and ripple around him and wetness drips down my thighs. With my heart racing, I hear nothing but the sound of my blood thundering in my ears. Thighs tingling and core clenching, I'm consumed by pleasure as they fuck my mouth and pussy to the same relentless pace. Time loses all meaning.

West rolls his hips, sweeping his engorged tip across my G-spot at the same time Xander sinks all the way into my throat. My climax rockets through me like a bullet train, rendering me incapable of holding myself up. But they do it for me as they fuck me through every single tremor. And I lose myself in the euphoria of giving them complete control. They dominate my body in a way I've never allowed anyone to do before, at least not willingly. Their groans and growls and whispered words of praise, telling me how beautiful I am and how well I take them both, take me to a level of euphoria I've never experienced before, and a sensation of freedom envelops me.

When my second orgasm hits, it's nothing short of life altering. I will never be the same again.

CHAPTER
SIXTEEN

WEST

Zeke takes a seat in my office, his biceps straining at the fabric of his T-shirt and a thin film of sweat coating what little skin he has on display. I prefer him shirtless for his post-workout routine, when he comes into my office with his protein shake to talk through our plans for the day.

He chugs half his shake in one go before placing the cup on my desk. "So, how was last night?"

His question alone makes my cock twitch. "It was good. Better than good, actually. We fucked her bare." His brow furrows in a scowl, making his deep brown eyes seem even darker. "She's clean and she's on birth control, so why the fuck would I bother with a condom? I couldn't wait to feel her, Zeke. And fuck me." I drag my bottom lip through my teeth because remembering her snug, wet cunt is making me hard.

"That was reckless, West. She could have been lying about her birth control."

It *was* reckless, which is unlike me. But for some reason, Lily makes me want to take risks. "She had an implant in her arm. I felt it. I didn't let my dick completely take over."

His only response is a grunt. I look up at the ceiling and blow out a breath. The sooner he gets out of his head about the whole Lily situation, the better for all of us. "You should have joined us."

He shakes his head. "Not yet."

I narrow my eyes. "Why? I know you like her."

He shifts in his seat and picks an invisible piece of lint from his sweatpants. "I do, huh?"

"Correct me if I'm wrong, but wasn't it *you* who invited her to our booth the other night?"

He grunts, refusing to make eye contact with me. "So?"

"When was the last time you did that, Zeke? I can't remember. Can you?"

"So, I think she's hot. I'm not avoiding her, West. I'm just ..." He sighs, and I wait for him to continue. "I've been looking into her."

"Okay." Zeke does background checks on all the women we allow into our lives, so I'm not surprised. "And?"

"She checks out. Graduated from Columbia eighteen months ago. Came third in her class."

Impressed, I whistle through my teeth.

Zeke nods, running a hand through his hair. "On a full academic scholarship. Like she told us, she now works in the mail room at Grayson."

"So she got a full scholarship and graduated third in her class. So why the fuck is she a bike messenger?"

He shrugs. "Everyone I spoke to at Grayson says she loves her job there. And she's had a couple of articles published. I guess she's trying to break into publishing but hasn't made it yet."

"Anything else?"

"She lives with her friend, Jen Broughton, whose father is managing partner at a law firm here in Manhattan. And you might be interested to hear that Lily had a clear STD screening three weeks ago," he says with a frown of disapproval. I know what he's thinking—I should have checked that for myself before I fucked her without protection. And he's right, but I was too damn pussy drunk. "Nothing else of note."

"So we have nothing to worry about."

He runs his tongue over his teeth but doesn't say anything.

"Zeke?"

He clicks his tongue as though he's thinking. "She does have a connection to one of our previous house guests."

"Who?"

"Bree Reid."

"Bree?" I groan. She came highly recommended from a friend who owns an exclusive sex club. He told us she was into multiple partners, and she worked out okay for a few weeks. Until she became obsessed with Xander and would get crazy pissed if Zeke or I so much as touched him. It wasn't the smoothest of endings. Of all the people connected to Lily, it had to be her. "Really?"

He nods.

"Isn't Bree way older than Lily though?"

"Four years older, but she took a few years off between high school and college, remember?"

"Oh, yeah. To travel." I roll my eyes, recalling how she spun that particular line. She had no idea that Zeke would do a background check and find out she was in and out of rehab for eighteen months, treating her raging coke addiction. But we didn't hold that against her. "Were they friends?"

"Not as far as I can tell. They were in the same sorority, but from all accounts, they didn't really get along."

I scrub my hand over my face. "So, it's not an issue then?"

He shrugs. "Probably not."

A knock on my office door stops the conversation from going any further. We both know it's Lily because Xander doesn't knock. Zeke takes his protein shake and stands. "I'll leave you to it."

"You really don't have to."

"Maybe later." He opens the door to Lily's smiling face, offers her a curt good morning, then maneuvers around her and disappears down the hallway.

She glances over her shoulder. "Is he okay?"

"He'll be fine."

She wanders into the room, Xander's T-shirt skimming the middle of her thighs. "He seems so different from how he was at the club the other night. Are you sure he's okay with me being here?"

"Yes, I'm sure." I watch her with curiosity, expecting her to take a seat on the edge of my desk or on the chair opposite, but she does neither. Instead she walks to me and looks down at my lap.

"You want to sit?"

She bites the inside of her cheek, the way I've discovered she does when she's trying to hide her nerves. "Yeah."

"So sit, princess."

She perches herself on me, her sweet round ass nestled against my cock. "Thank you."

"You're welcome. You're also aware there's a perfectly good chair over there?"

She sighs. "I know, but I figured you'd be way comfier than an old chair."

I nip at her shoulder through the T-shirt. "That chair is a priceless antique."

She giggles. "That's what I said. Old."

I glance at the papers on my desk. They can wait. But my

cock is growing harder by the second, and he hates to be kept waiting. I brush her hair back, exposing her slender throat and trailing my teeth from her ear to her collarbone. She shivers. "For future reference, Lily, you should know that coming into my office barely dressed is only going to end one way."

She flutters her eyelashes at me and wraps her arms around my neck, acting coy when we both know she's anything but. "Oh. And what way is that, West?"

"You bent over my desk with a part of me inside you."

She clenches her thighs together, and I can fucking smell her wet pussy. I press my nose against her throat and inhale. "You smell like sex, princess."

Her skin blooms with heat. "I haven't showered yet. I was on my way to take one, but I don't know how to work the fancy shower in my room. And Xander went for a run."

"That's why you came in here?"

Sinking her teeth into her bottom lip, she nods.

"Then why did you sit on my lap?"

She giggles again. "Well, that was purely because you look really sexy in your suit and tie." She glances around the room. "Is this where you make your billions?"

I trail my fingertips up the inside of her thigh. "One of the places, yeah."

"Hmm." She traps that sexy bottom lip between her teeth now, and I want to pull it out with my own. "Where you make all your big business deals happen?"

I brush a fingertip over her bare pussy, and a growl rumbles in my chest as my cock strains uncomfortably against my zipper. "You know what else I make in here?"

She dusts her lips over my jaw, teasing me. "What?"

"Bratty little girls come. Especially ones who walk around with no panties."

I pick her up and bend her over my desk before she can take

another breath. Pulling up her T-shirt, I expose her bare ass to me and give it a light spank that makes her squeal. Unable to resist the creamy expanse of soft flesh, I dip my head and sink my teeth into her backside, then give her another quick smack.

I place one hand between her shoulder blades and free my aching dick with the other. Nudging at her entrance, I grin as she squirms and whimpers. "Already a slut for my cock, huh, princess?"

Not giving her a chance to answer, I drive inside, grabbing onto her hips so I can hold her in place while I fuck her as hard as I want. I've gone weeks without any kind of release, and since I met her, it's all I can fucking think about. She's unlocked something in me.

She pants out my name, and I lean over her, sucking on the sweet skin of her neck and marking her for my own.

I growl against her ear. "Your pussy is addictive, princess. You're fucking addictive. I think I'm gonna keep you."

I thrust hard and hit that sweet spot, the one that makes her mewl like a feral kitten, and then I roll my hips, rubbing my crown over it.

"Oh, fuck. West!"

"I know, princess. You like that, don't you?"

"Hell. Yes," she gasps.

Her pussy walls ripple around me, and I know she's close to losing herself. I slide my hand between her thighs and strum her clit with my thumb, sending her hurtling over the edge. She comes hard, her body shaking as she moans out my name. A few more thrusts inside her tight cunt has me falling over that cliff right alongside her.

CHAPTER
SEVENTEEN

LILY

I stuff a few spoonfuls of cereal into my mouth and grab my backpack from the counter.

I can feel Xander frowning at me even though I'm not looking at him. "You should really eat a proper breakfast, shorty. Especially for a job as physical as yours."

"I'll grab a bagel from the deli," I assure him.

"We have bagels right here."

"I know, but I'll be late if I don't leave now." I check my watch and groan. I'll be late even if I do leave now. Although the early morning orgasm in West's office was worth it.

"We'll drop you," he insists, crossing the room and wrapping his arms around my waist.

"I should just ride there. I don't want to become dependent on your car."

"Why not?" West asks as he walks into the kitchen with Zeke close behind him.

"Because I can't, that's why. If I start getting shuttled around in cars all the time, I'll become soft."

West comes up behind me, wedging me between him and Xander. "I don't like you riding that death trap around the city anyway."

"Betty is not a death trap," I protest on her behalf. She has almost gotten me killed once or twice with her faulty brakes, but that's beside the point.

"Take the car to do your deliveries," West suggests.

I snort. "Don't be ridiculous." I glance at Zeke, hoping for backup, but he just watches the three of us, an intense expression on his face.

"Why is it ridiculous, shorty?" Xander asks.

"Because I am a *bike* messenger. I'd never get anywhere with city traffic, and I'd get parking tickets every time I stopped. Besides, it's wasteful and bad for the environment to drive around in a car all day."

Resigned, Xander shakes his head, and West plants a kiss on the top of mine. "We'll take you and the death trap to work this morning." He checks his watch. "Or you'll be late."

"And whose fault is that?" I murmur.

"Entirely yours, brat." He swats my ass on his way to the coffee machine.

I GRAB my parcels for the afternoon and go to the bike shed in the lobby of the Grayson News building. I glance around, sure that I left Betty in her usual spot, but she's not here. Nobody in their right mind would steal her.

I pop my head out of the small space and jerk my chin at the security guard. "Hey, Stan. Did you see anyone walk out of here with my bike?"

"Yeah. Your friend, Mr. Archer. He told me to tell you that he took it."

What the hell? "And you just let him? How am I supposed to make my deliveries?"

He passes me and goes over to the corner of the shed, pointing at a brand-new bike. "He left you this one as a replacement. That's some friend you got there."

My eyes widen at the sight of the top-of-the-line electric bike. "He left me that?"

"Sure did. She's a beaut."

"She's not Betty," I grumble.

"Yeah. Lucky for you, huh?" Laughing, he nudges my arm and leaves me alone with Betty 2.0.

Left with no other option—for now—I grab the fancy bike and spend a full five minutes cursing West before I accept what I already knew. This thing is a dream; with its effortless handling and ridiculously plush seat, I find myself falling in love. With the bike.

As much as I want to be pissed at West, the fact that I get my packages delivered in half the time it usually takes, without causing any accidents, makes it impossible.

I THROW my hands in the air. "You can't just buy me a four-thousand-dollar bike, West."

He rolls his eyes and turns his back to me, pouring himself a Scotch while he watches Zeke chop carrots like it's the most fascinating thing in the world.

"And where did you put poor Betty?"

He turns and frowns. "Betty?"

"Her bike," Zeke explains.

I blink at the back of Zeke's head. I don't know why I'm so surprised that he remembers. I guess he pays more attention to me than he lets on.

West scoffs. "You mean the death trap?"

"I mean my beloved bicycle that I've had for six years and who has been with me through ..." I swallow the words on the tip of my tongue. "A lot," is all I whisper.

Xander wraps me in a hug. "Relax, shorty. She's downstairs in the basement."

"Oh." Some of the tension eases out of my body. "You still can't just buy me an expensive bike like that."

West sets his glass down on the kitchen counter and pinches the bridge of his nose. "Why the hell not?"

I open my mouth, then close it again. For the Unholy Trinity of billionaires, four grand is nothing. It would be like me dropping my pocket change into a panhandler's collection cup. But that's not the point. "You just can't. It's too much. You've known me for less than a week."

Xander buries his face in my hair and chuckles darkly. "But we know the most intimate parts of you."

I squirm in his arms. True.

"You're our girlfriend, Lily. Why the fuck can't we buy you a gift?"

I gape at him. "Your ... girlfriend?"

Zeke turns now, brandishing the vegetable knife like a villain from an '80s slasher flick. "Aren't you?"

I frown.

"You live with us. You have sex with—" He clears his throat. "With West and Xander. So what the fuck else would you call yourself?"

"I don't know. I hadn't really thought about it," I admit, unable to tear my eyes from Zeke's intense gaze.

Xander kisses my neck. "Do you want to be our girlfriend, shorty?"

My cheeks burn. "I do."

"For appearance's sake, you'll be my girlfriend if anyone

asks questions," West says matter-of-factly, then takes another sip of his Scotch.

I swallow hard. Have I thought this through? Do I want to be West Archer's girlfriend? Not publicly. "Questions? Who will ask questions?" I can't have my picture popping up in some gossip column.

"Work mostly." He searches my face with narrowed eyes. "When we drop you there in the morning or pick you up for lunch. Better to say you're only dating one of us than all three."

"Okay." I nod. "No paparazzi stuff or anything though, right?"

"Fuck no," Zeke growls.

"We manage to fly under their radar for the most part," West says.

"Then I guess I'm your girlfriend." My lips spread into a grin that falters when I realize how ungrateful I've been acting. "And um, thank you for the bike. It was actually very thoughtful."

The wink West gives me ignites a fire in my ovaries. "You're welcome." He turns back to Zeke. "You need any help there?"

Zeke hands him a head of broccoli without so much as a word.

With Xander's arms around me and his mouth nuzzling my neck, I watch West and Zeke prepare dinner, their forearms occasionally brushing. While they work, they chat quietly. I'm unable to hear what they're saying, but I do hear West's soft laugh just before he runs his hand down Zeke's jaw to his neck. Their brief kiss definitely involves some tongue, and I can't help the way my body reacts to watching them together. Their dynamic is tender and sweet. And so damn hot my panties grow damp.

"Do they ever ...?" I whisper to Xander.

He presses his lips to my ear. "Sometimes. I get horny as fuck watching them together."

I giggle. "Me too."

"A horny Lily and at least an hour until dinner." He hums against my skin. "Hmm. What's a guy to do?" Without waiting for a response, he hoists me over his shoulder and carries me from the room.

CHAPTER
EIGHTEEN

LILY

"Your usual." Our server places my favorite sandwich down in front of me, and my stomach growls.

"He is so into you," Jen says with a wicked grin.

"He is not."

"Is too." She pops a french fry into her mouth.

"So, how are you and Trey?" I take a bite of my delicious lunch.

She sighs dreamily, her eyes practically glazing over. "He is sooo hot, Lil. I mean, like freakishly hot. And that man's dick should come with a health warning, I swear."

Snorting a laugh, I place my hand over my mouth and try not to spray her with chewed-up bits of chicken and avocado. "So you two living together hasn't been a bad thing?" Two weeks have passed since we had to leave her apartment, which is a long time for Jen. The woman has an innate fear of commitment.

"Not at all. In fact, I'm kind of sad I'll be moving back home tomorrow. Speaking of which." She arches a perfectly shaped eyebrow at me. "Will you be coming home too?"

Chewing my sandwich, I look up at the ceiling.

"Lils?" she prompts.

I wrinkle my nose. "No."

"You're staying with the three hot billionaires in the Park Avenue penthouse? Shocker." Smirking, she rolls her eyes.

"You don't mind, do you?"

She shakes her head. "Not at all. You were going to move out anyway. And if I was getting dicked down by the Unholy Trinity every night, I wouldn't leave either."

My face burns. "I do not get *dicked down* by all three of them," I say in a harsh whisper, darting my eyes left and right to make sure nobody heard her.

She tilts her head and stares at me.

My lips curve up at the corners. "Just two."

She shrieks with laughter. Once she calms down, I put my hand on her wrist. "Is that bad?"

"Hell no! You're out there living your best life, girl. You enjoy those fine pieces of man meat while you can."

Relieved, I take another bite of my sandwich. She's totally right. There's no way this arrangement can last forever, so I should enjoy it while I can. How many women get the chance to date three men as hot as Xander, West, and Zeke? Although I can't really count Zeke. Despite the connection we seemed to have, and even though he said he was on board with the whole arrangement, he hasn't touched me and has barely spoken to me since I moved in.

Jen steals a potato chip from my plate. "So, how's your article coming along?"

I swallow and wash my food down with a gulp of soda. "The last one I was working on didn't pan out, but I'm researching a new one. Julian thinks it could be promising."

"You could just publish it yourself. Online or something. Julian doesn't get to decide what you write."

"Um. He's the editor of the magazine I want to work for, so he kind of does," I remind her. "And I do want to publish my own stuff one day, but I want to be with a reputable publication first. To prove I can do it, ya know. And Grayson's is one of the most widely circulated magazines in the country."

"Well, you are sleeping with the guys who are about to own it. Just tell them to make Julian put your article in the next issue."

I shake my head. "You know that isn't how I want to do this, Jen. What's the point of working my ass off all this time? I want my article to be in there because it's good, not because I'm getting *dicked down* by the boss."

"*Boss-es*," she corrects me.

I grin at her. "Eat your fries."

XANDER and West messaged me to say they were working late, so I know they aren't home when I get back to the apartment, but the music coming from the den tells me Zeke's here. I go to find him, hoping he'll tell me what he wants for dinner. I hate choosing what to cook. Having to decide what to make is one of the worst parts of adulting.

I walk into the room to find him wearing only a pair of tight suit pants. His hair is damp like he recently took a shower, and my breath catches in my throat at the sight of his bare torso. He's always kept his shirt on around me before. "Wow." Realizing I just said that out loud, I slap my hand over my mouth while he closes the gap between us.

"Zeke, your tattoos are beautiful." I instinctively reach out to trace the lines of ink adorning his chest and abs, but he grips my wrist before I can touch him, squeezing hard enough to make me wince.

"I don't like being touched," he says with a throaty growl.

"West and Fitch touch you."

He sneers. "They've known me forever."

"So, it's a trust thing, then?" I ask, raking my eyes over the intricate works of art.

"Does it matter?"

"It matters to me." I'm surprised by the sudden knowledge that I would give anything to earn his trust.

"You getting a good look there?"

My eyes travel back to his, which are smoldering with anger and ... something else I can't identify. "I could stare at them all day. They're incredible."

"You think I don't know what you're really looking at, buttercup?"

Buttercup? He makes the term of endearment sound like an insult. But I have no idea what he's talking about, and my frown deepens. "What?"

He steps forward, and now his chiseled body is only a few inches from mine. Heat radiates from his skin, warming me even through my tank top. A pulsing sensation builds between my thighs.

"You heard me." His voice drops another octave, its steady cadence making goosebumps prickle along my forearms.

What the hell is this guy's deal? "Why did you lie, Ezekiel?"

His scowl deepens. "What?"

"You lied to me. When I asked you if you wanted me here, you said yes."

A muscle in his jaw twitches. "So?"

"It seems like you don't want me here at all." I shrug, trying to pull off an Academy Award-winning display of disinterest.

His head falls back, and he lets out a dark, arrogant laugh, then fixes those fiery eyes on me again. "And why do you say that, buttercup? Because I don't want you looking at my scars?"

I roll my eyes. Asshole. "What scars?"

He lowers his mouth to my ear, and his hot breath ruffles my hair. "The ones all over my fucking chest."

My eyes drop back down, and sure enough, the veneer of ink covers a cluster of thick, twisted scars. A lump of emotion clogs my throat, but I swallow it down. They must have been carved into his flesh long before he got the tattoos. How did he get them? Are they the reason he doesn't like to be touched? I open my mouth to tell him that I didn't even notice his scars. I mean we all have them, some are just on the inside. But before I can utter a word, he wraps a hand around my throat, cutting off my words and my air.

"You don't want to fucking play with me, Lily, because I will eat you alive." His grip relaxes just enough for me to speak.

Instead of reassuring him about his scars, I give him snark. "That would require some touching though, wouldn't it?"

He grunts a response, a humorless smirk pulling the corner of his mouth upward as a wicked glint flickers in his dark eyes. "*I* will touch *you* whenever and wherever the fuck I want."

Pretending his hand isn't still locked around my throat, I place my hands on my hips. "Is that so?"

"That's the deal you signed up for."

"Is there anywhere I'm allowed to touch you?"

He lets go of me. "Forearms. Or below the waist is fine."

I glance down, unconsciously running my tongue over my lip when I see the clear outline of his hard cock straining against his pants. He wants me, but he won't admit it. I wish I knew why.

A menacing growl vibrates in his chest. "You want a taste, buttercup?"

Not taking my eyes from his impressive bulge, I nod.

He inhales deeply, his abs tightening and the thick muscles of his thighs growing taut. He has an incredible body, and I want to feel it for myself. I want him to let me in. I need him to let me in. "Then go ahead." He grits out the words like they pain him.

Not giving him a second to change his mind, I drop to my knees. He flinches when I trail my fingernails over his zipper. I bite down on my lip to stifle a giggle and look up to find him gazing down at me with an expression of unrestrained hunger. My insides contract with white hot pleasure. I've never seen him like this, at least not with me, and it fuels my courage. Still, my fingers tremble on his zipper. And when I reach into his boxers and free his magnificent cock, he trembles too. His entire body shudders as he lets out a deep groan. It's possibly the hottest sound I've heard any man make—ever. This is my way in with Zeke. This is how I get him to trust me.

Wrapping my hand around the thick base, I squeeze. Precum leaks from the slit of his crown, and I dart out my tongue and lick it off, stifling a moan as his taste fills my mouth. He hisses out a breath. I want all of him inside me, but I want to draw this out for him too. I'm going to give him the best head he's ever had in his goddamn life.

"You taste so good." I wrap my lips around the tip of his cock, and he grunts appreciatively, rocking his hips forward, but I pull back, taunting him just a little.

Huge mistake.

Zeke snarls, the animalistic sound vibrating through him and into me, and fists his giant hands in my hair. "Don't fucking toy with me."

I take a deep breath through my nose right before he shoves his cock all the way into my mouth, hitting the back of my throat and making me gag. Tears stream down my cheeks. Saliva dribbles down my chin. He pulls back an inch, and I take the opportunity to suck in air, preparing for him to drive inside again, which he does half a second later, barely giving me any time to recover.

I place my hands on his hard thighs, my fingertips digging into his taut muscles and holding me steady while he fucks my face. Ezekiel Cavanagh is wrong if he thinks this is going to break me. So very wrong. I relax my jaw and my throat, the way I was taught a long time ago. Tears prick at my eyes for a different reason now, but I blink them away, anchoring myself to this moment right here. To Zeke's scent. His touch. His powerful hands on my head. The way they hold onto me, almost reverently as he drives his cock in and out of my mouth.

My heart leaps when I glance up and find him still staring down at me, a look of awe and desire on his face. His dark eyes shutter closed. "Fuck!" he grunts.

I continue to watch him, my eyes swimming with tears. A stray drop rolls down my cheek, and he wipes it away with the pad of his thumb. That one simple act makes my heart ache for him. My beautiful Zeke. So damaged, but so desperate for someone to love him. He and I have more in common than he will ever know. I blink away my tears and stare into his eyes. Edging forward, I swallow every single inch of him, my throat constricting around the crown of his cock. His eyes roll back in his head. His grip in my hair tightens.

"Mother ... fucker!" he growls, holding my head in place as thick ribbons of salty cum streak down my throat. I inhale through my nose and swallow again, and Zeke's thigh muscles tremble beneath my fingertips.

Our eyes remain locked as he slowly slides out of my mouth, and I lick the drool from my lips. "Where the fuck did you learn to suck cock like that, buttercup?"

I figure it's a rhetorical question, so I don't answer. What would he say, or do, if I told him the truth? Instead, I smile up at him, thrilled that, for a few seconds at least, I made him lose control.

He grabs my jaw, squeezing roughly. "Here I was, thinking you were a delicate little flower, Lily. But you're ..." His dark eyes narrow.

I'm what, Zeke? Tell me.

He doesn't finish his sentence. His Adam's apple bobs, and he looks away, breaking the connection between us as effectively as if he'd severed it with a knife. Releasing his grip on me, he tucks himself away and zips up his pants. Then, without another word, he stalks out of the room, leaving me alone on my knees.

CHAPTER
NINETEEN

LILY

Xander runs his fingers along my neck and rests his other hand on my thigh, sending shivers up and down my spine. I lean against his solid chest, trying to focus on the movie he chose for us all to watch, but I'm way too distracted by his hands and the fact that he, West, and Zeke are only wearing sweatpants. There's so much toned muscle on display, it's a wonder I can concentrate on anything at all.

"Is the movie boring you, buttercup?" Zeke asks after he catches me staring at him.

I squeeze my thighs together and squirm in my seat. "No. It's just I can't help thinking ..." My cheeks flame with heat.

Xander presses his mouth to my ear. "Can't help think what, shorty?"

"Um." I press my lips together.

West winks at me. "Use your words, princess."

Zeke switches off the TV and the three of them stare at me expectantly. Wetness seeps into my panties. They might not even be down for this. I moisten my lips. "I was thinking that there are way more interesting things that the four of us could be doing, is all."

"Holy fuck," Xander mutters.

Zeke narrows his eyes. "Such as?"

"We could go to bed." I sink my teeth into my bottom lip and flutter my eyelashes. *Please don't make me say more than that.*

Zeke opens his mouth, probably to taunt me, so I'm extra thankful when Xander jumps up, hoists me over his shoulder, and slaps my ass. "I think we all know what our girl is looking for."

I giggle as he jogs down the hallway, and when I see West and Zeke following behind us, a surge of adrenaline and anticipation makes my head spin.

Xander tosses me onto my bed. "Get her naked, Fitch." West's growling tone turns my legs to jelly.

Xander wastes no time in pulling off all my clothes until I'm lying on the bed, naked and staring up at the three of them.

Zeke's hungry gaze roams over my body. "Spread your legs, buttercup. Let me see our pussy."

My breath hitches and heat blooms beneath my skin. I do as he asks, opening wider. His gaze drops to the space between my thighs, and his harsh inhale makes me feel powerful and self-assured. "Motherfucker. That's fucking beautiful."

Xander nudges his arm, and a wicked grin spreads across his face. "Told ya."

West makes quick work of pulling off his sweatpants and tossing them into the hamper. "And already so wet for us, princess."

Xander takes his pants off too before flashing Zeke a knowing smirk. "Our girl tastes even better than she looks, Z."

Zeke merely grunts and takes a seat on the chair by the bed. I swallow a lump of disappointment. Maybe he likes to start off by watching.

Xander crawls onto the bed first, trailing his wicked mouth over my calves and my knees, along my inner thighs, all the way up to my soaking center. "So wet, shorty." With one long swipe of his tongue, he licks my seam. "And so fucking sweet."

West lies down beside me and cups my jaw in his hand. "As soon as we get you wet enough, princess, Xander is going to fuck you." He drags his tongue and teeth down my neck. "And then I'm going to fuck him while he's inside you."

The vibration of Xander's chuckle pulses through me. "That sounds so hot," I whisper.

West slides his hand down my neck, squeezing each of my breasts in turn. "Oh, it will be." He glances down at Xander, who's looking up at us, his eyes twinkling with delight. "Make her come like a good boy," West orders.

Xander sucks my clit into his waiting mouth, gently nudging the sensitive bundle of nerves with his tongue. Oh. That's so good. I reach down, intending to thread my fingers in his thick hair, but West catches my wrists and pins them above my head with one hand. "No, princess. Just lie back and take what he gives you."

I suck in a breath. Pleasure is rolling in my core, and he's barely even started. West kisses my lips, then he moves lower and sinks his teeth into one of my nipples. I moan and buck my hips, chasing the release that feels so close already.

"You like my boys teasing you, buttercup?" The deep timbre of Zeke's voice rumbles through me, and I whimper, my attention torn between West sucking and toying with my nipples and Xander's delicious mouth lapping at me.

Zeke laughs darkly. "I think she's had enough teasing, Fitch. He told you to make her come." His hand goes down to stroke himself, his intense eyes locked on the three of us. He's so sexy. I wish he'd join us, but before I can suggest it, Xander slides a thick finger inside me, and I moan his name instead. My back arches off the bed as heat and tingling pleasure sizzle down my thighs.

Xander groans. "Oh, you're squeezing me so tight, shorty."

West's tongue licks a path between my aching breasts. "Is she wet enough yet, Fitch?"

Xander murmurs against my sensitive flesh but offers no further response than that.

"I guess I'll find out for myself." West coasts his hand down my body, moving Xander's face out of the way. Another finger slides inside me, and the two men work in tandem, thrusting in and out.

"Yeah you are. So fucking wet, aren't you, princess?"

Unable to speak, I jerk my head up and down, gasping at the sensations flooding my body.

West runs his nose along my jawline. "Can you take a third?"

I moan my answer as wet heat rushes between my thighs.

"Good girl." Three fingers stretch me wide, two of West's and one of Xander's. Their hands work expert magic while West kisses my neck and Xander's tongue dances at my entrance. Without warning, my climax crashes into me, my pussy fluttering and rippling around them.

Xander grunts his appreciation and West bites down on my neck, sucking the sensitive skin as my hips buck from the force of my climax.

Once my body is done trembling, they slide their fingers out of me, and a rush of cum follows. I blush to the roots of my hair. West laughs softly, and Xander pushes himself up onto his forearms. "Definitely wet enough now, shorty."

I throw my head back, still coming down from my high. But before I can catch my breath, Xander is nudging my pussy with the crown of his thick cock. He sinks all the way inside me in one hard thrust, knocking the remaining air from my lungs.

He falls forward, resting all his weight on his forearms. He grunts, breath dusting over my neck. "Holy fuck, Lily."

I wrap my arms around him, clawing at his skin while he fucks me so hard that the bed shakes.

"Lube, buddy?" West says somewhere in the background, and I glance at Zeke in time to see him toss a small bottle toward the bed.

West positions himself behind Xander and weaves his fingers in Xander's thick hair. With a rough yank, he jerks his head back, and Xander winces. Wetness pools in my core as I watch them together, and when West sinks his teeth into the soft skin at the base of Xander's throat, his cock spasms inside me and excitement shudders through my entire body.

West growls. "Are you ready for me, boy?"

Xander hisses out a breath. Then his eyes lock on mine. "Are you ready, shorty?"

Breathless, I nod.

West's thick arms snake around Xander's torso and he sinks inside him, resulting in the impossible, pushing Xander even deeper into me than he already was. His eyes roll back and West pushes him forward, sandwiching him between the two of us.

West nails Xander while he rails into me, and the sheer intensity makes me dizzy. The pressure of the two of them driving into me pushes me up the bed and makes my breath stall in my lungs. My eyes flutter closed.

Fingers caress my throat, and I open my eyes to find Zeke lying beside us. "Breathe, buttercup." I nod, sucking in air. "You're doing so well taking them both."

His praise spreads heat through me like wildfire. Xander grunts loudly.

"You take my cock so fucking well, Fitch," West groans.

Xander increases the pace of his thrusts, causing West to do the same. I'm losing my mind from the waves of euphoric pleasure that crash over me.

Xander's mouth is on my neck, sucking and licking and biting. "You close, shorty?"

"Y-yes."

"Your pussy is gripping my cock like you'll never let me go."

I rake my nails over his shoulder blades. "I won't," I cry out as my climax takes hold, tearing through my body until my head is spinning and tears are running down my face.

"Holy fucking shit," Xander groans, driving his hips harder as he loses himself too.

West doesn't let up though. He picks up his pace while he watches me over Xander's shoulder, his stormy gaze holding mine. Xander shuffles like he's about to slide out of me, but West drives into him harder and lets out a throaty growl. "You're gonna stay inside her while I come."

I sink my teeth into my lip and try to focus on West's face, but I can't. Another orgasm is already stirring deep in my center. Xander's still hard, and now West is using brute strength to fuck us both into oblivion. My back bows as my third climax takes hold, pulsing through my body like a million tiny explosions. Then Xander bites into my neck, and stars flicker behind my eyelids.

"Jesus fuck," West shouts, his hips stuttering to a halt. He rests his forehead on Xander's back, keeping his weight on his hands so he doesn't crush us both.

Xander chuckles, his breath fanning my chest. "Fuck, that was hot."

West lifts his head and gives me a soft kiss on the lips. "You did good, princess."

Xander smiles against my neck. "So good."

My heart finally slows, and my eyelids flutter shut. I'm vaguely aware of West moving before Xander slides out of me. A soft groan of protest pours out of me, but then he lies beside me and slides an arm over my hip. Splaying his hand flat on my stomach, he pulls me closer until our bodies are flush.

A dreamy sigh tumbles from my lips, and I reopen my eyes to find West beside me too, lying flat on his stomach with his head turned my way. I smile at him.

"How are you so fucking perfect, Lily?" West's frown does nothing to take away from his handsome face. Before I can answer, Zeke crawls over him, peppering kisses along his spine. West's eyes roll back and mine widen with fascination. I've witnessed how hot Zeke and West are for each other, but they're both tops, so I'm eager to see where this is going. They've never done more than kiss in front of me.

Zeke lies flat on top of him, his heavy weight pressing West's huge frame into the mattress. He dusts his lips against West's ear, catching his lobe between his teeth and tugging gently, like a playful puppy. Or maybe a lion cub.

"Will you bottom for me?" Zeke asks in his low, throaty growl as he grinds his hips against West's ass. Dear mother of god, this is so freaking hot. Hot enough to rouse me from my post-orgasm haze.

West's mouth falls open on a groan, but he doesn't answer.

"Come on, West. It's been so fucking long since you let me fuck you."

"Lily and Fitch are right there, horndog."

Based on the heavy breathing coming from Xander, I'm certain he's asleep. Zeke must come to the same conclusion, because his eyes are on my face. As much as I'd love him to fuck me, I am a little tender. Plus, I'm more than a little interested in watching Zeke and West together.

I fake a yawn, and Zeke's lips twitch knowingly. "They're both beat. You fucked them both into oblivion. Come on. You know I can make you come so fucking hard."

"You do everything hard," West groans, but his eyes are dark with lust and there's a wicked smile on his face.

Zeke grinds against West and licks a path from his shoulder to his ear. "I'll be gentle this time. Promise."

West sucks in a breath. "You don't know the goddamn meaning of the word."

Triumphant. That's the only word that comes to mind when I see Zeke's smile. "You'll fucking love it."

TWENTY

WEST

Zeke's sexy-as-fuck mouth trails a path from the back of my neck down my spine, all the way to my ass. He licks down the seam, and despite the fact that I just came as hard as I ever have in my life, my cock twitches and my balls tingle.

He growls against my skin, and the sound travels straight to my dick. "You have such a hot ass, West. You should let me fuck it more often."

"Don't push your luck, Ezekiel." I hear the snap of a lid opening, and then his slick finger pushes against my asshole. He sinks in to the knuckle, twisting as he inches deeper.

The burning stretch sends hot rivulets of pleasure down my thighs, and I hiss out a breath when he adds a second finger. Zeke's lips are on my throat now, his weight on top of me while he slides his fingers in and out. "Relax. You know you can take me."

Fisting my hands in the sheets, I draw deep breaths through my nose, enjoying the endorphins that flood my body. He pushes his fingers deeper, massaging them over my G-spot, and my eyes roll back in my head.

He drags his teeth over my ear. "You love me fucking you, West. Admit it."

My cock is hard again, leaking precum from the crown. "You know I do." I grit out the words, my jaw clenched.

"Nobody but me. Ever. Isn't that right?"

I push my ass back into him, seeking Zeke's unique brand of pleasure laced with pain.

He growls, grinding his thick cock against my hip as he finger-fucks my ass. "Turn over. I want to look at you while I fuck you."

I snarl. I fucking hate being told what to do, but I'm too far gone. Too desperate to feel him sinking inside me, knowing he'll make it even better than what he's doing now.

He removes his fingers and I flip over. "Good boy," he says with a wicked grin.

Grabbing his hair, I yank his head back and he grunts. "Don't fuck with me, Zeke," I warn him.

He shakes his head from my grip, then climbs between my thighs and pushes them apart with his knees. "Just fuck you, yeah?" His cock is already slick with lube, and he presses the tip against my ass, edging in a little while he trails his tongue and teeth over my chest, lashing at the skin.

He inches deeper and I groan.

Holding his weight on his forearms, he lets his head fall back as he gives me more. "West, you feel so fucking good."

My balls tighten as the burn of him stretching me gives way to intense euphoria.

I pant out his name and pull him toward me, crashing his mouth to mine. Our tongues fight for dominance. Our teeth clash together. He bites my lip, drawing blood and then sucking it off. His cock pulses inside me as he fucks me into the bed.

Reaching between us, I grip my aching shaft in my palm. He breaks the kiss, his chest heaving and eyes darker than coal. "No. Let me make you come, West." He pulls out and drives into me again. "Like this."

I throw my head back and let go. My orgasm draws near, and my mouth falls open. Zeke slides his tongue inside again, stealing my breath and fucking me with unrelenting force. He sets a demanding pace that leaves us both gasping for air, our bodies slick with sweat as they grind and slap against each other. I bear down on him and band my arms around his back, digging my fingers into his hard muscles.

"That's it. Come with me, West." The way he grunts my name in my ear sets me off, and thick ribbons of my release coat our stomachs.

"You're such a good fuck." Zeke gives one final thrust of his hips and fills me with his cum. With his forehead on mine, our heaving breaths mingle. Our lips brush once, twice, then he smiles and turns his head. "You enjoy the show, buttercup?"

So, that's what this was? What an asshole.

Looking over, I find Lily watching the two of us, her mouth open in a perfect O. Her eyelids flutter closed, and she moans. The motion of her hand working her clit draws my attention down. She rocks into her hand, tremors shaking her body.

He turns his attention back to me. "I guess she did, huh?"

CHAPTER
TWENTY-ONE

ZEKE

West storms into the kitchen. Judging by the fine film of perspiration covering his toned chest and abs, he just finished his workout. My eyes are drawn to the V that disappears beneath his running shorts.

Snarling, he crosses the room in two strides and slaps his palms down on the counter. "Don't ever fucking use me again, Zeke."

My eyes narrow, confusion and annoyance prickling at my skin. "The fuck?"

His lips curl back over his teeth. "Don't pretend like you don't know what the hell I'm talking about."

I stand up and mirror his stance, planting my own hands on the counter and leaning forward. "I have no fucking idea what you're talking about." My nostrils flare as I try to keep a lid on my temper. "I would never use you."

His brow furrows. "No? So what the fuck was that last night?"

A cold wave of guilt hits me in the chest. "Last night?"

"You think I wouldn't realize that you were testing Lily by fucking me in front of her?" His gray eyes smolder with indignation. "To see how she'd react to the two of us together?"

"Why are you only bringing this up now?" I ask, but I know why. He never would have said anything in front of her, and I got the hell out of there before he came down from the high of his climax. West might be a top, but he loves it when I fuck him.

"You know why, you fucker," he shouts.

I suck in a breath and run a hand over my face. "It wasn't just about that." I stare into his eyes and drop my guard. My voice drops an octave. "You know it wasn't." He knows me better than anyone else on this entire fucking planet.

His jaw ticks. A vein in his neck pulses. "Don't ever fucking do it again, Zeke. I'm not a pawn in your fucked-up mission to prove that Lily isn't going to work out."

That slow-rolling guilt grows and gnaws at my gut. "I never said she wouldn't work out."

"No, but you're convinced she won't, right? So convinced of it that even though you can't take your fucking eyes off her, you've barely touched her since she moved in here over two weeks ago."

Rage courses through my veins alongside the gnawing guilt. My chest tightens. "I told you, she sucked my fucking cock yesterday before you got home." What more does he want from me?

He leans closer. "And you've barely spoken to her since. What the hell are you afraid of, Zeke?"

I slam my fist on the countertop. "Don't, West."

"Don't what? Don't ask why you refuse to fuck the woman you jerk off to in the shower every morning? When are you going to stop second-guessing everything and show her who you really are?"

A throat clears behind us. Motherfucker.

We both turn to where Lily stands in the doorway, a pained expression on her face. "I'm so sorry, but I really need some Tylenol."

"Are you okay?" West asks, his voice laced with concern.

"Yeah, just some cramps." She slips past us and heads to the medicine cabinet. "I'll be out of your hair in a few seconds."

Scrubbing my hands over my face, I sigh. "How much of that did you hear?"

She spins on her heel and arches one eyebrow. "Not much. Just that West thinks you should show me who you really are."

I run a hand through my hair and mutter curse words.

She grabs the bottle of painkillers from the cupboard and takes two with a glass of water. When she's done, she stands beside West at the kitchen island and studies me. "So who are you really, Zeke?"

Nope. Not going there. "You got your period?"

"Yup. Happens every month," she replies, one corner of her mouth curling up. "Who are you?"

"You always get cramps?"

"Not always." One eyebrow goes up. "So?"

West watches me, no doubt enjoying this.

I narrow my eyes. "You should probably go lay down or something."

"It's only period cramps. I'll be fine. They usually go away with a couple Tylenol and a little heat. Do you guys have a heating pad?"

I look at West, and he shakes his head.

"That's okay," she muses, then sinks her perfect white teeth into the pillow of her bottom lip and releases it with a sharp inhale. "You know what else is good for period cramps?"

West dips his head, running his nose over her hair. "Orgasms." She turns and smiles at him, but he gives her an apologetic look. "As much as I would *love* to help you out with that particular problem, princess, I have to shower and get to work."

He kisses the top of her head, and with a final pointed glance in my direction, he leaves Lily and me alone in the kitchen.

"So, what about you, Zeke?" She manages a steady tone, but her body language portrays her nerves. Body language betrays everyone. She has no idea what she just walked into, but the fact that she's still standing toe-to-toe with me is admirable.

"You want me to help with your cramps?"

"That too much for a big guy like you to handle?" Her defiant glare makes my cock twitch with the need to be inside her. "If you're worried about a little blood, I'm wearing a tampon and you only need to stay in the *clitoral* area. You do know where that is, right?"

Fucking brat. Slowly rolling my head on my shoulders, I fight the urge to grin. A thrill of anticipation travels straight to my balls. I stalk around the island and stop directly in front of her, inhaling her scent. So sweet and inviting. I curl a strand of her dark hair between my thumb and forefinger, and she cranes her neck to look up at me, a playful smile on her lips.

"You should be very careful talking like that around me, buttercup."

"I think I can handle you, Ezekiel," she says with a soft purr and a flutter of her eyelashes. "So are you going to help me out with my cramps or not?"

I search her face as she blinks up at me, her bright green eyes sparkling. She has no fucking idea what she's letting herself in for. But this has to happen sometime, right? At some point she'll see who I really am and run for the hills like all the others. Out of all of the women we've ever brought home, she's the one who needs to realize what I am sooner rather than later.

Before West and Fitch get more attached to her than they already are. I can't live with them resenting me for pushing her away. Decision made, I grab hold of her wrist, and my bruising grip makes her gasp.

"Come with me." Not giving her any other choice, I drag her toward my bedroom. She jogs to keep up with me, her breaths fluttering from her lips. Once the door closes behind us, her eyes dart toward the art adorning my walls, then her gaze falls on the super king-sized bed. She drags her bottom lip through her teeth and looks at me, wide-eyed and expectant.

I step forward, closing the gap between us. "Go take out your tampon."

The shocked look on her pretty face has me fighting back a grin. "W-what? No. Why?"

"Because I fucking told you to, buttercup. Now go. Bathroom's back there." I nod toward the far side of the room.

The spot between her eyes pinches together. "I can't do that. There'll be blood. Lots and lots of blood." She glances at the pristine white sheets on my bed.

I grip her jaw in my hand, squeezing hard until she focuses her horror-stricken gaze on me instead. Bending down, I bring my lips close to her ear, enjoying the way she shivers when my breath dusts over her skin. Her feminine scent fills my nose. I need her. Now. "I know how periods work, Lily. Now go take out your fucking tampon or I'll pull it out myself." Her breath hitches. "With my teeth."

A pink flush creeps over her nose and cheeks, obscuring the tiny smattering of freckles she has there.

"Now," I command, and she narrows her eyes, titling her chin in a show of defiance that makes my cock throb painfully.

"Fine, they're your sheets," she says with a sweet smile, before turning on her heel and storming into the bathroom. I'm pretty sure I hear her call me an asshole under her breath.

I take off my shirt and listen to the sound of the toilet flushing. A few moments later, Lily emerges from the bathroom, dressed exactly the same as before, in an oversized college jersey that stops at mid-thigh, but looking less bold than she did when she walked in there.

"Come here," I order, resisting the urge to make her crawl to me—for now. "And remember that you asked for this when I'm done with you. Don't go crying to West or Fitch."

She glares at me, and my aching cock weeps for her. But first, I need to taste. "Take off your clothes."

She doesn't hesitate to peel off her jersey, letting it drop to the floor beside her feet. She's not wearing a bra, and her nipples are already stiff peaks. I ball my hands into fists at my sides to stop myself from reaching out and squeezing the tempting buds. She hooks her fingers into the waistband of her black panties, and that's when she falters and throws another nervous glance at the white cotton sheets.

"Yes, those too, buttercup."

Her slender throat ripples as she peels her underwear down her legs and kicks them off. Sucking on my top lip, I allow myself a moment to take in every inch of her, to appreciate her lethal curves. I've seen her naked, but not like this—not just for me. She has a scar on her side, under her ribs. Another on the inside of her left thigh. Did someone put them there? Did someone mark her beautiful skin on purpose? Did she let them?

She squeezes her thighs together, and her voice is a hoarse whisper. "Zeke?"

"Lie on the bed."

She bites down on her lip, eyes full of excitement and more than a hint of fear, which only makes me harder. She's a woman full of sharp contrasts—compliant and defiant, confident but unsure, sweet but a little dangerous too. West might have been right—maybe she is perfect.

"Don't make me ask a second time."

She gets on the bed and scoots back until her head touches the pillows. Her cheeks are bright pink now, and that cute blush races down her neck and chest. So self-conscious about a little blood. I lick my lips. Soon she won't care.

I climb onto the bed after her. Spreading her legs with my knees, I crawl between them and run my nose up her calf to her knee, then her inner thigh. Her entire body trembles with nervous energy. I inhale deeply, and my balls tighten at her scent. Liquid arousal drips out of her, and the heady mix of her cum laced with that distinctive coppery tang makes me feral. Looking up at her face, I lick my lips. Dark green eyes stare back at me, her tits heaving with each heavy breath.

I brush my thumbs along her pussy lips and spread her wide open. "You smell good enough to fucking devour whole." I bite down on the inside of her thigh, making her whimper and moan and buck her hips.

She threads her slender fingers through my hair. "Z-Zeke." My name shudders out of her mouth on a plea. Whether it's to stop or keep going, I have no idea, but I suspect a little of both. I bite again, marking her this time, claiming her for my own. A sick thrill envelops me at the thought of how she'll look at these marks later and know that I gave them to her. I could mark her forever.

I bite down harder, and she squirms. The scent of her arousal grows thicker and stronger, and I need to taste her. Her clit is perfect, swollen and slick and begging for me to take a bite. I rub the pad of my thumb over it first, gently teasing her with the slightest amount of pressure. A keening wail rips out of her chest, and her back arches off the bed. "So fucking beautiful, Lily." I press more firmly. She writhes, lost in the moment, her earlier embarrassment about bleeding on my sheets forgotten.

"Oh. Oh, fuck." She rocks her hips, chasing more contact, and I give it to her in the form of my tongue running the length of her slit. She cries out, her hips almost shooting off the bed, and I hold her down with my free hand, keeping her exactly where I want her while I swirl my tongue over her supple flesh.

Her fingernails dig into my head, making my scalp tingle. I drink her in, her scent and taste flooding my nose and mouth. My tongue joins my thumb, and I work her clit with both, applying firmer pressure. Tremors wrack her body, and her thighs clamp around my head. I push one thigh back down, giving me more room to feast on her cunt.

Breathy pleas tumble from her lips as I carry her closer to the edge. I want to feel her silky heat wrapped around my length, but I'm going to make her come like this first. A quick, easy orgasm before I make her work for the rest.

Her breaths grow increasingly short and fast. Her fingernails dig into my scalp. I breathe her in and suck her sensitive clit into my mouth, flooding my senses with all things Lily. The animal-like craving already coursing through my body snaps its teeth, ravenous to have some part of me inside her right now.

I slide two fingers into her tight cunt and graze her sensitive flesh with my teeth. She screams my name, her inner walls locking my hand in place. Her head falls back and her body goes still, trapped under the spell of her orgasm. Whimpering and moaning, she covers my fingers and wrist with her juices, stained red with her period. I lap them up until the taste of her has my heart ready to gallop out of my chest. My cock throbs, desperate to claim her. Slipping my fingers out of her wet center, I push up onto my knees and settle between her thighs.

I wipe my mouth with the back of my hand and blood streaks across my knuckles. Her eyelids flutter as her climax continues rippling through her body, but when I bracket her hips with my hands, her gaze lands on mine. "You're an animal,

Zeke." The words leave her lips on a breathy moan. I rock my hips, coaxing every tremor from her as she comes down from her high, grinding against her soaking pussy and staining the gray fabric of my sweatpants with her blood and cum.

An animal? Not the first time I've been called that, but it is the first time anyone has said it the way she just did. Without judgment or revulsion. "You better fucking believe it, buttercup."

Her body sags against the mattress. She pants for breath, her hands fisted in the sheets. Thighs trembling. Like she needs a few minutes to recover.

I'm not going to give them to her.

CHAPTER
TWENTY-TWO

ZEKE

Without giving her any warning, I flip Lily over. She squeals in surprise, her body still wracked with tremors from her climax. I pull her up onto her knees so I can see her pussy dripping onto my sheets. Her whimpers are muffled by the pillow under her face. Reaching into my sweatpants, I free my aching cock and give it a sharp tug as I stare at her perfect cunt and ass, on display and waiting for me like the naughty little slut I know she is deep inside.

I spank her ass hard, leaving a bloody handprint behind. She groans out my name, and I can't wait much longer to bury myself inside her. My heart is thumping wildly against my ribcage, adrenaline thundering through my veins like it's my lifeblood.

I tangle my fingers in her hair, pulling her head back so sharply that she winces. "You're gonna take my cock now, buttercup. Every fucking inch of me on the first go." I drive inside her, bottoming out and filling her dripping cunt.

She makes a strangled sound, but her wet heat grips me tight. I pull out slowly, making her whine like a needy slut before I ram back inside, so hard that the bed rattles.

"Fu-oh!" she mewls. I yank her head back more and ride her hard, slamming into her over and over until tears roll down her cheeks and she's barely able to breathe. And when she seems as though she can't take any more, I bend over her, wrapping my free hand around her throat and railing into her like a man possessed.

I press my mouth against her ear, teeth nipping at her skin. I'm struck by an overwhelming desire to bite her, to become the animal she just accused me of being. She turns me into an animal, feral and famished, with a burning need to touch and claim every single part of her. I ravage her sweet cunt until she's panting for breath and whimpering beneath me. But it's still not enough.

I pull her up so we're both kneeling and spread her thighs wider with my knees, stretching her as far as I can while still being able to fuck her in this position. She's going to cum all over my sheets, stain them bright red with her release. My cock leaks inside her at the thought. "You're going to take everything I got, like my needy little whore."

Gripping her head and throat, I feel her try to nod. I increase my pressure, cutting off her airway as I drive in even harder, my hips slamming against her ass and making it bounce. Then I sink my teeth into her shoulder, biting down and breaking the skin. The tang of copper fills my mouth, the taste different than the blood from her pussy but just as sweet.

Her cunt ripples, milking my cock. I loosen my grip on her throat and let her suck in a breath. The rush of air ignites her climax, like oxygen feeding a flame. She comes hard, soaking my sheets and my thighs and trembling so much that her teeth chatter. I wrap my arms around her, holding her tight and roaring her name as my orgasm tears through me with the force of a freight train.

I let her go and she falls flat on the mattress, gasping for breath and clutching at her throat. I sway on my knees, my head spinning with the strength of my own climax. I'm seconds away from collapsing on top of her when a heaving sob escapes from her lips. The sound snaps me out of my orgasm-induced haze, and all I can do is watch helplessly as tears stream from her eyes.

Fuck!

Seconds drag like minutes, but she doesn't run. She doesn't scramble to get away from me. She doesn't do anything. Tentatively, I reach out and trail my fingertips down her spine, and she shivers. But she's still here. Lying between my thighs, covered in her blood and our cum, she looks so beautifully broken that my cock already aches to take her again.

"Zeke," she rasps, her throat clogged with tears.

"Yeah?" My own voice comes equally raw and thick with emotion.

Whatever she was about to say gets cut off by another sharp intake of breath. Before she can tell me not to, before she can run, I fall onto my forearms and press my chest against her back. A heavy sigh escapes her, and tension seeps from her body into mine.

We lie here like this for I don't know how long. Our hearts racing, breaths hoarse and ragged. After our chests stop heaving and the pulse in her neck is no longer throbbing, I press a soft kiss beneath her ear. The corner of her mouth curls into a faint smile. "That was so freaking intense," she whispers.

I hum my agreement against her skin. It was fucking incredible. I haven't felt a connection like that since ... Ever. Not with anyone other than Fitch or West.

"We're all sticky." She laughs, and the sound makes unexpected emotion well in my throat. I swallow it down and push myself up.

"Zeke?" The word is a protest, and she shivers at the loss of my warmth.

I grab the corners of the blanket and wrap her up like a burrito. "Stay there. I'll be right back."

Burrowing her head into the pillow and closing her eyes, she murmurs her agreement. I allow myself a second to look at her. Tear-stained cheeks and hair all mussed up from fucking. Fuck me, she's perfect.

TWENTY-THREE

LILY

Opening one eye, I watch Zeke change into a fresh pair of sweats and disappear from view. Where the hell is he going? I hope he's going to grab a clean set of sheets considering we all but destroyed this set. I can't even bear the thought of looking at the stains or the prospect of unwrapping myself from the duvet cocoon he made me. But despite how warm and comfy and spent I am, I'll have to do that soon.

Zeke walks back into the room with something clutched in his hands. He places whatever it is on the dresser, then goes straight to the bathroom. A few seconds later, the sound of running water drifts out of the open doorway. I guess I'd better get cleaned up too. I shrug off the covers and shiver as the cool air hits my damp skin.

Zeke comes back out of the bathroom and glares at me. "I thought I told you to stay right there," he says in his usual grumpy growl, but something about his tone is different. Laced with a hint of concern, perhaps.

"I need to get cleaned up." I sit up and wince at the sight of the blood-soaked sheets, my cheeks burning with embarrassment. "And all this."

He stares at them too, an unmistakable look of pride on his face as he surveys the damage. "I'll take care of the sheets." He scoops me into his arms, eliciting a tiny shriek of protest from me, but when he curls those huge biceps around my body, I practically melt into his chest. "After I take care of you."

Oh, well now my ovaries have exploded. I study his face, waiting for him to turn back into the grumpy, ice-cold asshole I've come to know, but he keeps his gaze fixed ahead. The scent of cinnamon fills the bathroom, reminding me of Christmas and pulling up long-buried bittersweet memories. Steam rises from the tub that's nearly filled to the brim with water and white bubbles. I press my cheek against Zeke's shoulder, careful to avoid his scars. "You have bubble bath?"

"I took some from Fitch's room." He sets me on the edge of the tub and dips his hand into the water. With a satisfied nod, he turns off the tap, then picks me back up and places me in the hot water before I can protest that I'm capable of climbing in by myself.

Any protest would have died on my lips as soon as my ass hit this water. A harsh moan tumbles from my lips as I sink into the soothing heat, and the relief that engulfs my aching limbs makes my mind go blank. Closing my eyes, I rest my head on the edge of the huge tub and sigh. "This feels so good."

Zeke mumbles something, but I'm too focused on my bliss to make out the words. A few seconds later, the sound of rustling clothing reaches me. Opening my eyes, I unashamedly stare at his toned and tattooed naked body. His cock hangs thick and heavy between his thighs, and I lick my lips at the remembered sensation of him filling me so completely.

"Move up." Without waiting, he steps into the tub behind

me and nudges me forward with his knees. I'm busy gawking at him over my shoulder. I never would have expected him to get in here with me. He usually avoids getting too close. Zeke gestures at his bloodstained torso and thighs and flashes a wicked grin. "You got us both a little messy."

Wrinkling my nose at the reminder, I scoot forward, making room for him to sit behind me. "I believe it was you who created most of that mess."

Once he's situated, he gathers my hair into his fist and drapes it over my shoulder, then wraps his huge arms around me, pulling my back against his chest. Unsure how to handle this new side of him, I tentatively rest my head on his shoulder. When he presses a soft kiss on my temple, a kaleidoscope of butterflies takes flight in my stomach.

The silence is broken by Xander's voice coming from somewhere outside our little bubble. "Hey, Zeke. You seen Lily?" A few seconds later, his horrified exclamation of "Holy fuck!" has me stifling a giggle. Strong arms band tighter around my torso, and the possessiveness in that small act makes heat coil deep in my belly.

Xander pops his head into the bathroom and arches one eyebrow at the pair of us before strolling inside. "Kinda looks like there's been a homicide out there." He tilts his head toward the bedroom.

"Lily got her period," Zeke says matter-of-factly.

Xander's knowing smile has me wondering what I missed. I turn my head to find a similar smirk on Zeke's face. "What's that look about, deviants?"

Xander perches on the edge of the tub and brushes a lock of hair from my forehead. "Zeke has a huge blood kink."

I sink my teeth into my bottom lip and skim my fingers over the bite marks he left on the inside of my thighs. "Well, now that makes sense."

Dusting his lips over the back of my neck, Zeke dips his hand between my thighs and cups my pussy. His groan rumbles through me, and he shifts his hips so that we both sink deeper into the water.

Xander's lips curl up at the edges, and I frown. "What else am I missing?"

Xander dips his head, brushing his lips over mine with the promise of a kiss that he doesn't deliver. He sits back, his blue eyes holding me captive. "Zeke here might love to cause pain, but what he loves just as much is to take care of you afterward."

Zeke grunts, his breath ruffling through my hair.

Xander grins. "And the more he makes it hurt, the better he'll take care of you after. Isn't that right, Z?"

"You'd know," Zeke replies.

"I would and I do. Enjoy being taken care of, shorty." He winks at me, then gives me a quick kiss on the lips. "I gotta go into the office for a few hours. You working from home?" he asks Zeke.

Zeke grunts again, and I feel him nod his agreement. Xander smiles at him before he walks out of the room. "You two have fun now," he calls out as he disappears from view.

"Are you staying home to take care of me, Ezekiel?" I snuggle into him and bite my lip to stifle a giggle when his cock twitches against my lower back.

"Does that surprise you, buttercup?"

"Um, yeah."

He flicks his tongue over my shoulder blade, his teeth skating tantalizingly across my skin. "I just told you I was going to take care of you, didn't I?"

"Yes, but ..." I bite down on my lip. "Was what Xander said true? Do you like taking care of people after you've hurt them?"

He circles the pad of his pointer finger over my clit, and my hips buck, chasing the pleasure he promises. He's trying to distract me—it's working like a charm.

"Zeke?" I pant, and he increases the pressure on the sensitive bud of flesh.

He doesn't speak. Instead he uses that wickedly sinful mouth to trail kisses and tiny bites all over my neck and shoulders while he brings me to another mind-blowing orgasm.

AFTER HE MADE me come in the tub, Zeke washed us both clean and I lay in his arms until the water got too chilly. Now he has me wrapped in a white fluffy towel standing in his bedroom. I squeeze my thighs together, conscious that I'm still bleeding. "I, uh, really need to go get my things."

"No need, baby doll." *Baby doll?* My heart swells. Then he goes to the vanity and takes something from it. A second later, he's standing before me with a devious smirk on his face. I'm about to ask him what he's doing when he drops to his knees, lifts my towel with one hand, and grabs my foot with the other. I offer a feeble protest.

"Relax." He presses a soft kiss on the inside of my ankle and places my foot on his shoulder. It's only now that I see the familiar blue packet in his hand. He must have grabbed it when he left the room earlier. He tears the package open with his teeth, and my stomach flutters so violently that I feel lightheaded.

"Zeke! I can do that, please ..."

He pulls the tampon from the wrapper, and my cheeks burn hotter. He looks up at me, eyes full of deviance and amusement. "I've already had my fingers, my tongue, and my cock inside your pussy, buttercup. Why are you all coy about me inserting a tampon?" With that, he pushes it inside me with one thick finger, and my eyes roll back in my head. That should not be hot!

When he's done, he presses a tender kiss between my thighs and stands tall again.

"Um, thank you," I whisper, my cheeks still burning with embarrassment.

He tilts his head, eyes boring into mine. "You're so fucking cute when you blush,"

"And you're very different when you ..." I don't finish the sentence because I'm not entirely sure what this new dynamic is between us.

Going over to his dresser, he wipes his hands and grabs a small jar from the top drawer. He comes back over and pulls the towel from my body, leaving me naked. Although the room is warm, I shiver. He unscrews the lid of the jar and scoops out a little of the contents with his pointer finger before rubbing it into the skin on my shoulder. I twist my head to see another bite mark.

"I broke the skin here," he says by way of explanation.

"Oh." I suck on my bottom lip as he rubs the ointment into my skin, his fingers moving carefully over the tender flesh while his dark eyes watch me intently. Xander was right about him; he does seem to enjoy taking care of people after he's hurt them. But while he did hurt me, the kind of pain he delivers is like nothing else I've ever experienced, and I'm open to a whole lot more of it.

CHAPTER
TWENTY-FOUR

LILY

Z eke pats his thigh when I walk into the den after I finish working on my article for the day. "Come here, baby doll."

Baby doll? He said it earlier in the bathroom, and it had the exact same effect on me then. Why do those two words make my panties wet? Maybe it's the way he says it, in that deep, commanding growl. Maybe it's just because it's Zeke.

Whatever it is, my legs shake as I make my way across the room. As soon as I'm within reach, he grabs my wrist and pulls me onto his lap, wrapping his huge arms around me and burying his face in my hair. He inhales deeply, and I bite my lip to stifle a giggle. I have no idea what happened to Zeke today, but whatever it was, I am so here for it.

When he lifts his head, I stare into his dark eyes, trying to read his thoughts. I fail miserably. "Thank you for making me a delicious lunch," I whisper. "You didn't have to do that."

He shrugs. "It was just a sandwich. Nothing special."

Just a sandwich, my ass. It was roasted chicken with a little skin still on it, bacon, avocado, and a smidge of homemade mayo on rye—my all-time favorite. "It was to me."

He gives a subtle shake of his head and rubs his left temple.

My heart rate kicks up a notch. "Is something wrong?"

"No," he says with a half snort, half laugh. "*Nothing* is wrong."

I shift on his lap. "I-I don't understand."

He bands his arms tighter around me. "It's ..." He sucks on his top lip and stares up at the ceiling for what feels like eternity. "You're too good to be true, Lily."

I open my mouth to speak, but no words come out. I can't work out whether that's a good thing or a bad thing. Before I can find my voice to ask, he fills the silence for me.

"Nothing about this ... about me ... about the way the guys and I are together ..." He rubs his temple again and takes a deep breath before continuing. "None of it seems to bother you. At all."

It's my turn to frown now. "Well, why would it? You were all open about what this would be. About your dynamic. I knew what I was getting into."

"Yeah, but there's a difference between people thinking they're okay with what we are and actually *being* okay with it."

"Well, that might have been your past experience." I take a chance and place my hand on his cheek. Happiness blooms in my chest when he doesn't pull away. "But I am okay with it. All of it. Better than okay," I assure him.

His tongue darts out to wet his lips, and an image of his mouth on me earlier causes warmth to pool in my core. I clench my legs together, and I guess he doesn't miss my reaction because the corner of his mouth curls up. He brushes back my hair and trails his teeth over the sensitive skin of my throat. "You were exceptional today, my little buttercup," he whispers. His hand runs up my legs to my thighs, fingers dusting across the bite marks he left there. I shiver on his lap. "You liked it when I marked you as mine?" He tugs my panties aside.

"Y-yes." The word leaves my mouth on a desperate moan.

"Does thinking about it make you wet?" he chuckles softly, his hot breath dancing over my skin. I try to squirm, but he holds me still.

"Does it?" he asks again, running a fingertip through my folds. "Or should I just find out for myself?" Flicking my tampon string, he curls his finger around the end and gives a gentle tug that moves it only the slightest fraction but makes me gasp.

"Yes!"

He presses a soft kiss on my collarbone. "Yes what?"

"Yes, it makes me wet."

Releasing the string, he places his finger on my clit instead, sparing my blushes. For now, at least. He rubs the hypersensitive bundle of nerves in slow, teasing circles. "Good girl."

I fist my hands in his shirt as pleasure coils in my gut. "Zeke," I whimper.

"You still got cramps?"

"No, but that feels so good. Please don't stop."

"Oh, I'll never stop." With a dark laugh, he sinks his teeth into my neck. My back bows, and he sweeps the tip of his tongue over where he just bit me, soothing the sting. "You're mine now, buttercup."

"I am?" I pant, a mind-blowing orgasm building deep in my core.

"Damn fucking right you are. That's the thing with me, Lily. I'm a fucking monster, but I'm your monster now." He presses harder on my clit, and searing hot pleasure skitters up my spine. "You kept on pushing me, daring me to let you in. And now that I have ..."

I rock my hips, arching into the euphoria he's giving me with only one finger. "W-what?"

"I'll never let you go."

"I d-d-oh, fu-oh!" My climax rips the words from my throat, leaving me unable to tell him that I never want him to.

"You look so fucking pretty when you come for me," he groans as he goes on massaging his finger over my clit, drawing out my orgasm for as long as he can.

"Zeke," I pant, my hands still fisted in his shirt.

He puts his finger into his mouth, eyes burning into mine as he sucks it clean. "You taste pretty fucking good too."

"Only pretty good?" Xander says, and we both look up to find him and West standing in the open doorway. "I'd say abso-fucking-lutely delicious, wouldn't you?" he asks West, who hums his agreement.

Despite the two of them having seen me come before, my cheeks still burn with embarrassment. "How long have you two been standing there?"

"Not nearly long enough, unfortunately," West says with a wicked grin. He strides across the room and leans down to give me a soft, lingering kiss. Then he turns his attention to Zeke, who licks his lips. West grabs Zeke's hair, tilting his head back and crashing their mouths together. I watch, transfixed. Zeke parts his lips, allowing West to slide his tongue inside, and Zeke's already hard cock twitches against my hipbone. The sight of these two like this is so damn hot. I want to slip my hand between my thighs and get myself off to the spectacle. But that would be selfish of me, right? Especially after Zeke just gave me an incredible orgasm. So instead I slide my hand into Zeke's sweatpants and squeeze the base of his shaft, making him groan into West's mouth.

West flashes me a quick wink before returning his attention to Zeke. Not all his attention though. With his free hand, he yanks my damp panties out of the way and flicks his thumb over my clit.

"Oh, fuck," I whimper. Working Zeke's cock while watching him get tongue-fucked by West as he plays with my pussy has me about ready to implode. That familiar tingle begins to spread, and I bite down on the inside of my cheek. Stealing a quick glance at Xander, I find him sitting on the armchair opposite us, palming his cock over his pants.

West wrenches his lips from Zeke's with a frustrated groan. "Princess," he grits, his voice thick and raspy. "I'm gonna need you to turn around and straddle him."

Resting one hand on Zeke's bare shoulder, I keep the other wrapped around his thick cock and position my knees on either side of his hips. His eyes burn into mine and his jaw clenches, but he doesn't protest. Even if he doesn't trust me yet, he trusts West completely.

As soon as I'm in place, West kneels on the sofa behind me, his knees pressed against the outside of Zeke's thighs and his chest flush at my back, sandwiching me between the two of them. West slides his hand over my hip and stomach before dipping it into my panties and toying with my clit again. Zeke's gaze is firmly on West now, his eyes dark with longing. West resumes their fiery kiss, and I grow wetter by the second watching these two powerful men devour each other.

I pump Zeke's dick harder and grind my ass against West's hard length. West continues rubbing my clit, circling it in a dizzying rhythm with the perfect amount of pressure. I rock into his hand, causing it to brush against Zeke's shaft. When I swipe the pad of my thumb over the crown of Zeke's cock, collecting the precum beaded there, a deep groan rolls through his body. West groans too, and they swallow each other's sounds.

Curling my fingers into Zeke's thick hair, I gently tug his

head back. He grunts and threads one of his hands through West's hair and the other through mine, holding us in place and arching into the pleasure we're bringing him. Dropping all his weight onto my back, West presses me flat against Zeke and wraps his hand around Zeke's length, directly above mine. The two of us move in unison, pumping Zeke's thick shaft as he shudders beneath us. We're so tightly woven together that I can no longer tell where one of us ends and the next begins. All three of us remain locked in this sweet, sinfully hot embrace. Zeke and I chase our climaxes while West pushes us closer to that edge.

My orgasm rolls over me, wave after unending wave. The hand on Zeke's cock goes still as the intense sensations render me immobile, and West takes control, milking Zeke's shaft while coaxing the last tremors from my body. A few seconds later, Zeke wrenches his lips away from West's with a harsh grunt, and thick ribbons of his cum spurt over West's knuckles.

West turns his head and grins. "You okay, princess?"

My head spins. "Uh-huh."

"You want to help me clean up?" he asks, lifting his hand to my lips.

Darting out my tongue, I lash it over his outstretched fingers and clean Zeke's cum from them, working my way from his fingertips to his knuckles. West's gray eyes turn stormy with desire. "You're so fucking sweet." Gripping my jaw tightly, he sweeps his tongue over my lips and groans when he tastes Zeke's cum.

"Holy motherfucker," Zeke mutters.

"Yeah, that was pretty fucking hot," Xander says.

West lets me up for air, and I glance behind me to see Xander standing right by us.

"Damn. It's my turn to cook," West says with a groan.

"I can help," I offer.

THE PERFECT FIT

He presses a kiss on the tip of my nose. "I can handle it. Stay here with Zeke and Fitch."

"Yeah," Xander says with a cheeky wink.

West untangles himself from me and strolls out, adjusting himself with a grimace. Xander flops down on the sofa beside Zeke and me.

Zeke turns me sideways on his lap so I'm facing Xander, who smiles at us both. "You two have a good time today then?"

I rest my head on Zeke's shoulder and sigh. "We sure did."

He chuckles. "I told you he was good at the aftercare."

Zeke grunts, but there's a hint of a smile on his face as he wraps his free arm around Xander's shoulder. I lace my fingers with Xander's and rest our joined hands in my lap. He turns on the TV and the three of us sit in silence watching *Forged in Fire* reruns while the delicious aroma of whatever West is cooking for dinner fills the penthouse.

CHAPTER

TWENTY-FIVE

LILY

"**Y**ou need to stop bending over counters like that, princess." West smacks my ass on his way past me.

I straighten up and fix him with the fiercest glare I can muster while trying not to laugh. "I'm cleaning. Kind of hard to reach the middle of the island if I don't lean over."

He winks, his gray eyes twinkling with amusement. "I need to get some work done before bed. You two behave yourselves." He gives me a soft kiss on the lips and leaves Xander and me alone to finish cleaning up after dinner.

My cell vibrates with an incoming call, and I glance at the screen, expecting it to be Jen calling for our usual evening chat. My heart stutters to a stop. Pressing the side button to decline the call, I dart a glance at Xander. Luckily, he's facing the other way, so he didn't notice my reaction. He turns around, a dish towel casually slung over his shoulder and a dirty dinner plate in his hand. "You not answering that?"

I look down at the counter, unable to lie while looking him

144

in the eyes. "It was just someone from work about swapping a shift. I'll call back later."

He nods and goes back to loading the dishwasher.

~

I WAIT until after dinner and head to my bedroom to return the call from earlier. Wiping my sweaty palms on my legs, I wait for him to answer.

It takes him way too long to pick up, and I'm starting to panic when I hear his voice. Relief floods my body and weakens my knees. I sink onto the bed, breathing his name like a prayer to the heavens. "Nico."

"Hey, Lily Pad." His familiar voice washes over me and tears prick at my eyes.

"Is everything okay? Are you ...?" My heart thumps violently.

"I'm fine. Everything's okay."

Taking a deep breath, I will my body to calm down. "Then why are you calling me on this number? You know you could get us both killed."

"I'm in New York."

Air whooshes out of my lungs, and I lie back on the bed before I fall down. What the hell is he doing in New York? My mind races with possibilities, none of them pleasant.

"Lil?"

I remember to breathe and take a gulp of oxygen. "I'm here."

"I want to see you." I imagine the scowl darkening his handsome features, marring the face I know as well as I know my own.

"No. It's too dangerous."

"Please. I miss you. It's fucking hell without you."

A single hot tear tracks its way down my cheek, my heart aching at the sadness in his voice. "I miss you too."

"So, can I see you?"

"What if someone sees us together?"

"Nobody will. I have a suite at Excelsior. Room 925. Meet me there tomorrow."

"I'm not sure I can get away." I sniff back the tears threatening to escape. "I have work, and ..." I stop short of telling him about West, Zeke, and Xander.

"Please. I'm only here for two days. I can't come to New York and not see you, Lil."

I close my eyes and will my heart to stop racing. It's way too dangerous, but how do I refuse him? Especially after everything he's done for me.

"Okay. I could probably get away from work for an hour around two. Does that work for you?"

"I'll make sure it does. But I gotta run. Bye, Lil. Love you."

"Love you too," I whisper, but he's already gone.

Julian Barnes, the editor of *Genevieve* magazine, calls my name as I walk past his office. "You got a minute?"

Nervous excitement skitters up my spine. I spin on my heel and head inside, closing the door behind me. He's leafing through a stack of papers, and as I step closer, I realize it's the research for my article. My breath catches in my throat. My future at this magazine is literally in his hands. I mean, I know I'm sleeping with the new owners, but that is *not* how I want to make a name for myself as a journalist.

"This is good," he finally says, and I practically fall into the chair opposite his desk. "Real good stuff. You've been thorough."

"I triple-checked all my facts. I just have a few more interviews to do, and then I think I'll have it all wrapped up."

"I'm thinking of putting it in the August issue. That work for you?"

That means my article will be out in July and will be published in the most purchased issue of the entire year. Hell yeah it works for me. Shifting in my seat, I fight to keep myself from jumping up, throwing my arms around his neck, and planting a noisy kiss right on his lips. "Sure."

"Keep up the good work, Lily."

I beam with pride. Julian is my hero. Youngest ever editor in chief of a major magazine, he started his career with hard-hitting but accessible pieces, and his work is incredible. He's also super fair and supportive of all his staff. And although I'm not on the staff yet, just a freelancer, he's been really supportive of me too.

His eyes narrow on my face, and I suddenly feel uncomfortable. "You know there's a rumor you're dating West Archer?"

I squirm in my chair. "Is that a problem? I mean I don't discuss work with him, and I would never—"

"It's not a problem for me." He shrugs. "I don't care who you date. Plus, I'm well aware that you could've asked your new boyfriend to make me put you in the magazine, but you didn't. I respect that."

He respects me. I smile so widely my cheeks hurt. "I'd never ask for a favor like that. I want my writing to speak for itself."

"And it does. I just want you to know what people are saying before you head back into that viper's nest out there. And if you do start working here permanently, you'll need a thick skin if you're dating the boss."

The prospect of working at this magazine fills me with excitement. "I wouldn't be dating the boss though, would I? More like my boss's boss's boss?"

He laughs loudly. "Remember that humor when I'm making you stick to insane deadlines."

"It would be an honor to stick your insane deadlines, Julian. I really appreciate the opportunity you're giving me."

"You have talent, Lily. The honor will be all mine. Now get the hell out of here." He nods toward the door.

I scurry out of his office, unable to keep the mile-wide smile from my face, but it falters when I run into Handsy Andy, *Genevieve*'s PR man, in the hallway.

His upper lip curls into a sneer. "Hey, Lily."

"Hey," I reply breezily as I press the call button for the elevator.

Standing too close for comfort, he leans down, and a shudder runs down my spine. "You know, we never did get that drink you promised me."

I take a deep breath and remind myself that there are plenty of people milling around. I'm perfectly safe. "I never promised you a drink, Andy." I told him I'd think about it when he had me cornered at an office party last Christmas.

Fury radiates from him. "You too good for me now that you're fucking West Archer?"

"Fuck you." I step into the elevator that arrived right on time and leave Andy seething. Just before the doors close all the way, I flip him the bird and promptly forget all about him.

I'm going to be in the August edition of *Genevieve* magazine, I have three insanely hot boyfriends that I get to go home to tonight, and most exciting of all, I'm about to see Nico.

My KNEES TREMBLE when I step inside the lobby of Excelsior, and I pull my beanie hat down further and glance around. The lobby is empty except for an elderly couple drinking coffee and a young woman feeding a baby.

Pressing a hand on my stomach to quell my nerves, I raise

my hand to knock on the door of room 925. Nico would never betray me, but what if *he* found out about us?

Willing him to hurry up and open the goddamn door, I glance down the corridor. Finally the door opens, and his familiar face creases with a huge smile. Pulling me into the room, he wraps me in a giant bear hug, nearly squeezing the life from me in the process, but I hug him back just as fiercely. All the memories we've shared flood to the surface, and I cling to him, tears streaming down my face. I convinced myself I could hold it together, but it's been over two years since we last saw each other, and seeing him now only makes his absence in my life all that much more acute.

"Hey, Lily Pad," he says, his tone gentle as he brushes the moisture from my cheeks with his thumbs. "Don't cry."

"I-I miss you so much."

"I know." He hugs me again, this time even tighter. "I miss you too. It's fucking awful back home without you."

"I'm s-so s-sorry I left you."

He pulls back and looks down at me, his dark brown eyes full of sorrow. "Don't be sorry, Lily Pad. I'm glad you got out. I'm glad ..." His Adam's apple bobs harshly.

I wipe my cheeks and focus on the fact that he's here right now. "Why are you even in New York?"

"Pop has asked me to oversee some business. I'll be here once a month, which means I get to see you."

"You will?" Equal parts of joy and anxiety wrestle in my stomach, and I swallow down a wave of nausea. "Do you think he knows?"

"He has no idea, I swear. If he did, he'd have a fucking army scouring this country looking for you."

He's got a point. "I wish I was strong like you."

"Hey," he admonishes me. "It's different for me, and we both know it. That was no life for you. What he was expecting

149

you to do." His hands clench into fists. "I would never have fucking allowed it, sis. *Never*."

My lips curve, not quite a smile but an acknowledgment.

He looks me over from head-to-toe one last time, like he's assuring himself that I really am here, then holds up one finger and goes into the kitchen. When he comes back, he's holding two mugs of coffee. He gestures toward the comfy sofas and we both take a seat. "So tell me all about your life here in New York."

"It's good. Great, actually. I'm still a messenger, but I'm working on a story for a magazine. They're publishing it next month."

"They are?" His face lights up with pride.

"Yeah." I look down and pluck a stray piece of lint from the sofa cushion. "It's something I'm really proud of. I'll let you know when it's out so you can read it."

"I'm so fucking proud of you. You were always destined to be amazing."

"Was not," I say with a blush. He's the amazing one. I'm just a coward who ran away from all my problems.

"Anything else going on with you? You meet a guy yet?"

Oh god. "Kind of." I take a small sip of my coffee. "It's still early." I hate not telling him the whole truth, but how do I tell my twin brother that I'm dating three men at the same time? And that one of them is a guy our father once tried to kill.

I hate keeping all these secrets, but it's the way I've lived my entire life. Always protecting somebody's secret, and now I keep my own. Not only for me, but for Nico. If our father ever found out about what he did for me, he'd surely kill him.

"Is it serious?"

I press my lips together. "It might be."

"Well, if you ever want to get married, have babies,

anything like that, those papers you have will stand up to the highest level of scrutiny. I promise you that."

"I know." I nudge his arm with my elbow. "They got me through four years of college, so I figure they can get me a marriage license, should I ever need one." He grins at me, and my face burns with embarrassment. "Not that I'm even thinking about that," I insist. It isn't like I can marry all three of them, even if I wanted to. Pretty sure that's illegal in all fifty states. "I only say that because you brought it up."

One corner of his mouth curves and he snorts. "Things must be a lot more serious than you let on."

"Stop!" I sink back against the plush cushions and stare out the window, thinking about the guys and how I'll have to make up a story about what I did this afternoon. It breaks my heart that when they ask me how my day was, I won't be able to tell them about the best part of it—seeing my brother for the first time in two years. I can't even tell them I have a brother. Swallowing down a lump of complex emotion, I redirect my attention to Nico. "Anyway, enough about my love life. How's yours?"

He sighs heavily. "Complicated."

"Can't you get out too?"

He shakes his head. "Both of us disappearing would look way too suspicious, you know that. He'd come after you too."

"I'd take that risk if it meant you could get out. We could go somewhere together." A pang of guilt blindsides me as soon as the suggestion leaves my mouth. Although I've only known them for a few months, I can't imagine leaving the guys. However, my heart breaks knowing that my wonderful brother can't be with the person he loves just because he happens to love another man.

"One day Pop won't be in charge anymore, and then maybe Dean and I can ..." He shrugs.

"You think he'll wait for you?"

"He's not exactly waiting. He's my second-in-command." He twists his wedding band around his finger, seemingly without thought. "I spend more time with him than I do my wife."

"How is Belinda?"

"She's happy with the way things are. For now, anyway. I try to knock her up once a month, and she spends a small fortune on handbags and personal trainers in an attempt to make up for the fact that we can barely stand each other."

"I hate that he forced you to marry her."

"Belinda and I knew what we were signing up for. We're both fine. We'll figure it out in our own way. As soon as we have a kid, we can divorce and she can go live her life however the hell she wants to."

"What if she has a girl?"

He drops a soft kiss on my forehead. "By the time she's grown, things will be different."

We chat a little more about trivial things and the series we're both currently binging on Netflix before he tells me he has to leave for his meeting. "Stay as long as you want. Nobody except Dean uses this suite."

"Where is Dean?"

"He'll be at the meeting."

"Give him my love, won't you?"

He winks at me. "Yeah."

I study my brother in his perfectly tailored suit. He's always immaculately turned out, exactly like I was expected to be. His thick black hair is cut short, and I've never seen him with even the slightest bit of stubble. He looks way too young to live the life that he leads. He might only be twenty-four, but he's wise beyond his years. "You two make a very handsome couple."

He laughs out loud at that.

"I hope I get to come to your wedding one day."

He inhales a deep breath. "Me too, sis."

I FIND West in the kitchen making dinner. "Sorry I'm late. It was my turn to cook tonight. You need me to do anything?" Now I feel even more guilty that my extended lunch to see Nico made me late with my deliveries.

"Nah, I've got it. I was home early, and I enjoy cooking." He glances up from the raw chicken he's cutting. "But come here."

"Where?" I say, feigning ignorance.

He licks his lips. "Right here, princess."

I step closer and grip the back of his neck, barely brushing his lips with mine. "Here?"

He growls. "Unless you want chicken guts in your hair, give me your fucking lips."

Smiling against his mouth, I curl my fingers in the hair at the nape of his neck. "These lips right here?"

He sucks air through his teeth. "I'd much rather kiss your other lips, princess, but I'm making dinner here."

I snort a laugh. "That's not what I meant."

He tugs my bottom lip between his teeth for a brief moment, then slips his tongue into my mouth. My body sags against him, and I whimper. I'm such a slut for this man's kisses. For anything from any of them. I have no idea why the universe chose me to be the luckiest girl on this planet, I'm just glad that she did.

He breaks the kiss, leaving me wanting more. Using lips and teeth, he works his way up my jaw to my ear. "I'll definitely be kissing those other lips later."

"I sure hope so," I say, wrapping both arms around his neck. God, I love him. I love all three of them. I wish that I could tell him who I really am. But what if he blames me for my father's mistakes? What if he only sees me as Carmine Constantine's daughter and he doesn't remember the little girl who begged her father to spare his life?

"Something wrong, princess?" The concern in his voice makes my breath catch in my throat.

"Everything's good." It's just a small lie, right? It doesn't hurt anyone, and it protects the people I love most in the world. Nobody can ever know what Nico did for me, and nobody can find out that Liliana Constantine is still alive. West, Xander, and Zeke can never know why I left, because if they were to ever start a war with my family, I fear there would only be one winner. My father.

TWENTY-SIX

XANDER

"Hey, you got that PR guy's email address?" I ask West as I walk into his office.

He looks up from his laptop. "Which PR guy?"

"The one from Grayson News Corp. What was his name? Andy or something? We met him at that meeting a few weeks back. I'm sure I took his card, but I can't find it."

He glances back at the screen and rubs a hand over his stubble. "Check the meeting minutes. I asked them to include everyone's contact details."

I take a seat in front of his desk. "You got an important meeting today?"

His gaze drifts back to me. "Grayson board meeting. They're being given a draft of our proposals for expansion today, so ..." He stretches his neck and sighs.

"Ah, is that why you're wearing your lucky suit?"

A faint grin flickers over his face. "It's just a suit."

It's not *just* a suit at all. It's a dark gray three-piece Tom

Ford. Not only does it make him look even more handsome and powerful than usual, but it fits him perfectly, hugging his huge biceps and shoulders, not to mention his magnificent ass and thighs, like a second skin. I adjust my cock in my pants, trying to give myself a little more room and some much-needed relief, but it doesn't help.

"Hey. Can I borrow your laptop charger? Mine has given up even trying to work," Lily says as she breezes into his office wearing nothing but a smile and, from the looks of the way it dwarfs her petite frame, Zeke's shirt.

"Sure, it's in the bottom drawer." Without looking up, West nods at the cabinet next to his desk.

My semihard cock grows as I stare at Lily's fine ass while she's bent over rummaging in the drawer. I glance at West, but his attention is fixated on his screen. How the fuck has he not noticed her? Ass in the air, cute pink panties on display?

A few seconds later, she gives a triumphant cry and stands, charger in hand.

"Hey, shorty." She turns and offers me one of her beautiful smiles. I hold out my hand. "Come here."

Her eyes bounce between West and me as she approaches. She giggles when I grab her arm and yank her into my lap.

West finally looks up and glares at the two of us. "My meeting starts in five minutes."

I bite back a grin. He knows that his bark won't stop me, and I'm always down for his bite. And now I have an incredibly hot and soon to be incredibly frustrated West on one side of the desk, and the super sexy, always horny and ready for action Lily on my lap. I'm gonna have so much fucking fun.

Lily twirls a lock of hair between her finger and her thumb. "What meeting? Anything exciting?"

"A board meeting with Grayson News Corp," I answer when he doesn't.

"Oh." She sits up straighter. "Is the takeover almost complete?"

"Merger," West replies coolly. "Despite what Jensen Michaels would have you all at Grayson believe."

She flushes. "I know. I'm sorry. I just ... I've been hearing takeover for so long now." She straightens her shoulders and lifts her chin. He doesn't intimidate her even a little, and I love that about her. "So, is the *merger* almost complete?"

"Soon." He types something on his keyboard. "Just a few more wrinkles to iron out."

"And everyone will keep their jobs, right?"

A muscle twitches in his jaw. "Everyone who wants to."

She frowns. "What does that mean?"

He really looks at her for the first time since she walked in. The scowl on his face softens. "It means exactly what I said. If people want to remain employed by us, they will. If they want to leave, they're free to do so."

"And Jensen Michaels?" West bristles at the name. "What will happen to him?"

"Why do you care?" he asks, his jaw tight.

She holds his gaze. "I'm just curious."

"He doesn't want to stay on, but he'll receive a considerable severance package," I tell her.

She leans against me, seemingly satisfied with that response. I brush back her hair and trail my lips over her neck. "Tell me how your article is coming along."

She wiggles in my lap. "Really well. Julian said he's going to publish it in next month's issue."

I slide my hand between her thighs. "He is, huh?"

She shifts her hips. "Please tell me none of you had anything to do with that."

I tug her panties aside and brush my fingertip over her clit. "Not a thing, shorty. We wouldn't do that to you."

"West?" She says his name on a moan.

"It has nothing to do with us, Lily," he confirms, proving that he's not as engrossed in his work as he seems.

"Good."

I circle her clit, and she wraps one arm around my neck, arching her back and rocking into my hand. "You gonna tell us what it's about yet?"

She shakes her head. "You can read it along with everyone else."

"Aw, Lily. We're not like everyone else though, are we?" I sink one finger inside her, and she moans.

West snarls. "My meeting is about to start."

"Good. I'm gonna fuck our girl while you fuck with the board."

CHAPTER
TWENTY-SEVEN

LILY

"I swear you're both going to pay as soon as I've finished this call," West says in that low throaty tone of his that turns my legs to jelly. As if they're not already trembling enough from Xander silently finger fucking me while West is on his conference call—with the board of the magazine where I hope to have a permanent job someday. Surely this is not a good idea, even if West's mic is on mute.

"Should we leave?" I whisper to Xander.

"Fuck no." Laughing, he stands and perches me on the edge of West's desk. "Making West mad is like my favorite hobby, shorty. And he's going to be so fucking pissed when he has to watch me eat your pussy on his desk."

I shriek in protest, but Xander has already dropped to his knees. He pushes me back until I'm sitting in the middle rather than on the edge, a wicked grin playing on his lips.

"Fitch," West warns.

Ignoring him, Xander slides my panties down my legs, wads them into a ball, and tosses them across the desk. I'm able to turn my head enough to see West's expression. Oh shit, he's pissed. I press my lips together to stop myself from laughing. Still glaring at us, he tucks the panties into his pocket. The look in his eyes promises retribution.

"Lie back, baby," Xander orders, and I drop back onto my elbows. West angles his laptop in the other direction, ensuring that I remain out of view from the camera.

Xander pushes my thighs apart, spreading me wide and placing my feet on his shoulders. "Oh, she's so fucking wet, buddy," he groans.

West grunts in annoyance. But then he reaches between my thighs, his hand out of view of the screen, and slides his pointer finger down my center, collecting some of my arousal on the tip before leaning back. I glance over at him, mouth open in shock as he rests his chin on his hands, with that same finger resting on his top lip. He inhales my scent, and the sexiest groan I've ever heard rumbles in his throat.

Holy fucknuggets. That's so hot.

"You smell amazing," Xander growls, bringing my attention back to him. He trails tiny bites over the tops of my thighs, dragging his teeth across my sensitive skin before he concentrates his skilled tongue on my wet slit. I let my head fall back between my shoulder blades and moan loudly, hoping that West still has his mic on mute. The sound of a board member droning on about profit and loss continues to fill the room, so he probably does.

Xander sweeps his tongue over my clit, and I hiss out a breath, rocking my hips upward to chase the friction.

"Holy fuck, Lily," he says my name with a grunt. "You're fucking delicious."

"You two are so fucked," West mutters.

"Please," I beg now as Xander brings me to the brink of an orgasm.

"I got you, shorty." He slips two fingers inside me, and my back almost bows in half.

"Holy fu—"

"Jesus fucking Christ," West growls, his voice sending shivers down my spine. I tilt my head to look at him. His laptop sits in front of him, seemingly forgotten, all his attention on me.

Blood thunders in my ears as Xander feasts on my pussy with all the skill of a sexual maestro. He thrusts his fingers in and out of me, murmuring words of praise and encouragement against my sensitive flesh.

"Oh holy, oh—"

"Mr. Archer. Sir?" A loud voice cuts through my moans just as I'm about to fall over the edge.

West clamps a hand over my mouth and pinches my nose, stealing my breath. He clears his throat. "Sorry, Campbell. Some of my employees were having a little trouble with something."

"Everything okay?"

"Yeah, I'll just finish the job myself as soon as we end this call," he replies coolly. My lungs scream for oxygen as my climax rockets through my body.

"Just give me five seconds," West says, then releases his grip on me. "Breathe!" he commands. I suck in ragged breaths, and a scream tries to wrench its way out of my throat.

Then his hand is over my mouth again, but he doesn't pinch my nose this time. I inhale deep, calming breaths. He talks to the board members, his voice steady and commanding. I look between my thighs to see Xander grinning at me, my cum all over his face. He winks at me, and I blush. He moves his fingers, reminding me that they're still inside me. He pushes deeper, rubbing over that sweet spot, and I whimper against West's hand.

"Everything okay, Mr. Archer?" someone asks.

SADIE KINCAID

He ignores the question. "Tell me about the projections for the next quarter."

Xander goes on finger-fucking me while West finishes the meeting, with his hand still silencing me. I do my best to stay as quiet as possible, but it's not easy when they both have their hands on me. Even West's palm flat against my lips is hot as hell.

After what feels like forever, West finishes his meeting and closes the laptop with a loud snap. He stands and leans over me, brushing my hair back from my face. I whimper shamelessly as Xander goes on working me, keeping me teetering on the edge. "You're such a naughty slut," West says before he presses his lips against mine and gives me a soft upside-down kiss. "Did you like our board members hearing you come?"

"They d-didn't."

He holds my face in his hands, thumbs on my cheeks and his fingertips cupping my jaw. "Pretty sure they did."

"It wasn't my f-fault."

"Don't worry, I'm going to punish him too," he says with a wink and releases me. He walks around the desk until he's standing beside Xander. "Stop," he orders, and Xander does so without question, leaving me on the brink of a mind-altering orgasm.

I groan my frustration, and West glares at me, so I press my lips together and focus on stopping my thighs from trembling. He takes my hand and pulls me off the desk.

Xander looks up at him expectantly.

"You stay on your fucking knees, trouble," West barks.

I swallow down a whole giant-ass knot of trepidation. Teasing West seemed like such a good idea a few minutes ago, but now I'm not so sure. I look to Xander for some reassurance, and he shoots me a conspiratorial wink. But who is he conspiring with?

162

CHAPTER
TWENTY-EIGHT

WEST

My cock is so fucking hard it's about to bust the zipper on my pants, and Xander was right—this is my lucky suit. Lily's dark lashes flutter over her pink cheeks as she blinks up at me. My hand is wrapped around her wrist, and I yank her closer until her perfect tits flatten against my chest. Her breath stutters.

I dust my knuckles over her cheekbone. "That was an important meeting, princess." She sinks her teeth into her juicy lip. "And not only did I leave it a half hour earlier than I was supposed to, but I have no fucking clue what happened during most of it."

"Sorry," she whispers, feigning innocence when we both know she's a sinful temptress and she loves to push my buttons just as much as Xander does. Pair of brats.

I glance at him kneeling patiently on the floor, and his wicked grin makes my cock twitch. I need to fuck one of them soon. Ass, throat, or pussy, I don't even care. I just need to fill one of them.

"I really am, West," she adds with a seductive purr, and my mind is made up.

"You will be." I spin her around and bend her over my desk. Her shirt rides up so that her juicy ass is on full display for me. I smile at the expanse of creamy white skin right before I spank her.

"Ouch," she yelps.

I place a hand between her shoulder blades, holding her in position while I dole out her punishment. I spank her again, and the sight of my red palm prints on her backside fills me with pulsing need. With a possessive grip on the back of her neck, I hold her down and punish her perfect ass. Over and over, until I'm feral with desire. Desperate. We both are. She cries out when my palm lands in the exact same place, but she whimpers and mewls too, grinding her pussy against my desk and pushing her ass back into my hand. Writhing and panting and shaking, she begs me to let her come.

I don't let her.

Releasing my grip on her neck, I unfasten my pants and free my aching cock, watching the tears run down her cheeks. I bunch her shirt up around her shoulders and wrap my hand around my shaft. My fingertips mark a path along her spine and down the seam of her ass. She shivers. I haven't fucked her there—yet. And I won't today. Not when I need to fuck hard. This girl has me in a chokehold, and it both terrifies and excites me at the same time. I've never allowed any woman to have this kind of power over me before. But Lily Sloane has wormed her way into my ice-cold heart, and I'll be fucked if I ever let her leave. I slide my hand lower and drive two fingers into her pussy.

"West!" she cries.

I pull my fingers out of her and stifle a groan when I see

them coated in her thick arousal. "You're fucking drenched, princess."

She whimpers. One glance at Xander reveals that he's waiting patiently like the good boy I've trained him to be. His hooded eyes are full of longing. I hold out my fingers and command him to suck.

He wraps his lips around them, greedily sucking her cum until I pull back and leave him gasping and desperate for more. "You want to watch me fuck our girl, Fitch?"

His eyes widen, pupils blown and obscuring the bright blue irises. "Yeah."

I nudge the crown of my cock at her pussy entrance, and she keens, back bowing as I inch deeper. Tremors wrack her entire body. She's so fucking close to the edge. So am I.

Thrusting forward, I bottom out and slam against her ass. She cries out a word that I can't make out, and I don't let up. I continue driving into her sweet pussy as it clamps around me like a vise. I can't stop. I want to be deeper inside her even though there's nowhere else for me to go. I pound her so hard that my balls slap against her clit. She's going to have bruises on her thighs from the way I'm fucking her over this desk, but I can't be bothered to care. I'm going to fucking lose myself in her and there'll be no going back. There's already no escaping how I feel about her.

"West," she cries, and it only makes me fuck her harder. The sturdy oak desk creaks. Papers scatter to the floor. My empty coffee mug tips over. She claws at the wood, her back bowed and her hot cunt rippling around me. So close to ecstasy. To oblivion. To me. She screams my name, and her orgasm vibrates through her. I grab her hips, holding her still, and give her every-fucking-thing I've got, driving into her harder and faster as I chase the high that comes from the sweet relief of being buried inside her. Of losing myself in everything that is her. She is fucking perfect.

"Jesus fu-uck, Lily!" The force of my climax steals the breath from my lungs. My legs are fucking trembling when I pull out of her, and despite how hard I just was on her, she still whimpers at the loss of me. I stagger back a few steps, and my gaze is drawn to Xander, then to her pussy, which overflows with my cum as well as hers. "Clean her up."

He shuffles forward on his knees, but right before he gets his mouth on her, I thread my fingers in his hair and tug his head back until he's staring into my eyes. "And then it's your turn, brat."

CHAPTER
TWENTY-NINE

LILY

An appreciative whistle greets me when I enter the kitchen. "Wow, you look hot, shorty."

Cheeks heating at his praise, I grab my purse from the counter.

Zeke glares at me, his jaw working as he crosses the room. "I'm not sure I'm going to let you leave the penthouse alone in those jeans, buttercup."

I glance down at my outfit. Skinny jeans and a sparkly tank top. "What? Why?"

He skims a hand over my backside and growls. "Because I can see every fucking curve of your ass." He squeezes hard, making me gasp. "Are you even wearing panties?"

Before I can answer, he pops open the button of my jeans and shoves his hand inside. "Zeke!" I protest, but my body instinctively leans into him.

His fingertips brush the soft cotton material, and he arches one eyebrow.

"It's a G-string. And do you mind?" I pull his hand out and refasten my jeans.

Dipping his head, he trails his teeth down my neck as another dangerous growl rumbles in his throat. "Yes, I do mind, buttercup. I don't want anyone looking at what's mine. And when you try to go out with your perfect fucking ass on display like that, it makes me want to lock you in your room and remind you who you belong to."

A gasp sticks in my throat. His possessiveness is kind of hot, if totally unnecessary. I'm theirs and he knows it. It's been two months since our *arrangement* began, and I'm completely head over heels for all three of them. Despite knowing how much it's going to hurt when this comes to an end, I let myself fall in love with them a little more each day. How could I not when they're so caring and smart and funny? Not to mention insanely hot and attentive and they have magical mouths and hands and …

I tip my head back, allowing Zeke better access to my neck. His heavy grunt reminds me that I haven't responded to his threat to lock me in my room. "You think I could forget who I belong to, even for a second?"

"Her ass isn't exactly on display, Zeke," West says. Walking up behind me, he grabs my hips and pushes himself up against my back. "But I agree, it is fucking perfect."

Wedged in the middle of their two hard bodies, I squirm as wetness and warmth pool between my thighs. "I need to catch the uptown subway."

West looks at me like I'm an idiot. "I don't fucking think so. Our driver will take you."

"But I like the subway."

"No fucking way, buttercup."

Looking for support, I glance across the room at Xander. "You take the car or you don't go," he says with a shrug.

Admitting defeat, I sigh. The problem isn't the car, it's actually a far more comfortable way to travel, but what if I get too used to it? It isn't my car. This isn't my real life—not forever, anyway. "You're all way too overprotective. The subway is perfectly safe."

Zeke bands his arms around my waist and pulls my body against his. "Are you still arguing about this?"

"No, I'll take the car."

"And this too." West holds his black Amex card in front of my face.

I snort out a laugh. "I know I'm a poor struggling wannabe writer, but I can afford to buy myself a few beers, I promise."

West presses a soft kiss beneath my ear. "Take the fucking card, princess."

"I can't." I shake my head. "You already give me free room and board."

"Take the damn card and buy you and your friend some drinks and some food to soak it all up with. You understand me?"

"But—"

He slides the card into the ass pocket of my jeans. "The pin is two-four-zero-seven."

Not wanting to argue about it anymore—it isn't like he can force me to use it—I acquiesce. But the fact that he trusts me with his card and the pin number means the world to me.

TWIRLING MY METAL STRAW, I scan the bar waiting for Jen to arrive. We haven't been out together in over two months, not since that fateful evening at Marché de Viande. A dreamy sigh escapes me at the thought of the three smoking hot men I'll be going home to later. And they aren't just hot; they're funny and

SADIE KINCAID

kind and generous. Nothing at all like the men I thought they were before I met them.

I smile at the sight of Jen's flaming red hair bobbing through the crowd but groan inwardly when I notice she isn't alone. She offers me her best "oh shit I'm so sorry I ruined our first night out in months" smile and pulls me into a hug. "I'm sorry," she whispers in my ear. "I ran into her outside my building and she asked me where I was going. I couldn't shake her off."

I give her a reassuring pat on the back before ending the hug. "Bree." I force a smile for our unexpected guest. "How are you?"

She wrinkles her perfect tiny nose at me, and I fight the urge to roll my eyes. Bree Reid was the president of our sorority back in college. She's four years older than Jen and me, and while she adores Jen, she can't stand me. Probably because Jen comes from a rich family and her dad is a named partner at a prestigious law firm, and mine ... well, as far as Bree's concerned, I have no family. Not that I'm saying she's an elitist snob or anything. But she's an elitist snob.

"I'm great. Daddy just bought me an apartment near the meat packing district. It's so chic. You should come see it." She makes a point of turning away from me and directing that last part at Jen. "And you, Lily? Still a bike messenger?" Her tone drips with disdain.

I straighten my shoulders, about to tell her that I'm goddamn proud of my job when Jen answers for me. "Lily's article is being printed in *Genevieve* magazine next month."

Bree snorts like that means nothing to her.

"It's a super exclusive deal. It's totally her big break," Jen goes on, and I flash her a grateful smile. She's my biggest cheerleader and always has been, ever since we met on our first day at Columbia.

Bree glances around the bar, pure disinterest seeping from her pores. "Don't tell me you're still dating that waste of oxygen bartender? Jacob?" Her surgically altered button nose wrinkles over my ex-boyfriend's name, and a swell of anger rolls in my chest.

Jacob is not a waste of oxygen. He's a nice guy—and that's exactly why we didn't work out. Not a single throat necklace during our entire nine-month relationship. When it comes to guys, it seems I'm genetically programmed to seek out the morally gray variety, which is unsurprising really. If I saw a shrink, I'm sure they'd tell me I have *daddy issues*. And I would laugh and tell them they had no freaking idea.

Jen answers while I'm still trying to come up with a reply. "No, she's dating West Archer." I shoot her a warning glare, but she sticks her tongue out at me.

That little nugget of information certainly gets Bree's attention though. I swear I've never her seen her lost for words. Her usually beautiful face pinches with a mixture of disbelief and envy. "You are not," she eventually says. "West Archer doesn't date."

I open my mouth to reply, but once again Jen beats me to it. "He damn well does. Lily's living with him, aren't you, girl?" She nudges my arm.

My cheeks burn. "Um, kinda."

"And his partners too? Xander and Ezekiel?" She says their names like she knows them personally. Given that her father is a rich banker, she probably does.

I shrug. "Yeah."

"Liar," she spits.

Bitch! I pull West's black Amex from the back pocket of my jeans and hold it up. I really didn't plan on spending a cent of his money, but I can't possibly pass up the opportunity to prove to Bree that I'm not lying. "He's such a sweetie. He gave me his card and told me to have a great time. Drinks are on me, ladies. What'll it be?"

Bree narrows her eyes. "A bottle of Dom."

I swallow hard. Shit. That will cost almost a thousand dollars in a bar like this. I don't want to spend that much of his money. "How about a cocktail?" I suggest instead.

Bree folds her arms across her chest. "If you're really dating West Archer, prove it. He can afford a bottle of Dom. Unless you're on an allowance?" she says with a sneer.

Why is she such a complete twatwaffle to me?

"No, he won't mind," I say as breezily as I can. "A bottle of Dom and three glasses coming right up."

AFTER BUYING NOT one but four bottles of Dom Perignon and drinking one of them by myself, I can barely stand let alone walk to the car that Xander sends for me when I text him. I never should have tried to keep up with Bree and Jen. I should have known better. Groaning loudly, I put my head in my hands, but it spins violently, and I slump against the wall outside the bar.

"Come on, lightweight." Jen wraps an arm around my waist and bundles me into the back of the car.

"Come with me," I whine, grasping at her top. "We can take you home."

She laughs. "I can't. Trey's taking me to some club. You could have come with us if you could handle your alcohol. Now I have to take *Bree*," she whispers that last part, and it makes me giggle.

"Champagne makes me dizzy," I slur. Leaning my head back, I close my eyes. The vehicle starts moving, and I reopen them to find Bree standing on the sidewalk, glaring at the car.

Cuntface.

West is waiting for me outside the apartment building. Oops, he looks mad. I shrink back against the seat, but he climbs in after me and pulls me out of the car, scooping me into his arms and striding toward the entrance with a curt thanks to his driver thrown over his shoulder.

I hiccup. "Sorry."

He presses the button for the elevator. "For what, princess?"

I trail my fingers over his jawline. "How did you know I was here? Are you sh-pying on me?"

He arches a beautiful thick eyebrow at me. I trace my fingertip over one and smile. Have his eyebrows always been this perfect? It's like they're manicured. "The driver called and told me you might not make it from the car to the penthouse without assistance."

"So, you're my assistant," I say with a grin.

He laughs softly.

"I can't afford to pay you." I drop my head on his shoulder as he steps into the elevator, and the world immediately starts to spin. "I have no money."

"You can pay me in kisses," he says, pressing one to my forehead.

"Kisses," I snort, and then gasp when I remember that I bought four exorbitantly expensive bottles of champagne using his credit card. "I spent all your money."

"You did, huh? Wow. Must've been some night."

I wince. "I bought four bottles of Dom Perignon. But it wasn't for me. It was for this girl from college. She hates me and she said things and then, and then she looked at me like I was crazy ... I'm sh-sorry."

"I gave you my card so you'd spend some of my money, princess. It's fine."

"I'll pay you back. Might take about five years, but I will. Promish."

"We'll see. But let's get you to bed first."

"I love you, West Archer," I say with a dreamy sigh. Closing my eyes, I press my face into his neck and inhale his masculine scent.

I'm pretty sure I didn't mean to say that aloud, and I'm also sure that he squeezes me a little tighter and presses a soft kiss on my forehead.

My eyes snap open and my head spins when the elevator doors open to the penthouse. I squint at the four men looking at me with a mixture of amusement and concern. "Why are there two Xanders and two Zekes?" I whisper.

Xander tips his head back and laughs. "Fuck, shorty. How much did you drink?"

"Not mush." My stomach lurches. "I'm gonna be—" Vomit spews from my mouth. All over West. I'd be mortified if I wasn't about to die of alcohol poisoning.

He doesn't put me down though. Instead he walks straight to the bathroom and gently sets me on the tiled floor beside the toilet. "Look after her while I get cleaned up."

A second later, Zeke and Xander are sitting on either side of me, and when I vomit again, with my head in the toilet this time, one of them rubs my back and the other holds my hair while they both murmur words of comfort. At least I think that's what they are. I can't seem to make out what they're saying over the echoing sounds of my own stupidity.

WHEN I WAKE up the next morning, I'm dressed in a white cotton T-shirt that clearly belongs to one of the guys, and I have no recollection of putting it on. I do remember projectile vomiting all over West and then into the toilet bowl. I throw my arm across my eyes and groan. I am never ever drinking champagne again.

"How you feeling, shorty?"

I open my eyes and realize I have hot man muscles on either side of me, and when I look up, I see that all three of them are in bed with me. Xander's perched on one elbow, and Zeke and West are still asleep. I roll onto my side to face him.

"My head is pounding. And I feel so embarrassed. I was so freaking drunk." *And I told West I loved him. Idiot!*

"Nah." He shakes his head. "You were cute and funny."

"I was sick on West." I close my eyes as a wave of shame washes over me. "Was he mad?"

Suddenly, there's an arm slung around my waist and West pulls me closer to him. "No, I wasn't mad, princess." He kisses my shoulder. "Go back to sleep. You'll feel better in a few hours."

"I'm sorry I spent your money," I add.

He nips my shoulder now. "I told you I gave you the damn card so you would spend my money. Now go back to sleep or I'll spank your drunken bratty ass."

Xander winks at me, and despite my throbbing head, I smile. Snuggling against the pillow and pulling Xander closer, I shut my eyes and drift off again, feeling happier than I ever imagined I could be.

CHAPTER
THIRTY

WEST

"You know this is just a way for him to feel like he's got a bigger dick than us, right?" Zeke grumbles as we wait in Jensen Michaels's office. "Like we couldn't have signed these papers in our lawyer's office."

I stretch my neck, feeling the tension already growing. Xander squeezes my shoulder and winks at me, reminding me that this will all be over soon. After merging three giants into one supernova—Hellsgate Media—we will be the owners of the largest media organization in the western world.

"It'll be fine, buddy." Xander gives Zeke a reassuring pat on the back. "And this is the last time we have to see the slimy prick. This time next week, it will be done."

Zeke rolls his eyes but nods.

"Besides, we all know our dicks are way bigger than his, right?" I add.

That gets a laugh out of him just as Jensen and his secretary walk into the room. The asshole's face twists with contempt as he takes a seat behind his desk. I understand why he hates us.

He's wounded and acting out. Like a dying animal striking out one last time before being willing to accept defeat.

"Are you three out of your fucking minds?" Snarling, he tosses a stack of papers onto his desk. If I had to guess, I'd say they're the new contract terms I drew up yesterday.

Zeke bristles beside me, but I shoot him a warning look. He doesn't need to smash Jensen's face into the desk, despite how much he wants to.

I narrow my eyes at Jensen. Thieving fucker. "It's a fair deal given our recent discoveries."

"It's fifty-seven million less than we agreed." Spittle collects in the corners of his mouth.

Leaning forward, I plant my hands on his desk. "You stole your employee's pension funds, asshole. Funds that we are willing to replace so that no one will ever know what a lying, thieving piece of shit you really are."

"That amounted to thirty-two million dollars. I was going to put it back as soon as the sale went through."

"They'll be our employees, not yours. We will be the ones to put it back."

"And the extra twenty-five million?" He bangs his fist on the desk like an angry toddler.

"Call that our compensation."

His face turns beet red, his mouth opening and closing like a fish on a line.

Xander chuckles and crosses his legs, resting his ankle on his thigh. "Careful, JM, you'll give yourself another cardiac event if you keep foaming at the mouth like that."

"Fuck you, you—you little bastard fuckers," he sputters.

"Or we can just tell the Feds what you did," I suggest.

"You greedy bastards. Don't you have enough money without—"

"Without what? Legitimately earning more? We've worked

for every single fucking cent we have. Never stolen anything from anyone." With a humorless laugh, I add, "Unlike you."

His scowl makes his eyes appear tiny, like pinpricks on his face. "You might be buying this company, but Grayson News Corp and *Genevieve* will always be *mine*. It was my name that started all this from nothing. My fucking name!" He stabs his pointer finger into his chest.

"But it won't be Grayson News Corp for much longer." I stand, ready to leave, and Zeke and Xander follow suit.

He sneers. "My employees will remain loyal to me long after I'm gone. You better watch your back, West. You'll never be able to trust any of them, never know if they're fucking you over just because I asked them to. I have people in every department of this building."

"Yeah?" I lunge forward, and he flinches. With a vicious smile, I straighten his tie. He knows we won't reveal his pension scam because the investigation will hold up our merger, but that doesn't mean he has any power here. "You might own a few people in this building, fuck-knuckle, but we own people all over this city. So *you* should be the one watching your back."

"You think Lily's in the den?" Xander asks as we step out of the elevator leading to the penthouse.

Zeke rolls his eyes, but I don't miss the flicker of a smile on his face. Xander's like an excitable puppy where Lily's concerned, but I get it. She's hard not to be happy around. She brings something new to our dynamic and makes coming home even more enjoyable. It's like she's always been here, and the thought that one day she might not be, that she'll decide to leave once our three months are up, fills me with a sensation of dread that I've never experienced over a woman.

She told me she loved me a few nights ago, right before she threw up all over me. Ever since, I've wanted to ask if she meant it or if it was the champagne talking. She gives her body to us completely, but I can tell how fiercely she guards her heart. I understand her need to do that. The three of us are a lot.

Not hearing anything, I glance down the hallway. She always has the radio on when she's in the kitchen, so she's not in there. "Let's go check," I say, heading in the direction of the den.

We're home earlier than expected. Maybe she's working on her article, the one she's been so secretive about. Sure enough, Lily's sitting on the sofa, head bent over her laptop as she types furiously.

"Hey, shorty," Xander says, seemingly unable to resist running over to her and jumping onto the sofa beside her.

She lets out a yelp of surprise and slams her laptop shut. "Jesus, Fitch!" Her cheeks turn a bright shade of pink, and she places her hand over her heart. "You scared the hell outta me."

With a giant smile on his face, he takes her hand and laces his fingers through hers. "Sorry."

"What were you working on?" Zeke sits in the armchair and eyes her with curiosity.

Her throat thickens as she swallows. She brushes a strand of hair from her face and narrows her eyes at him. "My article."

Xander shifts onto his knees and bounces. "You gonna tell us what it's about?"

Lily shakes her head. "I've already told you, it's a secret project. I haven't told anyone about it except my editor."

I perch on the arm of the chair beside Zeke, watching her intently now too.

"You can tell us though, right?" Xander trails his fingers along her collarbone.

179

She hugs her laptop to her chest and grins at him. "You can read it when it's published, like everybody else."

Xander's fingers drift down to her ribs, and she squirms beneath his touch. "But I already told you, we're not like everybody else, are we, shorty?"

She clamps her lips shut, but a giggle escapes when Xander begins to tickle her.

"Are we?" he asks again, still tickling her.

Squawking with laughter, Lily squirms to get away, but he straddles her, keeping her in place on the sofa as he continues his onslaught. Her squeals and giggles fill the small room and make both Zeke and me smile.

Her arms go slack around the laptop, and Xander wrenches it from her grasp with a cry of victory. "West," he calls over his shoulder, holding out his prize. I jump up and snatch it from him, but the screensaver is already in place when I open it.

"Password, princess?"

"N-no," she stammers between laughs.

"Tell him and I'll stop." Xander's words are muffled by her neck.

"Never," she squeals as he pins her arms above her head with one hand and goes on tickling and kissing her. Her back bows as tears of laughter run down her face. "Fitch!"

I step closer to them, and she looks up. "Give me your password, Lily."

Xander eases up a little, but my temptress merely grins and shakes her head at me.

"You know I could just crack it if I really wanted to?" I remind her. It would take me a few days, but I could do it.

"Yes," she says with a soft purr that bypasses my brain and goes straight to my dick. Then she arches one perfect eyebrow at me. "But that would be a gross invasion of my privacy, and you wouldn't do that, right?"

Grumbling, I drop the laptop onto the empty armchair beside me.

Her smile turns triumphant. "Thought so."

"You know you're about to pay for your disobedience though, right?" She sinks her teeth into her lush bottom lip, and my cock throbs. I'm going to enjoy sinking my own teeth into every fucking part of her body very soon. The perfect way to relieve any tension.

Her green eyes sparkle. "Oh, I sure hope so."

I rock my head from side to side. "Let her up, Fitch."

Fitch throws me a grin over his shoulder and stands, holding out his hand to her. She takes it and allows him to pull her up.

Zeke stands now too, and the sexual tension in the room is elevated about two thousand notches. He steps up beside me. "How long you think we should give them?"

Fitch arches an eyebrow. "Them?"

Zeke runs a hand over his jaw. "Seems only fair to even the odds, don't you think? Three against one would be no sport at all."

"Sport?" Lily's beautiful face pulls into a frown.

Xander licks his lips and tightens his grip on Lily's hand. Wide-eyed and innocent, she looks between the three of us.

Zeke curls a strand of her hair between his thumb and forefinger. "You're going to run, buttercup, and we're going to hunt you down."

She shivers. "Hunt us down?"

"I think two minutes should be enough," Zeke says, ignoring Lily's puzzled expression.

"Wait, what happens when you catch us?" Her tits heave under her tight tank top, and all I can think about is tearing it from her body and sucking on her nipples. My cock is harder than an iron bar.

Zeke laughs darkly. "What do you think?"

The blue of Xander's eyes is barely visible around his blown pupils. "They'll fuck us until we can't walk," he answers for us.

Lily sucks in a stuttered breath. "Oh."

I start unbuttoning my shirt. I get hot when I hunt. "You're going to need a safe word, princess. You know what a safe word is for?"

She blinks at me, her bright green eyes growing dark. "I do. But why will I need one?"

"It's the adrenaline," Xander says with a dark chuckle.

Her mouth opens, but it takes a few beats for her to speak. "The adrenaline?"

"When you're running from us, your adrenaline will spike even though, logically, you know you're not in any danger." I unfasten the last button and work on my cufflinks. "Maybe you'll even want to be caught." Xander nods. The little brat always wants to be caught. I tilt my head and watch Lily, but other than showing curiosity, she doesn't react. "But your body will still respond the way it's programmed to."

"Fight or flight," Zeke adds.

She nods her understanding, and something tells me she knows exactly what he's referring to, as though she's had direct experience with it. "So, even if you want what's happening, you may struggle. You might fight us ..."

"Scratch. Bite," Zeke offers with a wicked glint in his eyes.

I rake my eyes down her perfect body. This is going to be so much fucking fun. "And I won't lie, we both love it when our prey doesn't make it easy."

"So I need a safe word. I get it." Without showing a flicker of uneasiness about what we just said, she turns to Xander. "What's yours?"

He smirks. "Abercrombie."

Lily rolls her eyes. "Figures."

I discard my cufflinks and shrug off my shirt. "So, what's it to be, princess?"

"Marshmallow," she replies without hesitation.

I want to ask her the significance of that word, but not as much as I want to hunt. "You both have two minutes to run and hide."

Lily gasps. "Hold up a second. What about—"

"One minute fifty-eight seconds." Zeke's dark tone makes me shudder, and I'm not the one who needs to be afraid.

Xander tugs her hand. "C'mon."

Lily resists. "But what—"

Zeke's deep voice cuts her off once more. "One minute fifty-three seconds."

"We need to go, shorty." Xander pulls harder, and she stumbles after him.

She gives us one final glance, confusion and excitement in her eyes, then jogs out of the room with Xander by her side.

"You timing this?" I ask Zeke.

He looks at his watch and grins. "Kinda."

"You want Fitch or Lily?"

He gives me his full attention. "Fitch. You know how much I love chasing his hot ass down." I nod. Primal play is my thing. I've done it countless times with countless women, but I've never enjoyed hunting anyone as much as Fitch. However, something about chasing Lily down and fucking her senseless when I find her makes me hard as fucking iron. I lick my lips. That look on her face—the perfect mix of fear and lust—was incredible. She's gonna taste so fucking good when I get my mouth on her.

"Besides, it's probably best if Lily's first time is with you. You'll ease her in gently and she feels safer with you."

Placing my palm on the back of his neck, I press my forehead against his. I hate that he keeps questioning himself where she's concerned. "She feels safe with you too, Zeke."

He swallows hard. "I know that. I just don't want to scare her too much on her first time with this."

"You won't."

His soft sigh brushes my lips. "Just go after Lily and leave Fitch to me, yeah?"

"Okay." Pressing my lips to his, I give him a brief kiss. "One of these days, I'm gonna hunt *you* down. And when I catch you ..."

A grin tugs at the corners of his mouth. "You'd never catch me, old man."

I slide my hand down his muscular back. "One day, Zeke."

He dusts his lips over mine again. "One day, West."

CHAPTER
THIRTY-ONE

XANDER

My eyes dart up and down the hallway, ears straining for the sound of approaching footsteps. I thought about heading to the roof, but it's pouring rain. So instead of running, I'm trying to outsmart them. Staying one step ahead. My heartbeat thumps a steady rhythm. A shadow flashes in my peripheral vision, and I run, my feet slapping against the marble floor as they carry me to the other side of the apartment. If I can get to the gym, I can sneak through there and double back.

If Zeke's chasing me, I have a shot, but if it's West ... He slams me into the wall and knocks the air from my lungs.

Pinning my arms behind my back, he drags his teeth along the skin of my neck, taunting me with the promise of what's to come. "Gotcha, brat."

A shiver of excitement shudders up my spine. "I thought for sure you'd have gone for Lily." He's so fucking good at primal play, like a goddamn bloodhound sniffing out his prey.

SADIE KINCAID

"But I wanted you," he says before sinking his teeth into my neck.

My cock leaks precum from the tip. "Fuck, West," I groan, filling the hallway with the sound of my need for him.

Quiet footsteps pad somewhere nearby, too heavy to be Lily's.

"Is Zeke gonna be pissed that you caught me?" I ask, knowing he'll be doubting himself.

West twists my wrists in his grip and pain lances through my shoulders. I snarl and curse, which only makes him squeeze harder.

"You have more pressing things to worry about, brat. Like how hard I'm gonna fuck you for even mentioning another man's name when I have my fucking hands on you."

Pleasure and pain roll through me in equal measure. I fucking love jealous West. His hand slides up my back, rough fingertips digging into my skin. He grabs the nape of my neck and pins me flat to the wall with the full weight of his body. He's the same height as me, but he's thirty pounds heavier on account of the weight training he does every morning. I could put up a fight, maybe even knock him on his ass and pin him to the floor with his hands above his head. My cock stiffens at the memory of the times I've done exactly that and how he punished me for it after. But tonight I don't feel like fighting back. I just want West Archer any way he comes. Literally.

His hand slides to my throat, and he tilts my head back. "Shall I fuck you here in the hallway, Fitch?"

I push my ass back, rubbing it over his hard cock. "Fuck me anywhere you like, West."

He tugs at his belt and grunts. "You're a fucking manwhore, you know that?"

I grin, making him yank my head back further. "Yeah, so what?"

186

He smacks my ass. "You let just anyone fuck your tight ass, Fitch?"

"Maybe." I let out a wicked laugh. I might not want to physically fight him tonight, but I live to push every single button this man has, and he has many.

His response is little more than a growl as I feel him finally freeing his huge cock from the confines of his pants. He fists his hands in the front of my shirt and tugs it open, sending buttons skittering across the marble floor.

"Asshole," I mutter.

"You're testing every last fucking shred of my patience tonight, Fitch." He yanks the shirt down my arms and pulls it off, breaking my cufflinks in the process.

"You know you bought me those cufflinks, right?"

He pins me flat to the wall again, the hot skin of his chest scalding my back. "So I'll buy you another pair, you fucking brat." Sinking his teeth into the back of my neck, he opens my pants and tugs them down over my ass. Once he's satisfied that I'm exactly how he wants me, he holds his left hand in front of my face. "Spit, baby, because it's the only fucking lube you're getting."

I resist the urge to roll my eyes because fuck me, this is going to hurt like a motherfucker. I collect as much saliva as I can in my mouth and spit into his open palm.

"Good boy." He pushes the crown of his thick cock inside me, and my spit does little to ease the way. I press myself flat to the wall until there's nowhere left for me to go.

He inches inside me, stretching me open and dragging his sinfully hot mouth along my ear. "Holy fuck, West."

"I would have brought lube, but I knew you'd be a little brat for me and need it like this."

He inches in further. Pain, laced with the kind of pleasure sick fucks like me get from being hurt like this, hurtles through my body. "Oh fuck!" My nails scrape down the paint on the wall as he rocks his hips and sinks deeper. "Is that all you've got?"

"Fuck, Fitch," he groans, and the sound vibrates through his chest and into me. "Why do you have to fucking push me?"

I rest my forehead on the wall and suck deep breaths through my nose. "Because I love making you lose control."

Zeke is all passion and fire and heart once he lets someone in. My chaos. He gets off on pain, but then he makes up for it by being as sweet as a fucking kitten after. But West is pure ice. My peace. Calm and controlled, rarely letting emotion cloud his decision-making. He only hurts me when he loses control, so the pain he gives me comes with the satisfaction of knowing that I'm the one who caused him to let go of the reins, if only for a little while.

He pulls out and sinks in deep again, his hot breath on my ear and his free hand gripping my cock. "You're mine. You got that? Mine."

"I've always been yours." He squeezes my shaft hard, and burning hot pleasure coils at the base of my spine. He pumps me faster, the rhythm of his hand matching his thrusts. Blinding specks of light flicker behind my eyelids.

"I fucking love losing control for you, Fitch," he groans against my neck. His hips still—and so does his goddamn hand —as he comes.

I pant for breath, stranded on the ledge of the orgasm his body promised mine. "You're a fucking jackass."

With a laugh, he bites down hard on my shoulder blade, sucking the skin and no doubt leaving a huge fucking hickey. Marking me as his. I usually love it, but I'm pissed. I reach for my cock to finish myself off, but he snatches my wrist and makes a tutting sound. I'm going to headbutt him in the fucking nose if he's not careful.

A soft but demanding growl rumbles out of him. "Turn around."

"What?"

He pulls back, giving me space to move. "Turn around. I want to taste you."

I spin around, my eyes narrowed.

He tips his head to the side and flashes me a wicked grin. "Do I ever leave you hanging?"

"Yeah." That's a lie. He always gives in eventually, but *eventually* is the key word. He's been known to edge me for hours, and I don't think I can take that tonight. Not when the need to come feels like a thousand knives slicing me open.

He shakes his head. "Lucky for you, I want to suck your cock more than I want to punish you right now."

Dropping to his knees, he wraps his hand around my throbbing length and darts his tongue out, sweeping it over my crown and licking precum from my slit.

I tip my head back and let out a long, low moan. "I have no idea how you're so fucking good at that when you get barely any practice."

He squeezes the base of my shaft tighter and mutters something I don't understand before he takes me all the way into his mouth. I thread my fingers in his hair but resist the urge to fuck his throat. He hates that. Instead, I look down and watch the most powerful man I know suck my cock. The sight alone is enough to make me nut in his mouth. "Fuck, West."

He looks up, and the bastard winks at me. The back of my head hits the wall, and my hands fist tighter in his hair as I rock forward and come down his throat. He swallows every last fucking drop, and I'm still gasping when he stands and presses his forehead against mine.

"It's so fucking hot when you get on your knees for me."

He pulls my pants up and refastens them, then kisses the

three prongs of the trident tattoo on my chest. "You and Zeke are the only men I'd ever get on my knees for. You know that, right?"

I place my palms on either side of his handsome face. "I know. It's the same for me." As much as I enjoy making him jealous, he knows he has nothing to worry about. He and Zeke are it for me, and now Lily too. I'm happy to go the rest of my life fucking, and being fucked by, nobody but the three of them.

Grabbing my hands, he kisses the insides of both my wrists. "You want to come to bed and watch some trashy TV?"

My knees nearly buckle at the amount of love that rushes through me, but I force myself to stand up straight and grin. "Can we bring snacks, because I'm fucking starving?"

He chuckles. "You go get cleaned up. I'll get the snacks."

CHAPTER
THIRTY-TWO

LILY

I step out of the elevator and into the private parking garage full of the most expensive, high-end cars and motorcycles I've ever seen in my life. My heart races faster than the Ducati I pass, and I brush my fingers over its supple leather seat.

Sucking in a lungful of cool air, I head for the highlighter-yellow Lamborghini. I can't help but smile as I trail my hand along the hood. This must be Xander's.

The sound of the elevator going back up has my stomach rolling. My pulse thunders against my pressure points. How the hell do they know I'm down here already? Glancing around, I scout for a good place to hide, but the garage is a massive square. And to make it worse, the entire room is lit by bright fluorescent lighting. Could I have picked a worse place to run to?

With my blood thundering in my ears and my legs propelled by fear and adrenaline, I jog over to the line of cars farthest from the elevator and crouch behind the one at the very back. I lock my eyes on the shiny silver doors, my heart fluttering in my throat while I wait for them to open. The elevator only has three stops: the penthouse, the lobby, and here. A red L appears in the small window above the elevator, and I swallow a thick knot of fear and excitement.

He's almost here.

I tell myself that it might just be Xander coming down here to hide with me, but my body trembles and fear becomes my dominant emotion.

The elevator pings.

My heart hammers uncontrollably.

The doors open.

Blood screams in my ears.

Zeke steps out with a wicked smile on his face.

I almost fall on my ass.

"I know you're in here, buttercup," he sing-songs, and it's one of the most frightening sounds I've ever heard in my life. Do I want to play this game to its end?

Marshmallow. That's all I need to say, and this will all be over.

So, why don't I say it? Why do I stay right here with my lips pressed tightly shut and my hand over my mouth, waiting for Zeke to find me?

THIRTY-THREE

ZEKE

I know she's down here. I can fucking smell her. Her fear. Her arousal. I lick my lips and taste her in the air.

I step further into the brightly lit garage, seeking a glimpse of her. "Come out and I might make it easier on you."

Silence.

She's good at this. The first time I hunted Xander, he gave himself up because he couldn't stand the terror of waiting for me to find him. He said it was better to face the consequences than think about what they might be.

My fingers curl around the worn leather of my switchblade. I never would have gotten it from my room if I'd known I'd be chasing Lily instead of Xander. But now I have it, and she's in here somewhere. Pure adrenaline thunders through my veins, making my cock throb as well as my temples. There's no stopping this thing now. Not unless she says her safe word.

Walking along the center of the garage, I glance up and down the rows of cars. "Where are you, buttercup?" I tilt my head, straining to hear some sound from her. Her breathing or maybe a movement, but there's not a peep. She really is good at this. I pass by the silver Porsche and smile. But not good enough. Part of her sneaker is reflected in the rim of the 911 Turbo.

My heart rate slows, and I close my eyes for a second, savoring the moment before I let her know she's beat. My chest tightens and my balls draw up as I round the black SUV she's crouching behind. I figure I have one more second until she realizes I'm onto her and runs. I want her to run. I want her to fight too.

I take a few steps closer, and she bolts, darting out from between the cars so fast she's practically a blur. But I was anticipating her every move, and she's nowhere near quick enough to escape me. She's racing toward the elevator when I tackle her and throw her against the hood of the Bugatti. She lands with a thud and lets out a yelp, but I cut the sound short with my hand around her throat. "Gotcha, buttercup."

Pushing her back, I wedge myself between her thighs. With both hands, she shoves at my chest. I don't budge. A heady mix of excitement, pure animal lust, and the triumph of victory pumps through my veins. I feel fucking invincible right now. A truck couldn't move me from between her legs. Only one thing has that power, and I glare at her, daring her to say it.

"Fuck you!" She spits out the words, her eyes dark and full of anger-tinged desire.

"No." I fist my hand in the front of her dress and pull hard, tearing it down the middle and exposing her panties and bare tits. "But I *am* gonna fuck *you*."

"The fuck you will," she screeches, lashing out with her arms and legs and scratching my lip in the process. It stings, and I dart out my tongue and taste blood.

"Oh, Lily, you're going to regret that." Widening my stance so her legs are spread so far apart that she has no leverage to kick, I tighten my grip on her throat and slam her head back, pinning her to the car with brute strength.

Her hands curl into talons and she lashes out again. Before she makes contact, I grab both her wrists with one hand and pull a pair of cuffs from my back pocket with the other. I snap them open, and her eyes go wide.

"This ain't my first rodeo, buttercup. You think I wouldn't stop off and get a few little surprises for you? Like I told you upstairs, I love it when you fight." I pull her up and pin her wrists behind her back with ease before slapping the cuffs on her. She struggles throughout, screaming at me to stop as I push her back against the hood, crushing her arms under her. Now she's trapped and completely at my mercy.

"No! Stop!" she protests, her head whipping from side to side.

I adjust my grip on her throat so I can hold her head still. "You will fucking look at me when I fuck you, Lily."

She hisses like a feral kitten. "You're a fucking animal."

My cock leaks in my pants. I knew she'd fight a little, it's only natural, but this is way more than that. This goes a whole lot deeper than the innate human reaction to danger.

"Yes, I fucking am, buttercup." I tug her panties aside, tearing a hole in the fabric. "And you have no fucking idea how hard it makes me to see you like this."

I slide my finger through her wet folds and bite down on my lip so hard I draw blood when I feel how wet she is. "Oh you want my cock, don't you, my little baby doll?"

She gnashes her teeth at me, and my laugh only makes her fight harder. "I fucking hate you," she screams, her voice hoarse.

I slip one finger inside her. "You hate that too?"

She responds with an animalistic snarl, but her back arches off the car, telling me everything I need to know. I add a second finger. "How about that?"

"Fuck! You!" The words echo off the concrete walls of the garage and send searing hot pleasure down my spine.

Adding a third finger, I curl them upward and brush her G-spot. Muttered curses fall from her lips, like she's too far gone to scream at me. Despite what she says, she's painting the hood of the Bugatti with her sweet fucking cum. Squeezing her slender throat, I work her hard, and soon she's trembling for me. Her orgasm is so close I can smell it.

That's when I stop and slide my fingers out of her. Her body sags and she gasps for air.

I bring my fingertips up to her mouth and coat her lips with her arousal. "You look so fucking beautiful all wrung out for me."

She lunges for me, and I pull back, but her teeth graze the tip of my pointer finger.

"You'll pay for that, buttercup."

"The fuck I will!" she spits.

I have no idea what happened to the sweet girl who lives in the apartment upstairs. Logic tells me I should stop this before I fuck something up, but my aching cock won't let me.

She hisses. "Is this all you got? I expected more from you."

The disdain in her tone causes something to snap inside of me. Freeing my cock from my pants, I drive into her, bottoming out on the first thrust and filling every millimeter of her tight cunt.

With a ragged scream, she accepts all of me. Despite the vitriol pouring from her mouth, my sweet Lily is still in there. And that's when I realize she hasn't been talking to me. Her body is mine, but her mind is somewhere else entirely.

"Lily." I pull out and drive back in, trying to anchor her back to me.

She closes her eyes and tries to wrench free of my grip.

"Lily! Look at me when I'm fucking you, baby doll."

Her eyes snap open and focus on mine. She shivers.

"Good girl."

Her throat constricts under my palm, and I relax my grip a little as I pull out again and thrust back inside her. Her eyes flutter closed, and she breathes out my name.

Now I got her. I take out my knife and press the button to release the blade. The sound makes her blink, and when her eyes lock on the metal glinting in the harsh lights, she freezes.

"You know your safe word, Lily?"

"Yes."

"Good girl." I trail the tip of the blade between her breasts and over her nipple, following its path with my tongue. Her heart hammers against her sternum. Her tits heave with every breath. My cock pulses as I go on nailing her to the hood of the car and she spasms around me. She's so close to oblivion, and I want her to fall the fuck apart as she comes undone for me.

I trail the knife lower. It bites into her nipple, and she screams her pain. Pain that makes her pussy gush around my cock. "You gonna come like a good little whore?"

"Y-yeah." Her walls flutter around me, signaling that she's right there, and I sink the sharp edge into her soft flesh, watching as it slices her open. I lick the blood from her wound as her back bows in half. She drenches my cock with her sweet juices and screams my name.

The coppery tang of her blood on my tongue. The scent of her release thick in the air. The way her pussy squeezes my cock like I'm the only thing tethering her soul to this earth. All of it combines into an earth-shattering explosion. I come inside her with a roar that is drowned out by the deafening sound of blood rushing in my ears.

THIRTY-FOUR

LILY

Every inch of my body aches. I lack the energy to say a word as Zeke pulls me up from the hood of the beautiful car he just fucked me on. If what we just did can even be called fucking. It felt like nothing else I've ever experienced in my life. Like so much more than anything I've ever done before.

His strong hands glide over my arms almost reverently, completely at odds with the man who rutted me like a lust-blinded animal a few moments ago. He unfastens the handcuffs, and I sag against his broad chest.

He gently circles my wrists with the pads of his thumbs and forefingers, soothing the chafed skin. "I got you, buttercup," he murmurs against my hair. "You did so good."

I mumble incoherently, so tired I could sleep for a week.

He hoists me into his arms and cradles me close to his chest. "Let's get you upstairs" are the last words I hear him say.

When my eyelids flutter open again, I'm in Zeke's bed, and he's wiping me down with a warm cloth. I look down to see the small knife wound just above my ribs, and the memory of him cutting me sends a fresh jolt of electricity between my thighs. What the hell is wrong with me?

"It stopped bleeding, but I'm going to glue it, okay? It won't scar."

"It won't?" I ask, surprised at the disappointment that washes over me.

"No, buttercup. Did you want it to?"

"I don't know." I shake my head, still woozy from whatever the hell happened in the basement. "Kind of. Is that weird?" I graze my fingertip over the wound. "I kinda like having a permanent reminder of you."

He sucks in air through his teeth. "Jesus fuck, Lily."

My cheeks flush with embarrassment. "What? Is that crazy?"

He dusts his lips over the cut and looks up at me with fire burning in his dark eyes. "No, baby doll. It's hot as fuck."

"Oh."

He trails featherlight kisses down my body as he wipes the blood and cum from my skin. His lips feel so good on me. His hands work quickly and tenderly, and something profound and carnal and long forgotten makes tears well in my eyes. "I love you, Zeke." The words fall from my lips before I can stop them. Holding my breath, I brace myself for his reaction.

"I know you do, buttercup. I love you too."

My heart swells with relief and joy. Of course he loves me. I feel it every day. With an unabashedly wide smile on my face, I let my head sink back into the pillow and enjoy the way he caresses and massages my limbs until all the aches from earlier have all but disappeared. All too soon, his heat disappears.

"I'm going to get the glue so I can seal that wound. I'll be right back."

I whimper anyway but keep my eyes closed and wait

patiently. True to his word, he's back a moment later. "This won't hurt."

"Well, it seems I'm quite partial to a little pain anyway."

"You took it all like a fucking warrior. Your first time too. I thought for sure you were going to use your safe word."

I open my eyes to find him staring at me, his beautiful dark eyes peering into my soul. "Maybe, you're my safe word, Zeke."

He frowns. "That's not—"

"I mean, I feel safe with you. Always, no matter what. Even when you had the knife, I knew you'd never cause me real harm." I shake my head and throw my arm over my face, aware that I'm babbling. "It sounds crazy, and I can't explain it, but it's the truth."

He tugs my hand and uncovers my face. "It doesn't sound crazy, buttercup." The deep rolling timbre of his voice soothes me. "And that fact that you feel safe with me means more to me than you can ever know."

He rolls onto his back, pulling me with him. "Don't you need to glue my wound?"

"It's all done." I glance down and see the cut has been sealed, expertly by the looks of it. Just how much practice has he had doing this? He wraps one arm around my back and shuffles me so that I'm lying on top of him like he's my human pillow. I have nowhere to lay my head except for his chest.

"Um, Zeke." I wriggle in his grip.

He takes hold of my right hand and places it over his heart, then puts his on top of it. "It's okay, baby doll."

I swallow the sob that wells in my throat and lay my head on his broad chest. We lie together without speaking for a long time, his heart thumping against my palm and his fingertips trailing gently up and down my spine.

"Who hurt you, buttercup?" he asks, cutting through the silence like his blade sliced through my skin.

A lone tear rolls down my cheek. "Someone who should have protected me."

His arms band tighter around me. "Did what we just did help?"

"It did, yeah. Kind of cathartic. Is that strange?"

"Not at all. But where is he now? The man who hurt you?"

I almost tell him the truth. It wants to pour out of me like syrup from a jug, slow and deliberate. But I can't. "He no longer exists in the life I've built for myself." Before he can question me further on my vague answer, I add, "Who hurt you, Zeke?"

"Someone who should have known better." He lets out a deep sigh, and I think that's going to be the end of the conversation, but he keeps talking. "He was my foster brother and the first guy I ever loved. At least I thought I loved him, but I had no idea what that really meant back then. He was nineteen, and I thought the sun rose and set with him." He gives a self-deprecating laugh.

"How old were you?"

"Fourteen."

My heart breaks for a young adolescent Zeke. "What happened?"

"Turns out he was just experimenting." He snorts. "With his sexuality. With his fetish for cutting things open. People get kind of freaked out when their kids start slicing open their family pets, not so much when it's just the new foster kid."

"I'm sorry that happened to you."

"Don't be, buttercup. I moved to a new foster home and met West and Fitch, and I made a promise that no one would ever fucking touch me or hurt me again unless I wanted them to."

I flex my fingertips, feeling the ridges of scars hidden under his beautiful tattoos. I hate that someone hurt him that way. "Thank you for letting me touch you."

He grips my chin between his thumb and forefinger and

angles my head so he can look at my face. "It takes a whole lot of trust to allow someone to slice you open with a knife. Thank you for giving me that."

I love him so much. "It was beautiful. Thank you."

His Adam's apple bobs as he stares at me intently, like there's something he wants to say but can't. Or won't.

My stomach growls, and I wrinkle my nose. "You mind if we grab a bite to eat?"

He drops a tender kiss on my forehead. "Whatever my girl needs."

THIRTY-FIVE

WEST

"I know what it means, Mason, just get it done." I pinch the bridge of my nose. "I want all the paperwork complete by the fifth. We go live on the sixth."

"Okay, West. I'll have it pushed through."

"Thank you." Sighing, I hang up. Merging three media companies into one conglomerate is turning out to be a way bigger headache than I anticipated.

"You okay there, buddy? You need a little relief?" Zeke asks with a wicked grin. He's so much more relaxed now that Lily's in our life. Whatever happened between them the night before last changed them both. I saw the wound over her ribcage, so I know he cut her, and it seems like it brought them closer together.

I should get her over here and make her work from my office all day every day. Have her at my disposal so she can offer me some of that relief Zeke's hinting at whenever the fuck I like.

Instead, I arch an eyebrow at Zeke. "Are you offering?"

He tilts his head, his eyes roaming over my body. "I could

give you something, but probably not what you're looking for right now."

"Mr. Archer." My secretary's voice fills the room via the intercom on my desk. "You have a visitor."

I check my watch. I'm not expecting anyone, but my heart rate kicks up a notch. Please be Lily. I press the button to answer. "Who is it?"

"A Ms. Reid."

"Oh, fuck no," Zeke grumbles.

"Bree Reid?"

"Yes, sir."

I take my finger off the button so Zeke and I can speak privately. "What the fuck is she doing here?"

"Fuck knows. But I don't want to see her," Zeke says, his lip curled in disgust. "She's fucking loco."

I glance between him and the phone on my desk. Curiosity wins out. "Send her in."

Zeke groans and mumbles something unintelligible under his breath.

"Oh, stop your fucking grumbling."

Bree walks into my office in a cloud of perfume clutching a Hermès bag over her arm. I offer her a seat, which she accepts, throwing Zeke a look dripping with disdain as she settles in the chair. He glowers at her in return.

"What can I do for you, Bree?" I ask, forcing a smile.

"Actually." She crosses her legs, and her short skirt rides up, exposing the top of her stockings. I focus on her face. "I'm here about what I can do for you."

Interest piqued, I lean forward, steepling my hands under my chin. "And what's that?"

"I'm kind of surprised you don't already know this to be honest. You must be getting rusty, Ezekiel." She throws a glance his way, and her fake laugh drips sarcasm and contempt.

He snarls. "What the fuck is that supposed to mean?"

She glances at her manicured fingernails. "You usually check out the women you *experiment* with, don't you?"

My temper flares. "Is this about Lily?"

"Yes. Well, if that's even her real name."

Zeke leans forward now too, his dark eyes shooting daggers at Bree. "What the fuck are you talking about?"

"I'm talking about how an orphan from Brooklyn can afford to go to one of the most prestigious colleges in New York."

I frown. "She had a scholarship."

Bree shakes her head. "Did she though? Because the organization that paid her tuition dissolved as soon as she graduated, and it only ever funded one student—Lily Sloane. What kind of scholarship does that?

"She never had a job, either. Not the entire time we were there. Someone was funding her lifestyle, paying her bills. She used to sneak off to meet him sometimes. I caught a glimpse of him once. Young. Handsome. Rich. She couldn't keep her hands off him."

I snarl. Bree always had a jealous streak, and that's all this is. It has to be. "How the fuck do you know any of this?"

"I followed her on one of her little excursions once. I was curious about what she was up to, and I was the sorority house president. I had access to information that other people didn't."

"Weren't you screwing the dean too?" Zeke asks, his tone dripping with contempt.

She smirks. "See, you did such good homework on me, Ezekiel."

I scrub a hand through my hair as questions with no answers race around my head. "Why are you even telling us this? Why do you care if Lily has some mysterious benefactor?"

"Because I care about Xander, and I would never want to see his name dragged through the mud."

My frown deepens. "Why would it be?"

She rolls her eyes, making it seem like Zeke and I are missing something important. It pisses me off more than I care to admit that she might know something about our girl that we don't.

"Lily is writing an article, yes? One that's she's finally able to get published after two years of trying?"

"So?"

"It's no coincidence that she's writing it for the magazine that Jensen Michaels still owns, and that she just happened to meet you all at the same time she came up with this new exclusive article that's going to be her big break?"

The hairs on the back of my neck stand on end. "You're saying she's writing this article about us?"

She lifts one shoulder and glances back down at her manicured nails. "An exposé, to take the three of you down from the inside. What better way to do that than from your bed, West?"

"You're fucking lying," Zeke growls.

"Am I? My company does some of their PR. I hear things. And you know I was out with her a couple of weeks ago, don't you?" She directs her attention back to me. "She was waving your credit card in people's faces, offering to buy anyone who would listen a bottle of Dom at your expense. She was bragging about how she had you three wrapped around her little finger."

"No." I shake my head. That sounds nothing like Lily.

"Why are you all so blind when it comes to her? She got so wasted that Jen and I had to pour her into your car."

Bile burns my esophagus.

"You're lying." Zeke shouts the words this time.

"Are you really willing to bet your reputation on that, Ezekiel?"

I suck in a breath. This can't be true. Lily would never do

that to us. Whatever her article's about, it can't possibly have anything to do with us.

I glare at Bree, who smiles like she didn't just try to tear our world apart. "Get the fuck out of my office."

Smirking, she stands and slings her overpriced bag back over her shoulder. "You should look into her is all I'm saying. I'm sure you'll find that there's more to Lily Sloane than meets the eye."

With that, she stomps out, leaving Zeke and I to stare at each other for several seconds.

"You remember how she jumped when we came home early the other night and she was working on her article? She snapped her laptop shut like she was terrified we'd see it."

Zeke scowls. "We gave her a fright. Fitch jumped on her."

Gritting my teeth, I stretch my neck. I'm so fucking tense. "Michaels warned us he had spies on the inside. He specifically told us to watch our backs."

Zeke chews on his bottom lip for a second, then shakes his head. "He's a snake backed into a corner."

"Yeah." That doesn't stop an uneasy feeling from settling into the pit of my stomach. Lily is just a little too perfect, and experience has taught me that if something seems too good to be true, it almost always is.

"Who do you think this mysterious benefactor is then?" Zeke's face is lined with worry now too.

"You mean the young good-looking guy she couldn't keep her hands off of?"

"Yeah. That one."

I bare my teeth. "Find out."

CHAPTER

THIRTY-SIX

LILY

I glance up and down the crowded sidewalk one last time before I step out of the hotel. I've had that creepy feeling of being watched all morning, but it must be in my head. Nobody knows about Nico. Hell, nobody knows who I really am, and the fact that I'm still breathing is proof enough of that.

This is the second time I've met with Nico in as many months, and as much as I adore seeing my brother, I feel so guilty lying to the guys about him. I'm just not sure if I can tell them yet. Our three months are almost up. I have no idea what happens next, and I'm too scared to ask about it. Although what we share feels like it's gone far beyond our original agreement, what if it isn't?' What if they fall in love with every single woman they do this with?

"Marshmallow?" The voice stops me in my tracks.

I spin around and my heart almost stops beating at the sight of his familiar face. It's dangerous and reckless, but instinct makes me run to him. I throw my arms around his neck. "Doc?"

He wraps his arms around me, and I bury my face against his shoulder, stifling a sob at the memories that are invoked by seeing him after all these years. He guides me to a nearby doorway, out of view from the street.

A sudden wave of panic makes my knees buckle. "What are you doing here? Is *he* here?"

"Relax, Marshmallow. He's back in Vegas. I'm here with Nico. Just making sure things go smoothly. It's so good to see you. You look great." He tousles my curls. "I like your hair like this. It's just like your mom's."

My cheeks heat. "It's good to see you too."

He steps out and glances at the street, then back at me. "I should really get moving. This is too dangerous. I'm sorry, but I saw you and ..." His eyes turn glossy with unshed tears.

"I'm glad I saw you." I pull him in for one last hug. "Take good care of Nico, won't you?"

"Always, Marshmallow. You take good care of yourself. Remember that right hook I taught you?"

"Sure do."

He swallows like he wants to say more but can't. "Bye, kid."

"Bye." I watch him walk out of the shadows and back onto the street, taking a piece of my heart with him. But staying apart is the only way we all get to stay alive.

THIRTY-SEVEN

XANDER

Lily's in the den putting the finishing touches on her article, and I sneak up behind her, trying to catch a glimpse of what she's writing. When she's not with one of us or at work, she has her head bent over her laptop, but she refuses to give us a single clue as to what it's about.

When I get close enough to see her screen, all I see are pictures of puppies. I jump over the back of the sofa and land next to her with a thud. Shrieking, she slams her laptop shut and hugs it to her chest.

"Xander! Please stop doing that to me," she gasps, but her eyes are full of amusement.

I laugh and give her a kiss on the cheek. "I thought you were working, not looking at pictures of cute puppies. Or is that what your article is about? Cutest puppies of New York?"

Rolling her eyes, she reopens her laptop and unlocks it with her fingerprint. "Not exactly." She shows me a picture of Rottweiler puppies snuggled up in a pile.

I tilt my head. "Aw. They are cute."

She nods, a huge smile on her face. "You like dogs."

"Who doesn't?" I wrap my arm around her shoulder as she scrolls through more images.

"Some people don't," she says in a sad tone, but before I can pick that apart, she goes on. "I always wanted a Rottweiler puppy."

"You did?"

"Yeah, I'd call him Snowflake."

I bark out a laugh. "Snowflake? A huge black Rottweiler named Snowflake?"

"Yeah." She giggles. "I like the irony."

"I've always wanted a dog too, but West and Zeke won't let me get one." That isn't entirely true. If I insisted, they'd jump on board, but their objections always manage to talk me out of it. Apparently puppies are a big responsibility.

"They're so mean."

I kiss her sweet-smelling neck. "But if you were to ask for a puppy ..." I trail my kisses lower.

"They'd tell me I was crazy," she says in a breathy tone.

I stop kissing her neck and stare into her bright green eyes. "No. They'd do anything for you, shorty. We all would. Don't you know that?" She bites down on the soft cushion of her bottom lip, eyes shining as she blinks at me. Holy fuck, she has no idea how much we need her, want her, love her. My chest tightens and I struggle to breathe. Is someone sucking the air from the room?

"You would?" she whispers, her dark eyelashes fluttering against her pink cheeks.

I take her laptop from her hands and place it on the couch, then pull her onto my lap to straddle me. My fingers caress her cheeks, brushing her hair from her face. "I love you, shorty. I can't believe I never told you that before today, because I think

I've loved you from the moment you handed me your roach-infested backpack."

"I love you too, Xander."

I dust my mouth over hers, and her warm breath mingles with mine. She tastes of coffee and chocolate, and I want to devour her whole. My fucking phone rings before I can. Pulling it from my pocket, I read the text from West. *We need you here at the office. It's important.*

Squeezing my eyes closed, I sigh. "I gotta go, shorty." I give her a quick kiss, barely refraining from sliding my tongue into her mouth and taking what I need from her.

"Wait a fucking minute, you've had a PI following Lily and you never told me?" I scowl at Zeke and West. "What the fuck?"

"I told you what Bree told us about her, Xander," West says, trying to justify this shitshow.

I slam my fist on his desk. "And I told you she's a crazy fuck-bucket who can't be trusted."

"We know she is, but I asked Zeke to check out what she said anyway. Just to be sure. I didn't know about the PI until just now."

I retrain my glare on Zeke. He scowls back. "Since when do either of you ever question my methods? I get shit done, and you don't usually give a fuck how I do it."

"Because this is Lily we're talking about, you asshole. Fucking *Li-ly*." I overenunciate her name to remind him who we're discussing here. There's no fucking way Bree is right about her. No way in hell.

A throat clears, and we all turn our attention to Spencer, the PI standing awkwardly in the corner.

Zeke sighs and glares at me. "Tell us what you found, Spencer."

"Your girl went to the Valencia Hotel. Took the elevator to the presidential suite, then went into a man's room. Stayed for an hour and left."

West bounces on his toes. Spencer's about to get a punch in the face if he's not careful. "You're telling us that she went into some guy's hotel room and stayed for an hour?"

"An hour and six minutes to be exact."

West's hand balls into a fist at his side, and I grab his forearm before he literally kills the messenger. "There could be a perfectly reasonable explanation."

"Who the fuck was he?" Zeke demands.

Spencer's Adam's apple bobs, and my stomach sinks. The fear on his face is scaring the shit out of me.

"Who?" West barks.

Spencer winces. "Nico Constantine."

West's face turns an unnatural shade of gray. Zeke kicks a chair, sending it flying across the office. I put my head in my hands. What the fuck, shorty?

"Nico fucking Constantine?" West spits the name out like poison.

Spencer nods. "Then on her way out, she ran into another guy who's affiliated with Carmine Constantine. I grabbed a picture." He takes his cell phone from his coat pocket and presses a few buttons. A second later, we all get an alert notification.

My heart breaks at the image on my screen. Not because she's hugging some guy I've never seen, but because she wears a look of sheer joy on her face. This isn't some casual acquaintance; he means something to her.

Zeke slams his fist down on the desk. "You have anything else to share?"

Spencer clears his throat. "No, that's everything."

"Then get the fuck out."

Spencer quickly follows Zeke's command, leaving the three of us alone with the bomb he just dropped.

West sinks into a chair across from me. "Nico fucking Constantine," he says again with a shake of his head. "What the actual fuck?"

"You think she's fucking him?" The mere thought of anyone's hands on Lily makes me burn with jealous rage, an emotion I've never felt before in my life.

Zeke barks a humorless laugh. "Why the fuck else would she spend an hour alone with him in his hotel room, Fitch?"

West scrubs his hands over his face and looks up at the ceiling. "She might not be fucking him, but she's definitely up to something."

"You think she knows what went down between us and Carmine Constantine?" I ask.

"Who knows? But that was fourteen fucking years ago." He gives me a pained look and shakes his head. "I don't know how that could have anything to do with now."

I sink into an empty chair like a deflated balloon. "He have any connections to Jensen Michaels? You think he's trying to fuck up our deal somehow?"

West frowns. "The deal's as good as done. And what the fuck would the Constantines want with a media company?"

"What the fuck do they want with Lily?" I retort.

West scowls. "Whatever it is, she's been lying to us all along. She's been meeting that Constantine piece of shit all this time and never once mentioned him. I'd guarantee he's the guy who paid for her college. The one she couldn't keep her hands off of. She's been fucking the three of us and then sneaking off to his hotel."

"Maybe it's something to do with her article?" I know I'm

clutching at straws, but there's no way I can believe that our girl's been pretending with us all this time.

Zeke sighs. "*Genevieve* doesn't publish features on the fucking Mafia, Fitch."

My head is spinning so fast I feel like I might throw up. Lily wouldn't do anything to hurt us. She fucking loves us. "So we do what?" After a long moment of silence, during which tension infuses the air and makes it difficult to breathe, West sits up straight and twists his head from side to side. "When we get home tonight, we ask her about her day. And if she fails to mention spending an hour in Nico Constantine's hotel room, we'll know that she's a fucking liar."

THIRTY-EIGHT

LILY

I'm preparing dinner when West sneaks up behind me and wraps his arms around my waist. "Hey, princess. Something smells good."

My hands are covered in sauce, so I rub my cheek against his. "I'm making lasagna."

"No, not that." He runs his nose along my jawline. "Pretty sure it's you."

Zeke strides into the kitchen and rolls his eyes. "Oh, let her the fuck go, West."

"Yeah, I'm starving. Let Lily make dinner, and then we can fuck her after," Xander adds with a cheeky laugh.

West slaps my ass and takes a seat with the others at the island.

"You do anything interesting today, buttercup?"

I freeze for a second, but then I remember that they always ask me about my day when they get home. Guilt sits on my chest like a lead weight every time I lie to them, and it's making

216

me paranoid. "Just work. It was all kind of boring really. Tell me about your day."

Xander starts telling a funny story about a cold call he got from a guy offering to help him grow his business, but once he figured out who he was speaking to, the guy asked for a job. I only half listen, my mind wandering to Nico and Doc and all the secrets I'm keeping from the men I love most. I wish more than anything that I could just tell everyone the truth. It feels like the burden of carrying so many secrets by myself will crush me if I don't. But how do I confide in them without putting them and other people I care about at risk?

I swallow down the confession that's forever perched on the tip of my tongue and join their conversation instead.

CHAPTER
THIRTY-NINE

ZEKE

I pace up and down Julian Barnes's office, unable to sit calmly like West, who's taking point on the questions. Lily's been lying to us, and I have no fucking idea why. Surely Bree was wrong about this though. She can't be writing an exposé on us. She wouldn't.

"What exactly can I help you with?" Julian asks.

"Lily Sloane is writing an article for your magazine, yes?"

Julian eyes him warily. "Yeah."

"What's it about?"

He scowls. "That's between Lily and me."

West bangs his fist on the desk. "What the fuck is it about, Julian?"

"I just told you, it's between Lily and me."

"If you like your job here ..."

"If I like my job, what? Are you fucking threatening me, Mr. Archer? Otherwise, allow me to remind you that you might own this company, but I am still the editor of this magazine. As long as my name is on that issue, I will not be bullied by men who can't handle that their girlfriend has a life that doesn't revolve around them."

Let me beat the shit out of him, West. Just say the fucking word.

"That's not what this is," he says, his tone a little calmer. "I just want to know what her article is about."

"Ask her."

"I'm asking you."

"And like I already said, I'm not telling you. So, please leave. I have a magazine to run."

I bounce on my toes, ready to tear this prick a new asshole, but West stands and shakes his head at me, leading me out of the office.

I stop just outside Barnes's door. "What the fuck was that?"

"There are other people we can ask," he says, keeping his tone level while his eyes tell me to drop it. "Let's go."

He stalks down the hallway, and I fall into step beside him, ignoring the worried glances of the staff as we pass. West stops at an office at the end of the hall and walks inside.

"Andy," he barks.

The guy in question sits behind his desk, twiddling a paper-clip, and he looks like he's about to shit his pants. "Y-yeah?"

"You have your finger on the pulse around here, right?"

That makes Andy sit up straighter, and he puffs out his chest like a peacock. "Yeah."

West closes the door behind us and takes two menacing steps forward. "What article is Lily Sloane working on?"

Andy swallows, his eyes darting between the two of us. "Why? What have you heard?"

Fuck. I don't have the time or the patience for this. "That it's about us." I narrow my eyes. "An exposé."

Licking his lips, he leans forward. The way his head bobs up and down reminds me of a weasel. "That's what I heard too."

"So she is writing about us?"

SADIE KINCAID

He shrugs. "Julian's keeping it pretty close to his chest, but yeah, that's the rumor. I mean it makes sense that he wouldn't tell anyone if it's about his new bosses. An article in your own magazine wouldn't look good, would it?"

"Motherfucker," West mutters.

"If I hear anything else, I'll be sure to come straight to you, Mr. Archer. And if you'd like me to keep tabs on Lily for you, you know, keep a note of who she speaks to and stuff, just let me know. I'd be happy to oblige."

His lascivious grin has me seeing red. "You stay the fuck away from Lily."

His hands shoot up in the air like I'm pointing a gun at him. "Okay, okay. No worries, bro. But you should know that you have some enemies in this office. But not me! I'm on your side. One hundred percent loyal."

West merely grunts at the guy, then looks at me and cocks his head toward the door.

I wait to speak until we're alone in the elevator. "You think he was telling the truth?"

West pinches the bridge of his nose. "All I know for certain is that the only two people who know what the article's about aren't talking. And two separate people connected to this magazine have told us that it's about us. What the fuck else are we supposed to think?"

"Maybe we could hack into her laptop and see this article for ourselves." It's a longshot. "You can do that kind of shit, and if you can't, I know a guy."

West shakes his head. "It would take a few days, and the article comes out next week. We need to fix this now, Zeke."

"So, she's just been playing us all along?" I blow out a breath. "What I don't get is how she could have planned this. She had no way to know we'd end up living together."

"Think about it. How she met all three of us on the same

day and then showed up at our club that night. She could have orchestrated the whole thing."

"But she couldn't have known we'd be there that night."

"Maybe she went every week until she bumped into us. Or maybe she got lucky on the first try." He levels me with a stare. "Think about it, Zeke. The way she's just too fucking perfect for us. How easily she adapted to the three of us and how she fits in with each of us like the missing piece of a puzzle. Like she's ..." Clenching his jaw shut, he shakes his head.

"Too good to be true?" I finish for him. "So, how the fuck do we handle this?"

"We fucking cut her loose. We let her go and we discredit her. We make sure that nobody believes a single goddamn word that comes out of her mouth ever again."

Considering his idea, I nod. "And how do we do that?"

"The launch party tomorrow night. How about we show Lily exactly who she's fucking with?"

CHAPTER
FORTY

WEST

I stare at my monitor, a pencil gripped between my fingers so I can take notes, but the pages of numbers swim before my eyes. I can't focus on anything other than how quickly everything has fallen apart. Lily isn't who we believed she was. When I first heard Bree's story, I was convinced that her jealousy drove her to cause trouble for us, but it turns out I'm not as good a judge of character as I thought.

It tracks that I was wrong about Lily this whole time. She's been sleeping in our beds, letting us fuck her every single night, making us fall in love with her. All for a fucking story. She did say that nothing would ever stand in her way of becoming a writer, so I guess she didn't lie about everything. The worst part about the whole mess is her involvement with the Constantines. I can hardly believe she'd crawl into bed with a pit of vicious snakes, but I saw the fucking proof with my own two eyes. My pencil snaps in my hand, snapping me from memories of Carmine Constantine—memories that are better off left in the past where they belong.

LILY STARTLES, then smiles brightly when she comes out of the bathroom to find me sitting on her bed. She is one hell of an actress. "I didn't think you'd all be home until later."

I narrow my eyes, searching her face for any hint at all that she knows we're onto her. But what the fuck do I think I'm gonna find? She played us all for months now. I'd admire her if I wasn't so preoccupied with fighting the urge to wrap my hands around her throat and forcing her to tell me the truth. "Zeke and Xander aren't back yet."

Stepping closer, she bites her lip. "So we're alone?"

My traitorous cock throbs. I need to get out of this room before I end up with a part of me inside her. "I have to work."

I get up to walk out and she turns to the vanity. "You work too hard, West."

The way she says it snaps something in me. Before I even know what I'm doing, I'm standing right behind her. "Yes, I do work hard, Lily. I have busted my ass for every single fucking thing I have."

I sense that she's about to ask what the hell's gotten into me, but I don't give her the chance. "Come here." Wrapping my hand around her slender throat, I pull her back against my chest. Why shouldn't I take what I want from the lying little bitch? She should suffer the way she's made us suffer.

I yank her towel off with my free hand, and her breath hitches, causing her tits to jiggle. She eyes me in the mirror, her cheeks and chest flushed pink with arousal. Like anything about this is going to be about her. My hands fumble on my belt and zipper as the need to hate-fuck her surges through my veins.

She shivers, and I don't know if it's from fear or excitement. And I don't fucking care. Finally freeing my aching cock, I kick her legs apart, spreading her open for me. With a tight grip on her throat, I drive inside her. A gasp tumbles from her juicy pink lips, and her eyes shutter closed. She places her hands on the vanity for support as I rail into her. Blinded by my rage, I drive into her with punishing thrusts and try to rid myself of all the anguish coursing through me. I want to hurt her. Make her suffer. Make her weep. Fucking make her bleed.

Except that I don't. I can't.

I slow my pace, and she sags against me, a soft groan tumbling from her lips. I run my nose over her neck and inhale her sweet scent. My cock pulses, and the desire to make her moan my name while I fill her with my cum consumes me. She has some kind of fucking hold on me that I can't seem to break. I slide my free hand between her thighs and swirl my fingertips over her swollen clit.

"West," she rasps. "I love you."

My heart cracks open. *Fucking liar.* I rock my hips, driving deeper into her tight, hot cunt. "Why did you have to be so fucking perfect for us?" My instincts take over, and I get lost in the feel of her in my arms.

She's too busy soaking me with her release and squeezing me like she'll never let me go to answer. *Fucking liar.* As soon as the last drop of cum drips out of me, I pull out and zip up my pants, but her hand on my arm stops me before I can walk out. "Are you sleeping in here tonight?" She looks at me with eyes full of the emotion she just spoke of, and the pieces of my heart tremble, desperate to be pieced back together. If only the one person who held those pieces hadn't turned out to be an illusion.

"I can't. Too much to do before tomorrow."

The look of disappointment that settles over her face appears so real that I almost buy it. "Well, I'm really looking forward to the launch." She expertly trades her dejected expression for one of pride. "It's so huge for you guys. It's huge for the magazine."

"Yeah. Huge. Get some sleep."

FORTY-ONE

LILY

I slick on a final coat of lipstick and check my reflection in the mirror. Smiling to myself, I smooth my hands over the fabric of the same red dress I wore the night I met the guys at Marché de Viande. It seemed only fitting to wear it tonight. Like we've come full circle. I guess we have.

Butterflies swirl in my stomach. Establishing Hellsgate Media is akin to conquering the world, and I'm so proud of them. And if I'm honest, the shy high school nerd with braces is also excited beyond belief to be their guest for the evening.

And after tonight, I will put on my big girl pants and initiate a conversation about our *arrangement*. Our three months will be up in a few days, and I don't want it to end. I don't think that they do either. While it's outside the norm to have my heart stolen by not one man but three, our relationship feels so effortlessly right. Except they didn't steal it, did they? I gave it willingly.

Chewing on the inside of my cheek, I wonder how the hell I got so lucky? West, Zeke, and Xander are any woman's dream,

226

and having the love of all three of them feels like I've somehow cheated at life and come out the victor.

I grab my purse and head for the elevator. A car is waiting for me downstairs, and the guys are waiting for me at the club. Without warning, anxiety churns in my gut, and I fight to swallow it down. Everything will be fine. So what if every single person in the media world is going to be there tonight? It doesn't matter if rumors fly about my article being published because I'm dating West Archer because I know the truth.

The truth.

It sits like a lead weight in the pit of my stomach. Maybe I can tell the guys that I don't feel well and spend the night curled up in bed watching trashy TV instead. I could wait for them to come home and celebrate with them then.

I shake my head. No. I must go. And then tomorrow, before I ask them if I can stay, if we can make our arrangement permanent, I will tell them who I really am. Even if it means losing them.

All I can do is hope that they have it in them to love Liliana Constantine as much as they love Lily Sloane.

RAIN HAMMERS the roof of the limo roof as it pulls up outside the nightclub. The ride was short but lonely, and I can't help but think of how the four of us could have put this spacious interior to good use. There's always the ride home. A thrill of excitement shoots through me, and I smooth the fabric of my dress over my hips and peer out the window at the crowd gathered outside.

Everyone who's anyone in the world of media is here tonight, many of them still awaiting entry under the shelter of their umbrellas. I spot Julian standing near the entrance with some of the writers from *Genevieve*, as well as Handsy Andy, the

PR guy. Ugh! Ignoring him, I grin and wave frantically at Julian, but of course he doesn't see me because of the tinted windows.

Excitement and anticipation swirl in my stomach, and I wish the guys were with me so I wouldn't feel so self-conscious about stepping out of this limo on my own. *Take a deep breath, Lily.* They'll be there when I get inside.

I've never been interested in being the center of attention, and in recent years I've shied away from any kind of limelight at all, but tonight feels different. I'm proud of what Xander, West, and Zeke are doing. I'm honored to stand by their side and beyond freaking blown away by the fact that I get to go home with all three of them at the end of the night.

The car rolls to a stop, and the door is pulled open a few seconds later. Driving rain lashes my face when I step outside. I was hoping the driver would offer me an umbrella, but I should have thought to bring one for myself like all the people in line did.

The red carpet squelches beneath my heels, and a scowling bouncer steps in front of me as I reach the doors. "It's a private event, Miss."

"I know. That's what I'm here for. I'm on the list, name's Lily Sloane." I go to walk past him, but he bars my way.

"You don't get in without a ticket. I'm sorry."

"What?" I gape at him, then peer over his shoulder, hoping for a glimpse of one of the guys. Surely they're here by now.

"You're blocking the entrance. Please move."

I blink away the torrent of rainwater that runs into my eyes. "I'm with the owners. West and Ezekiel. Xander? They're expecting me."

"I wasn't told about you, miss." He shrugs. "Now please move."

"Please. Just ask inside. They're expecting me."

He rolls his eyes like his patience is growing thinner by the second, but guess what, buddy, so is mine. I'm soaked and my hair and makeup are ruined. He roughly grabs hold of my arm and jostles me. "You need to leave."

"Take your goddamn hands off me," I snap, wrenching from his grip. "You'd better go get one of your bosses out here right now."

Another bouncer, burlier than the first, approaches, and I realize we're creating a scene. The people in the lines, including my would-be colleagues from *Genevieve*, are murmuring and staring at me like I'm a circus act. "What's the problem here?" the second bouncer asks.

"She says she's with Mr. Archer and the owners."

The burly one looks me over from head to toe and shakes his head. "News to me."

"Are you freaking kidding me?" I shout. "Just go get one of them. If they find out you left me to stand out here in the goddamn rain, heads will roll."

They exchange a wary look, and the original bouncer must think there's some truth to my words because he goes inside the club. I turn back to the street to see if the car's still there so I can take some shelter from the driving rain, but it's already gone. Folding my arms over my chest, I shiver and wait. A few seconds later, my heart soars when I see Zeke step outside with the bouncer by his side.

"She says she's with you, Boss." The one next to Zeke points at me.

The other bouncer stops me when I bound forward, yelling Zeke's name.

He studies me but shows no sign of recognition. His face is completely blank, like he's faced with a stranger. Then he shakes his head. "Nope. Not with me."

Is this some kind of joke? I frown at him. "Zeke?"

He takes a step closer. I smell his distinctive cologne, the

229

one I find so comforting when he has his giant arms wrapped around me. Instinctively, I edge forward, seeking his reassurance and warmth. My teeth are chattering from being cold and soaked to the bone. But his face twists in an angry scowl when he says, "Go home. You don't belong here."

My head swims with confusion and fear. What is this? Did he discover the truth about me? In desperation, I lunge for him and grab his hand, but he shrugs me off. He gives me a look filled with such revulsion, and I feel it like a punch to the solar plexus. It's like my touch disgusts him. Like I mean nothing to him and never meant anything at all. As though those hands that know me so intimately are strangers to me.

Tears merge with rain and drip from my face as my heart is torn from my chest, leaving behind a gaping hole. It shatters into a million tiny fragments at his feet and leaves me gasping. "Zeke, please?" I hate the desperation in my tone, hate myself for pleading with him in front of all these people while he pretends that I don't exist. But I'm so confused. I don't know what else to do.

He dips his head, bringing his face close enough for me to hear his spiteful voice and see the fiery rage dancing in his eyes. "You are a lying, cheating whore, Lily. Nobody wants you here." He blinks and the fire is extinguished, leaving a void so dark and empty that I'm afraid I will fall inside and be lost forever.

I dimly register him speaking to the bouncers. "Put her in a cab and get her the fuck out of here." Without another word to me, he strides back inside the club.

The bouncer is looking at me differently now. His eyes are full of pity, and I can't stand it. He signals a cab and guides me to it. I can hear whispers and not-so-muffled conversations about how embarrassed I must feel and what a disgrace I am, but it all washes over me. I'm practically numb when I climb into the cab, shivering from both the cold and the shock.

When the driver asks where I'm going, I give him Jen's address. I need to go somewhere that someone won't pretend I don't exist. What the hell just happened? Did they learn my identity, and if so, why did he still call me Lily? If they would just let me explain ...

Fumbling with my purse, I pull out my cell phone and check for a message from Xander or West telling me that Zeke has lost his mind and I'm not to listen to anything that comes out of his mouth. There's nothing since the last text from West instructing me to meet them at the club.

I dial his number, and it goes to voicemail. So does Xander's. I even try Zeke's. After leaving three equally incoherent voice messages, I grip my phone with both hands and wait for one of them to call me back.

FORTY-TWO

XANDER

"Jesus fucking Christ." I suck in a deep breath to cool the burning in my lungs, but it doesn't help. I listen to her voicemail again, and just like all the other times, a fresh welt is sliced across my heart. She's barely coherent over the sound of her teeth chattering and her sobs. I imagine her freezing and shivering in the back of a cab in her soaking wet dress, wondering what the fuck happened. We should have talked to her. I should have stopped them ...

"Stop fucking torturing yourself, Fitch," Zeke barks as he takes a fresh bottle of water from the fridge.

He's right, listening to this on repeat is fucking torture. I would rather stick needles in my goddamn ears than hear her cry like that again. The raw pain in her voice makes me want to throw up. Nobody is that good of an actress. "We fucked up. We never should have done that." I sink to the floor, my head in my hands.

West sighs. "She lied to us, Xander. What the fuck were we supposed to do?"

"We could have fucking talked to her like normal fucking human beings," I shout. "What if this is all some big fucking misunderstanding? What if there's an explanation for all of this that doesn't involve the woman we love, who has shown us nothing but love and kindness, royally fucking us over?"

"Why would we talk to her, Xander?" West shouts back. "She had plenty of fucking chances to come clean about whatever the fuck she's been hiding, and she didn't. She lied to our fucking faces that day she met Nico Constantine in his hotel room. So we just let her lie to us some more? Get some juicy sound bites for her article?"

"Fuck that," Zeke growls.

I glare at them, rage at the injustice of the situation simmering in my veins. I watched Zeke earlier. I saw the pain on her face when he destroyed her in front of all those people. And West held me back from going to her. "You didn't have to be so fucking cruel, Zeke," I yell. "You didn't have to fucking eviscerate her in public like that."

He crouches down, his face twisted with anger. "No? You think she's not going to fucking eviscerate us when her article comes out in two days?"

I press my lips together before I say something that I can never take back. I love him and I always will, but he's the cruelest person I've ever known when he thinks he's been wronged. He stares at me, and I try to forgive him. And I almost do after I see the pain in his eyes and consider his deep-seated fear of betrayal. But I can't. Not yet, anyway.

I jump up from the floor and head to her bedroom. Being surrounded by her things is gonna hurt like a motherfucker, but I need to feel it. I need to feel something that has to do with her, even if it's only pain.

"Fitch!" Zeke calls after me, but in a resigned tone, West tells him to leave me be.

Yeah, leave me be, you heartless fucking bastards.

CHAPTER
FORTY-THREE

LILY

"Drink this, honey." Jen hands me a mug of chamomile tea, and I wrap my hands around it so that the heat I usually find soothing warms my palms. But nothing is soothing to me right now. Everything is sharp and jagged and painful. Even breathing hurts.

She climbs onto the bed and wraps her arms around me. My head throbs from the constant crying and lack of sleep, and I sniff as another fat tear rolls down my cheek.

Jen squeezes me tighter, concern radiating from her. I literally fell into her arms last night when I got here, a drenched sobbing mess. It was a full ten minutes before I could even talk enough to tell her what happened.

I glance at my phone again, pathetically hoping for a text or a call to tell me this has all been some awful mistake, but it remains conspicuously silent.

"What am I gonna do, Jen?" I suck in a shuddering breath that makes my heart physically ache.

"*We* are going to go over there and demand they speak to you and tell you what the fuck is going on."

"No." I shake my head and wipe my dripping nose. "If they won't answer my calls, they're not going to let me into their building."

"The fuck they won't. I'll call the cops if I have to."

"And say what? That they're heartless bags of donkey shit? I don't think that's an actual crime."

"No. I'll tell them they have all your stuff."

I throw my arm over my face and groan. "My stuff. I need it back. Especially my laptop."

"Then we'll go over there. I'll borrow my dad's car."

Another sob bursts out of me, and I cling to her. "I don't want to. Can't I stay here?"

She gives me an apologetic smile. "If you send me by myself and I see one of those selfish dickwads, I'll probably scratch his eyes out, so it's probably best if you come to keep an eye on me. Besides, you deserve to know what the fuck their deal is. And we won't leave until we have answers."

"Maybe our time was just up?" But I don't believe that for a second. If that was the case, why not just tell me? I would've been crushed, but still … To humiliate me like that in front of my peers and people I hoped to work with one day was beyond cruel. It doesn't gel with the men I know at all. Maybe I didn't know them. Maybe the men I thought I knew have simply mastered the art of conning women they want to fuck, and they have zero qualms about tossing those women aside when they're done with them.

Of course, there's a strong chance that they found out the truth about who I really am. It's the only logical explanation for the way they treated me. But fear of what that could mean for me is too paralyzing, the consequences too dire to consider. If they do know and they confront him ... No. I can't face the choices I'll have to make if that happens, not on top of losing them. Not right now.

Despite my resolution not to consider it, my mind races, and another huge sob bursts out of me. I'll have to leave New York. Jen. My job. My dreams.

"Finish your tea and then have a nice hot shower. I'll call my dad and tell him I need the car."

"Okay," I mumble, too exhausted to argue.

~

JEN TURNS off the engine of her dad's SUV and unclips her seatbelt, but I place my hand on her arm. "Wait here. I'll go on my own."

She frowns. "You sure?"

Nodding, I look out the window at the imposing building. I sent Xander a text to say that I was on my way over and needed my stuff. He read it but I didn't get a reply. Nausea churns my stomach, and I clamp my lips shut. If I see them, I need to be alone. Another tear rolls down my cheek, and I swat it away, furious with myself for all the crying. But I don't know how else to release the visceral pain that engulfs me. I know it's not scientifically possible, so why does it hurt like my heart is literally breaking inside my chest? Why does every single heartbeat feel like it's going to be my last?

"If you're sure. I'll be right here, honey. Call if you need me."

I nod again and climb out of the car. Dread thunders through my veins like it's the iron in my blood, and I can hardly breathe as I make my way to the entrance of their building. Foolishly, I still feel a tiny glimmer of hope that one of them will see me and realize what complete fuckwits they're being.

"Ms. Sloane." The doorman gives me a curt nod. "Your things are here for you." He opens the door to the building and indicates a small pile of neatly stacked boxes along with my suitcase and backpack sitting in the lobby.

I sway on my feet and tears blur my vision, but I notice the stupid electric bike leaning on the wall. Is that supposed to be my parting gift—my consolation prize?

I swallow down a thick knot of emotion. "Where's my bike?"

"It's right there, miss."

I glare at the doorman. "No. *My* bike. The one I came here with."

He blinks at me, confused.

"Where is my goddamn bike?"

He shakes his head. "I'm sorry, ma'am, but I don't know what you're talking about."

I storm through the lobby toward the elevator, and he chases after me. "Miss, you can't go up there."

"I don't want to go up there. I want my goddamn bike back," I screech, wholly aware that I look and sound like I'm in the throes of a mental breakdown, but I don't care. I don't want their charity. I don't want anything from them. I never even want to see them again. "I just want Betty." I sink to the floor, drop my head between my knees, and sob.

I hear the faint buzzing of a phone and then the doorman's voice. "She says she wants her bike."

A fresh wave of anger and hurt washes over me. They're watching? Those sick fucks. Renewed by my fury, I stand and wipe the tears from my face, glaring at the doorman even though I know he's simply a pawn in whatever twisted game they're playing. "Her name is Betty."

"Betty?" the doorman says with a puzzled look on his face. A second later, he ends the call and flashes me a sympathetic smile. How many other women has he watched this happen to? "Your bike will be here in a moment. Would you like me to help you with your things?"

I haul my backpack onto my back, pick up a suitcase, and straighten my shoulders. "No, I don't need any help."

CHAPTER

FORTY-FOUR

WEST

Xander walks into the kitchen holding today's mail in his hand, and my heart sinks. Today's the day we discover the true depth of her betrayal.

"Is that it?" I nod at the advanced copy of the magazine that was FedExed here at my request.

His knuckles are white around the glossy pages. "Yeah," he rasps. "I almost opened it, but I ..." He shakes his head and runs his free hand through his hair.

Zeke steps up beside me, arms folded across his chest. "Open it, Fitch. Let's see what the hell she wrote about us," he says, his voice little more than a throaty growl.

Xander swallows, his eyes darting between mine and Zeke's.

"Do it," I bark, ready to get this over with. I can't assess exactly how much damage control will be needed until I see what she wrote, and I want to get a jump start on that before it hits the shelves tomorrow.

Xander's fingers tremble as he unfurls the pages and opens

the magazine. He scans the contents section, a frown pinching his dark brows together.

Zeke rocks on the balls of his feet. "You see it?"

Xander grunts and flicks through the pages, frantically searching for the evidence of Lily's betrayal.

My heart is in my fucking throat, blood thundering in my ears, and all I can do is wait. My fingers twitch with the effort of not tearing the magazine from Xander's hands. When his blue eyes widen and his skin turns whiter than snow, I'm forced to swallow the bile that burns my esophagus.

Zeke bristles.

"How bad is it?" I force out the words.

Xander's eyes remain fixed on the page, and his mouth opens but nothing comes out. A look of horror twists his features. What the fuck did she say about us?

"Fitch!" Zeke's harsh tone doesn't seem to penetrate Xander's haze. His knees buckle and he sinks to the floor. The pages of the magazine rustle loudly in his trembling grip, and Zeke snatches it away. Xander drops his head into his hands and lets out an anguished wail.

Concerned for him but needing to know what elicited such a reaction, I jerk my chin at Zeke. He holds up the offending article so we can both read it. The headline stands out in neon pink writing.

The True Horror of the New York City Puppy Trade

The words blur together, and I nearly join Xander on the floor. "What the fuck?" I whisper.

"Nothing ..." Xander groans, his voice muffled by his hands. "Not a single fucking word about us."

Blinking to clear my vision, I quickly scan the article, looking for any mention of us. Any justification at all for the way we treated her. But Xander's right. There's nothing.

My eyes drift to the bottom of the second page—by Lily Sloane.

My Lily. Our sweet, beautiful Lily.

What the fuck have we done?

FORTY-FIVE

XANDER

I blink at the double-page spread, torturing myself with the pictures of pitiful-looking mama dogs, surrounded by their litters and locked in flea-infested cages. This is what Lily was writing about. Of course it was never about us. Why the fuck would she write an exposé on us? She fucking loves us.

Well, she *loved* us. And we royally fucked it all to hell and back.

West has his head in his hands while Zeke paces up and down the kitchen.

"So she wasn't writing an article about us. She wasn't trying to fuck up our deal. But she *was* hiding something," West says. "Her connection to Nico Constantine. What the fuck is that about?"

Zeke stops pacing. "I'll look into it."

"Because you did such a stellar fucking job last time." I snort. The pain that's etched on his face makes me want to take it back, but I don't. They fucking caused this. I should have trusted my gut and forced them to speak to her.

"I didn't have enough time. I'll ..." He clears his throat. "I'll find out."

I shake my head. I don't have time for Zeke's guilt right now. I want our girl back, and I want her back today. "Your PI said she looked really happy before and after she met this guy, right? That's why he thought she was going to his room to get laid?"

Zeke frowns. "Yeah."

"So, he's obviously someone she cares about. I don't believe for a single fucking second that she was cheating on us. Where would she have found the time or energy? So he must be a relative. Brother, cousin, uncle?"

West hurries out of the room, muttering under his breath.

Zeke and I stare at each other for a few beats before we go after him. We find him in his office, firing up his computer.

"What is it?" I ask.

"I read something a few years back ..." He types on his keyboard, his eyes narrowed on the screen. "Constantine had two kids. Twins."

"Yeah, and?" Zeke replies.

"The daughter. I'm sure I read that she died."

"What does that have to do with Lily?" I ask.

He doesn't answer. Both Zeke and I stand behind him as he searches for whatever answers he's looking for. He clicks on an old newspaper article and brings up a picture of eighteen-year-old Liliana Constantine. Her hair is straight and only shoulder-length, plus she has braces on her teeth. She's certainly filled out over the years, but there's no mistaking our girl. Jesus fuck, shorty.

"You think he faked his daughter's death?" Taking a closer look at the screen, I scan the article for any clues as to why she kept this from us.

West sits back and runs his hands through his hair. "Knowing that twisted fuck, I'd bet she faked her own."

"So Nico Constantine is her twin?" Zeke asks.

I stare at a second picture of her and her brother. She has a fucking twin, and she never mentioned him to us. She must really hate him. Or she adores him and is trying to protect him. I can't imagine our girl hating anyone, not even us, despite how much we deserve it. "It would make sense that she lied to protect him."

"This is so fucked up." Zeke paces the length of West's office. "She's a fucking Constantine. I should have done my due diligence. I should have dug deeper, but everything she first told us checked out. Everything! She was some broke girl from Brooklyn, not a Mafia princess and an heiress to the biggest goddamn hotel chain in America."

I shake my head. "Lily's not an heiress though, is she? Liliana Constantine is, and she's fucking dead." If only our girl were here, we could get some answers. "You think she had any idea about what her father did to us all those years ago?"

West leans back in his chair and sighs. "I have no fucking clue what to think anymore."

FORTY-SIX

LILY

Betty creaks loudly as I stop at the light, and I can't say I blame her. How quickly did I discard her when something newer and shinier came along? I now know first-hand how much that stings. I've decided that's the most reasonable explanation for what happened with the Unholy Trinity. I'm still breathing, so they can't know who I really am.

"I'm sorry, girl." I pat her handlebars and sniff back tears. "You know I love you."

A black SUV comes to a stop beside me, the back window rolled down. "Lily."

My heart jolts like I've just been hit with a defibrillator. I stare straight ahead, refusing to give him the satisfaction of acknowledging his presence.

"Lily," West says again. "Can you please get in the car?"

To my relief, the traffic light changes and I pedal forward, but my damn knees shake, making it more difficult than it should be.

"Please, shorty?"

I ignore Xander too, but the car continues driving alongside me. Tears swim in my eyes, blurring my vision and making me wobble.

"For the love of god, can you get in the damn car so we can talk to you?" Zeke shouts.

I pull on my brakes and come to a halt, causing the cyclist a few feet behind me to curse as they swerve around me. Their car stops too, and horns blare in protest. Turning, I glare at them and fervently wish for them to burst into flames. "Fuck you." I flip them the bird too, just to make sure they get the message.

The car door is thrown open, and Zeke jumps out. Shit-eating bastard. He reaches for Betty's handlebars, but before he can touch me or my bike, I punch him in the jaw. He staggers back, his lip split open and bleeding. Whoops, didn't intend to do that. I mean he deserved it, but still.

His eyes narrow, and I push aside my guilt and give him a triumphant smile. "Crawl back to your limo and leave me the hell alone."

He wipes the blood from his lip with his thumb and his tongue darts out to lick away the rest. An unwelcome memory of his mouth doing unspeakable things to me makes me sway, but I think I manage to steady myself before he notices. I expect him to start raging at me, but his shoulders droop. "Lily. I know we don't deserve a second of your time, but please, get in the car and let us explain."

I swallow down the tears that threaten to burst out of me. Three days have passed, and the pain of what they did hasn't lessened at all. I deserve answers, and I don't care if they think they've won if I get into this car. I need to close the door on this part of my life, and I can't do that until I face the three of them. I hop off my bike and thrust her into Zeke's hands. "Fine. You can give me a ride home."

They look both intimidating and kind of awkward all squished together on the bench seat when there's so much room in this car, but Xander moved from his spot when I climbed in, allowing space for Betty and me. And if one of them tried to sit near me now, I'd scratch his eyes out.

I clasp my hands together so they don't see them shaking. My legs tremble too, but I plant my feet on the car floor. It's little comfort that they all appear as nervous as I am. "So?"

West speaks first. "We're sorry."

I rear back like I've been slapped in the face. "Sorry? Fucking sorry. Oh, that makes everything okay then, doesn't it?"

"I'm not done," West says through gritted teeth.

"We're all so fucking sorry, shorty," Xander adds, his eyes pleading with me.

"I didn't get into this car for an apology." The pain of their betrayal burns in my chest, but I manage to keep my voice even. "The time for sorry has passed. I want an explanation. That's all I'm interested in." I cross my arms and legs and sit back. "I'm listening."

Silence fills the small space as they glance at one another, and I'm contemplating jumping out while the car's still moving when West finally speaks. "The article you were writing ..." He grimaces. "Somebody told us that you were writing an exposé on us."

A fucking what now? I clamp my lips together.

"It was an ex-girlfriend of ours. We should have known she had an ulterior motive," Xander adds.

The anger already simmering inside me threatens to boil over. *An ex-girlfriend. And they believed her?*

Xander runs a hand through his dirty blond hair. "We didn't believe her, shorty."

Zeke leans forward. "Not at first. But then, some of the things she said made us ..."

"Curious," West finishes for him when he can't seem to find the word.

Do they know the truth? Are they going to tell him I'm still alive? Sweat trickles down my back and my pulse spikes.

West clears his throat. "Then someone at the magazine confirmed it was true."

I glare at him. Who the hell told them that? Nobody except Julian even knew what my article was about.

"Come home with us and we'll talk about this properly, princess."

Princess? That word snaps my last shred of restraint. These arrogant, conceited assholes know nothing about me or who I really am, so at least there's that. I'm still safe here in New York. But they chose to believe some other woman, a woman they no doubt screwed over if their actions with me are any indication, rather than give me a chance to explain.

"I am not your fucking princess, West. I am not any of your fucking anything anymore. You all left me standing in the rain looking like—like a fucking lunatic!" Losing my composure, I screech the final few words. The mere memory of that night cuts like glass. I take a deep breath before continuing in a calmer tone. "You showed me who you really are that night. And you know what? I don't even care why you did it. I don't give one iota of a fuck why you didn't speak to me like grown-ups instead of blindly trusting whatever your ex told you about me—"

West cuts me off. "We didn't blindly—"

I hold up my hand. "Do *not* interrupt me when I gave you the courtesy of listening to what you had to say." A thick vein pulses in his temple, but he keeps his fat mouth shut. "I am done. There is *nothing* any of you can do to change what you did. Nothing you can say to alter the fact that you are three of the worst human beings I've had the displeasure of knowing.

And I don't give a monkey's fucking buttcrack about how much money you have or how powerful you are. I hate you. I hate what you turned me into. I hate that I shed a single tear over any of you." Gritting my teeth, I swipe the back of my hands over my cheeks and glare at them.

"Now leave me the hell alone and go ruin someone else's life." I press the button to speak to the driver. "Stop this car and let me the hell out. Now!"

"Lily?" Xander pleads.

His expression even more emotionless than usual, Zeke presses the button on his side of the car and gives the driver the go-ahead to stop and let me out.

"Fuck no. We aren't ending things like this." Xander reaches for me just as the car rolls to a stop, and I jerk away.

West puts a hand on Xander's thigh. "Let her go, Fitch." Then he gets out and opens the door for me. Tears stream down my face as I climb out, hauling my battered old bike out with me and wishing I could bring myself to hate them as much as they deserve.

FORTY-SEVEN

ZEKE

I bring the SUV to a stop outside the club where four of our bouncers are shuffling impatiently, wilting in the hot July sun. I roll my window down and signal them to jump in. They file into the back seats and exclaim their gratitude for the AC pumping through the vents. While Xander and I are more than capable of handling this ourselves, it doesn't hurt to have a little extra muscle in situations like these. They're more than happy to tag along, knowing they'll be well compensated for their time.

A half hour later, we arrive at the first of four puppy farms that Lily highlighted in her article. The other three are being paid a similar visit right now, but this is the biggest and most lucrative, which is why we're handling it ourselves.

The guy sitting in the small booth outside the steel gate adjusts his Celtics cap and scratches his thick red beard. "Can I help you?"

"We've come for some puppies." Xander grins.

The guard hesitates.

"Let us the fuck in," I say with a snarl.

He leans forward and eyes the men in the backseat, then looks back at me. "I can't."

Removing my seatbelt and grabbing his head in one fluid motion, I smash his face into the small console in the booth. "How about now?" Blood gushing from his nose, he fumbles with a series of buttons. A few seconds later, the gates open, and I tap the side of his face. "Good boy."

It doesn't take long to find the owner cowering in a corner. The guard must have called ahead. "I own these premises now, and this place is no longer in business," I tell him. When he just gapes at me, I snarl. "Do you understand me?"

He nods furiously. I motion for the bouncers to surround him, wishing I could have them beat the living shit out of him. But we don't want the cops sniffing around, so I let him go with nothing more than a slap to the head.

Before we left the apartment, I placed a call to the local shelter. We're longtime patrons of the charity that runs it, and Carly, the CEO, was more than happy to accept all the dogs we're relocating today. The puppies will find new homes quickly. The older ones are unlikely to be adopted, but they'll have a good life with Carly and her team, and our recent donation will fund the facility expansion necessary to accommodate today's influx and then some.

This is what Lily was doing all along. I swallow a thick knot of regret that hasn't left me since we discovered the severity of our fuckup. The one that bubbles into my throat every time I think about her. Every time I picture her face drenched with rain and tears.

My knees buckle, and I place my hand on the wall beside me to hold myself steady.

"Hey, Zeke. Look at this guy." Xander walks toward me with a big goofy grin on his face and an equally goofy slobbering ball of dark fur in his arms.

"No. Not happening." I shake my head. "We're not getting a fucking puppy, Fitch. Put it back."

"Aw, but he's so cute," he says, and the damn thing licks his nose. "Anyway, he's not for me. Meet Snowflake." The pup yawns and lets out a sound that can only be compared to a Wookie howl as Xander waves his paw at me.

My lip twitches—even I have to admit the stupid dog is adorable—but I roll my eyes. "You think a dog is going to fix what we did?"

"Not entirely." His grin is replaced with a look of anguish. If I were a better man, I would have let him keep his fantasy a little longer, but nobody would accuse me of being a good man. Besides, the hope he found in this shithole would have been crushed eventually, and I'm of the belief that staying in reality hurts a whole lot fucking less than being bitch-slapped by it. Loving and losing Lily taught me that. She took the tiny bit of goodness and optimism I had with her. "But it's a start, right?" Somehow, despite his own heartache, Xander still has both qualities in abundance.

Exasperated, I shake my head. "Just go make sure everything's taken care of back there so we can get the fuck out of here."

He clutches the puppy tighter and mutters "Fine," before skulking off like a sullen teenager. I rub my right temple and look around the room. If only Lily had told us what she was working on. If we'd just fucking asked her. Goddamn it, we should have listened to Xander. He was the only one willing to believe the best of her. That infuriating goodness and optimism is what allowed him to see the fucking truth of her—she's the

SADIE KINCAID

best person the three of us have ever known, and we ruined
ourselves when we ruined things with her.

I thought the cages in this room were empty, but a movement in the far corner catches my eye. Not wanting to spook
whatever is in there, I approach slowly and crouch down in
front of the steel frame. A big black Rottweiler glances up at me,
her massive body filling the small space. She's lying on her side
and barely acknowledges my presence, but the defeated look in
her eyes kills me. She looks like she's just waiting for death to
come.

"I know that feeling, girl," I say quietly. Her ears twitch, but
she doesn't move. The door creaks when I carefully open the
door, but the dog still doesn't move. I reach inside and lightly
run my fingertip across the top of her head. When she offers no
resistance, I scratch behind her ear and a deep sigh leaves her
body. Then she tilts her head, pushing it against my hand, and I
chuckle. "You like that, huh?"

"She's probably had at least fifty puppies in this place,"
Xander says as he crouches beside me. I'm pleased to see that
he's no longer holding the furball. The Rottweiler sits up and
gives a soft woof. "They take them away from their moms too
early, you know. And the mamas fret for their babies."

Her soulful brown eyes glisten like she understands what
we're saying. "Is that true, girl? Do you miss your family?"

She cocks her head to the side, and Xander chuckles. "She
likes you."

I tilt my head too, studying her as she watches us both.
People have way too much fucking power over animals. "You
want to come home with us?" She gives me a full bark this time.

Grinning, Xander nudges my arm. "What are we gonna call
her?"

"She kinda looks like a Stella to me."

254

"Stella?" He snorts a laugh, but she barks again and her stumpy tail wags once.

I give Xander a smug look. "Well, *she* likes it."

Stella steps out of the crate and turns so she's leaning against both of us. And just like that, we have ourselves a dog.

FORTY-EIGHT

LILY

I thank the server for my coffee before turning my attention back to the man across from me.

"Thanks for agreeing to meet with me, Lily," Julian says, smiling.

I eye him suspiciously. Was he the one who lied about my article? I have no idea who I can trust any more. I mean he did ask to meet me for coffee to discuss whatever it is he has in mind rather than inviting me to his office, which I appreciate. I don't think I could handle walking past all those people who witnessed my public humiliation. "Can I ask you about something?"

He takes a quick sip of his coffee and then nods. "Sure."

"Did West Archer, or anyone, ask you about my puppy farm article?"

He frowns. "He did come to see me, actually."

"And?"

"I told him to go to hell. He might own the magazine, but as long as I'm the editor, he can read the exclusive scoops along with everyone else."

I'm filled with relief knowing that my instinct to trust him was spot-on.

"But he wasn't the only one interested in that article," he adds.

I lean forward. "No? Who else?"

"Andy asked about it, which isn't that unusual given that he's the PR manager. Or at least he was."

"Was?"

"He left yesterday. No explanation. No notice and no job to go to as far as I'm aware. I told him he won't be getting this month's salary if he didn't work his notice, but he quit anyway. I thought I'd never get Handsy Andy out of there, considering his mom is on the board."

I stare at him, open-mouthed. "You knew we called him that?"

He grins at me. "It's my magazine, Lily. I know everything."

"And was there anyone else interested?"

"Yeah." His frown deepens. "Bree Reid cornered me in the coffee shop by our building one morning. You know her, right? She owns the PR company we sometimes use."

I swallow hard. "Yeah, I know her. Why was she interested in my article? What did she say?"

"She just said she knew you from college. She'd heard you were writing something for me and asked what it was. I told her it was an exclusive and nobody but you or I would know the content until it went to print."

I know she doesn't like me, but why the hell would she care what I write about?

"You know she used to date West Archer too, right?"

No, I did not freaking know that. "She's the ex?" I mutter.

The fact that she's the person they believed over me stings even more.

"Huh?"

"Nothing." I gesture toward the menu, desperate for a subject change. "The waffles are delicious if you want some food."

"I already had breakfast, but ..." He licks his lips. "You want to split some?"

I wrinkle my nose. "I already had breakfast too."

"Come on," he urges.

I roll my eyes like it's a hardship to eat half a plate of delicious waffles. "Fine."

Julian goes to the counter and orders, then settles back in his chair. "So, I didn't just ask you here to talk about your jackass ex-boyfriend and eat waffles."

"That jackass is your boss," I remind him.

He shrugs. "He's still a jackass for the way he treated you."

My heart warms. There are good men in this world. A few, at least. "Thank you."

"And I hope that him owning the magazine won't affect your decision to take a job there. As features writer?"

Happy tears fill my eyes. This has been my dream for so long. "What?"

"I always knew you were a great writer, Lily, but your last article really proved it. You know how much feedback we've had about it? It's been huge. And did you hear that all the puppy farms you featured in your piece have been closed down?"

"What? No!" This is the best news. It makes me prouder than I ever dreamed possible to know that an article I wrote had that kind of impact.

"So. You want to start Monday?"

I swallow down a knot of emotion. Damn those three

assholes for ruining my life. I worked hard for this chance, and they shit all over it. "You know I can't, Julian."

He grimaces but doesn't look surprised. "You'll have nothing to do with him. He has no say in the running of *Genevieve*. I hate the prick for what he did to you, but he's actually been reasonable where the magazine is concerned. He won't interfere."

"It doesn't matter." I shake my head. "I can't work for Hellsgate Media. Ever."

"They own three-quarters of the market, Lily. You're cutting yourself out of a hell of a lot of opportunities."

I blink back tears. I know he's right.

He places his hand over mine, squeezing gently. "This is your dream."

He's right about that too, but ... "I can't, Julian. Nobody will ever let me forget what happened."

He scoffs. "Fuck 'em."

"Nobody will ever believe that I got the job on my own merit."

"You're wrong." He shakes his head. "Everyone at that magazine knows what a good writer you are, and that has fuck all to do with West Archer. You hold your head high and you rock that job like you were born for it. Because you were. And I know you are strong enough to not give a damn what anybody else thinks."

"Thank you for the amazing opportunity, Julian, but I can't."

The hope in his eyes disappears, and he sits back with a sigh. "I knew you were going to say that."

Before he can try and persuade me further, our waffles arrive, distracting him with their sugary goodness.

I TRUDGE down the hallway toward Jen's apartment, my heart heavy at having to turn down my dream job. But I will never work for any of those men. I can't believe how a three-month relationship managed to fuck up my life so royally.

I'm too busy plotting extravagant ways to get my revenge, plans I will never put into action, to notice the man standing outside the apartment until I'm practically on top of him. It's the wriggling black and tan ball he's cradling in his arms that steals most of my attention though. Despite my crappy morning, I smile. Who can resist a puppy? Especially one as cute as this one, with its nubby tail wagging and tongue hanging out.

"Well, aren't you adorable?" I coo, giving the pup a scratch on the head.

"Lily Sloane?"

I tilt my head. "Yeah?"

"Thank god," he huffs, then dumps the puppy in my arms. "This is for you."

The bundle of fur licks my face. "What?"

"Need you to sign here." He holds out a pen and clipboard, like my hands aren't full of baby Rottweiler.

"No. There's been some mistake. I didn't order a puppy." I hold the squirming dog away from my body, trying to hand it back.

"No mistake. I definitely have the right name and address." He shakes the pen and clipboard at me.

"I am not signing that. You need to take him back." The puppy licks my face again, and I sputter.

The delivery guy groans. "You folks make my job so fucking difficult." With that, he turns and walks away.

"Hey!" I shout after him. "I'm a delivery person too." Why I feel the need to explain myself to a complete stranger, I have no idea. "But you can't leave me with this dog."

Ignoring me, he leaves me alone with the incredibly inconvenient, if utterly adorable, animal.

I fumble in my pocket for my keys. Why doesn't he have a collar and a leash? At least then I could put him on the floor without fear of him bolting.

"Where the hell did you even come from?" Finally getting the door open, I stumble into the apartment and put the dog on the floor. He scampers off in the direction of Jen's bedroom, and I curse under my breath. Pacing up and down the tiny apartment, I go on muttering every curse word I can think of while rubbing my sweaty palms on my jeans. What the heck am I going to do? Pets aren't allowed in the building, but even if they were, I can barely take care of myself right now. Who would be stupid enough to send me a pup—

I am going to kill him.

Xander goddamn King is the only person who knows that I've always wanted a Rottweiler. Is this his idea of a fucking joke? I stomp my foot on the floor and scream at the top of my lungs.

The pup comes running out of Jen's room, tripping over his too-big feet. Righting himself from his tumble, he cocks his head and stares at me like I've lost my mind. Maybe I have.

I drop to my knees, and he prances over and burrows his giant puppy head into my neck. "I'm sorry, boy." I quickly lift his paws and check his parts, confirming that he is indeed a boy. "You're so adorable, and if I had a house with a yard and the money to feed and care for you, I would keep you in a heartbeat."

His little nub wiggles back and forth, and he stares up at me with his bottomless brown eyes. How can anyone ever be cruel to such amazing animals? I really do wish I could keep him. Way to break my heart all over again, Xander.

Asshole.

CHAPTER
FORTY-NINE

XANDER

"I'll need the figures from the last twelve months, Kristin," I tell the new PR manager for *Genevieve* magazine. She's already better than the last one. We should have strung him up by his balls and left him for the rats after he lied to us about Lily. I had to physically stop Zeke from doing exactly that, but we can't go around killing our own employees. That would be bad for business.

I'm on the phone with Kristin, listening to her run through our new marketing strategy when my door bursts open and slams into the wall with such force that the window behind me rattles in its frame.

"I'll call you back." I end the call and give Lily my undivided attention.

"Are you out of your goddamn mind?" she shrieks.

Well, that wasn't what I expected, but now that she mentions it ... I am out of my mind. Out of my mind wondering what she's doing without me every second of every fucking day. I'm still trying to figure out how to respond when she gestures wildly, and I bite back a laugh at the makeshift leash in her hands.

"Is this some kind of sick joke? Sending me a goddamn puppy?"

The puppy flops onto his butt and grins at me, his tongue hanging out of his mouth, and I can't help but grin back.

"Xander!"

"What? I saw him and he sounded exactly like the dog you said you'd always wanted. So I got him for you."

She plants her hands on my desk, her body shaking with rage. Her perfect juicy tits strain against her T-shirt with each heaving breath. "Don't pretend like you did this to be sweet."

I frown. "I thought you'd like him."

"There is no way in hell that you're so far removed from the real world up here in your ivory tower that you didn't realize that having a puppy costs money. A lot of money. Money I don't freaking have." She tosses the leash at me. "How the hell do I keep a puppy when I don't even have a goddamn apartment, Xander?"

I rub a hand over my jaw. "I didn't think—"

"Yes, you did think." She sneers. "You wanted to show me something else that I couldn't have. Is that it? Twist the knife a little more?"

"Lily, please." The fact she could believe me to be so cruel cuts me to the bone.

"And then I had to spend forty bucks that I couldn't afford on a cab so I could bring him back to you."

I didn't think of that either. "I swear—"

"I don't want to hear it. Just leave me the hell alone, Xander."

She spins around and marches toward the door, but before she walks out, she turns and fixes me with her fiercest glare, pointing a finger in my direction. "And if anything bad happens to this dog, if you don't find him a true loving home where he'll be cared for every day of his life, I'll report you to the police, the humane society, the FBI, the CIA, Congress, NASA, and any other organization I can think of." Her pretty face incandescent with rage, she storms out of my office.

"Well, that definitely didn't go to plan, Snowflake."

He lifts his leg and pisses on my desk. Yep, that's exactly what I deserve.

A second later, West walks in. "Was that—?"

"Yep."

"What the fuck happened?"

I look down at Snowflake. "I sent her a dog."

Irritation darkens his handsome features. "Jesus Christ, Xander. What the fuck were you thinking?"

My body shakes with pent-up rage. "Don't you *Jesus Christ* me, West. At least I fucking tried *something*, asshole. What the fuck have you done? This is all your goddamn fault anyway. You and Zeke believed that fuckbucket, Bree. You wouldn't listen to me when I told you we should just sit down and talk to Lily like normal fucking people would. You and Zeke treat me like I'm a fucking child, but I was the only one of us who wanted to act like a man, and I was stupid enough to let you talk me out of it. I was stupid enough to—fuck!" The last word is ripped from my chest. Closing my eyes, I take several deep breaths. "We lost her, West. We fucking lost her."

West drops his head to his chest and sighs. "I know, Fitch," he says, his voice full of despair. I hate that I blame him. The truth is that I could have spoken to Lily myself. I'm a grown-ass fucking man.

Snowflake rubs his head against my leg, and I smile down at him. "I know I shouldn't have sent her the puppy. I wasn't thinking straight. I hoped he would be a cute surprise and didn't stop to consider it."

He stares at the adorable bundle of black and tan fur at my feet and arches an eyebrow. "Is that leash made from—"

"Panty hose? Yeah." Reaching down, I untie them from the dog's neck and wrap them around my fist, then lift my hand to my face and inhale, desperate for her scent.

They smell of dog and laundry detergent, but I hold onto them anyway.

"Um, Lily doesn't wear panty hose. Those are probably Jen's."

"Ugh!" I fling them away, and West laughs. I have no idea how he can laugh when I'm as miserable as Scrooge before the ghosts' visits.

I rest my forehead on my desk, and a second later, I feel West's fingers running through my hair. "We'll get her back, Fitch. I'll fix it. I promise." I wish I shared his optimism. "What are you doing with the pup?"

"His name is Snowflake." I sit up and lift him into my lap.

"Xander, no. We already have one dog."

I shrug. "Now we have two."

FIFTY

WEST

I wait for the man in front of me to get his latte, then join him at his table when he sits down.

He frowns at me, his eyes darting around the nearly empty coffee shop. "Uh, can I help you?"

"Every day for the past two weeks, I've had a package sent to my office at XWZ buildings."

He shrugs. "Yeah, so?"

"And every day, someone other than Lily Sloane delivers it. Can you tell me why that is?"

He bristles. "You get your parcel on time, right? What's your problem?"

"You see ..." I run a hand over my jaw. "I don't give a fuck about the parcel. I want Lily to deliver it."

"You think that's likely to happen now, you sicko?"

"I admire you for protecting her, Craig. I want to protect her too." I lean forward and lower my voice like I'm letting him in on a secret. "You see, Lily is my girl, and I need her to deliver all of my packages from here on out."

"And just who the fuck are you?"

"West Archer." The corners of my lips curve upward. "You've heard of me, yeah?"

He rolls his eyes. Everyone in this city knows my name. "What the hell do you want with a sweet young kid like Lily?"

I glare at him. She's *not* a kid. "Have her deliver all my packages, Craig."

"Not a chance, you sick fuck."

Closing my eyes, I take a deep breath and then level him with a look. "I assure you that she is in no danger where I'm concerned. I just want to check in with her."

He snorts.

Looks like I need to play dirty. "And if you don't want me to check in with my friends at the IRS and tell them about all the deliveries you do off the books"—I pause and watch the blood drain from his face—"you'll have Lily deliver my packages. Am I making myself clear?"

He looks away, his teeth grinding together, but he eventually nods.

"I'm gonna need you to use your words, Craig."

"Yes," he spits.

"Good boy." There's a smile on my face as I leave the coffee shop. All I need is to spend some time with her and make her see how sorry we all are. How much we miss her. I can fix all of this, I know I can. If I can just get her to listen to me.

CHAPTER
FIFTY-ONE

LILY

I read through my route for the day, and my stomach drops when I see the location of the last delivery on the list. "Craig, there's one here for the XWZ building." I've only worked here for two weeks, but I like this job. He's a good boss who didn't ask any awkward questions about why I left my previous one.

"Sorry, kid. Got no one else to do it. You'll have to take this one."

I look around at everyone filling their backpacks. Surely one of them can swap with me. "But Craig, we agreed. Can't someone else do it?"

He sighs. "I told you I got no one else."

Tears prick at my eyes, and he frowns. "What's your deal with that place, anyway? You in some kind of trouble or something?"

I shake my head. "No, nothing like that. It's ... Please, Craig. I'm begging you." It wouldn't be so bad if it were just the building, but the delivery is for the devil himself. He's had packages sent to his office every day since I started here, and until now, Craig has been cool with my flat-out refusal to take them.

"Deliver the package." He turns toward his office.

"I can't."

He doesn't stop but calls over his shoulder, "Then you'll be looking for another job, kid, and it would be a damn shame to lose you."

∾

"Can you please just sign it?" I give the security guard my biggest, sweetest smile. "Please? It only needs a signature. It doesn't have to be Mr. West's," I lie.

"I can't help you, ma'am. More than my job's worth," he says with a grim shake of his head.

Goddamn you to hell, West Archer! Grumbling under my breath, I haul Betty to the elevator. Her busted wheel makes a strange squeaking noise with every rotation. I was so distracted by the thought of coming here today that I crashed into a post and fell into a muddy puddle, scraping my cheek on the pavement. I ignore the gawking faces of the employees I pass. I don't give a tiny rat's ass what they think of me or that I have mud and mascara streaks on my face. They can all go straight to hell alongside their three megalomaniac bosses.

By the time I get to the top floor, my emotions are about ready to boil over. Rage bubbles in my stomach, threatening to burst through my chest at any moment, but it's tangled up among all my other emotions. The most pervasive being shame. I'm ashamed that I was such a damn fool. That I believed three of the most powerful men in the country could want me for more than just a little fun and that I allowed them to turn me into a crying, trembling mess almost every hour of every day. But riding shotgun with my anger and mortification is overwhelming misery. It's not enough that these men humiliated and betrayed me, now they feel the need to continue making my life a goddamn misery. And for what? Their own twisted amusement?

The elevator doors ping open, and I stumble forward, pushing my broken bike out with me. I scan the empty hallway, my heart racing at the recollection of the last time I was here. I came to visit West and Xander at work, and I distinctly remember feeling like the luckiest girl in the whole goddamn world. Hindsight can be a sick son of a bitch.

Then I see him. His huge frame fills the hallway as he saunters toward me, a smile on his arrogant, entitled face. But then he sees my busted bike, my torn jeans, and his smile falters. "Lily?" He picks up his pace until he's practically jogging down the hallway toward me. No doubt he'll make himself feel all self-righteous with his show of concern.

I throw the parcel at him, and he catches it with ease, his brow furrowed. I stumble back from him. Screw the signature. I don't care. I don't fucking care.

"Lily," he says again. "Are you hurt?"

"Screw you, West. Yes, I'm fucking hurt." My words echo down the empty hall. "You nearly cost me my job today with your bullshit." Tears drip from my eyes, and I swat them away with the back of my hand. I hate that he's seeing me cry, but I'm done with trying to hide what a complete mess their little power games have turned me into. "I get that a few hundred bucks a week means nothing to you, but this is the only goddamn job I have. So the next time you think it will be fun to drag the poor stupid bitch you and your friends messed with over here just so you can admire your handiwork, do me a favor. Remember that this might be a game to you, but it is my fucking *life,* you entitled, conceited, entitled, self-obsessed, entitled prick!"

Spinning around, I drag my bike with me, but the stupid wheel grinds to a halt, refusing to move any further.

"Piece of shit!" I kick it over, and it hits the floor with a metallic crash. Tears blurring my vision, I stomp toward the elevator, vaguely aware of West calling my name again. He's probably trying to tell me to take my piece of crap bike with me, but I ignore him. This is the last time I will allow him or his two psycho friends to get to me—the last fucking time.

CHAPTER

FIFTY-TWO

ZEKE

"Thank fuck you're home. Where the hell have you been?" Xander asks, his brow furrowed.

Same place I always am lately, but he doesn't need to know that. "What's up?" Shrugging off my coat, I scan the entryway. Why haven't the dogs come to greet me? "Where's West?"

"In his office. I've never seen him like this, Z." I follow him down the hallway to West's office. We stop outside the closed door, and Xander lowers his voice. "Something happened today." He scrubs a hand through his thick hair. "With Lily. He started drinking as soon as he got home." He shoots me a worried look. "Whatever happened, it was bad. He's had almost an entire bottle of Scotch."

I push the door open. He's slumped over his desk, muttering incoherently to himself, the two dogs sitting at his feet. I give them both an appreciative pat on the head and pick up the almost empty bottle of fifty-year-old Macallan. "You couldn't drink yourself into a stupor with the cheap stuff? You had to take my twenty-five-thousand-dollar bottle of Scotch?"

He lifts his head, his red eyes swimming with tears. His tie hangs loose around his neck. "We broke her."

I perch on the corner of his desk. "I know."

"We fucking broke her, Zeke. We ruined her life." A heaving sob wracks his body.

I glance over at Xander who's gaping at the broken man before us. "He'll be fine," I assure him.

"No." West shakes his head. "I ... we fucking broke her ... and she was perfect. She was ..." His head drops back down on the desk.

I place my hand on the back of his neck and squeeze. "Then we'll fix her, West."

He sniffs loudly. "We can't."

"Z?" Xander says, his lip trembling.

"He'll be fine," I assure him again. "Help me get him to bed."

Together, Xander and I lift a grumbling, sobbing West up from the chair. Each taking one arm, we drag him out of his office to the nearest bedroom, which happens to be mine. He rambles incoherently the entire time and is still going when we lie him down on the bed.

Turning, I put my hand on Xander's shoulder and kiss his forehead. "Go get some sleep. I'll take care of him."

His blue eyes swim with tears. "I'll help."

"You know I'm good at taking care of people." Knowing I'm right, he gives me a faint smile. "Go get some sleep, baby. No point in both of us being awake all night."

He glances between me and West, who's now passed out.

"Go. Take care of the dogs."

Xander's head drops in defeat, and I wrap my arms around him, pressing his face into my neck. His tears scald my skin. "He said he'd fix it, Z."

Squeezing my eyes shut, I nod. "I know."

"What if he can't?"

I squeeze him tighter but don't respond. I don't do false promises.

After finally persuading Xander to go to bed, I strip West down to his boxers, then kick off my shoes and climb into bed next to him. Sitting up with my back against the headboard, I pull him into my arms, resting his head on my chest. He grumbles a drunken protest, but he's too wasted to offer any kind of resistance.

I brush his damp hair back from his head and cradle him in my arms. "Shut up, you drunk fucker."

His pathetic glare almost makes me laugh. Seconds later, he passes back out.

I've only ever seen him cry once before in my entire life, and that was when Xander almost died from appendicitis. We might have broken her, but she broke us too. We've been living in a void since she left. No, not living, existing. Barely. Every spare hour I have is spent on her. Looking into her past, checking in on her. I've become her stalker, obsessed with all things Lily.

That's how I knew she saw West today. I watched her leave our building, and she looked destroyed. Xander was working from home, so it could have only been West who put that look of torment on her face.

Maybe it's time I stop watching her from the shadows. Time for me to fix this. For her, for Xander and West. For me.

~

WEST GROANS and rolls onto his side, waking me up. I stayed up watching him like a hawk until the sun came up before I finally fell asleep. Rolling onto his back, he throws his arm over his eyes.

"How are you feeling?"

"Like shit," he snaps.

I lean up on my elbow and study his face. "Well, you downed almost a whole bottle of Scotch."

"That's not why I feel like shit, Z."

"No?"

His Adam's apple bobs. "Not the only reason, anyway."

I trace my fingertips over his chest. "You're not the reason she left."

He shakes his head. "So, why do I feel like I am? I should have listened to Xander. I should've—"

"We both should have."

He turns his head and looks at me. "You think I don't know that you just go along with whatever I want to keep me happy, Z? You always have."

I shrug. "I thought she betrayed us too. It's not all on you."

He runs a hand through my hair and tugs my head back. "Thank you for looking after my drunken ass."

I wave off his thanks.

"What the fuck did I do to deserve you?" It's not one of those rhetorical questions people who love each other ask. He's genuinely looking for an answer. And I suddenly understand why he's always telling me that I'm too hard on myself. Always trying to keep me out of a self-loathing spiral. He never lets me forget how loved I am, by both him and Xander.

I trail kisses across his chest, and he groans, his fingers still threaded through my hair. When I move lower, teeth and tongue swirling over his hard abs, he hisses out a breath.

I rub my palm over his cock, and it grows harder at my touch.

"Zeke," he warns, but I don't stop. Moving lower, I shove his boxers down and grip his shaft. I lick a path from the center of his stomach all the way to the base of his dick.

His fingers dig into my scalp. I tug on his thick cock and precum beads on the slit. Darting out my tongue, I lick it off, letting the taste of him fill my mouth.

"Zeke, don't."

"Why? Because you think you don't deserve this?"

"No," he grits out. "Because you don't do this."

He's right. But why don't I? He and Fitch are two of the three people I've ever truly loved. Why should the prick who fucked me up be the only man I've done this with? "I would do anything for you."

I wrap my lips around the end of his cock. It's been over twenty years since I gave a blowjob, but I've had enough of them to know what to do.

"Motherfucker!"

Suppressing a smile, I take him to the back of my throat.

"Oh, that feels so fucking good." He loosens his grip on my hair. I know how desperate he must be to hold my head still and fuck my mouth the way he does with Xander and Lily.

I shift my weight until I'm lying between his thighs and swirl my tongue across the crown of his cock, moving down his shaft and back again. His free hand fists in the sheets. Reaching up, I push a finger into his mouth, and he sucks, coating it with his saliva. I love that he knows me so well. When I slip that finger into his ass a few seconds later and press it against his G-spot, he grunts my name and comes down my throat. I swallow every fucking drop he gives me.

FIFTY-THREE

WEST

"Hello, West." Her soft sultry voice fills my ear.

I rub a hand over my face. "Alison, I need a favor."

"A favor? From me?" She laughs. "You must be desperate."

"Well, yeah, I am." Beyond fucking desperate to fix at least some of the damage I caused.

She laughs again, and I can picture her sitting at her desk, tossing her long blond hair over her shoulder, getting such a kick out of this. "What can I do for you?"

"I need you to give someone a job."

"A job?" She snorts. "You have like three billion employees. You give them a job."

"I would if I could, but she won't take one from me."

"Oh, West," she purrs. "Have you been a naughty boy?"

Sighing, I pinch the bridge of my nose. "Look, she's a great writer. She'd be an asset to your magazine."

"So give her a job at yours. If she says no, offer her more money. Everyone has a price."

Regret grips my throat. "Not this girl, Ali."

"Oh, West." Her tone is serious now. "Has someone broken your ice-cold heart?"

"A job, Ali."

She hums but doesn't say anything.

"Did you see that puppy farm piece in *Genevieve* last month?"

"Yeah, I read it."

"That was her."

She's silent for several seconds, and I'm opening my mouth to beg when she asks, "That's who you want me to offer a job to?"

"Yes, Lily Sloane. But she can't know I had anything to do with it."

She lets out a loud breath.

"Ali, come on. You read the article; you know she's a good writer. She's a great person too. Sweet and loyal and ..." The words stick in my throat, and I cough to clear it. "Do this for me and I'll owe you." I hold my breath and wait for her to give me an answer.

"Fine," she eventually says, and my heavy exhale makes her laugh.

"Thank you."

I end the call and rest my forehead on the cool desk. My head throbs, partly due to the aftereffects of drinking almost an entire bottle of Scotch last night, but mostly with the knowledge that we've lost her. We had the perfect woman, and she loved each of us equally. With everything she had.

Now everything is broken.

And I can't fix it.

CHAPTER
FIFTY-FOUR

LILY

I open the door and scowl at the messenger who delivered the puppy to me a few weeks ago. What the hell are those assholes up to now? I really thought that they were going to leave me alone after my visit to West two days ago. Especially after his ten-minute rambling drunk-dialed voicemail.

"Lily Sloane?"

I roll my eyes at his snarky tone. "You know I am."

"You can never tell in this game," he says, and I'm pretty sure one corner of his mouth lifts slightly.

"Whatever." Leaning against the doorframe, I cross my arms over my chest. "What delights do you have for me today?"

"This piece of crap." He steps out of sight.

Trepidation causes my stomach to sink, but my heart leaps when I pop my head out and see what he's brought me. "Betty!"

His forehead wrinkles, but there's definitely a smirk on his face now. "You got pissed off when I brought you an adorable puppy, but you're overjoyed by this pile of junk?"

SADIE KINCAID

"She is *not* junk." I yank her handlebars from his grasp and wheel her inside, dimly registering the lack of metallic protest.

He arches one eyebrow. "She?"

I tip my chin up. "I said what I said."

He puts his hand on the doorframe and leans in. "You wanna get a drink some time?"

I blink at the sudden change of subject. Is this some kind of test? "A drink? With you?"

"Yes. And yes." His grin showcases a set of perfect white teeth.

I tilt my head and consider his proposal. I mean, would there be a better way to piss off the Unholy Trinity than to start dating the guy they use to deliver stuff to me? "You look way nicer when you smile."

He licks his lips. "And you'll look way nicer with those legs wrapped around my neck."

"Ugh!" I slam the door in his face. Scrubbing the last thirty seconds from my mind, I turn my attention to Betty. She looks like she has two brand-new wheels, and her frame is all straightened out. A sob wells in my throat. Which one of them did this? And why? I haven't been able to stop beating myself up for leaving her behind since I calmed down later that day, and I hoped for the best—that they would find it in their hearts to send her back to me in the same condition I left her. But by this morning, I'd given up hope and figured they hauled her to the dumpster. Why would they go to the trouble of having her fixed?

Forever imprinted on my memory, West's voicemail plays in my head. If I weren't intimately familiar with his voice, I wouldn't have recognized it. I could hardly decipher most of his drunken rambling, but he kept repeating how sorry he was and how it was all his fault.

My ringing phone jolts me back to the present, and I grab it off the kitchen counter. Not recognizing the number, I debate whether to answer, but curiosity wins out. "Hello?"

"Lily Sloane?"

"This is she."

"My name is Alison Steadman. I saw your article in *Genevieve*, and I was wondering if you have half an hour to come in and chat about working here at *Ignition*?"

I stop breathing, certain I misunderstood. I replay her words in my mind. Holy shit, she's asking me to come in for an interview at the second-most read magazine in the country.

"Lily?" she says, and I realize how long I've been silent.

"Hell yes!" I clap my hand over my mouth and take a deep breath, then manage to answer more calmly. "I mean, I'd love to. When would be good for you?"

"Does today at two work for your schedule?"

On the inside, I'm celebrating like I won the lottery, but I keep my voice even. "It does."

"Perfect. You know where we are, right?"

I cycle past your building every damn day. "Yes, I'm familiar with the building."

"Wonderful. Then I'll see you today at two."

As soon as she hangs up, I toss my phone onto the couch and squeal at the top of my lungs. Pumping my fists and shaking my hips, I dance around the apartment. Alison Steadman wants to chat about me working there. "Fuck yeah!" I clamp my hand over my mouth. I might be alone, but these walls are thin. I go on dancing but sing quietly to myself.

I might have a new job. Betty is back. And between the severance package I got from my mail room job at *Genevieve* and what I saved from my last two weeks' pay at my new job, I have enough for a deposit on an apartment in Brooklyn. It's tiny but it's mine, and I move in next week.

Life is finally looking up.

CHAPTER
FIFTY-FIVE

LILY

Even after two days, I still smile every time I let myself into my new building. I've never lived on my own before. It's so liberating. Taking out my shiny new key, I open the front door, and my heart almost stops beating. I scream, which only makes him smile.

"Zeke? What the hell? How did you even get in here?" He's sitting at the tiny breakfast bar in my little kitchen, hands casually resting on the countertop.

"I'm a man of many talents, Lily."

"Yeah? I didn't figure breaking and entering was one of them."

"You'd be surprised at the extent of my skill set."

I put my hands on my hips. "How did you even know I moved here?"

"I made the mistake of not being thorough in my research on you once before, Lily. It cost me everything, and it will never happen again. I know everything there is to know about you now."

I sure hope not because then you and I could be in a whole heap of danger. "Highly doubtful," I say instead, crossing my arms over my chest.

The corner of his mouth curls up. "I know you got your pussy waxed two days ago and your nails done later the same afternoon."

My cheeks burn with mortification, and I hate giving him the satisfaction of knowing he's right. My new job came with a small advance, and I decided to treat myself to some long overdue grooming. "You're stalking me now?"

"Keeping a careful eye on you," he corrects.

Yeah, same thing. "You know there are laws against that kind of thing, right?"

He stands suddenly, and his broad frame seems even bigger than usual in my tiny kitchen. "There isn't a law in this land that could keep me from you, baby doll." His declaration is made with such confidence that I'm unable to fight the urge to roll my eyes. Conceited asshole.

Closing my eyes, I rub my forehead. I am so not in the mood for his games. "What the hell are you doing here, Zeke? If you're looking for —"

He cuts me off midsentence "I'm not here for forgiveness, Lily."

"You're not?"

"I'm not looking for redemption. More like retribution."

My eyes follow his to the counter, and that's when I see his knife. The one with the worn leather handle. Anxiety bubbles in my stomach. "R-retribution?"

He reaches for the knife, and his huge hand swallows the handle. "Not for me, buttercup." He drops to his knees at my feet. "For you."

My heart begins to pound in my ears. What the hell is he doing? Too shocked to form words, I gape at him.

He pulls his shirt off over his head and holds out the knife. I blink at him and recall the sharpness of that blade, the endorphins that raced through my body as it sliced my skin. How he took care of me after. How he told me he loved me. He was vulnerable and honest and everything I now know he isn't.

Tears prick at my eyes, and I blink them away. "Get out of my apartment."

"Not until you give me what I need, Lily."

"And what's that? You want me to cut you? Will that make you feel better?" What the hell is his end game? Zeke never gives anyone power over him, not even Xander or West.

"I want you to make me feel something, Lily. I've spent the last two months completely numb, and I can't fucking stand it anymore."

"I'm not cutting you, Zeke."

"Why not?"

"I don't want to. Why would I?"

"I'm already bleeding. Every single second without you is torture. I need you to make it hurt so I can feel something real. Mark me so I can remember that you belonged to me once, even if I didn't get to keep you."

I swallow the lump in my throat. "Zeke, no."

"We fucked up, baby doll. Monumentally fucked up. I'll never forgive myself, so I would never expect you to forgive us ..." His eyes swim with tears, and all my resolve melts away. Seems I'm a complete sucker for a messed-up guy who shows his emotions. I can feel the anguish radiating from him. This isn't some line to get me back, and although that shouldn't matter after what he did, it does.

He watches me intently, as though he's searching my face until he can find a crack in my carefully constructed armor. A tear runs down my cheek, and I swat it away. And there's the crack.

His dark eyes narrow. "But I swear we will spend every single second of the rest of our lives trying to make up for it." He grabs my wrist and places the handle of the knife in my open palm, then closes his fingers around mine and pushes the tip of the blade against his chest.

"I don't want to hurt you, Zeke," I say, a sob catching in my throat.

"Then come home, baby doll. Please. Come home or cut me right now."

"You can't give me an ultimatum like that. It's not fair."

"It's not an ultimatum, Lily. When I think about your face that night—when I remember how cruel I was to you and how much pain I caused, I can't fucking breathe. I need you to make me feel some of that pain."

"It's not comparable." I shake my head. "What you did ..." My words are lost in the maelstrom of emotions crashing together inside me.

"I told you I was cruel." His head drops for a few beats before he fixes his black eyes on mine again. "I'm a sick fuck. I know what I did was unforgivable, but I'm selfish enough to ask you to look past it anyway. When I'm hurt, I don't know how to handle it. I lash out. And I felt betrayed, Lily, but I should have known better. Because you are the best person I've ever known, and having your love, even for just a little while, is the single greatest accomplishment of my life. But now you know that the people I allow to see me at my worst are the people I love the most."

His words are scrambling my senses. "Zeke, please," I whimper.

"Come home, buttercup," he pleads, yanking my hand closer until the tip of the blade pierces his skin. A drop of deep crimson blood trickles over his pectoral muscle. "Come home or stick this fucking knife in my chest so that I can remember what it feels like to be alive."

CHAPTER
FIFTY-SIX

WEST

The elevator doors open and Zeke steps out. He glances around nervously, and it sets my teeth on edge. Something's going on. He looks terrified, but he also seems oddly happy. And then I see why.

I swear my heart stops beating when she steps out behind him. She flicks her dark curls over her shoulder and folds her arms across her chest. Our eyes meet, and I stand frozen, certain I'm dreaming and will wake up at any minute.

"Shorty?" Xander's voice cuts through the uncomfortable silence. He's standing at the other end of the hallway, looking as shocked as I feel.

"Hey," she says so quietly I almost don't hear her. Then the four of us stare at each other for what feels like a fucking eternity. *Say something, asshole. Go pick her up and carry her to bed. Fucking chain her to the goddamn frame if you have to.*

The sound of thundering paws breaks the silence for us, and Snowflake charges down the hallway.

Letting out a delighted shriek, Lily crouches and holds out

her arms. The stupid mutt jumps straight into them. Okay, maybe he isn't as stupid as he looks, considering he did the exact same thing I wish I could have done.

"Oh my goodness." He places his paws on her shoulders and licks her face like it's a prime rib, and her giggles fill the hallway. Content that he's tasted enough of her face, he drops to all fours and sticks his head between her thighs, which only makes her laugh harder. Forget every bad thing I've ever said about him, the damn dog is a genius.

"Snowflake. No." Zeke commands. The obedient pup backs off a little, his little nub whipping back and forth and his tongue hanging out.

Lily brushes the fur from her jeans and stands up slowly. "You called him Snowflake?"

"That's what you wanted to name him. How could we call him anything else?" Xander takes a tentative step toward her.

A quiet sob falls from her lips, and she brushes a tear from her cheek. Zeke stands behind her, his hands stuffed in his pockets as though he wants to touch her but he's not sure if he's allowed. I know exactly how he feels.

Before Xander reaches her, she's distracted by a movement behind him. A split second later, Stella comes into view and warily eyes Lily, her head low and her tail wagging just a little.

Lily gasps. "And who is this?"

"This is Stella. She's Snowflake's adoptive mom," Zeke says, holding out his hand and beckoning the dog over. She goes straight to him, and he scratches behind her ear.

"Stella," Lily repeats, a look of wonder on her face. "Can I pet her?"

"Sure." Zeke looks at the dog with an expression I never saw on his face until the day we brought her home. "She's a little nervous around people, but we told her you're one of the good ones."

Lily's entire face lights up as she crouches back down and holds out her hand for Stella to sniff. In no time at all, Stella decides she likes our girl and happily steps into Lily's arms, smiling her doggy smile as Lily rubs her back. "You told her about me?"

Xander squats down beside them. "Of course we did. She wouldn't be here if it wasn't for you, shorty."

Lily looks between Xander and Zeke. "She's from one of the puppy farms?"

Zeke nods.

"You ... you saved her? You were the one who had those places shut down?"

"It was all of us," Zeke replies, nodding in my direction.

She looks back at me, and her eyes swim with tears as she pushes herself to her feet. "You too?"

I swallow the ball of emotion lodged in my throat, but my voice is still little more than a croak. "Yeah."

"Are you back, Lily? For good?" Leave it to Xander to ask the question I know we're all waiting to have answered.

Clearing her throat, she gives a small shake of her head. My heart bottoms out. Is that a no? "I think we ... we need to talk."

Relief washes over me. It's not an outright no. Talking is good. I'd much rather fuck her into submission, but beggars can't be choosers. We'll talk things through and *then* fuck her into submission.

"West made roast lamb," Xander says.

Lily looks at me and licks her lips, and I push down all the memories of that tongue on my neck, my chest, my cock. "I thought I could smell your signature dish."

"It'll be ready in about twenty minutes." I recognize the purple bag in Zeke's hand. "You want to put your things away first?"

"Your room is still how you left it," Xander adds hopefully.

"I, uh, I don't know."

"Lily," Zeke says softly. "Please? Just give us one night?"

Looking pained, she finally nods, and I wonder what he did to get her here. Whatever it was, I owe him.

~

WE EAT AN AWKWARD DINNER. Despite coming here to talk, Lily seems as reluctant as the rest of us to bring up any of the things we should be discussing right now, including her true identity. While I believe she never had any intention to hurt us, she still hid who she was. She still lied.

"Anyone else finding this super awkward?" Xander asks as he pushes his carrots around his plate. Lily bites her lip and glances at the three of us, her face flushing pink and obscuring the tiny smattering of freckles across her nose. He stares at her then, his bright blue eyes trained on her face. "What if we start with telling you how sorry we are?"

"You all already told me that," she says quietly.

I let my fork clatter to my plate, and she looks over at me. "But you don't believe us?"

Her eyes brim with tears, and the memory of how cruel we were to her that night causes a fresh wave of crippling guilt to wash over me. "I do believe you're sorry ..."

Xander props his elbows on the table and leans forward. "But?"

Her slender throat works as she swallows. She sets down her fork and takes a deep breath. "It doesn't change what you did or how humiliated I was. It doesn't change the fact that you refused to give me *any* opportunity to explain my side of the story."

Xander reaches for her but then pulls his hand back. "But—"

"But nothing, Xander. You all turned your backs on me. I stood in the lobby of this building, the place you made me believe was my home, sobbing like my life was over, and you sent your goddamn doorman to bring me my things." She doesn't bother to wipe away the fat tear rolling down her cheek. "It wasn't until you saw my article that you knew Bree lied about me. You believed her with no real evidence, while my word meant *nothing* to you. And that's when I realized that I didn't mean anything to you either." Her voices cracks along with my heart. Surely she can't actually believe that. She pushes back her stool.

"But you lied to us about who you really are," I tell her. "We know that you're Liliana Constantine."

Her eyes go wide, and for a long moment, the kitchen is silent but for the sound of her harsh breaths. "No." She shakes her head. "You don't get to put this all on me. I know I kept my true identity a secret, and I know I should have told you about my past, but I lied to protect someone I love. To keep myself safe. But *if* you'd asked me, if you had come to me with what Bree told you—" She gasps, tears running freely down her face now. "If you'd come to me, I would have told you the truth."

Shame gnaws a hole in my gut, and I respond before I can think about what I'm saying. "It's easy to say that now, isn't it? But the truth is we'll never know."

Her jaw drops, and she glares at me as though she's about to tear me a new one. I wish she would. I wish she'd rage at me. Throw a goddamn plate at my head or something, because all this tension is too fucking much.

She doesn't though. She wipes the tears from her cheeks and stands straight, shoulders rolled back and chin lifted. "You're right, West, I guess we never will." Then she walks out of the kitchen.

I ignore Xander and Zeke's fierce glares and drop my face into my hands.

"You fucking asshole," Xander yells.

Zeke remains quiet, but I feel the anger and frustration pouring from both of them. It's inescapable. And I don't blame them. I am a fucking asshole.

"Go fix it, West," Zeke says quietly.

With a heavy sigh, I push back my stool and head off to stop our girl from running away. Blood thunders in my ears. She's not leaving ever again. If necessary, I will tie her to her fucking bed.

CHAPTER
FIFTY-SEVEN

LILY

I feel his presence in the room without needing to turn around and see him. My skin bristles with anger and nervous anticipation. I've spent the last two minutes throwing my things into my bag and telling myself I never should have come back here. But that's not entirely true. I needed closure. Without it, I have zero hope of moving on with my life.

I laugh even though I feel like crying. Seems I'm still lying to myself. Because that's not why I came back here at all. I swallow down a sob and spin around to face my personal demon, my lip curled in a sneer. "You come to make sure I don't steal anything on my way out?"

He kicks the door closed and stalks toward the bed. "No, because you're not going anywhere, princess."

"Excuse me?"

"You heard me." He steps closer, and now we're only inches apart. Heat from his body warms my skin, and my knees tremble. My head spins. I haven't been this close to him since ... I can't think about that now.

"You think you can stop me from leaving?"

He tucks my hair behind my ear, then slowly trails his fingertips down my neck, and my mind is overwhelmed with memories of his hands on me. Heat coils in my center. "Oh, I *know* I can," he replies with an arrogant smirk.

I jerk away from his touch, but that only makes him step even closer than before. "You're a conceited douchebag." I blush at the tremor in my voice.

He shrugs. He is such an asshole. "Maybe I am, princess. But I let you go once, and it will never happen again."

I snatch my bag from the bed and hoist it over my shoulder. "Pity you don't get a choice, jackass."

He dips his nose to my neck and inhales deeply. Like an animal savoring his prey before he devours it. A shiver runs the length of my spine. "I will cuff you to my fucking bed if I have to, Lily, and there's not a thing anyone can do to stop me."

Holy fucknuggets. I need to get out of this room. "You're insane." Scoffing, I try to push past him, but he remains standing in front of me like an immovable wall of muscle and arrogance.

He grabs my wrist and yanks me forward until our bodies are flush. "Yeah, I am, but only because I almost ruined the best thing that ever happened to me."

I roll my eyes and shake my head. "If you're talking about us, there's no *almost* about it. You did ruin it, numbnuts."

Those sinfully dangerous lips inch closer, and my traitorous body trembles for him. "So why did you come back here tonight?"

I suck in a shaky breath. "B-because Zeke ... he made me."

"No." He stares into my eyes—into my goddamn soul—and shakes his head.

"Y-yes."

His hand slides to the nape of my neck. "You came back here because you know that what we have is worth saving."

I open my mouth, but no words come out. I need to get out of here. Away from his hypnotic eyes and far away from the tantalizing erection currently pressed against my abdomen. That thing makes me lose at least a hundred IQ points.

"I could drop to my knees right now and tell you how sorry I am, princess ..."

He damn well should. It's the least he could do. "But?"

He grins wickedly. "I've already told you many, *many* times how sorry I am, so now I'm going to show you."

What an arrogant jerkwad. "The hell you are."

"Yeah, the hell I am. But don't worry, I'll still be on my knees."

Is he suggesting ... I shake my head. "N-no, West." My legs tremble harder than my voice.

He takes my bag from me and tosses it into the corner of the room. "Oh yes, Lily." Grabbing hold of my hips, he drags me against his rock-hard length and presses his lips against my ear. "And afterward he'll show you just how much he's missed you."

Then he drops to his knees, and I gasp at the sudden turn of events. What's about to happen was one of the many scenarios that ran through my head on the way over here, and it was also pretty high on my list of most anticipated outcomes, but he can't—

His fingers slide beneath my dress, lightly dusting across the backs of my knees. Oh, fucknuggets. "West, you can't just—"

"Lily." His eyes burn into mine. "Stop fucking talking."

I open my mouth to tell him to go straight to hell, but he picks me up and tosses me onto the bed, rendering me speechless. Grabbing my hips with a bruising grip, he pushes himself between my thighs and pulls me to him until my knees are wedged against his waist. I suck in a stuttered breath, and before I can let it out, his mouth crashes down, his tongue sliding against mine as he takes what he wants. I try to wrench away but he's too strong. I bite his lip, but he only growls and kisses me harder, his weight pinning me to the bed. I'm powerless to stop him, but not because of his superior strength. No, I'm powerless because I realize how much I want this too. Maybe this is the closure we need.

I melt into his kiss, my hands fisting in his thick hair and pulling him closer, giving him unspoken permission to claim me. He breaks the kiss and hovers his lips barely an inch from mine, palming the back of my head and holding me still. A wave of regret washes over me. If only it was this easy. We both know it's not, and if he's forgotten that … "But you don't know who I really am."

"I love you, Lily. You're my fucking girl, and that's all I care about right now."

His lips find mine again. Closing my eyes, I revel in the sensation of his hands on me, loving the way his kiss devours me whole. His hands roam over my body with fervor, grabbing at my dress and grunting in what I can only imagine is frustration before his hands slip beneath the soft fabric. He tugs my bra down and squeezes one of my breasts, flicking the turgid peak of my nipple with the pad of his thumb. My pulse races. Wetness slicks between my thighs.

"Fuck, princess," he groans, breaking our kiss. His tongue darts out, licking his lower lip. I bite mine. Excitement and nervous energy fight for dominance. Our eyes lock for a fraction of a second, and whatever he sees in mine sends him into a frenzy. Before I can take another breath, he's yanking my panties down my legs so roughly that I'm pretty sure I'll have friction burn, but I help him by kicking off my sneakers so he can drag my underwear all the way off. He drapes my legs over his broad shoulders and pushes up my dress, exposing my bare pussy to him.

He breathes out my name as he trails rough bites and kisses up my inner thighs. "I missed you so fucking much." I curl my fingers in his thick hair, pulling him closer to where I need him. "I know, princess," he groans. "Just let me taste all of you." His tongue snakes up my thigh, and I buck my hips, desperate for a little friction to sate the growing ache in my core.

He runs his pointer finger up my center, making me squirm and moan. "Damn, princess. So fucking wet for me already, aren't you?"

"Jackass," I groan, my fingers curling tighter in his hair as I try to tug his mouth closer.

He laughs softly, and his warm breath dusting over my wet folds makes me shiver. "Not the worst thing you've ever called me." Then he trails his hot tongue from my slick opening to my clit, and I yell his name.

That has him laughing harder. "I love how fucking desperate you get for me when my mouth is on you."

"It's not on me right now," I snap.

"You want me?"

Fucking hell yes, I want him. I never stopped.

"Lily?" My name leaves his lips on a plea.

If I had any restraint at all regarding this man, the very last thread of it just snapped. "Yes, West. I want you. Now."

"That's my fucking girl." He sucks my clit into his wickedly talented mouth and swirls his tongue over the sensitive bud. My back arches off the bed, but he wraps his forearms around my thighs and holds me in place so he can maintain full control as I come apart and scream his name.

"Can you believe these two started without us?"

Still trembling from my orgasm, I look up to find Xander

pulling off his clothes. Zeke is close behind him. He shakes his head and glares at West's back like he's mad, but there's a wicked smirk on his face.

West rocks back onto his heels and wipes his face with a single sweep of his hand. "You okay with a little company, princess?"

My eyes dart between the three of them. We were supposed to talk, but West and I already put that plan on pause. Might as well enjoy the rest of the night. "Hell yes."

Xander lies on the bed and pats the empty space beside him. "Get your ass up here, shorty."

I scoot back on my elbows until my head is resting on the pillow beside him. He brushes his knuckles over my cheek. "It's so fucking good to have you home."

I swallow a knot of emotion, still unsure whether I am home. But I don't have a chance to voice that before he seals his mouth over mine and licks a path along the seam of my lips. I open for him, and he slips his tongue inside, swirling it against mine and swallowing my ardent whimpers.

"Did you get her nice and wet for us?" Zeke asks, and West hums his agreement. Without warning, two thick fingers slide through my wet center, and my back arches off the bed.

Xander places a hand between my breasts and pushes me flat to the mattress, then finally lets me up for air. "Steady, shorty." He grins wickedly. "You're gonna want to pace yourself if you're taking all three of us tonight."

I glance down to see that it's Zeke with his hand between my thighs. His dark eyes flash with desire while he toys with my clit. "All three of you?" I whisper, the thought alone making wetness rush between my thighs.

Xander hums and trails his lips lower as he squeezes my nipple between his thumb and forefinger. When Zeke slips two fingers inside me, my cries fill the room.

Zeke growls. "Oh, you made our girl so fucking wet, West."

Then his fingers are gone, but his mouth is on me before I can protest, covering me with kisses and tiny bites as his tongue swirls over my sensitive flesh. "Best pussy I've ever eaten."

"Zeke!" Another orgasm threatens to wash over me.

"Only pussy I'll ever eat again. You got that, buttercup?" He nips the top of my thigh, and hot pleasure sears my core. Xander kisses me again, his hand sliding down my body to flick my clit while Zeke devours me like he's a starving man eating his first meal in months.

Starbursts of intense pleasure explode inside of me. And when I think I can't take anymore, West joins in, adding another set of hands and lips to the mix. They're everywhere, and I can no longer tell who is doing what to me. All I can focus on is their sinfully delicious mouths kissing and eating me and six different hands grabbing and grasping and rubbing and kneading.

My orgasm slams into me like a tsunami, and a scream bursts out of me, my back nearly bowing in half. And even as I shake and plead with them to stop, they keep going, kissing and sucking and biting and touching. The three of them swap places until I've tasted myself on all their lips. When I come again a few moments later, I almost pass out with the force of the climax they wring from my body.

FIFTY-EIGHT

XANDER

Lily's limp body is shaking uncontrollably, and she can barely breathe by the time we're done eating her. I run my fingertips over her jaw. "You know we've barely gotten started, right?"

Her green eyes flash. "You haven't?"

"No. And seeing as how it was Zeke who brought you home to us ..." I dip a finger into her dripping pussy and pull it out again, and she watches me place it in my mouth and suck it clean. "I think he should be first to fuck this sweet pussy. How about you?"

She looks up to see Zeke already settled between her thighs, his cock in his hand and his eyes fixed on her wet center.

Her bottom lip quivers and then she throws her head back. "Please, Zeke."

He pins her thighs flat to the bed and drives his monster cock inside her. She keens, biting into her plush bottom lip as he sinks balls-deep. Seeing the way he stretches her wide has me desperate to fuck her too. I squeeze one of her full tits instead, twisting a little, and she yelps. Zeke falls forward, bracketing her hips with his hands, and then he fucks her so hard the bed rattles off the wall. I'd tell him to take it easy on her, but I understand his burning need to fuck her so hard that she'll still feel him inside her for the rest of her life. I want it too. Our girl is going to find it difficult to walk tomorrow, but there's no chance that any of us, her included, are willing to stop what's about to happen.

Zeke nails her to the mattress. She sinks her fingernails into his shoulders, and his abs tighten the way they do when he's about to come. With a roar, he empties himself inside her.

When he rolls off her, completely spent, I lie on my back and pull her over to straddle me. Planting her hands on my chest, she steadies herself, and their cum drips onto my abs. I gather some onto my fingers and lick it off. My cock throbs. "You and Zeke taste so fucking good together."

Her eyelashes flutter against her pink cheeks, and I swipe my thumb back through the sticky mess on my stomach and hold it to her lips. "Taste."

Sucking my thumb into her mouth, she swirls her tongue around the tip before releasing it with a pop. "Such a good little slut for us, shorty."

She opens her mouth to say something, but all she can do is moan after I grab her hips and impale her on my cock. Sinking into her pussy feels like coming home. I've missed this so fucking much. She's so hot and wet. So snug, milking me with her hungry squeezes. "You feel so fucking good full of his cum."

West crawls onto the bed behind her. I know exactly what's going on in that devious brain of his, and I'm here for it.

Lily bears down on me as he settles behind her. Tilting her head back, she grants him access to her neck, and he takes full advantage, trailing his teeth over her sensitive skin. Then he drags his pointer finger through the cum still on my abs and flashes me a wicked grin.

CHAPTER
FIFTY-NINE

LILY

West flicks his tongue over the spot on my neck where he just bit me, and I whimper. Xander's fingertips bruise my hips, and it only makes me ride him harder, chasing the delicious blend of pain and pleasure they all offer me in different ways.

West slides his finger between my ass cheeks, pressing gently against my entrance. I flinch. "You ever been fucked here, princess?"

"No," I admit in a whisper.

Xander slows his movements, holding me steady as West inches his finger inside me. I gasp out a breath at the unfamiliar intrusion. He bands one muscular arm around me, pulling me back against his hard chest as he edges in further.

His name comes out in a breathy moan.

He growls, his hot breath dusting over my skin. "You like that?"

"Y-yeah."

"So are you gonna let me fuck this virgin ass? Because I'm fucking desperate to be inside you. To fuck you with him."

Fierce waves of euphoria crash over my body, and I pant for breath as he pushes his finger deeper, my muscles clenching around the two of them. Then Zeke is kneeling beside us, and he cups my jaw. "Relax, baby doll. You can take them both."

"Are you gonna let me fill you with my cock too, Lily?" West asks again, tweaking my nipple and sinking his finger deeper.

"Yes!" I gasp.

He presses his lips to my ear. "Good girl."

I shiver at the idea of what's about to happen, and Xander gives my waist a reassuring squeeze. "You'll be fine, shorty. It might hurt at first, but you just gotta breathe and let him in. Okay?"

I nod. "Okay."

Zeke distracts me with a soft kiss, but I still jolt when West places the crown of his huge cock, already slick with lube, against my dark hole. I wince, my eyes watering at the burning stretch, but Zeke goes on kissing me while West and Xander shower me with praise. Their hands roam my body, their words soothe my pain.

"Relax, princess." He spreads my ass cheeks and gives me another inch.

I wrench my lips from Zeke's. "I can't, West. You're too big."

"You can do this, baby doll," Zeke promises. "We've all got you. We'll never let anything bad happen to you." He circles my clit with the pad of his pointer finger. "You're ours now, Lily. Every fucking part of you."

"Love you so goddamn much, shorty." Xander's voice is strained, likely from the effort of holding back the urge to fuck me while I adjust to West's girth in my ass.

West hums his agreement, his lips dusting over my skin. "We were completely lost without you."

My muscles relax, and the burning gives way to bone-deep pleasure. "I can take a little more."

West groans. "That's my good fucking girl."

"You're squeezing me so tight, shorty. Fuck!"

"Just do it, West," I groan. "You're making it hurt more by going slow."

Zeke shoots him a look, and West tightens his grip on me, pushing his cock so much deeper into my ass. I let out a guttural sound that I don't recognize, and he whispers more praise in my ear. "You're such a good girl taking us both, Lily."

The pain is like nothing I've ever felt before, but it hurts so good as it curls through my core, mixing with the pleasure and forming an all-new sensation that makes me feel invincible. Like I'm experiencing the euphoric high of a new drug for the first time.

I throw my head back. "Fuck. Me!"

"Yeah, we're gonna." West releases a dark laugh, and they move in unison, setting a deliciously steady pace that has pleasure snaking up my thighs and coiling deep in my core.

I look into Xander's bright blue eyes. "You like that, don't you, shorty?"

I can't speak with all the stimulation consuming my mind, so I nod.

Zeke goes on rubbing my clit while he trails kisses over my breasts and neck. "That's good to know, because you look incredible being fucked by my boys, buttercup." He presses his mouth to my ear. "And I can't fucking wait to fuck you with them too."

My orgasm burns through my veins like gunpowder lit by their combined fire, and a rush of cum floods my pussy. I shudder and tremble, sandwiched between all three of them as I experience the most mind-blowing climax of my life. They hold my boneless body upright while Xander and West continue fucking me until they reach their own climaxes a few moments later.

XANDER and I lie face to face with Zeke's chest against my back and West's arm draped over Xander from behind, his hand resting on my ass. My body aches and my pussy and ass throb like they have their own pulse, but I smile contentedly.

Zeke brushes my hair from my neck. "You okay, buttercup?"

"I'm so okay."

"Say you're back for good, shorty."

"Oh, she's back for good. She's never fucking leaving this penthouse again," West grumbles.

Dread washes over me. "I want to stay, but I have some things to tell you all first. Then you can decide if you still want me."

West leans over Xander and cups my face in his hand. "There is *nothing* you can tell us that will change how much we want you, Lily. Nothing."

"You don't know that," I whisper.

"We do, baby doll. Because we lost our fucking minds without you, and we can't go through that again. So you're ours no matter what."

"No matter what," West repeats.

Xander winks at me. "You're our ride or die."

Despite my concern that they'll change their tune tomorrow, I can't help but smile. For tonight at least, I will enjoy being the luckiest woman on earth.

CHAPTER
SIXTY

LILY

Sitting in the kitchen eating pancakes the next morning, I feel all their eyes on me. Last night was beyond incredible, but there's still so much they need to know about me.

I put my fork down and clear my throat. "I guess I should tell you who I am, huh?"

"We know you're Liliana Constantine." Zeke says the name so nonchalantly, as if it can be spoken openly without dire consequences. The name holds too much power, and I've spent years trying to forget it. But I should have known that I couldn't hide forever.

"I am. Or I was. She died in a boating accident six years ago."

West leans forward and studies my face with narrowed eyes. "You faked your own death?"

I nod. "My brother helped me. Nico got my papers, my new identity. Women in my family don't have access to such resources, so I couldn't have done it without him."

"So you just disappeared and left it all behind? And your father bought it?" West looks skeptical.

"It helped that witnesses saw me go overboard. But Nico and I had holidayed on that island since we were children. There was a small cave, and we hid some diving gear there. Nico's best friend, Dean, was waiting on the other side of the island. I followed the coastline, and he took me back to the mainland." They risked so much to help me escape, rescued me from horrors they didn't even know about. I squeeze my eyes closed for a second. Now isn't the time to dredge up the memories I've kept buried so deep in the hopes of never reliving them again.

I take a deep breath and continue. "I used my new identity and flew back to the States while my brother mourned my disappearance. My father's men were still searching the area for me, but they eventually gave me up for dead."

Xander tilts his head. "And you never went back home?"

"Nope. I came to New York. Figured it was far away enough from Vegas that I wouldn't run into anyone from my old life. Maybe I should have gone to some backwater town in the middle of nowhere, but all I ever wanted was to become a journalist, and Columbia and New York were my dream. Nico set up a trust to administer my scholarship and made sure there was enough for me to get my degree, but beyond that, I had nothing from my family. I wouldn't have even taken that much, but I couldn't get a genuine scholarship in my new name and ..." I shake my head. "I guess I'm a hypocrite for taking my father's money to pay for college, but I didn't see any other way."

Xander places his hand over mine and gives it a reassuring squeeze.

"Faking your own death, though? It's ..." Zeke sucks on his lip.

"Extreme?"

Zeke nods. "Kinda."

"Let's just say that the future my father had mapped out for me was so bleak and terrifying, even my actual death would have been a welcome relief." I swat away the tear rolling down my cheek.

Xander squeezes my hand again. "No more secrets, shorty."

I nod, ignoring the voice in my head telling me that we've barely even scratched the surface of my secrets. There are so many that I can't share now, maybe not ever. "I was eighteen. I wanted to go to college like my high school friends, but women in my family don't get to do that. We marry and we have babies. And I guess that's not the worst life, not if you get to choose your husband, but my father had plans for me. I was going to marry Giovanni Santangelo."

Zeke blanches at the name. "The former head of the Mafia?"

"Yeah. I was to be his virgin bride and give him many heirs. It didn't matter to my father that he was fifty-eight years old."

West scowls. "He wanted you to marry a man who was forty years older than you?"

"Yeah, but that wasn't the worst of it. I could have dealt with that if he would've been a good husband and father, but Giovanni was the vilest man I ever met. We used to sometimes go to his house on Sunday afternoons, and every single time, there would be a crying woman leaving as we arrived. Always beaten and bruised. He used to laugh with my father about how much he enjoyed making them bleed."

Zeke snarls, but Xander lays a comforting hand on his arm.

"Three weeks before our wedding was due to take place, Nico and I overheard him talking to one of his guards about the depraved things he planned to do to me on our wedding night. About how I would never leave his house again. He planned to keep me as his prisoner."

West's hands ball into fists. "Jesus, Lily."

"We both knew then that I couldn't marry him. I begged my father to find someone else for me, but he refused. And when Nico told him what we'd overheard, he just laughed, telling me it was all I was good for." I press my lips together at the intense betrayal I still feel. The weight of those emotions used to threaten to crush me, but in the years since I learned the truth of my heritage and my true birthright, I've taught myself how to breathe through the pain. I was eleven when I discovered why Carmine Constantine, the man who claimed to be my father, hated me, so I shouldn't have been surprised about his willingness to hand me over to the head of the Mafia or that he didn't give a single fuck what happened to me after.

Zeke runs a hand over his beard. "So your father has no idea you're alive?"

"None. If he ever found out, he'd have Nico and Dean killed for helping me. That's why I couldn't tell you. I couldn't put their lives at risk, not after everything they've done for me."

"And Dean can be trusted?" West asks.

"Yes. He'd never betray Nico. He loves him more than anyone in the world."

He hums, his eyebrows pinched together like he's deep in thought. "And Giovanni? What happened to him?"

"Murdered in his bed about two months after I disappeared. Somebody slit his throat. When I first found out, I liked to imagine that it was my father who did it, finally stepping up to at least take some vengeance for me, but I suspect it was my brother."

"Holy fuck, shorty. That's some life you've lived."

"Yep. So, you still want me?"

Zeke walks around the island and wraps his arms around me, dropping a tender kiss on the top of my head. "More than anything, baby doll."

"I met you once, didn't I?" West asks, drawing both mine and Zeke's attention back to him.

My breath catches in my throat. "Yeah. I didn't know if you'd remember me."

Both Xander and Zeke frown. "You met before?" Xander asks.

West rubs a hand over his stubble. "I didn't have any idea it was you until just now." He sighs and directs his attention to Xander and Zeke. "It was the day we found out Carmine had stolen our entire casino investment. When I confronted him, he put a gun to my head. He would have pulled the trigger too, except a little girl came running in, clutching a teddy bear under her arm. She begged him not to kill me."

Tears fill my eyes. That happened fourteen years ago, but sitting here watching West relive it, it feels like yesterday.

Cupping my chin in his hand, Zeke turns my head so I'm looking at him. "And he listened?"

I shake my head. "Never."

"But ..." Xander frowns again.

West sucks in a deep breath. "He turned his anger on her instead. He cracked her across the face with the back of his hand ... her little head snapped right back." His skin pales, and he drops his eyes to the counter. "And I fucking ran out of there. I left her." His eyes swim with tears when they meet mine. "I left *you*. I should have taken you with me."

"He was my father, West. You wouldn't have made it two steps with me. If you hadn't run when you did, he would have killed you. I can promise you that."

West still doesn't appear convinced. His eyes are so full of anguish, and I wish I could make him see that he had no choice. "I never knew what happened though. Why my father almost killed you that day."

His Adam's apple bobs. "The three of us had worked our

311

asses off from the moment each of us left high school. We wanted to get into the casino business. We saved every single fucking cent we earned for six years to get our investment together. And then your father stole it. Just like that." He snaps his fingers. "We thought about going back to kill him, but ..."

Zeke squeezes me tighter. "We were just kids, and he was a made Mafia man. We left town the same day he tried to kill West."

"We swore we'd make him pay one day, but then we moved on to bigger things. We created XWZ and never looked back," West adds.

Zeke takes a step back but keeps his arms around my waist. "Wait. Did you recognize West when you met him?"

"Yeah. As soon as I walked into his office at XWZ that day. But I never thought I'd see you again. That night in the club, I should have walked away as soon as you came to the booth. But then you all invited me for dinner, and you were so sweet ... how could I tell you without revealing who I really was? I mean, I always planned to someday ..." Sniffling, I shake my head. This whole situation is fucked up and emotional, and I am so fucking tired of crying.

"Lily." West's voice cuts through my internal chatter, and he walks around the island to stand on the other side of me. He wraps me in a hug and presses his lips against my neck. "You saved my fucking life, princess. Twice. Once a long time ago, then again when you walked back in here last night. I'm so fucking sorry that I never came back for you and rescued you from him."

"Well, if you had come and rescued me when I was ten years old, this relationship right here would be all kinds of fucked up, now wouldn't it?"

I feel him smile against my skin.

"I could get behind calling you Daddy though," I add with a giggle.

Zeke and Xander laugh, but West groans. "Don't fucking tempt me, princess."

"You kind of are like our daddy though," Xander says with a cheeky wink.

Even Zeke hums his agreement. "Yeah, you're a lot older than us."

"I'm two fucking years older than you, Zeke."

"Almost four years older than me," Xander chimes.

"And fourteen years older than me. Biologically speaking, you *could* actually be my daddy."

The growl that rumbles through West vibrates through me too. "I'll be your fucking daddy, princess." He hoists me over his shoulder and spanks my ass hard, making me squeal.

"We have work to do today," Zeke reminds him, and he puts me back on my stool with a dramatic sigh.

"Yeah. You got that meeting with the new board of *Genevieve*," Xander says.

West heads over to Xander and wraps an arm around his neck. "And you've got dogs to walk."

Xander smiles up at him. "It's still better than a board meeting."

Humming his agreement, West runs his nose along the other man's throat.

"How about we take a little time before the next big merger?" Zeke suggests.

West eyes Zeke with curiosity. "But we never take time off."

"Yeah." Zeke bands his arms tighter around me, pulling me close to his chest. "But now we have a reason to spend more time at home."

West's stormy eyes roam over my face and chest, and goosebumps prickle along my forearms. "I just started a new job. I can't take time off."

Zeke brushes my hair back and trails kisses across the nape of my neck. "You won't have to, baby doll."

Xander runs his hands down West's chest. "I think Zeke's right about us though. We go through another merger like the last one and you might have a fucking coronary."

West takes Xander's hands in his, stopping them from moving any lower. "I'm as healthy as a fucking horse."

Xander chuckles. "Hung like one too."

With a growl, West palms Xander's neck and kisses him so hard, I swear I can feel his knees trembling from here.

CHAPTER
SIXTY-ONE

ZEKE

Our driver holds the car door open, and West and I climb inside. My ass has barely touched the seat when he gives me a smile that I haven't seen in a long time.

"So, how do you feel about meeting Nico and his buddy, Dean? I think we could have some mutual interests."

I grin back at him. Oh, how I love dangerous West. I've missed him. "I thought you'd never ask."

"When do you think you can get it set up?"

Sucking on my top lip, I mentally sort through my Vegas contacts. I know just the man who can get me a call with Nico Constantine. "Give me until the end of the day, and I'll have a meeting sorted. If he's the kind of guy Lily seems to think he is, he should be desperate to speak with us as soon as we mention her name."

West offers me a faint nod, but he's distracted.

"You okay?" I ask.

He licks his lower lip. "Thinking about last night."

My lips curl. "I thought about last night twice in the shower this morning."

That gets me a laugh, but then he's serious again. "Thank you, Z. For whatever you did to bring her back to us."

I shrug. "I figured it was about time I fixed something for a change instead of fucking it up."

He slides his hand to the back of my neck and forces me to look him in the eyes. "You don't fuck anything up. Ever."

I look away, unable to handle his gratitude.

Grabbing my jaw, he turns my face back to his. "You fix *everything*, Zeke. When are you going to realize that? Why is it you're the one I always ask to get shit done? I never have to question your methods because you always fucking come through for me. No matter what."

My throat's too clogged with emotion to offer a response.

"And that's why I know I'll be talking with Nico Constantine by the end of the day."

I clear my throat. "You're a smooth fucker."

Leaning back, he runs a hand over his jaw and stares out the window. I can hear the cogs turning in his brain. Lily's father thinks she's dead. With her dating West, or any one of us, it's only a matter of time before the press gets ahold of her picture from somewhere.

WEST IS COOKING dinner by the time I get home. Walking up behind him, I rest my chin on his shoulder and eye the pork chops he's seasoning. My stomach growls.

He laughs. "Won't be long."

I press a kiss between his shoulder blades and take a seat at the kitchen island. "Where are Lily and Fitch?"

"In the den. Making out last I checked." He glances at his Rolex. "Probably made it to third base by now."

Lucky fucker. But those two being distracted means we can have the conversation we need to have. "We're gonna need Fitch to drop her at work tomorrow morning. You and I have a video conference at nine-thirty."

He turns and arches one eyebrow. "With Nico?"

I nod. "I know a pit boss who works at one of the Constantine casinos. It took some convincing, but I eventually got a message to Nico. My guy confirmed he received it loud and clear."

Smiling, West wipes his fingers on the dish towel, then crosses the kitchen and steps between my spread legs, placing his hands on the counter on either side of me. "You promised me by the end of the day."

I snort. "I promised I'd have the meeting sorted by the end of the day, jackass."

He runs his nose along my jawline and grinds his cock against mine. "You have any idea how much it turns me on when you get shit done like this, Zeke?"

Sliding a hand through his hair, I tug his head back and lick my lips. "Enough to let me fuck you later?"

He grins wickedly. "Not tonight, big guy. I have other plans."

I yank his hair harder, my fingers digging into his scalp and making him wince. Licking a path along the column of his throat, I smile to myself as a groan rumbles out of him. And when I sink my teeth into his skin, he grinds his thick cock even harder against me.

Gripping the lapel of my jacket, he tips his head back and allows me to bite harder. "Jesus fuck, Zeke. You better not give me a hickey."

I flick my tongue over the teeth marks I left on his skin.

They'll fade in a few minutes. He doesn't mark easily, but even when I do take things too far, the man can grow a beard in a day. I pull back and lick my lips. "You taste fucking delicious."

He twists his head to the side. "Do I have a hickey?"

"No. But you stand there much longer rubbing up against me and I'll give you one the size of an apple." He ignores my threat, keeping his fingers tangled in my hair, his body still flush with mine. I growl. "I mean it West."

He laughs darkly before licking along the seam of my lips and sliding his tongue into my mouth. West's kisses are rough and dominating. It's the only time I ever allow him to take control when it comes to my body, and he takes full and frequent advantage.

By the time he comes up for air and gives me a wicked grin, my cock is leaking precum. "Dinner."

"Fucking tease," I grumble.

WEST GOT me so worked up before dinner that as soon as we were all done eating, I carried Lily to my bed, knowing that he and Xander would follow. Then he and I fucked our little brats together. Now they're lying between us, and my baby doll's perfect ass is pressed against my cock. All I can think about is fucking her when she's this close.

"Hey," Xander says with a loud yawn. "Seeing as how we don't keep secrets now, isn't there something we need to tell Lily?"

I shoot West a worried glance. We're not exactly keeping our meeting with Lily's brother a secret, but it's safer not to involve her until we know that he's on board with our plan.

She yawns and her eyelids flutter. "What is it you need to tell Lily?"

"You remember when Jen met Trey?" Xander says.

"Yeah."

"Well, we kind of paid him to take her off our hands for the night so we could have you to ourselves."

That sure wakes her up. "What? But she's ... they're dating now! You *paid* him?"

Xander offers her a sheepish grin. "I know it sounds bad, but it was only for that one night, shorty. Their relationship is real. He really likes her. He told me."

"You're unbelievable," she says with a shake of her head, but there's a soft smile on her lips.

"He was also in on the whole apartment thing," West adds, and I roll my eyes. Why are we telling her all this?

Her eyebrows pinch together in a cute frown. "The apartment thing?"

"Yeah. There were never any roaches," West admits.

"What?" she shrieks. She sits up, her mouth hanging open and her eyes darting between the three of us. "I had nightmares about roaches for days after. You assholes." She crosses her arms over her chest. "Why on earth would you do that?"

I pull her back down, and she resists a little, wriggling in my grip, but as soon as my arms are around her, she stops. "You know why, baby doll. Because we wanted you here and we wanted it to happen fast."

"But ..." She presses her lips together. "You could have trusted me to come to that decision on my own."

"We weren't willing to take that chance, princess."

"Do you always get what you want?" she asks, snuggling into me. I guess she's too high on orgasms to actually be mad at us.

I nip her shoulder. "Always."

"I knew there was something weird about that whole roach nest thing," she grumbles. "You're all insane, you know that?"

Xander kisses her forehead. "Yep, and proud of it."

"I guess it's not the worst thing you've ever done," she adds.

West shoots her a pained look. "Not even close, princess."

I nuzzle her neck, and she purrs like a kitten. "Consider it a reflection of how much we wanted you, buttercup."

Xander dusts his knuckles over her cheekbone. "From the first moment we met you, we all knew you were something special."

West runs his fingers over her hipbone. "The perfect fit."

CHAPTER
SIXTY-TWO

WEST

"Hey, princess. Come in here."

She pops her head through the open doorway and smiles. Fuck me, I love that smile. Am I really about to wipe it from her face and possibly risk never seeing it again? "I have something I need to tell you." Looks like I am.

She saunters in wearing knee-high socks and Zeke's old football jersey. Jesus, is she trying to fucking kill me? Her eyes narrow as she searches my face.

"Come here." I pull her onto my lap.

"What is it?" she whispers.

I brush her dark curls behind her ears. "Last night when we were telling you about some of the shady shit we pulled, I left something out, something Zeke and Xander don't even know about."

She looks at me, waiting. I wrap my arms around her waist

so she can't run out of the room when she finds out the truth. "Your job at *Ignition* ..."

"No, West." Tears well in her eyes. "Please tell me you didn't."

I swallow a thick knot of regret. "I knew you'd never take a job with Hellsgate."

She tries to climb off my lap, but I hold her tighter. "No." She shakes her head. "I love that job."

"Lily, please listen to me. Let me explain."

She glares at me, all defiance and fire, and even though I would have sworn it wasn't possible, I fall even more in love with her. "Alison Steadman is an old acquaintance of ours. I knew you'd be a good fit for her magazine, and that's why I reached out to her."

"But I thought I got that job because she liked my writing. Because she saw my article."

I brush away the tear on her cheek. "You did, princess. She and I have a rule that we don't steal each other's employees. She wouldn't have come knocking on your door because she thought you worked for me, so I asked her to give you a chance. But I never asked her to make you features editor. You got that job all on your own." Another tear runs down her face, but at least she's no longer trying to run away from me. I press my forehead against hers. "I'm sorry."

She sniffs. "Is there anything else you need to tell me? Any more secrets?" The meeting I'm about to have with her twin brother in an hour is at the forefront of my mind, but she saves me from having to answer. "Because I can't keep doing this. Every time I think we have a solid foundation, you pull the rug out from under me. Promise me there'll be no more bombshells, West."

I grab her wrists and wrap her arms around my neck. "I can't promise that, princess, because I plan to surprise the hell out of you for the rest of your life. But I can promise all your surprises will be good from now on. Can you live with that?"

She rolls her eyes, and I cup her chin in my hand. "You did not just roll those pretty eyes at me, did you?"

"You deserve way worse than an eye roll, West Archer."

"Have I ever told you how hard you make me?" She rolls her eyes again, and I laugh. "Oh, I see, you want to play? Has Fitch been teaching you all the best ways to earn yourself a punishment?"

Feigning innocence, she bats her eyelashes. "No."

I trail my lips over the sweet skin of her neck, humming my response. Then I lift her off my lap and smack her fine ass. "You need to stop teasing me and get ready for work."

She places one hand on her hip and glares at me, full of that fire I love so much. "I was on my way to shower when you called me in here."

I turn her around by her shoulders and slap her ass again, making her squeal. "Go."

"Are you riding to work with us this morning?" she calls out over her shoulder.

"No. Zeke and I are working from home."

She turns and gives me her full attention. "So Xander and I get the car all to ourselves?" Little minx.

"If you fuck him in the car and sit at your desk with cum dripping out of you all day, I will give you the spanking of your life when you get home tonight."

She flashes me a devious smirk. "Is that supposed to be a deterrent?"

Before I can answer, she strolls out of my office. If I didn't have this meeting with her brother, I'd chase after her and fuck her where she stands. Then I'd ride to work with her so she'd have to sit at her desk with my cum dripping down her thighs.

CHAPTER
SIXTY-THREE

LILY

I stare at Alison Steadman, my arms folded over my chest. I admire her so much, and I love this goddamn job. I will put dog poop in West's protein shake if he's ruined this for me.

"Yes?" She frowns. She's probably not used to people barging into her office like this.

"I know."

She rests her hands on her desk in front of her and leans forward. "Know what?"

"About West asking you to give me this job."

Laughing, she shakes her head. "I knew he'd tell you."

I fling my arms down by my sides, acutely aware that I'm acting like a belligerent teenager. "So you didn't see my article on the puppy farm? That's not why you hired me?"

She pushes her chair back, crosses her legs, and fixes me with the infamous Steadman stare that I've only heard about until now. "Take a seat, Lily."

I do as she asks, anxious now that she's using that boss bitch tone she does so well. She's freaking amazing.

"While I might be willing to do West Archer a favor now and then, do not insult my integrity by suggesting that I would risk my magazine. I wouldn't do that for anybody. Yes, I agreed to give you a job because he asked me to. But I could have given you a job making coffee or sorting paper clips. I gave you the features position because you are an insightful writer."

I sink into my chair. "Oh."

"I made you features editor because you impressed the hell outta me in your first week."

My cheeks burn. "Oh."

She tilts her head to the side, a smirk playing on her lips. "Oh."

"Thank you, Alison. I'm sorry about storming in here, but he told me—and then I thought—and I just love it here so much."

She holds up her hand, and I take it as a signal to stop babbling. "I get it. I understand needing to make it on your own merit. And I admire that about you. Believe me when I say that I wouldn't insult you by blowing smoke up your ass, no matter who your boyfriend is. Okay?" A little of her Jersey accent slips in, and it makes me smile.

"Okay. Thank you."

"You're welcome. Now get back to work. You owe me an article by noon."

I jump up from my chair. "It will be ready by eleven, boss."

CHAPTER
SIXTY-FOUR

ZEKE

I glare at West's computer screen while we wait for the call from Lily's brother.

West gives me a side eye, and I realize I'm grinding my teeth, but I'm on edge. What if this guy turns out to be as big a prick as his father? What if he doesn't give a shit about Lily after all? And then I'd have to track him down and kill him too, along with her evil bastard of an old man. From the moment Lily told me about how she faked her own death to escape him, I've been dreaming of ways to make him pay. Sick, twisted ways that feed all the depraved parts of my psyche that I rarely let out to play. I know in my bones that her father is the man who hurt her. The man she was fighting off that night in the basement when I fucked her on the hood of my car. So if her brother is *anything* like him, he will be added to my list of people to torture and kill.

A notification pings, telling us that someone has joined the meeting room. West glances at me. "Will you relax?"

"I am relaxed," I snap.

He rolls his eyes and refocuses on the screen. A figure sitting at a desk in a suit and tie comes into view. "Thank you for agreeing to meet with us, Mr. Constantine."

"Well, when someone starts throwing around my dead sister's name, it tends to get my attention, as I'm sure you know."

West nods, and I glare at the figure on the screen. Nico adjusts his shoulders, clearly as agitated as I am.

"Are you alone?" West asks.

Nico's eyes dart away from the screen, and he clears his throat. "No."

"This is a delicate matter."

Nico leans forward, his lip curling in a snarl.

A growl of frustration rumbles out of me, and I lean forward now too. "Look, fuck-knuckle. Do you trust whoever is in that room with you enough to have a conversation about your sister?"

West shoots me a warning look, but I'm not the diplomatic type. That's why he handles all the important meetings.

"The only person in this room is my second." Nico's tone loses some of its hostility. "I trust him with my life, and my sister's, if she were still here. So let's cut the bullshit and tell me why the fuck you're talking to me about Liliana."

West runs a hand over the thick stubble on his jaw. "Well, Lily lives with us. She's my ..." His tongue darts out to moisten his lips. "*Our* girlfriend."

Nico frowns, his eyes bouncing between whoever's in the room with him and the camera. "What the fuck does that have to do with me?"

I shoot West a look, telling him to tread carefully.

"We both know the answer to that. We want to discuss a solution to the problem that Lily faces. The reason she can't be who she's supposed to be."

He looks offscreen again, then returns his attention to us. "So, you're both dating her?"

Glancing at each other, we nod.

Nico frowns. "Prove it."

How the hell are we supposed to do that? I could grab a pair of her panties from the bedroom, but what would that prove? And why did my mind go straight there?

Fortunately, West isn't thinking with his dick. He grabs his phone and pulls up a selfie of the four of us smiling at the camera. He holds it to the screen, and Nico's eyes soften. "We love her, Nico. We'd do anything to protect her. Anything."

"As would I."

"So, are you up for meeting with us to discuss how we might keep her safe? You know, in the long term?"

Lily's brother releases a heavy sigh. "If you're talking about getting rid of my father ..." I'm sure I notice the corners of his mouth curling up ever so slightly. "Then I'm all in."

Yeah, I think I'm gonna like this guy.

SIXTY-FIVE

XANDER

"So, you're sure we can trust this guy?" I ask, pacing West's office and chewing on a hangnail.

"Well, we're about to find out," West says, shooting me a look that warns me to stop fidgeting, and I will as soon as Lily's brother gets here. Security called a few minutes ago to let us know he was in the building. But for now, it's worrying and pacing time.

Zeke grunts.

West sighs. "Will you both fucking relax?"

I stop pacing. "You know Zeke has no chill."

West arches one eyebrow. "And you?"

"I'm just hungry." My stomach growls to prove my point.

Zeke rolls his eyes. "You're always hungry."

I perch on the edge of West's desk. "Well, I could barely eat my second bagel this morning because I fucking *hate* lying to Lily, and you two fuckers know it."

Zeke strides across the office until he's standing right in

front of me. "Which is why we didn't tell you about our meeting with Nico until we had to."

"Besides, we're not lying," West adds.

"Sure feels like we are," I mutter.

West shoots Zeke a look, and before I can ask what it's about, Zeke is sliding his arms inside my suit jacket. With a rough grip on my waist, he yanks me close and runs his teeth over my throat. "How the fuck do you stay in such good shape when you eat two bagels every day for breakfast?"

I hiss a breath. "Stop trying to distract me. It won't work."

He glances down at my crotch. "But it's already working."

I sink my teeth into my lip and glance up at the ceiling, willing my cock not to get any harder. "Fuck you."

His tongue lashes at the sensitive spot on my neck that makes my knees buckle. I'm suck a fucking manwhore for him. "I'm gonna fuck you on West's desk as soon as this meeting is done."

The sound of West's secretary's voice fills the room, announcing Nico's arrival. I push Zeke off me and straighten my clothes before perching on the edge of the desk and crossing my legs to hide the bulge in my pants.

Nico looks a little like Lily, but not as much as I would've expected. His dark brown eyes are most notable, so different from her glowing green. His second-in-command, Dean, strolls in beside him, and it's clear they're very close. Like the way West, Zeke, and I are close. I don't know that anyone else would notice, but my gaydar is finely tuned. Dean's eyes rake over my body a fraction of a second longer than they should, and the warning growl that comes out of Zeke has me biting back a laugh.

Once the introductions are complete, Nico takes a seat opposite West while Dean remains near the door. "Where's Lily?" Nico asks, glancing around West's office.

"She's at home," I tell him.

"Is she okay?" His tone is laced with genuine concern, and any worries I had about his motives dissolve instantly. He obviously loves her.

"She's good. Maybe you could come see her after we're done here," West suggests.

Both Nico and Dean smile at that suggestion, but Nico's the one who answers. "We have to be back in Vegas by morning, but it would be great to see her."

As we're wrapping up the meeting, I realize that I like these guys. I appreciate how much they love our girl and that they clearly have her back. However, I don't like that West and Zeke are going to be involved with a plan to take out a made Mafia man. Although this won't be the first time the two of them have gotten a little blood on their hands. They've walked a fine line between doing what they think is right and doing what the law says is right for as long as I've known them. And if I'm honest, I must admit that I wouldn't have them any other way.

"So, shall we let Lily know we have company for dinner?" I ask.

"Let's surprise her." West grins. "She always cooks too much food anyway."

SIXTY-SIX

LILY

S tella and Snowflake scamper out of the kitchen, their loud barks announcing that my men are home.

"Where are you, shorty?" Xander calls.

"In here." I tug off my apron and toss it aside before leaning against the counter, self-consciously rubbing my hands over my bare stomach and hips. Is greeting them wearing only a tiny pair of pink panties too much?

"We have a surprise, baby doll," Zeke calls out.

So do I. I press my lips together to stifle a giggle. Zeke walks into the room first, and upon seeing me, his mouth drops open, but then his face turns gray. He stops in his tracks so abruptly that Xander bumps into him, and now his eyes are greedily raking over my almost naked body.

"Motherfucking fuck," Zeke groans.

"Abort! Abort!" Xander shouts, spinning on his heel and herding West out of the doorway.

Meanwhile, Zeke runs over to me and pulls off his jacket, then drapes it across my shoulders.

Well, this sure didn't go as planned. "I'm sorry," I whisper. "I thought it would be sexy, or at least a little funny."

Zeke catches my eye, and his are twinkling with amusement. He fastens me into his jacket and wraps his arms around my waist, resting his hands on my ass. "Coming home to you wearing nothing but your panties is sexy as fuck, baby doll. But tonight we have guests."

Gasping, I swat him on the chest. "Oh my god. Did they see? Why didn't you warn me?"

He purses his lips and lowers his head, his shoulders shaking.

"Are you ..." I suppress a growl. "Are you *laughing* at me, Ezekiel?"

He snorts. My grumpy Zeke snorts with laughter. I gape at him, all my irritation gone at the sight and sound of his uncharacteristic mirth. Soon we're both doubled over, giggling and holding onto each other to keep from collapsing on the kitchen floor, and I have to squeeze my thighs together so I won't pee myself.

"What the fuck, you two?" West's voice carries across the room, and I look up through tear-filled eyes to see him standing in the doorway, grinning at the pair of us. "You need to put some clothes on, princess."

I wipe the tears from my eyes and glance at Zeke, who's still bent over, one hand gripping the kitchen counter for dear life. West ushers me out of the room with a warning to Zeke to pull himself together.

"Why didn't you tell me we had guests?" I ask when we reach the safety of my bedroom.

"Because it was supposed to be a surprise. And fuck me, but it was." He unfastens Zeke's jacket, and his eyes roam the contours of my body. "Promise me this is how you'll greet us every night from now on."

I fold my arms across my chest and scoff. "I think not. I just almost gave a group of strangers a peep show!"

West's eyes drop to my boobs, which are now squeezed together beneath my arms, and licks his lips. "Are you trying to fucking kill me?"

"Shouldn't I get dressed?" I whisper. "I don't want to keep your guests waiting."

His eyes crinkle at the corners as he offers me a warm smile and runs his fingertips down my arm, making me shiver. "They're your guests too, princess. And they're definitely not strangers." Then he gives me a hard swat on my ass and tells me to get dressed.

Zeke is waiting for us in the hallway, and the look of amusement on his face elicits another giggle.

West glances between the two of us, his lips twitching. "Are you two done?"

Zeke snorts one more laugh, then closes his eyes. When he reopens them, his usual serious demeanor is perfectly in place, and he nods. Rolling my eyes, I nod too.

Waiting for West to go ahead, I lace my fingers through Zeke's and whisper, "I've never ever seen you laugh like that."

"It's been a long time, baby doll." He gives me a peck on the cheek. "Thank you."

My chest swells with pride that I was able to bring out that rare side of him. "So who are these guests who aren't strangers?"

Waiting for us at the end of the hall, West gestures toward the den. "You're about to find out. And when you do, you'll understand why Zeke almost pissed his pants at the sight of you in nothing but those sexy little panties."

I enter the room, and my heart almost stops beating when he stands. "Hey, Lily Pad."

"Nico!" Dashing toward him, I throw my arms around his neck. He embraces me, and tears drip down my cheeks. When we finally pull apart, I just stand and stare at him, unable to believe that he's really here. That Xander, West, and Zeke brought him to their apartment. "This is the best surprise ever."

"Don't I get a hug too?" Another voice pipes up from behind me, and I spin around.

"What?" I shriek, launching myself at Dean. I'm sobbing while he rubs my back and tells me how good it is to see me again.

I don't know how long it takes me to get over my shock at their presence, but as soon as I do, I bombard all five of my favorite men with questions—what, how, why are they here?

"Sit down and breathe before you pass out." West guides me to the couch and goes to pour drinks.

Zeke takes a seat beside me and grips my hand tightly as Dean and Nico sit on the couch across from us. I hope they know they don't have to hide who they really are from anyone in this room. After handing everyone their Scotch, West perches on the arm of the chair next to Xander and runs a loving hand over his hair. With that one simple touch, he manages to make my brother and his lover visibly more comfortable, and I love him even more for it.

"This is the best surprise ever," I repeat, my smile threatening to split my face in two.

"Well, we're hoping that it can happen more often, shorty."

Just like that, the reality of the situation sinks in. As incredible as it is to have all the people I love most in one room, it isn't safe. And not a single one of them understands why. "That would be great, but it can't happen. It's too dangerous, no matter how careful we are."

Zeke squeezes my hand, and West shakes his head. "It can,

princess. Soon we won't need to be careful. Your time of living in fear of your father finding you is almost over."

I blink at him. "But if he finds out what we did ..." I look to Nico now. "You know what he'll do."

"Not if we do it first, Lily Pad."

It takes my brain a few beats to register what he just said. Is that why they're here? Are they conspiring to— "No." I shake my head. "It's too dangerous, Nico. You know it is."

"It's been a long time coming. We both know that one of us should have put a bullet in his head years ago."

"B-but—" I suck in a deep breath to calm my racing heart, but it doesn't work. "Can't you just wait him out a few more years? Maybe he'll step down. Wouldn't that be safer, easier than killing him? I mean he's not just anyone. He's Carmine Constantine. He has an entire army and God knows who else at his disposal."

Nico scowls at me. "You think that I, of all people, don't know that?"

Dean chimes in. "He's sending me away, Lil."

That gets my attention. "To where?"

"Italy." He shrugs. "Your father still has use for me, he just doesn't want me here."

There must be another way. "Then just don't go. Nico, tell him you need Dean as your second. Tell him—"

"I've tried. I think Pop knows about Dean and me. At least he suspects."

"If he knew for sure, I'd already be dead." Dean says that so nonchalantly; like it isn't preposterous for a man to be killed simply for loving another man. But then, in my father's world, it isn't outrageous—it's normal.

"So, you're going to kill him. Both of you?"

Nico's eyes dart around the room. "Zeke and West are going to help."

"No." I shake my head. "No." I look at Zeke sitting beside me. "You don't know this world. You can't just go to Vegas and kill Carmine Constantine and walk out again."

Zeke lifts my hand to his lips and kisses my knuckles. "We know what we're doing, buttercup."

"Trust us, princess," West adds.

My heart feels like it's being crushed in a vise. Carmine Constantine is a powerful, violent, cruel man. They have no idea what he's capable of. "When is this happening?"

"Soon," West answers.

"Soon?" I wail. "How long is soon?"

"A week or two at most," Nico replies.

No. I need more time to convince them how crazy this is.

Zeke rubs a hand over my back. "Nico will let us know when the time's right, and we'll go to Vegas. We'll be on the jet and back home with you, Fitch, and the dogs within a day, baby doll. I promise."

I wrench my hand from his. "You can't make that kind of promise, Zeke. Nobody can." What I wouldn't give to rewind my life one hour and be back in the kitchen with him laughing so hard he couldn't breathe.

"We know what we're doing, princess," West says, his eyes dark as they burn into mine.

"No." I shake my head. "You really don't. None of you do." I stare at Xander, sure that he'll see sense. "You must see how crazy this is."

He leans forward with his hands clasped between his spread thighs. "It'll be fine, shorty."

I turn my pleas to my brother. Of all the people in this room, he knows what Carmine Constantine is capable of. "Please don't do this."

"I have to, Lily Pad. I can't go on living like this. My whole life is a fucking lie. The *only* thing that keeps me sane is

Dean." He places his hand on Dean's thigh. "And now Pop's sending him away because he knows it will break me. We can end this for good, sis. With West and Zeke's help, I know we can."

I can't breathe. They're crazy. But how do I deny my brother the chance at a life like the one I've found, one I'm only allowed to live because of the sacrifices he made for me?

My head is spinning. I know that Carmine must die. It's the only way. Because if he knows about Nico and Dean, there's every chance he's having them followed. And that means the likelihood of him finding out that I'm alive grows stronger with each passing day.

"Did I smell your incredible fried chicken when we came in earlier?" Xander asks, changing the subject and effortlessly relieving the tension in the way that only he can.

I take a deep breath and accept what I need to do next. Then I let it all go and focus on enjoying a meal with my five favorite people on the planet. "You did."

"So let's go fucking eat."

SAYING goodbye to Nico and Dean was heartbreaking. They stayed for hours after dinner, and we talked about everything except Carmine and their crazy-ass scheme to kill him. It would have been sad to say goodbye anyway, but knowing the danger of their plans for the near future makes me feel like I can't breathe.

Stepping up behind me, Xander wraps his arms around my waist and rests his head on my shoulder. "I'm worried about them too, but Zeke and West are the smartest men I know. They'll be just fine."

I lean back against his hard chest, wanting to believe him.

He tugs at the waistband of my jeans and nuzzles my neck. "You still wearing those sexy-as-fuck panties under here?"

"Yeah."

"I almost passed out when I saw you standing there like that. For a second I forgot your brother and his friend were coming in right behind us."

"Yeah, I don't think I'll be doing that again."

"Oh, no, shorty." He tugs open the button of my jeans. "We'll never bring guests home again. Ever. You can walk around this apartment in your underwear whenever the hell you want."

I let my head drop back against his shoulder, and he slides his hand into my panties.

"Are you two coming to bed?" West's voice cuts through the quiet of the kitchen.

I sigh. I'm so mad at him and Zeke, but I don't want to fight with them. Especially if ... A sob wells in my throat.

"They'll be fine," Xander whispers. "We'll be there in a minute," he calls over his shoulder.

The guys are already under the covers by the time I'm done in the bathroom and ready to crawl into bed.

Xander pats the space between him and West. "Saved your spot, shorty."

I climb over West, and he shuffles back, giving me space to slip under the covers.

Zeke props himself up on one elbow and peers at me over Xander's shoulder. "Did you enjoy your surprise?"

"The part where my brother and Dean came to visit? Yes. The part where you and West have agreed to get yourselves killed? Not so much."

Growling, West wraps his arm around me and pulls me close. The heat from his skin warms my core. "We're doing this for you."

"But I don't want you to do it for me. I want you both to stay here, with me and Xander and our dogs, where we're all safe."

Xander laces his fingers through mine.

"And what if he finds out you're still alive? How safe would we all be then?" West snaps.

I close my eyes as guilt rolls in the pit of my stomach. "I'm sorry for putting you all in danger."

"No. You don't get to do that, baby doll. We should have taken our revenge on your father a long time ago. We won't walk away this time. You are not responsible for him being the man he is, but there's not a chance in hell that we'll let you spend another day of your life living in fear because of him." He reaches over Xander and cups my chin. "Do you understand me?"

I nod.

His scowl tells me he doesn't quite buy my compliance, but then his face softens. "Good." He lies back down and scoots forward, pushing Xander closer to me. His leg drapes over the two of us, and Xander wraps an arm around my waist, just below West's bicep. West burrows his face into my neck, and we lie in the darkness, a sea of bodies and limbs all fused together like one.

West is right—if Carmine finds out I'm alive, none of us will be safe. He'll assume that their importance in my life means they know the whole truth too, and that puts them in more danger than they realize. I'm the one responsible for this mess. I need to be the one to fix it.

~

I WAKE EARLY the next morning to the sound of Snowflake's soft snores. He and Stella are supposed to sleep in the den, but he sneaks in here in the middle of the night and curls up next to the laundry hamper, and occasionally in it.

"You need to go out, boy?" The reliable little pup lets out an excited bark.

"It's too early, Snowy," Xander grumbles.

"You sleep. I'll take him outside." I jump out of bed before any giant arms can haul me back in and offer to take him instead.

"Hurry back, princess," West says with a sleepy growl.

Snowflake rubs himself against my bare legs as I pull on one of the guys' sweaters and my sneakers. "We'll be right back, won't we, boy?"

He lets out a little woof and wags his tail, and I grab my coat from the hook in the hallway. Stella hears us passing by the den and ambles out to join us.

I give her a scratch behind her ear, taking comfort in her steady presence. "Morning, girl."

Opening the reinforced steel door that leads to the rooftop gardens, I'm hit by a blast of cold air. Undeterred by the chill, the dogs run out ahead while I pull my coat tighter and take my phone from the pocket. It's only 2:30 a.m. in Vegas, but that's not an issue. The person I'm calling rarely sleeps, or so I'm told. I dial the number I memorized six long years ago, and despite my confidence that one of them would have let me know if it had changed, my heart stops beating until I hear her voice— soft and sweet and reassuring. Nothing like the ruthless queen with ice in her veins that she's purported to be. Vicious and calculated, Ludovica Santangelo. The first and only female head of the Vegas Mafia. Niece of Giovanni Santangelo.

"It's me."

"Liliana?" My name comes out almost like a plea.

"Hey Mom."

"La mia dolce figlia." I can't help but smile. She's the only person who's ever called me their sweet daughter. "Are you okay? Are you safe?"

"I'm safe," I assure her. "For now, anyway."

"What do you need, Liliana?"

"I think it's time to show the world who I am."

CHAPTER
SIXTY-SEVEN

LILY

"Have a good day, princess." West gives me a soft kiss on the lips. Wrapping my arms around his neck, I cling to him like I might never get the chance to touch him again.

"Hey. We'll be okay," he says, eyes narrowed as they hold mine. I guess he can feel the anxiety in me, just like Xander and Zeke did when I left the penthouse half an hour ago. When I kissed them like it might be the final time. "And we have fun plans for later."

I raise an eyebrow, needing to maintain some semblance of normalcy and pretend that the world as we know it isn't about to change forever. "Do they involve me being naked?"

The corners of his mouth turn up. "Always, princess."

I run my fingers through his thick dark hair. "My favorite kind of plans."

"You're going to be late if you keep looking at me like that, Lily."

I roll my eyes and sigh. "You're right." Before I climb out of the car, I kiss him one more time and try not to think about the email that will land in his inbox in a few hours. The same one Xander and Zeke will receive.

The car doesn't pull away from the curb until I'm safely inside the building, and I stand in the lobby, watching it disappear. I roll back my shoulders, refusing to let fear and anxiety take hold. This is the way it has to be.

I spin around to head to the elevator, but two men in dark suits bar my path. They aren't familiar to me, but it seems that Carmine didn't want to waste time sending his best once he learned of my whereabouts.

"Liliana," the shorter of the two says, sneering.

"No." I try to push past them, but they block me.

The second one opens his jacket to reveal a pistol. "We can do this the easy way or the hard way, Liliana. Up to you. But whatever happens, you will be leaving here with us."

My heart kicks into a gallop. "Is that so?"

The shorter one licks his lips. "He'll pay us double if we bring you to him alive, but I'd be prepared to take a pay cut to snap your pretty little neck."

The lobby is already full of people coming to work for the day, and I hope nobody will try to intervene. I need to make sure I don't draw too much attention while going along with their charade by pretending to be the terrified little girl they've been told about. "And you expect me to just come with you? One scream and security will be over here in a heartbeat. You pull that gun out and the cops will be here too. I'm really not sure you've thought this plan of yours through."

The taller one scowls, but the other one merely laughs. "That's why we have ourselves a little insurance policy." He pulls his cell phone from his pocket and dials a number.

My stomach rolls violently as we wait for the call to be

answered. I know what kind of *insurance policy* tactics men like Carmine employ. It can't be West because he just left here. Xander and Zeke are safe at home. Aren't they? Please God, let them be safe.

"Ah, Sergei," the goon says, grinning. "Show Liliana what will happen if she doesn't come home to Vegas to see her Papa."

He turns the screen and shows me two men tied to chairs, blood streaming down their faces. One has his head held back and a knife at his throat as he struggles against his bindings. "Nico?" I gasp, my hand flying to my mouth. Another face fills the screen, obscuring my view of my brother and his best friend. It's one of my father's men, and this one I recognize. He's been my father's most trusted soldier for as long as I can remember. "Let them go, Stefano. Please. They've done nothing wrong."

Stefano's eyes crinkle with amusement. "Come home and they'll be safe."

I swallow hard. I always knew this would have to happen one day, didn't I? And I meant what I said to Ludovica this morning. It's time to let the world know who Liliana Constantine really is.

SIXTY-EIGHT

XANDER

I place my bowl of cereal on my desk and fire up my laptop, ready to work through the hundreds of emails awaiting my attention.

Right as I open my inbox, West calls. "Have you checked your email?"

"Just doing it now. Why?"

"There's an email from Lily." The panic in his voice has my hand shaking as I move the mouse to the email that came through six minutes ago. The subject line says *I love you*.

My finger hovers over the button, but I can't bring myself to press it. Once I do, it can't be undone. I can't unsee whatever she wrote. Anything that makes West sound like he's been sucker punched in the gut is nothing to joke about. "What does it say?"

"She's fucking gone, Xander."

I blink at the screen. "No. What. Where?"

"To see her father, I think. I dropped her at work three hours ago. I watched her walk into the building. She was safe. She was ..." He wheezes. "He'll fucking kill her."

Fuck, I've never heard him like this. "Relax, buddy," I say as calmly as I can with blood screaming in my ears. "Zeke, get the fuck in here," I shout. "West, come home. We'll take the jet and go to her. We can fix this. I promise."

"Xander, what if he ..." He doesn't finish the sentence. He doesn't need to.

Being the one to hold him together for a change is completely alien to me, but the fact that he needs me to keep my head calms me. "We'll get her. Come home."

Zeke runs into my office. "What is it?"

I nod to my laptop, and he comes to stand beside me. I still haven't opened her email. "West?"

"I'm on my way." The line goes dead, and I'm left with a confused-looking Zeke. I turn back to the screen and click on her message.

Hi guys.

Have I ever told you how much I love you? I'm pretty sure I have, but I'll say it here, in black and white for all eternity, I love you! All of you. Like I could never choose between any of you, and I'm super glad (and lucky) that I don't have to. You have made me feel a happiness that I never could have dreamed possible for myself. You made me envision a future that I never could before. I had one goal, and that was to be a writer, but now I have so many dreams and goals, and they all involve you.

That is why I can't allow you to go up against Carmine for me. There are still some things you don't know. Things that would put you in too much danger if you did. So let me deal with this, and then I can come back home to you all and tell you the whole truth. Every single secret. The ones that I've kept for far too long, the reason I've been a target for Carmine's hatred since the day I was born.

Please don't worry about me. I have more allies than you know, and I have a pretty solid right hook. I'll be home soon. I need to do this alone, so please don't come after me. I'll be back before you even have a chance to miss me. And if I'm not, know that you three are the only men who will ever have my heart. I'm sorry I didn't tell you the whole truth, but you've always known the most important truth I possess—I love you.

Always and forever, your Lily xxx

My heart drops to the ground.

Zeke lets out an animalistic howl. "She went after him?"

I can only nod. Glancing between him and the email, I wonder what the hell she was thinking. Although I want to be angry with her for doing it, I should have known that she'd never let West and Zeke put themselves at risk for her. She's the most selfless person I've ever met in my life.

Zeke sums up the situation with one succinct sentence. "Goddamn it all to hell."

CHAPTER
SIXTY-NINE

ZEKE

An indescribable rage, the likes of which I haven't felt for a very long time, courses through my veins like blood. Every cell in my body simmers with it, making every single move I make feel a thousand times more difficult than it actually is.

Closing my eyes, I grip the edge of the desk. My knuckles turn white. It might just be the only thing holding me up.

"Zeke?" Xander's voice comes from a distance. I can't focus on him. All I can think about is how she's walking into the lion's den; all I can feel is acute fear that I won't be able to save her.

His warm hand grips the back of my neck, grounding me.

I focus on his bright blue eyes that are filled with the same anguish I'm sure must be in mine. I swallow down all the emotion desperate to pour out of me. "I'm here."

"We need to think. Find out where she went and get to her as quickly as possible. West is on his way here."

I mentally check off the things we need to do. I know people in Vegas, people who can get me access to as many weapons as we need. I'll blow that motherfucker and his entire empire to pieces if necessary. "Make sure the jet is ready to go as soon as possible." Xander already has his phone in his hand, and he nods. "Check in with her office too. See what time she left. That will give us an idea of how far ahead she is." He nods again.

Redirecting his attention to me, I grip his face, if only to stop my hands from shaking. "I'm going to make some calls. As soon as West gets here, we'll be ready to go."

BY THE TIME West gets to the penthouse, I've arranged for a small arsenal of weapons to be at our disposal when we land at LAS. He comes straight to my office with Xander close behind him.

"Someone fucking took her, Z," Xander blurts. My veins expand with the force of blood hurtling through them, and I absent-mindedly wonder if this is what a stroke feels like.

West looks as strung out as I feel. "What the fuck are you talking about?"

"She never made it to the office. She's been clocking time on a big story, so they assumed she was working from home. But I knew West dropped her off, so I had the security footage pulled. As soon as she got to the lobby, she was stopped by two mean-looking fucks. She left with them two minutes later."

West pinches the bridge of his nose. "She left or they took her?"

Xander's face is etched with worry. "She walked out, but the footage is pretty clear. They weren't friendly."

My head spins. "But her email. It was sent like forty-five minutes ago."

West shakes his head, his jaw working, and I know he's as

fucked up over this mess as I am. "Maybe she didn't send it?" The look on his face tells me he doesn't buy that.

"No way." Xander pulls his phone from his pocket. "I know my girl's writing. Those are her words." His eyes go wide. "She sent it using Schedjunkie."

He looks up and must notice our blank expressions because he rolls his eyes. "It's an app we developed for our Hellsgate employees, but I downloaded it to Lily's phone for her to use. It allows you to schedule emails and messages ahead of time."

I rub my temples, trying to stave off the dull ache throbbing through my skull. "So she wrote the email before those guys took her from the lobby?"

Xander nods.

"She knew they'd come for her?" West frowns. "None of this makes any sense."

I am going to spank her ass so hard when I get my hands on her. If I get my hands on her. A violent swell of rage and fear washes over me, making me sway on my feet. I shake my head to clear my thoughts, focusing on what needs to be done and praying to a god I don't even believe in that we find our girl in time.

CHAPTER
SEVENTY

LILY

"Get your hands off me, asshole." I snarl at the man with the skull tattoo as he grabs my arm and drags me up the steps of Carmine's mansion.

He presses his face close to mine. "I cannot fucking wait to get the nod to put a bullet in your head, little girl."

Spittle hits my face, and I wipe it away with disgust. "You honestly think Carmine would let some pathetic little weasel like you have the honor of killing me?" I snort, and his cheeks turn purple with rage.

"Always so full of fire, Liliana." The voice of the man I hate more than anyone else in the world drifts through the open doorway. "You haven't changed a bit, have you?"

I spit at his feet. "Fuck you."

Raising his hand, he cracks the back of it across my cheek, causing my head to snap to the side and making my two kidnappers laugh.

"Do not speak to me like that, puttana!"

Memories assault me from being called a whore by the man who tried to turn me into one. The man who snuck into my room every night for almost a year and made me suck his disgusting cock. I balk at the mental assault. His stench. The feel of his flaccid penis filling my mouth. The bile that burned my throat when I gagged or even vomited, but nothing ever made him stop.

I glower, trying to make him feel all the hatred and venom I've been holding onto just for him. If I could let him experience even a fraction of it, then he would surely drop dead where he stands. "Where are Nico and Dean?"

He sneers. "Safe for now."

"I want to see them."

"And see them you will, Liliana. How else will you take their place?"

He dismisses the two men with a jerk of his head, then motions for me to follow him. Shivering, I step inside the house that has haunted my dreams for far too many years. The place I was desperate to escape and swore I'd never come back to.

"How did you find out?" he asks, eyeing me with curiosity.

"An old friend of my father's told me," I say, and it's not exactly a lie. When I was eleven, an old friend of my father's did tell me that Nico wasn't my twin and Carmine wasn't my father. Relief that I wasn't Carmine's nearly overshadowed the depth of my heartbreak about Nico. I was sworn to secrecy, and I've never spoken of it to another soul.

Without showing an ounce of emotion, he backhands me again. "*I* am your father. The man who raised you. The man who fed and clothed you."

Yeah. With my actual father's money, you psychopath! But I keep my mouth shut, if only because I can taste blood and my eye is throbbing where he's already hit me twice. There's nothing I can say to make him believe he's wrong and I'm right. He murdered his own brother in cold blood just to get his hands on more money, as if he didn't have enough already. A calculated monster who forced my mother to give me up. Although, he's not solely to blame for that. Her own family played just as much a part as he did.

"Who was this friend?"

I shrug. "I don't recall his name."

He snarls. "But you believed him over me?"

"Why wouldn't I?" I scoff. "It certainly explained how you could force me to do that sick, twisted shit you made me do. You always hated me. Do you think I didn't realize that was why you were marrying me off to Giovanni, because we all know what happens to women who share his bed, *Dad*. They end up hooked on pills to get through the day or jumping off a building. It was the perfect way to shut me up for good."

He leans close, his sour breath washing over me. His lip curls in disgust. "I should have killed you the moment you were born."

"Yeah, but you couldn't, could you? Because despite all of this"—I wave my hands at his opulent mansion—"you have no true power at all. The Santangelos forced you to take me in because Ludovica begged them to let me live. They forced you to keep her little secret quiet so it wouldn't mess up her marriage to Vito Morrone and ruin their precious alliance. A scared eighteen-year-old girl wielded more power than you." I laugh. "You couldn't even make your own fortune. You had to steal it from my father, your own brother. And you know why? Because he was smarter and stronger and one hundred times the man you are."

His face turns purple and he raises his hand to slap me again, but I punch him in the jaw, causing him to stagger back. My triumph is short-lived though. He barrels forward, crashing into me and pinning me against the wall with a hand wrapped around my throat. He squeezes hard, and I struggle to breathe.

"Boss?" A familiar voice makes us both turn. "Not here, eh?" Stefano says with narrowed eyes. "Let her see her brother before she dies."

Carmine grunts but releases me, and I rub at my tender throat. I follow the men to a darkened room at the back of the house, lit only by one bare low-watt bulb. The faint scent of copper that always seems present in this room makes me gag. I lost count of the number of men I saw walk in here and never come out. It's the same room where I first saw West Archer. The thought of him and Zeke and Xander gives me a fresh injection of courage.

"Lily Pad?" Nico shouts, and I rush to the back of the room where he and Dean remain bound to chairs. Dropping to my knees at their feet, I check them both over for injuries and find nothing serious. Their wounds were caused by someone who knew what they were doing. Someone who knows how to make the cuts and bruises appear worse than they actually are. "Are you both okay?"

"We're fine. We'll both be fine," Nico assures me.

I stand up and face Carmine and Stefano. "Let them go."

Carmine's lips twist into an evil smile. "Soon. Once you're dead. For good this time."

"No!" Nico and Dean shout in unison, struggling against their bonds. "Let her the fuck go, Pop," Nico adds.

I put my hand on my brother's shoulder and squeeze. "It will be okay. I promise."

He blinks a drop of blood from his eye, his face a mask of confusion. He isn't stupid. He knows something isn't adding up.

"Stefano has been waiting for your return, Liliana. Isn't that right?" Carmine turns to his second-in-command.

Stefano winks at me. "Sure have."

"You remember why we call him the surgeon, don't you?" Carmine picks up a scalpel and holds it to the light. "You know he can peel all the skin off a person's body while they're still alive."

Stefano grabs the blade from him. Not taking his eyes off me, he stalks across the room. I step back and bump into my brother's knees.

The unmistakable click of heels on marble echoes from the hallway outside, and Carmine turns toward the open doorway. "Who the fuck?"

I suppress a smile as Stefano reaches me. With Carmine's back turned and his attention focused on the noise outside, his most trusted soldier leans close to my ear. "Okay, Marshmallow?"

I nod, and then he winks at Nico and Dean, who I turn to see are both staring at the two of us with pure shock on their faces. But it's nothing compared to the look on Carmine's face when my mother strides into the room.

"Ludovica." The obvious tremor in his voice makes me want to fist pump the air.

"Carmine," she says, her voice dripping with disdain.

Carmine's mouth opens and closes. "What—how did you get past my guards?"

"Oh, I used that secret entrance. The one you use for your whores." She holds up a shiny silver key and he sputters. Then he turns and looks at Stefano, the only person other than him with access to the key for that door.

"What do you want me to do, Boss?" Stefano asks.

Carmine curls his hands into fists. "I want you to—"

"He wasn't talking to you," my mom says, breezing past him. "I think we should keep it as clean as possible. Perhaps a fight between father and son that escalated? Carmine pulled a knife, and Nico tried to defend himself and ... oops." She shrugs. "It was all a nasty accident. You and Dean witnessed the whole thing."

Carmine gapes, his eyes ping-ponging between my mother and Stefano.

"Did you really think I would allow you to take my daughter and not afford her some protection, Carmine? I should have had you killed a long time ago for what you did to me, to my Angelo, and to our beautiful Liliana." Her cool facade slips for a fraction of a second before she slots it firmly back in place.

Carmine spits at her feet. She laughs, but it's not a pleasant sound. It's cruel and mocking. "Did you not think it even a little strange that Stefano turned up on your doorstep looking for employment just a few days after you and my uncle took Liliana from me?"

"But he was sent by—"

"By a friend of my family, yes. But Stefano's family has been loyal to the Santangelos for almost a century."

"But he ..." Carmine blinks and redirects his attention to Stefano. "You've saved my life."

My mom scoffs. "How else would he have earned your trust for all these years, Carmine? Are you really as stupid as you look?"

Foaming at the mouth, Carmine lunges for her but doesn't get close. Stefano blocks his path and sinks the scalpel into Carmine's stomach, slicing upward. My childhood abuser slumps to the floor, clutching at the guts spilling out between his fingers.

I stand over him and watch the life drain from his body. "You should have just let me go, Carmine." He opens his lips to say something but chokes on the blood pouring from his mouth.

"I wanted *nothing* from you, but you couldn't just leave me to live my life in peace."

With a final sputter, the last flicker of light in his eyes is extinguished. I take satisfaction in knowing that mine was the last face he saw before the devil dragged him to hell.

CHAPTER
SEVENTY-ONE

LILY

Stefano makes quick work of freeing Nico and Dean from their bonds. Running straight to me, Nico wraps me in a hug.

"Lily Pad. What the fuck?" He squeezes me tight as Dean comes up behind me and does the same.

"Are you two okay?" I ask.

They step back. Nico nods but glares at Stefano. "Yeah, but what the hell, Doc?"

Stefano, or Doc as we've affectionately called him since we were innocent little kids and heard people refer to him as *the surgeon*, pats Nico on the back. "I'm sorry, boys, but I had to make it look real. Besides, I barely scratched either of you."

Dean wipes a streak of blood from a cut above his eye. "Tell that to my face, Doc," he says, but he's grinning.

"So, we're not twins?" Nico frowns. "Not even brother and sister?"

I shake my head. Smiling, I try to lighten the mood. "I was

born two days before you, by the way. So I'm officially the oldest now."

He looks down, sorrow clouding his handsome features.

I cup his face in my hands. "You'll always be my brother, Nico. No matter what."

Stefano wraps an arm around my shoulders and kisses the top of my head. "Can we save the family reunion for later? Ludovica has to get out of here before anyone notices she's gone, and we need to deal with all this. Nico and I will let the men know the new order of things."

"You think they'll accept it?" I ask.

"They'll have no choice." He shrugs. "I'll stay on as Nico's adviser for a while, and once the dust settles, I can finally go home."

The look he shares with my mom makes the hair on the back of my neck stand up, but the soft expression flickers on my mother's face and disappears as quickly as it arrived. Clearing her throat, she turns her focus back to me. "Come to the hotel as soon as you can, Liliana. We have things to discuss."

"I will." Swallowing a sob, I watch her slip out the door.

Stefano nods down at Carmine's body. "Let's get this mess cleaned up and you out of here before the cops show up. And I'm sure those friends of yours from New York will be here soon too, Marshmallow."

I shake my head. "I told them not to come. I'll call them and let them know I'm safe."

Nico and Dean share a strange look. "What?" I ask.

Nico wraps his arm around me. "Don't forget that I met them, Lily Pad. I saw the way they all looked at you." He chuckles. "I guarantee that they're already on their way here."

As much as I'd like to believe that they trust me enough to let me handle things myself, I know better. With a sigh, I hold out my hand. "I need to borrow your phone."

CHAPTER
SEVENTY-TWO

WEST

Cursing, I hang up after leaving yet another voicemail on Lily's phone. Is this karma for all the times she tried to call us after we abandoned her with no explanation?

"She'll be okay," Xander says, trying to convince himself as much as me. But the worry on his face makes me feel sick. Carmine Constantine is one twisted fucker. Our girl shouldn't be within three hundred miles of his cruelty.

"Can you go any faster?" As soon as the words leave my mouth, I wish I could take them back. I know Zeke is just as desperate to get to her as Xander and I are, but it feels like the car is barely moving. He could be going 200 miles per hour and it wouldn't be fast enough for any of us.

Justifiably pissed, he bares his teeth at me. "I'm going as fast as this old fucking jalopy will go, asshole. We'll get to her."

I force myself to sit back and close my eyes. I'm grateful he had a car waiting for us at the airport, and even more grateful that it contains enough of an arsenal to take out a small army.

But that gratitude is overshadowed by the tightness in my chest. A thousand sickening scenarios of what could be happening to her right now rush through my head at a million miles a minute. "What if we don't?" Opening my eyes, I look over and see his jaw clenched tight.

～

WHEN WE FINALLY ARRIVE AT the ostentatious golden gate of Carmine Constantine's mansion, the gates are wide open. We jump out of the old minivan before it comes to a complete stop and sprint down the driveway, but my footsteps falter as soon as I see two cop cars and an ambulance parked in front of the house.

My heart lurches so violently that I almost throw up. A cop approaches, and I'm vaguely aware of Xander talking to him, but I'm too busy looking for a sign of Lily.

Bile surges in my throat at the sight of Nico's battered face. I want to shout at him, demand that he tell me where she is, but the words get stuck. Noticing me, he excuses himself from the cop he's talking to and walks over.

"Where is she?"

He shakes his head. "She's gone."

Gone? She can't be gone. I glance at the ambulance, and that's when I see the covered body on the gurney. My knees buckle and black spots dance before my eyes, but a strong hand on my shoulder brings me back.

Nico's face is inches from mine, and his lips are moving. It takes me several seconds to make sense of his words, and when I do, my hands ball into fists. "She's alive, West. She went to her mom's hotel. We didn't think it was a good idea for her to be here when the cops showed up."

"Jesus fucking Christ! She's fine?" My lungs burn as I remember how to breathe. "Lead with that next time, asshole."

"Sorry, buddy." He laughs nervously, and his hand falls from my shoulder as he takes a tentative step back. "It's been a hell of a day. She used my phone to call you. I thought she left you a voicemail."

"A voicemail?" I glance at my cell but there's no voicemail notification. Then the rest of what he says registers in my brain. "Her mom's hotel?" I thought her mom died when she was a baby. Have I stepped into an alternate universe?

"Yeah, her mom. I told you, it's been a day. The Fontana. Biggest on the strip. You can't miss it."

I know the place. And I know who owns it. Jesus fucking Christ, Lily. "Who's that then?" I jerk my head in the direction of the ambulance.

He bows his head a little, playing the grieving son with the cops around, but I don't miss the way his lips curl up. "Dear old Dad."

"My condolences." Then I add, quietly, "Should I be thanking you?"

He shakes his head. "Wasn't me. You need to ask Lily what happened. I'm still trying to wrap my head around it all myself. It seems my sister is a whole lot tougher and smarter than I've given her credit for."

Damn right she is. His sister is the most incredible woman I've ever met. "Yep. She's something else."

He rubs a hand over his jaw and hums his agreement. "But know this, West." He gives me a hard look, and I see all those years of Mafia service in the set of his jaw. "As tough as Lily is, she's still my sister, and if you ever break her heart ..." He glances over at Xander and Zeke. "Any of you."

"We'd never hurt her, Nico. She means everything to us. I

might consider putting her on a leash after this little stunt she just pulled, but I'd die to protect her."

His eyes narrow. I'm not sure he appreciated the leash joke, but then the corner of his mouth curls up in a grin. "She's sure going to keep you all on your toes, West."

God, I sure fucking hope so. "I promise I'll never break her heart." *Ever again.* Shaking off the lingering guilt over the worst mistake I've ever made, I glance back at the battered old mini-van, then take in the mansion in front of me. I need to see my girl right fucking now, and that piece of shit isn't going to be fast enough. "You got a car we could borrow?"

"Sure. Garage is in the back. Keys are hanging by the door. Take whichever one you want."

"So you're telling me that Lily's mom is the head of the Mafia? Like the whole Mafia?" Xander leans over the center console from the backseat of the Lamborghini Urus I borrowed.

"If she owns this hotel, that's exactly who she is."

"This situation keeps getting weirder by the minute." Zeke frowns. "Why hasn't she called us and let us know that she's safe?"

"What if she doesn't want to see us?" Xander asks, and the atmosphere in the car changes on a dime.

"Nico said she tried to call me. He thought she left a voice-mail, but she didn't." We all glance at each other before I turn my eyes back to the road.

"Of course she wants to see us. She loves us," Zeke mutters. "And I don't give a fuck who her mom is, we're taking our girl home with us."

I bring the Lamborghini to a screeching halt and toss the keys to the valet as we run into the hotel. We don't know what room she's in, and there's no way a halfway decent hotel would hand a woman's room number to three strange men. This hotel is a shitload better than decent, and the woman in question is the owner's daughter, so I have no idea how we're going to find her, but I do know that nothing will stand in our way.

But before we can come up with a plan, we're approached by a smartly dressed guy with a shaved head and the squarest jaw I've ever seen. "Sirs, I believe you're looking for Ms. Constantine?"

Who the hell is this guy, and can we trust him?

Without waiting for a response, he tells us to come with him and walks away. With no other way to find Lily, we follow him through the lobby to a large private area. Finally, he stops outside an ornate black door and knocks softly before pushing it open without an invitation. Swallowing a ball of dread along with the acute concern that we might get our heads blown off, I follow him inside. We should have brought one of the dozens of weapons that were stashed in the back of the minivan, but it wasn't exactly feasible to sort through grenades and semi-automatics with the cops hanging around.

"West!" Lily's voice is like music to my ears. "Xander! Zeke!" She launches herself into my arms, and I bury my face in her hair, squeezing the life out of her.

"Thank fuck, princess. Are you okay?"

Her face is wet with tears. "I'm okay. They took my phone and I tried to call from Nico's but you must have been in the air and I was going to leave a voicemail but then a call came through and then the cops were on their way and I had to get out of there—" She gasps for air.

Snarling, I brush my fingers over the purple bruise blooming across her cheek. I fucking hate that someone hurt her. She shivers, which makes me feel like an ass. I push a dark curl behind her ear and cup her beautiful face in my hands. "It's okay. We're here now."

"Come here, shorty." Xander's voice is little more than a growl as he pulls her from my arms so he can hug her too. The distance gives me the opportunity to scan her body, and I'm relieved that she doesn't appear to have any major injuries.

Xander finally lets her go, but Zeke stays back and just stares at her.

"Hey." Her soft voice seems to break whatever spell he was under, and he reaches her in one long stride. Picking her up, he crushes her to his chest.

A throat clears, and we all turn to see an elegantly dressed woman with long dark hair and eyes the exact same color as Lily's. Her icy glare sends a shiver down my spine.

Lily blushes beet red. "Guys. I'd like you to meet Ludovica Santangelo. My mom."

CHAPTER
SEVENTY-THREE

ZEKE

Taking a seat at the huge table that dominates the room, I pull Lily onto my lap and bury my face in her hair. Ludovica eyes me suspiciously, and while I'm mindful that she's the head of the Mafia and I currently have my hands all over her daughter, I gotta say, I don't give the smallest sliver of a fuck.

I inhale Lily's sweet scent and squeeze her until she giggles and squirms. "Zeke. You're going to crush me."

I relax my grip just a little and press my mouth to her ear. "You are going to get the spanking of your life when we get home. Mafia princess or not."

She wraps her arms around my neck and offers me one of her sweet smiles. "I sure hope so."

My cock jumps at the thought of punishing her and taking care of her after. Maybe I won't even wait until we get home.

"Mr. Cavanagh, may I have a word with my daughter?" Ludovica says in a clipped tone. Of course she knows who I am. Given the fact I'm dating her daughter, I have no doubt she knows my shoe size and what color underwear I currently have on.

I stare back at her. "Go ahead. But she's staying right here."

"Zeke." Lily shoots me a warning look. Acquiescing to my girl's request and not her mother's, I allow her to climb off my lap. She sits in the chair next to mine and directs her attention at her mom. "You can say anything you have to say in front of Zeke, West, and Xander. I trust them."

Xander and West sit on either side of Lily and me, and Ludovica eyes us all before finally taking a seat. A tall man with a neat gray beard stands guard behind her. Tossing her long hair over her shoulder, she fixes Lily with a hard stare. They might have the same bright green eyes and dark curls, but where this woman has ice in her veins, my girl has straight fire.

"Tell me. What now, Liliana? Carmine is gone, and Nico will take his place as the new head of the family. But you are the rightful heir to the true fortune, the Constantine hotels and casinos." She arches one perfectly sculpted eyebrow. "A simple DNA test will prove it."

Lily leans back in her chair. "I'm going home. To New York."

Her mother frowns, and an inscrutable emotion flashes in her eyes. "You don't want any claim over your father's legacy?"

"Nico is the rightful heir because he's the best man for the job. Even if not by birth, he's my brother in every other sense of the word. I'll have some papers drawn up renouncing my claim on everything related to Constantine Holdings. And I'm sure he'll have a fairer and more tolerant reign than his father ever did. *My* father's legacy isn't the money he made or the casinos and hotels he built. Those things are tainted with the blood of all the people Carmine killed to get his hands on them. My father's legacy is sitting right here in front of you." Her back straightens and she tilts her chin up. "And I am going to change the world."

Fuck yeah you are, buttercup.

Ludovica's eyes crinkle at the corners, and her lips curl into the faintest hint of a smile. Maybe the woman is human, after all. "Then I look forward to watching that happen, Liliana. Or is it Lily now? Lily Sloane." The name rolls off her tongue like she's testing it to see how it tastes.

Lily hesitates, but when she speaks, her tone is totally confident. "Liliana is fine. I told you it was time to show the world who I truly am."

I look over at West and Xander. They look as confused as I feel, but we keep our mouths shut and continue to watch this scene unfold.

"Liliana Constantine is back from the dead then?" Ludovica asks.

"She is. A lot of good can be done with a name as powerful as mine. And like I said, my father's legacy will be greater than the things he built."

Ludovica's lips twitch. "And your mother?"

Lily fixes her eyes on the woman who birthed her and lets out a breath. "I'm sure she'll continue to watch from the sidelines like she always has."

"Protecting you," her mother adds with a frown.

"I don't need protection anymore." My sweet Lily laces her fingers through mine and Xander's, then looks past me to West.

"You will always have my protection, la mia dolce figlia, whether you need it or not." Her eyes well up, but she blinks quickly until they're clear.

Lily smiles at her. "Well, let's hope I never need it."

The man behind Ludovica bends his head. "Ma'am, you need to leave now."

Closing her eyes, she nods, and when she reopens them, her ruthless Mafia mask slips and shows the woman underneath, laying bare all the sacrifices she made to become what she is.

Fascinated, I watch the two women move together and stand facing one another as though they're peering into a mirror. Ice reflects fire.

"Thank you, Mom."

"Always, Liliana."

They exchange a brief hug, then Ludovica turns and walks away. Before she leaves, she throws one last glance over her shoulder. "Remember this, mia figlia—although the world will never know, you are my legacy too."

SEVENTY-FOUR

WEST

Everyone stayed quiet on the way to the jet. There are so many questions that it's hard to know where to begin, and none of us want to bombard Lily after the day she's had. We're going to ensure she can't sit down for a week when we give her the spanking she's due, but for now, we're going to give her space to heal and come to terms with everything that happened.

But after we take off, we're all surprised and relieved that she breaks the silence. "I'm sorry I kept another secret."

"Why did you?" I ask.

"Angelo Constantine wanted nothing to do with his family's Mafia ties, so he created his own legacy. He built Constantine Holdings from nothing and turned it into the most successful hotel chain in the country. Carmine had him murdered, his own brother, so he could take control of my father's wealth, and he killed everyone who knew my true parentage. Everyone except my mother and her uncle, Giovanni. And the only reason he didn't go after them was because he knew he'd never get away with it. Do you think he would have thought twice about killing me or anyone he remotely suspected of knowing the truth? He was terrified I'd take it all away from him even though I never wanted any of it."

"So Giovanni Santangelo was your great-uncle? And he wanted to marry you even though he knew you were his niece's daughter?" Xander shudders. "That's fucked up."

"Yeah, well he was a fucked-up kind of guy."

"And your real mom is the head of the fucking Mafia?" Zeke whistles.

"Yeah. Although when she had me, she was just an eighteen-year-old kid who was impregnated by a man who stood against everything her family represented. He was more than twice her age, but they were in love. He was going to marry her, and they were supposed to live happily ever after."

"So Carmine passed you off as his own child?" I ask, trying to wrap my head around the whole fucked-up situation. "But why?"

"My mom was forced by her family to give me up in order to protect her marriage to Vito Morrone—an alliance that sealed the Santangelos position of power. Carmine offered to raise me as his own daughter. I guess he wanted to keep me close so that I'd never come after my birthright if I ever discovered who my father was. He would have had me killed if it wasn't for my mom. She traded her silence about my father's murder for my life. Stefano told me she begged her uncle to find me a better family, but he and Carmine came to an agreement and she didn't get much choice in the matter. I guess she was as much a victim as I was. However, she knew better than anyone the kind of man Carmine was, and that's why she sent Stefano to watch over me. He infiltrated Carmine's organization and worked his way up to being his second."

Zeke's brow furrows. "So why didn't she help get you out

when you faked your death? Surely she was in a position to help you?"

Lily shakes her head. "She was still under Giovanni's control back then. She didn't take charge until after he died."

"And what about now? Why does she still keep you a secret?" I ask.

"Because she's still Vito Morrone's wife, and the alliance between those families is decades old. If anyone were to ever find out she has lied to the Morrones all this time and wasn't the virgin princess she was purported to be, then it would cause a rift that could tear the whole hierarchy apart." Lily blows out a breath and sinks back into her seat.

This is all a lot to process, and I'm a grown-ass man. I have no idea how Lily dealt with all of this at just eighteen. "And it was Stefano who told you about your real parents?"

"Yeah. When I was eleven." She bats away the tears on her cheeks.

"Come here, princess."

She stands and I pull her into my lap. Banding my arms around her, I hold her like I'll never let go.

"Carmine was the one who hurt you, wasn't he?" Zeke asks, his voice low and dangerous.

"It started when I was eleven and it stopped two hundred and sixteen days later," she says matter-of-factly. She counted the number of days that sick fuck abused her. Rage burns in my chest, and I wish I could bring the man back to life and kill him all over again. "But when Stefano realized what was happening, he fixed it so that Nico and I had adjoining rooms. I don't know if he ever let Carmine know that he knew, but it didn't happen again."

Burying my face in her neck, I take a deep breath and drink her in. She's ours now, and nobody will ever hurt her again.

"Are there any more secrets you're keeping from us, baby doll?"

She shakes her head. "I promise you that's everything, and I will never lie to you again. Please know that I only kept secrets to protect you. Because if anything ever happened to any of you —" Her words are swallowed by a gut-wrenching sob.

"You think we don't feel the same about you too?" Xander asks. "Do you have any idea how we felt when we opened your email yesterday?"

She sniffs. "I knew it would hurt, and I'm sorry, but if I told you what I was going to do—"

"We'd have chained you to your bed," I say with a hint of a smile. As pissed as I am that she cut us out, my prevailing emotion is joy. The woman I love is not only alive, but she's in my arms.

"We would have," Zeke agrees.

"I'm sorry, but I couldn't let any of you risk being hurt because of me. I couldn't have lived with myself."

Xander looks out the window, avoiding making eye contact with her.

"Xander?" She says his name on a plea, but he continues looking out at the clouds.

I release her from my embrace, and she goes to him, dropping to her knees at his feet. "Xander, please look at me. I'm sorry."

With a deep sigh, he turns to face her. "Get off your knees, shorty."

"Only if you're not mad at me."

He frowns. "I'm super fucking pissed at you." Her face falls, but he rubs the pad of his thumb over her cheek. "But only because I love you so goddamn much."

"I love you too."

"Did you really just tell our girl to get *off* her knees?" Zeke asks.

"Amateur," I mutter.

Xander's mouth drops open. "What? I was making a point."

"Kind of a dumbass move if you ask me. You can come kneel before me, buttercup," Zeke adds with a dark chuckle.

Lily flashes him a wicked grin, but before she can move, Xander puts his hand on the back of her neck and shakes his head. "Uh-uh, shorty. Come up here." He pulls her up to straddle him before he kisses her. I watch, and even though they're only making out, it makes my cock hard.

I glance at Zeke who raises an eyebrow at me. "We got five more hours to kill on this flight."

Grinning, we both pull off our clothes. "You ever had sex on a plane before, princess?"

CHAPTER
SEVENTY-FIVE

ZEKE—8 WEEKS LATER

L ily's eyes practically pop out of her head when she walks into the kitchen after getting home from work and sees the three of us in our tuxedos.

She blinks, her eyes wide and shining with excitement. But she always looks like that lately. She loves her job and recently published an article on the plight of New York's animal shelters that's already been nominated for awards. The media frenzy over Liliana Constantine's return from the dead has finally quieted down. Life has settled into a routine again, one that involves a whole lot of fun and fucking, but still a routine. However, there's one thing that's been nagging at me, and I know Zeke and Xander feel the same. "Where are you all going?" she asks.

I cross the room and slide an arm around her waist. "You mean where are *we* going, buttercup?"

Frowning, she glances down at her jeans and sweater. "Um. Okay. Where are we going?"

"We're going to the club," Xander says. "There's a dress on

your bed."

She swallows, her eyes bouncing between the three of us. "No. I don't want to go there."

Guilt crushes me. I knew she wouldn't want to. "You are, baby doll. We need to make things right."

Her pretty face turns bright pink, and she crosses her arms over her chest. "If you think I'm ever going to that place again, you're very mistaken."

Standing behind her, Xander pulls back her hair and kisses her neck. "Please, shorty?"

"You think I'm that easy?"

West smirks, and she glowers at him. "Don't even think about saying what you're thinking."

"Okay, princess. But we're going to the club tonight. A PR firm is throwing a big event. There'll be champagne."

"I'm never drinking champagne again," she reminds us.

I brush her hair back and cup her face. "Don't make us go without you."

She keeps her arms folded and taps her foot.

"What's the name of that PR firm again, Fitch?" West asks.

"Um. Reid Spencer, right?"

Lily's brow pinches in a cute-as-fuck scowl. "Bree Reid's PR firm? You're letting her use your club for an event?"

West arches one eyebrow. "Business is business, princess."

I stifle a grin. She's going to punch him in the mouth any second, and he deserves it. I rub a hand over my jaw and wince at the memory of being on the receiving end of our girl's mean right hook.

West brushes his knuckles over her cheek. "So we can either go alone, or we can go with the most incredible woman alive, who's going to be wearing a sexy dress, and we can let the entire world, including Bree Reid, know that you're our girl."

Her eyes narrow, and I give her one last nudge. "Your choice, buttercup."

She rolls her eyes dramatically. "Fine."

I CAN FEEL the tension in Lily as soon as we step out of the car. Not that I blame her. I'm strung tight as a bow myself. All I can think about is how cruel I was to her the last time we were here.

The flash of a camera blinds me. Damn paparazzi. I pull Lily behind me and scowl at the bouncers standing nearby. "Move these fucks out of here."

Xander shields Lily from the other side, and we hurry into the club. "I'm sorry, baby doll. The event was supposed to be private."

Glancing around nervously, she shrugs. West finishes speaking with our security team and jogs over to us. "They're gone now," he assures us.

She chews on the inside of her cheek, and Xander asks her if she's nervous.

She blinks at him, her eyes wet with unshed tears. Fuck, we are such assholes. "Kinda."

He wraps his arms around her and kisses the top of her head. "I promise not to leave your side the entire night. Okay?"

She's nodding against his chest when a bouncer approaches. "Your booth is ready, Mr. Archer." Lily's eyes widen on the man who just spoke, and my heart sinks.

Clearing my throat, I pull her from Xander's arms and into mine. "José, I'd like you to meet our girlfriend, Lily. You might remember her from the Hellsgate launch? When I was a complete fuck-knuckle and left her standing in the rain."

He nods, his eyes softening on her face. "I do."

"She ever comes here again, with or without us, she gets treated like a fucking queen. You got me?"

"I understand, Boss."

She gives me a shy smile. Fuck, I love this girl. I slide my hand to her ass, which is perfectly encased in a black leather minidress that fits her like it was painted on, letting every single person here know that she's mine.

West tilts his head at the doors leading to the main room of the club. "Shall we?"

I give Lily a quick kiss on the cheek and step back, allowing Xander to escort her. It will sting a whole lot worse if he's the one with his hand on her ass when we walk through those doors.

We enter the central area of the club, and just like everywhere he goes, Xander turns heads. This is his arena. PR is his domain. A world where image and appearance are king and one in which West and I prefer to take a back seat. Bree's eyes land on him, and she weaves her way through the crowd like a heat-seeking missile. I bite back a grin when her face twists into a hideous sneer. Yup, she saw our girl and she is pissed.

"It's so lovely to see you, Bree," Xander says with a fake smile. "And I think you know my girlfriend, Lily." He doesn't take his hand off Lily for a second.

Bree looks Lily up and down, and my hands ball into fists. I glance over and find West smirking at me. "Pretty sure our girl can handle Bree," he whispers.

Lily rests her hand on Xander's chest, and he pulls her closer. "Oh, of course she does. She made up a bunch of lies about me, remember?"

Xander's face lights with amusement. "You know, you're right, baby. I remember now."

Bree rolls her eyes. "I just told you what I'd heard."

Lily takes a step forward, closing the gap between her and

the other woman and making Bree flinch. "No. You flat-out lied, Bree. You knew exactly what you were doing. Because you're a bitch." Bree flinches again. "Yeah. I said it. I've known you were a bitch since we first met in college, but I was always too polite to say it until now."

Bree purses her lips. "This game is all about being able to talk in the right ears, Lily. I simply told West and Zeke what they were waiting to hear. It's not on me that they chose to believe me instead of you, now is it?"

I could kill the bitch for reminding Lily of that. But my fear that the plan will bite us all in the ass is soothed when Lily plasters a saccharine smile on her face. "I should be thanking you really."

"And why is that?" Bree's fingernails tap a nervous tempo against her leg, belying her bored tone.

"Because the make-up sex"—she tilts her head back and lets out a breathy moan—"especially with this one here ..." She turns and runs a hand through Xander's hair. "It's out of this world."

Bree's mask falls completely, her beautiful face twisting and showing a glimpse of what she looks like on the inside.

West steps forward and wraps his arm around the other side of our girl's waist. "Oh and thank you for bringing all of these lovely people here for us tonight, Bree."

Her attention goes to West, and she scoffs. "For you?"

West looks at Xander. "Did you not tell her?"

Xander slaps his forehead. "You know, I downright forgot. I've been so busy *making up* with my girl, it must have slipped my mind."

Hurt darkens Bree's features. "Tell me what?"

"All of your clients are now our clients." Xander flashes her his winning smile.

She opens and closes her mouth like a fish on a hook.

"We gave them a pretty solid offer." He shrugs. "One they couldn't refuse."

"No." She shakes her head, eyes wide with horror. "They have contracts."

"Naw." Xander rubs a hand over his jaw. "Nothing our attorney couldn't get us out of. Turns out most contracts are actually pretty meaningless." His lips twitch. "Who knew?"

"They are not useless." She stamps her foot, and I cough to cover my laugh. "I'll sue every one of them."

"We've already promised to cover their legal costs. You'll be tied up in court for the next twenty years." West looks down at his fingernails like he's already done with this conversation.

"Your daddy might be rich, Bree, but mine is richer," Xander says, flashing West a wink. "And we have a few hundred million to spare if it comes to it. We're more than happy to watch you walk away without a dime."

Her eyes dart between all of us and fill with moisture.

I throw my arm around Xander's shoulder. "Don't ever fuck with our girl, Bree. Try it again and we'll fucking end you permanently. You got that?"

With that, we walk away and don't look back. Once we're settled in our spot, the booth Lily sat drinking champagne with us the night we met her, I drape my arm around my girl's shoulders and put my hand on Xander's thigh.

Lily takes a sip of her champagne and sighs. "This night is turning out to be pretty incredible after all."

I drop a kiss on her forehead. "You know what else is incredible?"

She shivers. "What's that?"

My hand skims down her back. "Your ass in that dress."

She rolls her eyes, but I don't miss her laugh. Pressing my lips against her ear, I growl. "I'm going to fuck it when we get home, buttercup."

Her entire body shudders and she lets out a low moan that travels straight to my dick.

I lace my fingers through hers. "Can you forgive us, Lily?"

She offers me that sweet smile of hers. "I already did or I wouldn't be here."

I brush my fingers over her cheek. "You're so fucking perfect for us, you know that, don't you?"

West pulls back her hair and plants a kiss over her fluttering pulse. "Yeah. We're the perfect fit," she murmurs.

SEVENTY-SIX

XANDER

With my hands on Lily's glorious ass, I grind my hips against hers as we move in perfect sync to the thumping bass of the music. I steal a glance at Zeke and West sitting in the booth and suppress a grin when I see them watching us intently. I can only imagine the raging boners they're currently sporting. I'm so gonna get in trouble for this, but oh, it's so fucking worth it. Lily tips her head back, and I run my teeth along her throat, lashing her sensitive skin with my tongue. I love how she tastes. How she smells. My hard cock twitches against her stomach.

A soft moan falls from her lips, and I squeeze her ass harder. It's no surprise to me at all when West and Zeke appear at our sides not even twenty seconds later.

Lily spots them too and flutters her eyelashes, her arms still around my neck. West jerks his head toward the exit, his jaw clenched. "We're leaving."

"We are? Why?" she asks.

West looks pissed, but he isn't. He's horny as fuck. But it's Zeke who answers while West glares at the two of us. "Because you two little brats are about to get a good fucking, that's why."

Lily gapes at them, and I suppress a laugh.

"Now," West growls, and Lily clearly holds back her own giggle.

I place my hand on the top of her ass and guide her toward the back exit where our car will be waiting. "You're in so much trouble for grinding your sexy ass in front of all these people."

"What? Why? We were just dancing."

Zeke throws her a look over his shoulder. "You were practically fucking, baby doll."

ZEKE, West, and I sit in the back seat of the car, and I pull Lily onto my lap to straddle me. Giggling, she wraps her arms around my neck and rolls that sweet pussy over my aching shaft.

Reaching beneath her dress, I pull her lacy panties aside and drag my fingers through her slick wet center.

She grinds against me, her teeth sinking into her bottom lip as she stifles a groan. "Aren't we already in trouble?" she asks in a seductive whisper, feigning innocence when she's as big a brat as I am.

I grin as I slide a finger inside her. "You think I'd let either of these two stop me from fucking my girl when she's this wet for me?"

She moans out my name, and Zeke's dark laugh rumbles to my left. "You two are so fucked."

I unzip my pants and free my aching cock. "She's about to be." I yank her panties to the side and line my cock at her soaking entrance. Her whimpers and West's growl fill the car, fueling my need to take her right here, right now. Grabbing Lily's hips, I pull her down and sink into her hot dripping pussy. And fuck she feels so good squeezing me.

"Oh, god," she whines, throwing back her head as I fill her with every inch. My fingers dig into her hips.

"I'm so gonna enjoy punishing them for this when we get home, Z," West says, his tone hinting at the danger to come.

Sinking her teeth into her juicy bottom lip, Lily glances between them both, but I grip her jaw and turn her head so her entire focus is on me. "Who's fucking you right now?"

She sucks in a breath that makes her beautiful tits shudder. "You are."

I thrust my hips, driving deeper into her. "When I'm inside you, I want your fucking eyes on me. Do you understand me?"

Her cheeks flush and she nods.

"Good girl." Fisting my hands in the hem of her dress, I yank it over her head in one fluid motion and trail my lips across her collarbone, working my way down while I unhook her bra. Within seconds, her mouthwatering tits are right in front my face, begging to be bitten and sucked.

"Xander," she pants as I suck one hard nipple into my mouth and flick my tongue over the stiff peak. I'm vaguely aware of West and Zeke giving a running commentary on how hot we both are and how we're both getting fucked when we get to the penthouse, but my focus remains on my girl and the way she's riding me home like she's about to win the Kentucky Derby. Back arched from pleasure, her lips part on a series of desperate cries.

Her hot, silky cum slicks my cock, and her pussy walls greedily milk my shaft as she comes apart for me.

"Holy fuck!" I growl as she takes me over the edge with her, all heat and pleasure while my balls draw up and I fill her with my release.

With a contented sigh, she rests her forehead on mine. I'm still trying to catch my breath when Zeke lets out a feral sound. "Dammit, West. I think I'm gonna have to fuck them right here in the car."

CHAPTER
SEVENTY-SEVEN

LILY

Zeke kneels behind me on the floor of the limo, the coolness of his shirt soothing my overheated flesh. At some point in the last fifteen minutes, the car stopped moving and the engine turned off. As Zeke pushes me flat to the door, I peer out the tinted window at the parking garage in the basement of their building. He grabs my wrists and yanks them above my head. "Hold on, baby doll." His low growl vibrates through my body.

I do as he asks, tightly gripping the handles above the doors. "Such a good little brat." He laughs darkly as he proceeds to tie my wrists to the handles using my bra and panties. Devil!

He pulls at the restraints when he's done and gives a satisfied grunt, then slaps my ass hard, making me yelp.

"You're so fucked, princess. You too, brat." West says with a growl and another loud slap comes from behind me. Xander groans, and when I glance over my shoulder, goosebumps break out all over my entire body at the sight of him bent over the bench seat with one of West's hands fisted in his hair and the other bruising his hip while he drives inside him. Holy fuck-nuggets, that's so hot.

Before I can enjoy more of the show, Zeke grabs my jaw and turns my head back to face the window, then smacks my ass. "No watching them while I'm fucking you tonight, baby doll." He pulls my hair to one side and drags his teeth over my neck, making me squirm. "When I take this beautiful ass for the first time"—he spanks me again—"you'll only be thinking of me. Isn't that right?"

He pushes two fingers deep into my pussy, and I whimper. Rocking back, I pull on my restraints and lean against his hard chest.

"Isn't. That. Right?" he asks again, punctuating each word with a thrust of his skilled fingers.

"Y-yes!" My scream fills the car and mingles with Xander's groans.

Zeke slips his fingers out and slides them to the seam of my ass, circling my tight hole. I instinctively tense and inch forward until my chest is pressed against the door. But Zeke simply follows, the weight of his body sandwiching me between him and the window. I suck in a deep breath, and he pushes his finger farther into my ass. "I told you I was fucking this ass tonight, buttercup. And if you'd been a good girl instead of letting Xander take you in the car, I would've made you feel a little more comfortable. We would be doing this in bed with you spread open for me, and I would have used a half bottle of lube to get you nice and ready."

Another brutal swat stings my sore ass cheek. "But you were a naughty little whore, and now you're dripping with his cum."

I wince at the burning stretch of his finger in my ass. "So that's all I'm gonna use to fuck you with. Right here in this car with your luscious tits pressed against the glass and your hands tied with your own wet panties." He sinks his teeth into my shoulder blade, biting hard as he pushes his finger all the way inside. Pain and pleasure fight for control of my body, making me cry out. "And you can cry and beg me not to." Without warning, he drives his cock into my pussy, and stars flicker behind my eyelids. "But this ass is getting fucked no matter how hard you fight it."

I chant his name with each moan and whimper he pulls from me with the simultaneous motion of his finger and his cock. So deliciously full of him, I feel like it's too much, but I'll never get enough. White hot pleasure coils deep in my core, snaking and turning and desperate to burst out of me.

"Not yet, buttercup." He pulls out, leaving me empty and panting for breath. Seconds later, I shudder when his wide head presses against my asshole. He's coated with mine and Xander's release, but this is still going to hurt. There's nowhere for my body to go with the cold steel of the car at my front and a scorching, desperate Zeke at my back.

He presses his lips to my ear. "Safe word?"

"M-marshmallow."

"Good girl." With that, he pushes his cock into my ass.

I squeeze my eyes tightly closed as he stretches me wider than my body is prepared for. Tears leak from the corners, and the cheek that's pressed against the window slips on the glass. Zeke grunts. "That's it, cry for me, buttercup. You know that makes me want to fuck you harder."

"No. It hurts," I croak.

"I know it fucking hurts," he growls. "It's supposed to fucking hurt."

"Zeke!" His name is more of a gasp than a word as he pushes deeper. My head spins from the pain and euphoria gripping my body. The pain is winning out, but it must speak to something inside my soul because I have no desire to utter my safe word and make it stop.

He dips his hand between my thighs and presses the pads of his pointer and middle fingers on my clit, tipping the balance back to where I love it. Pain might be the thing that gets Zeke off like nothing else, but the happiness of the people he loves— me, West, Xander—is always his primary focus. And I adore him for that.

"Your ass is so fucking tight, Lily. I want all the way inside you."

"No, you're too big. I can't take any more," I rasp as tears keep rolling down my cheeks.

Increasing the pressure on my clit, he rolls his hips and sinks all the way inside me until his thighs are slamming against mine, and I shudder violently as intense pain gives way to searing pleasure. "That's it." He thrusts gently now. "I'm all the way in, buttercup. I knew you could take all of me."

"Fuck, Zeke."

He trails his tongue over my neck. "Such a good little whore for me. Does it still hurt?"

"Yes," I whimper.

With a groan, he gently thrusts in and out of me and continues to rub my clit. Then he sinks his teeth into the base of my neck, and that's my undoing. I come apart in his arms, shaking uncontrollably, my teeth rattling in my head as he fucks me through my orgasm.

"Motherfucking fuck!" His hips still as he empties his release into me. He rests his forehead on my shoulder, both of us panting heavily.

"You are fucking perfect, buttercup." Wrapping me in his arms, he slides his cock out of my throbbing ass.

～

Letting out a contented sigh, I burrow further beneath the comforter. West and Xander lie on either side of me, with Zeke behind Xander, his arm draped protectively over the pair of us. He and West cleaned us up when we got to the penthouse before making us hot chocolate with a shot of whiskey. A deliciously perfect end to a perfect evening. "I never want to leave this bed," I murmur sleepily.

"I can make that happen, princess," West growls in my ear.

I hum my agreement. "Maybe just for a little while?"

"Duvet day tomorrow?" Xander suggests.

"Christmas movies and hot chocolate with marshmallows and sugar cookies?"

"Christmas is six weeks away, buttercup."

"I know, but I'm in a Christmassy mood. Can we put our tree up early?"

Xander chuckles. "We'll need to get one first."

"A real one will die if we get it now, princess."

"Then we can get a fake one too? Then get the real one a few weeks before Christmas. Please?" When I was very young, Stefano and our housekeeper, Elena, always made the holidays special for Nico and me, and I hang onto those happy memories from my childhood while trying to forget the rest of it. This time of year has always been special to me, but Christmas in New York, with all the snow and the lights—it's beyond magical. And spending the holidays with my guys ... my heart flutters.

"Whatever you want, shorty." Xander's enthusiasm makes me smile, even as Zeke and West grumble a reluctant agreement.

"Don't be so grumpy. Christmas is so much fun."

West kisses my head. "I'm sure it will be with you. An excuse to spoil you with presents."

"You don't have to spoil me," I insist. "That's not why I love it."

"Your ass still sore?" Zeke asks with a hint of warning in his voice.

My cheeks heat at the memory of him unhinged and feral in the limo. "Yes."

"Well, if you don't want to get thrown over someone's knee and spanked, you will let us spoil you rotten for Christmas. You got that?"

"Yes, Sir," I whisper.

"Sir?" West growls. "Oh, I fucking like that word on your lips, princess."

Zeke laughs. "She didn't call you Sir."

A dark chuckle rolls through him. "Oh, she fucking will."

CHAPTER
SEVENTY-EIGHT

Christmas Eve

Zeke's fingers curl around mine and pull me from the car.

"Can I take off my blindfold yet?"

I recognize West's scent coming up behind me. His arm slips around my waist, his hot mouth on my ear. "Soon, princess. Have a little patience."

The biting wind whips my hair, and I shiver despite being wrapped in my coat and scarf.

"You cold, shorty?"

"A little." I shiver again.

Xander's arms snake around me from behind, and the heat of his body warms me.

"Keep walking," Zeke urges. The three of us shuffle awkwardly forward, the sound of late-night traffic humming in the background and the scent of the city in my nose. Where the hell are we, and what deviousness have my guys cooked up?

"Is this my Christmas present?" I bounce on my toes. "Because I have the best surprises planned for you." I giggle at the thought of the gifts I've picked out for each of them.

"Nope. Not a Christmas gift," West replies.

We come to a stop, and I turn my head in every direction, straining to hear anything that might offer me some clue as to where we are.

"You ready, shorty?"

"Yes!" I squeal, then remember to add, "Please."

The blindfold falls from my face, and I blink as the bright lights of the WXZ lobby come into focus. "You brought me to your building?"

West squeezes my hand in his. "Not our building, princess."

Xander presses his lips against my ear. "*Our* building."

I frown. "That's what I said."

"Look up," Zeke says, and my eyes follow his to the giant polished steel WXZ sign twenty feet above our heads. Except that it no longer says WXZ.

"WXYZ?" They changed their company name? "What's the Y for?"

Zeke brushes his lips over my knuckles while Xander rests his chin on my shoulder. I turn to West for an answer.

His eyes narrow, and I feel like I'm missing something obvious. "The Y is for you, princess."

"Me?"

"You, baby doll."

"I don't understand."

West smiles. "We changed the company name and drew up a new contract. The business is yours now too. We all have an equal share."

I shake my head. "No. I can't do that. I ... You three worked so hard for all this. I don't want it."

"We know, shorty, and that's exactly why we want you to have it. You're one of us."

"But ... this is too much."

Zeke turns my face to his. "Baby doll, we might not be able to legally marry you, but we found a way to tie you to us forever. This is purely selfish on our part."

"It was either this or knock you up," Xander says, chuckling.

"And we did consider swapping out your birth control," Zeke adds. His nonchalant shrug makes me believe he's serious, but before I can voice my outrage, West chimes in.

"But we figured you wanted to work on your career for a few years first."

I let out a quick laugh. "You boys don't do anything halfway, do you?"

Zeke smirks. "Never have. Never will."

"So, what do you say, princess? Will you be our business partner?" West takes a folded brown envelope from his jacket pocket and holds it out.

Chewing on the inside of my cheek, I glance at the building, then back at them.

Zeke tilts his head to the side. "You need us to get down on our knees, baby doll?"

Despite the cold weather, heat blooms beneath my skin. An image of the three of them on their knees for me makes me lightheaded. "Not out here in the street. But maybe when we get home."

West rustles the pages and Zeke produces a pen. "Not unless you sign."

"Come on, shorty. I'm freezing my nuts off here."

With trembling hands, I take the pen from Zeke and glance over the papers. "I promise you it's all completely above board," West assures me. "It makes you a quarter owner in everything. It makes you officially one of us."

I smile at the three men who've brought me more joy than I ever thought possible. "Forever?"

Their voices join together like a chorus. "And ever."

EPILOGUE

WEST—TWELVE MONTHS LATER

"Samson, no!" I shout as the runaway mutt charges into the den with one of my shoes clamped between his slobbering jaws.

"Are you being naughty again, baby boy?" I follow Lily's infectious laughter and find her with my shoe in one hand. The other hand scratches Samson's wiggling belly. His tongue lolls out of his mouth as he glances over, and I swear the little fucker is laughing at me.

I glance at Stella and Snowflake, who are curled up on the rug in front of the roaring fire. "Shouldn't you two be teaching the new guy some manners?"

Snowflake wags his tail and gives a soft woof. Stella, being Stella, closes her eyes, ignoring me completely.

"Aw, he's just learning." She gives him one final belly scratch, then orders him to go lie down beside his better-behaved canine siblings. I fight the urge to snarl when he does so without hesitation. Damn dog only listens to her and Zeke. It's like he's deaf to all voices that aren't theirs, especially

Xander's and mine. "I got your shoe back." She holds it out to me, a devious grin on her beautiful face.

Disgusted, I scowl at the slobber dripping from the sole. "I'll buy a new pair."

That makes her laugh harder, and she places the offending item on the floor. "I'll clean it off later. It'll be fine." She wipes her hands on her red flannel pants.

My eyes roam her perfect body, hardly any of which I can currently see thanks to the aforementioned red flannel. "The fuck are you wearing, princess?"

"My Christmas pajamas." She smiles brighter than the Christmas lights surrounding her.

I brush her dark curls back from her forehead. "You're fucking adorable, you know that?"

A sweet pink flush stains her cheeks. Despite how she's turned into an even bigger brat than Xander and all the filthy ways we fuck her, she still blushes so innocently when I compliment her. "You're not really mad at Samson, are you?" She flutters her eyelashes.

I glance over my shoulder at the snoring Saint Bernard mix she brought home six weeks ago after someone left him tied up outside her building for an entire day. He wasn't chipped, but I was convinced someone would claim him. Now I know why nobody did. He's a menace.

But he's our menace now. "No." I sigh. "Who can be mad at that giant ball of slobber and fur?"

She giggles, and I sit on the floor beside her. Leaning back against the sofa, I pull her onto my lap. "Just please tell me you don't plan on filling our gorgeous home with dogs."

She bites down on her lip and looks up at the ceiling as she hums softly. Six months ago, we bought a house in the Hamptons, right on Wainscott Beach. We wanted somewhere we could switch off from the city on the weekends, but we've spent almost all our time here since. There's something about having all four of us here that makes it feel like home in a way that nowhere else ever has. "I'm not sure I can make such an insane promise," she finally says with a shrug. "I mean what if I find another poor stray who has nowhere else to go?"

"Wrong answer, princess." Tickling her and nuzzling her neck, I soak in the music of her laughter. Who am I kidding? Our girl could bring home every stray in New York and none of us would do a thing to stop her.

She squeals and squirms in my arms, and I stop torturing her in favor of relaxing with her in my arms. Peace envelops me the way it so often does when she's near. I glance at the twelve-foot fir near the fireplace, decorated in red and gold. "The tree looks beautiful."

"Thank you. Xander and Zeke helped."

I arch an eyebrow. "Zeke?"

She laughs. "Mostly Xander."

I drop a kiss on her forehead. "Where are they?"

"I left them fooling around upstairs about fifteen minutes ago."

"Oh?" I nip her neck and slide my hand beneath her pajama shirt. "So I have you all to myself?"

"Seems like," she whispers. "Those two were super hot for each other."

One of the many things I love about her is that she's never threatened by our relationships with each other. "You didn't want to join in?"

She shrugs. "The dogs needed feeding, and they seemed to be doing just fine without me. So I finished off the lights on the tree. Anyway"—she tugs on my tie, pulling me closer—"you're home late, Mr. Archer."

I run my nose over her sweet-smelling throat. "I was tying

up a lot of loose ends so I won't have to work until after the new year."

Her eyes widen. "Really?"

I shake my head. "I won't so much as open my laptop."

Rolling her eyes, she swats my shoulder. "Liar."

Flipping her over, I position her across my knee and spank her. The dogs glance over at her squeal, but immediately go back to ignoring us. They're used to their mom getting her ass spanked and squealing like a brat. "Did you just call me a liar *and* roll your eyes, princess?" I smack her ass again.

"You two having fun without us?" I turn my head and grin at Zeke. Xander ambles in beside him.

When I pull Lily back up to a sitting position, her cheeks are as red as her pajamas. "Well, I was about to."

"You bring our gifts?" Xander asks me with a knowing smile.

"I did. They're in my briefcase in the hall."

"But all the gifts are under the big tree in the living room," Lily says as Xander rushes out, practically skipping.

"We got more." Zeke gives her a grin that rarely made an appearance before she entered our lives. He's always let Xander and me see the softer side of him, but that side was never truly soft. Watching him settle into life in this house with Lily and our dogs has brought me immeasurable joy. Before Lily, Xander and Zeke were the only two people in the world who truly mattered to me, and I would have done anything to make them happy. Who would've thought that one woman could be the answer for all of us?

"Thanks to your obsession with everything Christmas, we have four trees. Seemed like we needed more presents to go under them." I place a kiss on her forehead.

Xander comes back with my briefcase and pops it open. "We are doing this tonight, right?"

"Yes. No more waiting." Zeke sits on the couch behind Lily and me.

The spot between Lily's brows pinches together. God, she's so fucking beautiful. "No more waiting for what?"

Sitting on the floor next to us, Xander places the black bag in his lap and unties the gold ribbon. Lily watches him, probably assuming it's a gift for him, and she isn't wrong. There's a gift for each of us in there.

"Yours is the blue box. Zeke's is black. Lily's is green."

He grins at me. "And yours is gray."

Lily glances between Xander and me as Xander takes the four ring boxes out of the bag and passes them out.

Lily runs her fingertip over the soft green velvet. "W-what are these?"

I shrug. "Open it and see."

"Are these a gift from you?"

"From all of us, to all of us."

Her frown deepens.

Xander fidgets. Zeke sits perfectly still. The heavy knot of anxiety in my throat mirrors the tension radiating from them. What if she says no?

She snaps open the box, and her eyes immediately fill with tears. Her ring is made of four thick bands fused together, two platinum and two rose gold, each engraved with one of our names. She looks at us with tear-filled eyes that overflow with love for us. "It's beautiful," she whispers.

Xander opens his box to reveal his ring, which is identical to Zeke's and mine. The only difference between ours and Lily's is that ours are all platinum. He immediately slips it onto the ring finger of his left hand, and Lily sucks in a stuttered breath.

"That's where yours will fit too, princess."

Tears drip from her chin, and she opens her mouth, but nothing comes out.

Zeke leans forward, hands clasped between his spread thighs. "We might not be able to legally marry each other, baby doll, but we are committed to you and each other more than any marriage license can demonstrate."

She looks between Zeke and me. "You both have one too?"

I take out my ring and slide it onto my finger. "Sure do."

"The only piece of jewelry I'll ever agree to wear," Zeke says as he puts his on.

Xander jumps up onto his knees. "So what do you say, shorty? Will you be our wife?"

Zeke cups her chin in his hand and tilts her head so she's looking up at him. "Say you'll be our partner in every way, baby doll."

"Yes! Yes, I will," she squeals, almost jumping off my lap with excitement. I take her ring out of the box, and a lump of emotion lodges in my throat as I slip it onto her finger. Fucking perfect.

I had this idea a few months ago but worried Xander and Zeke would think I was crazy. When I suggested it, they both immediately jumped on board the second I said the word *wife*, and we spent the last few weeks designing the rings. Xander has hounded me practically every hour on the hour this past week, beyond ready for this moment right here. And in this moment, the four of us make sense in a way nothing else ever has. Together in everything. Always.

Lily holds out her hand, and the precious metals glint in the lights from the tree.

"Looks beautiful, Mrs. Archer."

Zeke snorts. "I don't fuckin' think so. Mrs. Cavanagh is way better."

"Actually, I think Mrs. King has a nice ring to it." We groan, but Xander laughs at his pun.

A wicked grin curves her lips. "Or you could all change your name to Constantine."

"Hell to the fuck no, princess. Not happening."

She bites on her lip and flutters those long dark lashes at me. *Brat.* "We could always hyphenate. Constantine-Archer-Cavanagh-King."

Xander roars with laughter. "Cack!"

"I'm not being called Mr. Cack, baby doll, not even for you."

Lily giggles like she knew exactly what acronym that would make. "How about we keep our own names then?"

"I'm just gonna call you Mrs. Archer anyway."

Zeke snarls. "And I'll call you Mrs. Cavanagh."

"Mrs. King."

She pretends to scowl, but her lips stay curved. "I guess I'll just have to answer to them all."

I pop open the top two buttons of her pajama shirt and push my hand inside, cupping one of her breasts and squeezing. She is fucking ours, and I would die for her happiness as easily as I'd take my next breath. "Damn fucking straight you will."

"West," she murmurs, tipping her head back.

Xander kisses her neck and slips his hand into her pajama pants. "Always so fucking wet and ready for us."

Zeke joins us on the floor and swallows her moans with his kiss.

Together the three of us strip off her clothes, kissing and touching her all over until she's whimpering and begging to be fucked. I sweep my tongue over the length of her pussy and groan as her sweet taste floods my mouth.

"You think our wife needs some cock?" Xander asks.

Lifting my head from between her thighs, I lick my lips. "I think she might. You think you can take all three of us, princess?"

"Please," she whines.

SADIE KINCAID

While our sofa is huge, it's not nearly big enough for the filthy things we're about to do to our girl. "Let's take this party somewhere a little more comfortable." Zeke sweeps her into his arms and leads us to the bedroom we share.

~

LILY

"This perfect little ass is mine, buttercup," Zeke says with a throaty growl as he gives it a hard slap.

"I call dibs on pussy." Xander tugs off his boxers, and now we're all naked.

Stepping up behind him, West nips at the back of Xander's neck, making him shiver. "That means your ass is mine, Fitch."

Zeke lies on the bed, his back against the headboard and his outstretched hand summoning me. "Come here, Mrs. Cavanagh. I need to fuck you. Now."

Anticipation skitters down my spine, and I bite my lip, holding his intense gaze as I crawl on top of him. He pulls my hair, tilting my head to his desired angle, and gives me an all too brief kiss. Then he spins me around, maneuvering me easily until I'm straddling him reverse-cowgirl style. "Lube," he barks, and a second later Xander throws him a bottle.

I can feel Zeke coating his fingers and cock behind me, but my eyes are fixed on Xander. He licks his lips and crawls between Zeke's spread legs. "You're so getting fucked, Mrs. King."

I tug my bottom lip through my teeth. "Is that a promise?"

Zeke grabs my hip with his free hand and tosses the lube to West. "Yes, it's a fucking promise, baby doll."

West stares at the three of us with hungry gray eyes, and a thrill of excitement runs through me. We've done this so many

404

times, but it never feels any less incredible to have all of them together like this.

Zeke's grip tightens on my hip as he slides a slick finger inside my ass, working it deeper and twisting before he adds a second, all to prepare me for his thick cock. So tender and careful even as he mutters about how desperate he is to fuck me.

Xander has a wicked glint in his eyes as he stares at the space between my thighs. "Spread her open a little for me, Z."

Zeke opens his thighs wider so that mine follow.

West crawls onto the bed behind Xander. "Jesus. You're fucking dripping, princess."

Xander drags two fingers through my wet center, and my moans turn to desperate whimpers. "So wet and needy." He pushes them into my pussy, and I sink my teeth into my lip, unconsciously stifling a loud groan.

Zeke removes his fingers from my ass and replaces them with the thick head of his cock. I hiss out a breath, the stretch burning despite how ready he's made me. "Let me inside you, buttercup," he growls.

Nodding, I inhale a deep, calming breath and relax my muscles, allowing him to give me more. Pleasure and pain lace together, and the feeling of fullness from Zeke being seated so deep inside me makes my head spin and my thighs tremble.

Xander's crown nudges my entrance. "You in, Z?"

Zeke holds onto my hips with both hands now, his fingertips biting into my supple flesh. "Yeah."

"You ready to take me too, shorty?"

I suck in another deep breath. "Uh-huh."

Xander groans appreciatively, sinking his thick cock into my pussy. "Good fucking girl."

My eyes flutter closed.

"Don't fuck her yet," West barks.

"Motherfuck," Zeke mutters, but they both go still, the only movement the throbbing of their cocks inside me. Their muscles tense, and I know from experience that they're holding back from driving into me until West says so. I love that their need for me is as strong as mine for them.

"Fuck, West," Xander hisses as he's pushed forward by West entering him, resulting in him thrusting deeper inside me. His tip brushes my G-spot, making me whine with desperation.

West grunts. "You love my cock, Fitch."

I open my eyes to see Xander's eyes rolling back in his head.

"Please?" Heat slicks between my thighs, every cell in my body vibrating with the need for them to deliver the mind-blowing orgasm they've stoked.

Zeke glides his hands up and down my sides. "Almost there, buttercup."

West winks at me over Xander's shoulder. "You're so fucking beautiful stuffed full of my boys' cocks, princess."

West drives hard into Xander, causing him to rail into me. "Oh, fu—oh!" I cry.

Zeke growls, rocking his hips upward and fucking my ass. Molten pleasure floods my body, turning my insides to liquid as I melt between their hard bodies. Zeke and Xander hold me up while the three of them work in perfect harmony, moving together like they've been doing this with me forever. My first climax comes quickly, crashing over me in a rolling wave. They don't stop as they fuck me through it, setting an exquisitely torturous pace.

"This ass is so fucking tight," Zeke groans.

"So fucking wet for us, shorty."

"So fucking perfect," West growls.

They go on fucking me, whispering praise and filthy promises of what's to come. I gasp in a breath and Xander seals his lips over mine, stealing my air and swallowing my screams.

Zeke and West lean forward, and their mouths clash in a fierce kiss.

Another climax builds in my core. I ride the glorious symphony as it heightens to a stunning crescendo, soaring higher and higher. My body trembles, my lungs burning with the need for air as Xander goes on kissing me. Grunts and groans, panting breaths and curses, the wet sound of Xander driving in and out of my pussy, skin slapping against skin. I can no longer tell where I end and they begin. We all move together like one entity, focused on the singular goal of attaining that fierce mind-altering pleasure. And we chase it hard, each of us falling over the cliff one after the other like a chain reaction.

I lie between their hard bodies, my head spinning and pleasure swirling through my core and limbs—soothed and satisfied, warm and safe in this solid unit we built. This is exactly where we all belong.

Exactly where we all fit.

～

ARE you ready for the next explosive installment of Sadie's bestselling Chicago Ruthless series? The Moretti's might think they have their happy ever afters, but there's one more Moretti out there with one hell of a grudge! Available to preorder now

Keres

DON'T MISS the next series in Sadie's Ruthless universe. You can meet the James brothers in Manhattan Ruthless. Book 1 is available for preorder now

Broken: Manhattan Ruthless

Also by Sadie Kincaid

Sadie's latest series, Chicago Ruthless is available for preorder now.
Following the lives of the notoriously ruthless Moretti siblings - this
series will take you on a rollercoaster of emotions. Packed with angst,
action and plenty of steam — preorder yours today

Dante

Joey

Lorenzo

If you haven't read full New York the series yet, you can find them on
Amazon and Kindle Unlimited

Ryan Rule

Ryan Redemption

Ryan Retribution

Ryan Reign

Ryan Renewed

New York Ruthless short stories can be found here

A Ryan Reckoning

A Ryan Rewind

A Ryan Restraint

A Ryan Halloween

A Ryan Christmas

A Ryan New Year

Want to know more about The Ryan Brothers' buddies, Alejandro and Alana, and Jackson and Lucia? Find out all about them in Sadie's internationally bestselling LA Ruthless series. Available on Amazon and FREE in Kindle Unlimited.

Fierce King

Fierce Queen

Fierce Betrayal

Fierce Obsession

If you'd like to read about London's hottest couple. Gabriel and Samantha, then check out Sadie's London Ruthless series on Amazon. FREE in Kindle Unlimited.

Dark Angel

Fallen Angel

Dark/ Fallen Angel Duet

If you enjoy super spicy short stories, Sadie also writes the Bound series feat Mack and Jenna, Books 1, 2, 3 and 4 are available now.

Bound and Tamed

Bound and Shared

Bound and Dominated

Bound and Deceived

ABOUT THE AUTHOR

Sadie Kincaid is a dark romance author who loves to read and write about hot alpha males and strong, feisty females.

Sadie loves to connect with readers so why not get in touch via social media?

Join Sadie's reader group for the latest news, book recommendations and plenty of fun. Sadie's ladies and Sizzling Alphas

ACKNOWLEDGMENTS

As always I would love to thank all of my incredible readers, and especially the members of Sadie's Ladies and Sizzling Alphas. My beloved belt whores! You are all superstars. To my amazing ARC and street teams, the love you have for these books continues to amaze and inspire me. I am so grateful for all of you.

But to all of the readers who have bought any of my books, everything I write is for you and you all make my dreams come true.

To all of my author friends who help make this journey all that more special.

Super special mention to my lovely PA's, Kate, Kate and Andrea, for their support and honesty and everything they do to make my life easier.

To the silent ninja, Bobby Kim. Thank you for continuing to push me to be better. And to my amazing editor, Jaime, who puts up with my insane writing process and helps me make each book better than the last.

To my incredible boys who inspire me to be better every single day. And last, but no means least, a huge thank you to Mr. Kincaid—all my book boyfriends rolled into one. I couldn't do this without you!